I0831751

TOWN BELL

Prequel to *Boy's Pond*

TOWN BELL

Prequel to *Boy's Pond*

WARREN J. STUCKI

Santa Fe

Sunstone books may be purchased for educational, business, or sales promotional use.
For information please write: Special Markets Department, Sunstone Press,
P.O. Box 2321, Santa Fe, New Mexico 87504-2321.

Library of Congress Cataloging-in-Publication Data

Names: Stucki, Warren J., 1946- author.
Title: Town bell : prequel to Boy's pond / Warren J. Stucki.
Description: Santa Fe : Sunstone Press, [2023] | Includes reader's guide. | Summary: "With the Cold War raging and espionage flourishing, a summer of innocent pranks turns deadly"-- Provided by publisher.
Identifiers: LCCN 2023033454 | ISBN 9781632935502 (paperback) | ISBN 9781611397215 (epub)
Subjects: LCGFT: Novels.
Classification: LCC PS3619.T84 T69 2023 | DDC 813.6--dc23/eng/20230809

LC record available at https://lccn.loc.gov/2023033454

WWW.SUNSTONEPRESS.COM
SUNSTONE PRESS / POST OFFICE BOX 2321 / SANTA FE, NM 87504-2321 /USA
(505) 988-4418

DEDICATION

To the friends of my youth—Doug, Mitch, John and Lee—you were the inspiration for this book. And to my wife, Linda—as always, her editing, suggestions and support proved invaluable.

PREFACE

The term "Cold War" was likely introduced in 1947 by Americans Bernard Baruch and Walter Lippmann when they used it to describe the emerging tensions between the two former World War II allies, the United States and the Soviet Union. Even though there was never a direct military engagement between the two superpowers, what ensued was nearly a half-century of rapidly escalating military buildup, global maneuvering, tense political battles and steely-eyed brinksmanship. Like a particularly virulent strain of the Spanish flu or Coronavirus, the Cold War rapidly spread outside of Europe (the continent of its origin) to nearly every region of the globe. Of course, the Soviets sought to export Marxism and the U.S.A. sought to contain it, with both countries forging numerous diplomatic alliances to achieve those ends. On the geopolitical map, the U.S.S.R. and communist sympathizing countries were often colored Marxist red and the U.S.A., and its allies were commonly painted a patriotic blue. For a few years, it looked like the whole world, one country after another, was going red, the so-called domino effect.

Not too surprisingly, the Cold War led to a space and arms race, culminating in a flood of new technology and weapons, including the A-bomb, the H-bomb and the ICBM rockets to deliver them. Suspicion and fear reigned supreme with each side fearing the other would develop first strike capability (a preemptive surprise attack that could totally annihilate the other) and ultimately employ it.

In a nutshell, this was a period of pervasive distrust and unbridled paranoia. Unfortunately, when one mixes unfettered neurosis with explosive advancements in military science and technology, it provides a remarkably fertile soil for the emergence of spies and the highly clandestine trade of espionage. Keeping up with the competition was vital and widely accepted as necessary for survival. And to keep up, it was crucial to know what the other side was doing and how they were doing it.

Everyone spied on everyone. France had agents in the U.S.A., China had agents in East Germany, Poland had agents in Great Britain, and Great Britain had their prolific and most effective M-16. However, the U.S.A. and the U.S.S.R. had agents nearly everywhere—in government, in industry, in the military, in atomic research and test facilities, and even within their own intelligence agencies, always looking for the double-cross. Double agents became feared as the new norm, and loyalties were frequently suspect and were often for sale, usually to the highest bidder.

Though certainly not limited to the Cold War, espionage came of age during those chaotic decades. Not only did it flourish, but was polished and refined to a deadly art, a lethal game of global cat and mouse.

Being only one hundred miles from the National Test Site at Yucca Flats, Nevada, it would almost be naïve to think that somehow southern Utah had escaped this pandemic of international intrigue. Undoubtedly spies commissioned by the Soviet Union frequently wandered in and out of the St. George area while keeping a veiled but close eye on the activities of the Nevada Test Site.

Within the borders of the United States, Cold War hysteria reached a fever pitch. Like noxious weeds after a wet spring, concrete bomb shelters and missile silos sprang up nearly everywhere. Disaster drills, complete with authentic air raid sirens, were rehearsed in almost every elementary and high school and also in many private homes. Many families had a written disaster plan and stockpiled food, water, guns, and ammunition. It seemed only a matter of time until the clack of Soviet tanks or the tramp of Russian jackboots could/would be heard marching down Main Street U.S.A.

Because of its geography, St. George, Utah, and Washington County were uniquely positioned to be caught up in this Cold War tsunami. As the crow flies, southern Utah was just a little over a hundred miles from President Harry S. Truman's newly created Nevada Test Site (NTS) at Yucca Flats. Eschewing major population centers for obvious reasons, the NTS was located so the prevailing winds would carry any radioactive products of detonation due east, away from the heavily populated west coast, and directly over the sparsely populated deserts of southeastern Nevada and southern Utah. In Washington County, gray ash and sometimes even the glowing hot remnants of the mushroom clouds could be seen drifting by, occasionally raining down solid radioactive particles, like hot pellets of hail from Dante's hell. Unable to shelter from these radioactive storms, range cows suffered severe radiation burns on their backs, and hundreds of grazing sheep perished.

As might be expected, Atomic Energy Commission (AEC) employees and scientists were a frequent presence in and around St. George, often whipping up patriotic support and/or assuring the populace the "Shots" posed no real danger. Radiation detection badges were casually clipped to the clothing of unsuspecting elementary school children, then quietly collected a month or two later. Any data generated from the badges was never revealed, at least not to the participants. Leukemia, as well as solid cancer rates more than doubled during the Cold War era and continued for many decades thereafter. Eventually, the citizens of southern Utah were collectively tagged with the dubious moniker, "downwinders."

Even America's youth were not immune to all this hype, this deluge of propaganda. In almost every town across the country young budding scientists and amateur rocketeers suddenly emerged determined to be the next generation of Cold War warriors. For Christmas, starter chemistry sets, light microscopes, alpha-1 ballistic rocket kits and self-assembly crystal radio sets were every bit as popular as Schwinn bicycles, roller skates or Lionel trains.

But in spite of this ongoing and swirling maelstrom of global intrigue, in some ways it was a simpler time. A shared family dinner was almost sacrosanct and most youth recreation was not commercial or organized into summer camps, but was the byproduct of active and fertile imaginations. Harmless pranks were usually tolerated, frequently associated with a quick but veiled smile, and not necessarily prosecuted as Class B misdemeanors.

And yes, my hometown of Santa Clara, Utah (just five miles west of St. George) was like this in the 1950s. And in spite of the looming Cold War backdrop, it was an idyllic, kind of a George Orwellian—uh—uh—what I meant to say, Santa Clara was very much a Norman Rockwellian kind of place to grow up.

1

PROLOGUE
CIRCA 1932

In the pre-dawn darkness, Judd and Howie crouched behind an overgrown tangle of Gewürztraminer vines. Overhead a thin slice of moon hung slightly askew, as though pinned to the dark sky by a blindfolded birthday boy. The glow of the Milky Way, coupled with the light of the slipper moon, gave off just enough light to make out the A-frame outhouse and behind it the ghostly, almost gossamer image of the big house. However, there was not sufficient light to see specific features, like a similarly shaped quarter-moon carved right into the door of the outhouse.

Somewhere off to the left and sounding a bit like a string quartet warming up for a chamber concert, a cluster of crickets screeched away endlessly, and directly behind them, probably up on top of the Red Sand Hill, a coyote wailed, sounding eerily like a jilted lover. Wafting on the warm night breeze, Judd could smell, in spite of his own sour mash breath, the spicy, fruity fragrance of overripe Gewürztraminer grapes.

Judd's Swiss ancestors, specifically his grandfather, had managed to bring the vines when they emigrated from Switzerland, some seventy-five years earlier. At first, those early Santa Clara pioneers cultivated the grapes for the making of wine, presumably to be used for the ordinance to commemorate the sacrifice and atonement of Jesus Christ, though undoubtedly there was a wee bit of "medicinal" use as well. And even though some years earlier, the Latter-Day Saints Church (the Mormons) had switched from sacramental wine to plain old tap water for this holy sacrament and had issued a very strict edict, the Word of Wisdom, prohibiting the imbibing of alcohol, grapevines still flourished in Santa Clara as did some covert brewing and bootlegging.

"Looks quiet," Howie whispered, as they surveyed the dark big house for signs of life.

"Yeah," Judd nodded, but made no effort to get up, "looks like the ole Gub's still in bed."

"Well, we better get going," Howie stood up, "cause he gets up about every hour - you know, he has prostate problems."

"What's prostate problems?"

"I don't know for sure," Howie replied, "but I think it's like diabetes; it makes you pee a lot."

Judd slowly shook his head. "Howie, maybe this is too much, specially after the truck fiasco of the other night."

Silently, Judd recalled how just two weeks earlier, and about this same time of night, they'd sneaked into Orson Gubler's backyard, shifted his 1932 Ford pick-up in neutral, and pushed it down Highway 91 for about a quarter mile or so.

"Nah," Howie shook his head in the dark, "that was nothing. It only took him a couple of hours to find it."

"Yeah, but only after he got the Sheriff involved."

"So, no one was hurt, and nobody knows it was us." Howie took a step toward the outhouse. "Come on, let's get going."

Staying low, and as much as possible to the shadows, Howie flitted back and forth like a Voror wraith, eventually flattening out against the outhouse wall. Reluctantly, Judd followed, but with less emphasis on caution. He looked more like a marine storming the beach at Okinawa.

For the next thirty minutes, Judd and Howie worked to loosen eight three-quarters-inch rusted nuts from their equally rusted bolts, anchoring the outhouse baseboards to the railroad ties (the ties formed a solid foundation for the outhouse around the refuse pit). More than once during the operation, they had to pause and pass the pint around—not so much for courage, but as a partial antidote to the powerful odor wafting from the crater.

Twenty minutes later, after they'd removed all the nuts and washers, the boys positioned themselves on either side of the privy. Grunting under the strain, they hoisted it off the bolts and ties, then backed it up a couple of yards, being extra careful not to slip and slide back into the fetid, semisolid hole. Once they were a safe distance behind the pit, they gently set the outhouse down again, aligning it with the path to the big house.

"You think this will do?" Howie asked, surveying the final position.

Without immediately offering an opinion, Judd walked around the little A-frame, eyeing it from several different angles. Within an inch or two, the privy was lined up perfectly with the path from the house, but now instead of resting directly above the six-foot-deep pit, it was approximately two yards behind that hole.

"Yeah," Judd finally answered, "that should do."

"Do you think there's too much light now?" Howie asked, glancing up. The sliver moon was already starting to fade, merging, and blending into the nascent glow of an impending dawn.

"Nah," Judd shook his head, "you'd never know it, 'less you were looking fur it."

"But—but, it's getting light—"

At that moment, coming from the big house, they heard a screen door banged loudly against its jamb.

"H—he's coming," Judd whispered, nudging Howie. "Let's go!"

Almost instantly, the two boys melted into the purple haze, disappearing once again into the tangle of Gewürztraminer vines.

Through the broad leaves and twisted branches, Judd managed to create a small portal. Squinting, he could barely make out the stumbling form of old Orson Gubler, clutching his crotch as he hurried down the path toward the outhouse.

Due to the whorl of Gewürztraminer vines, he didn't actually see the moment old Gub disappeared into the pit, but they did hear him scream.

"You little sons-a-bitches!

2

TWENTY YEARS LATER
CIRCA 1952

KA-BOOM!

An explosion ripped through the classroom, like it had been targeted by a M-3 Howitzer.

The cause of the blast, however, was not exploded cannon ordinance, but twelve pyrotechnic cherry bombs hurtled through open windows and exploding almost simultaneously.

A millisecond after the blast the subsequent concussion battered the windows, shattering one, then immediately launching razor-sharp shards, like tiny missiles, into the room.

The concussion also shook the walls and floor, tossing loose sheets of paper and lighter notebooks into the air, while heavier objects like textbooks and lunch pails simply toppled off desks and thudded to the hardwood floor.

With a loud crack, the aluminum tube attached above the blackboard and housing the geography maps was ripped from its wall brackets. It crashed down on Miss Miller's desk, scattering her notes and crushing her sandwich, but fortunately missing poor Stella by mere inches.

Thick black smoke from combusting nitrates, mixed with the rotten egg odor of burning sulfur, quickly filled the room. At first, the clouds swirled and boiled like gathering storm clouds, before surging forth and out the open windows.

Shrieking like an Irish Banshee, Miss Miller dropped her novel and her partially eaten Jonathan apple, diving under her desk like a marine into a foxhole. And even though her desk now protected her from further bombardment, she continued to couch and wail.

Standing as tall as he could, John Tobler Kunz (J.T.) balanced on his tiptoes so he could see it all unfold. He was shocked, no, more like flabbergasted at what he saw. He never expected any of this. The explosion was so loud and the room had filled with smoke so fast and—and all of that flying debris and—and the shattered window! It was total chaos. It meant trouble.

Five seconds later, the classroom door slammed open and Mr. Cannon and Mrs. Dorland, the other two Santa Clara Elementary teachers, burst into the classroom. Once inside they also paused, momentarily stunned by the degree of destruction. With mouths agape, they rapidly assessed the situation, then tripped over each other as they rushed to aid Miss Miller, who remained hunkered and sobbing under her desk.

Still peeking in, eyes wide with disbelief, J.T. inadvertently sucked in a lungful of sulfur-tainted air. Coughing and rubbing his burning eyes, he backed away from the window and turned to Mickey.

Suddenly, and way out of character, Mickey also seemed frightened and unsure. J.T. suspected this was even more than he'd expected.

"L—let's get the hell out of here." Mickey's voice quivered like a struck banjo wire. "A—and maybe we'd better split up."

Right away, everyone started to leave, but Mickey called them back. Already, he seemed to be regaining his composure. "Hold on a sec!" Everyone stopped and circled back around. "Okay, nobody tells nobody nothing 'bout this. We've gotta keep this mum. You understand?"

The boys nodded nervously, while glancing over their shoulders at the smoke still billowing from the classroom windows.

"Well, then," Mickey now sounded more confident as he once again resumed command, "well then let's pair up and get the hell outta here."

Quickly, Weird Willie paired up with a reluctant Alan and as was customary Curley joined his best friend, Greg. Briefly, Mickey looked at J.T. as though he might have a rational explanation for what had just happened, for this unexpected degree of destruction. J.T., however, remained silent.

"Okay," Mickey continued, "then let's get the hell outta here."

After correcting some initial confusion, two pairs had both headed east, each twosome raced off in roughly three different directions.

With Mickey leading, he and J.T. sprinted due south, directly across U.S. Highway 91 (Main Street), down Hafen Lane, heading straight for the Santa Clara River bottom and the relative safety of the dense ribbon of foliage flanking the small stream.

Giving no regard to bruises, scratches, or torn clothing, they crashed through the brambles of thorn and skunk bushes, busted through thickets of coyote and stink willows, and danced around dense stands of live oak and a battalion of sapling cottonwoods.

Eventually, it was not the thick tangle of vegetation that stopped them. No, what stopped them, was they'd finally ran out of breath. With chests heaving, like thoroughbreds after a run at Churchill Downs, they collapsed on the ground. Using the tail of his shirt, J.T. wiped the sweat from his brow, then looked around to get his bearings. No big surprise here. They'd ended up on the familiar banks of Boy's Pond.

The diminutive Santa Clara River (would be classified as a creek anywhere else in the world) originated thirty-five miles to the north, high in the snow-capped, granite peaks of the Pine Valley Mountains. When the Swiss/Mormon immigrants settled the Santa Clara Valley (sequestered in the far northeast finger of the Mojave Desert) they immediately decided in order to survive, they needed to harness this invaluable asset; the Santa Clara River being the only source of water for the entire region. So, in 1861, and without the aid of modern earth-moving machines, those early settlers constructed a rock and earthen dam across the little river, diverting the water into a series of feeder canals to supply the newly cleared and perpetually thirsty fields.

In one spot, where the north canal made a rather abrupt forty-five-degree turn in order to circle around a hillock of blue clay, the swift current obliquely impacted the bank, making the water churn and forming a standing whirlpool. The whirlpool, acting like an earthen router, relentlessly ate away at the bank, eventually creating a thirty-by-forty foot pond, six-foot deep in some spots.

Over the years, a desert oasis had literally grown up around the pond. The dense riparian foliage, consisted of skunk bushes, live oak, white river willows, and eventually huge arching cottonwood trees reigned over the pond. At the shallow end, occupying less than a third of the pond, a thick carpet of reeds and cigar-shaped cattails had taken permanent root.

Nearly, a half-mile south of town and well away from any dedicated municipal road, Boy's Pond was secluded and was almost always blessed with shade from the overhead canopy of cottonwoods. In late summer, however, the shallow end of the pond often stagnated and overgrew with green algae, producing a fishy, mossy odor.

On the other main irrigation canal, the south canal on the far side of the creek, a similar pond had been carved by the current and was designated Girl's Pond. It was not quite as deep as Boy's Pond and being across the creek was a little farther from town, but nevertheless it was an adequate swimming hole. At both ponds, bathing suits were considered optional, but it was absolutely understood Girl's Pond was totally off limits to the boys and vice versa. Pond-peeking, along with breaking the Word of Wisdom (smoking and drinking alcohol) and skipping church were well-established taboos for this little Mormon town.

"Nobody's coming," J.T. finally managed to get the words out after his breathing had slowed enough for conversation.

"Yeah," Mickey agreed, glancing over his shoulder, "it looks like nobody followed us." He removed his sweat soaked shirt, hanging it on a nearby skunk bush. "As long as we're here," he continued, looking around one last time, "let's take a dip. It's already too damn hot and it's only May."

"I wish you wouldn't use those words," J.T. said, frowning. "The church says we're not supposed to swear."

"What words?"

"You know."

"Well, let me just tell you this, dam is not a swear word; it's a thing and hell is a place. For your information, there's a dam across this here creek up a little further and it would play hell on our crops if it broke." Mickey's grin indicated he thought he'd made his point.

"Nah," J.T. shook his head, "it's not the same. Damn is from the word damnation, and we're not supposed to say it."

"You just did," Mickey laughed. "Are you goin' a take a dip or not?" Mickey stripped off his pants and socks.

"D—do you, do you think we hurt her?" J.T. asked, his face still drawn and pale.

"No way," Mickey forced a laugh, "but did you see her dive under the desk?"

"Yeah, but—but she was screaming!"

"Women always scream. That's what they do."

"But do—do you think she's hurt?"

"Nah, I saw the whole thing," Mickey shrugged, sounding confident. "She was already halfway under the desk when the map came down. Missed her by a foot and hit the desk."

"Are you sure?"

"Pretty damn sure."

"What about the flying glass?"

"Missed her too."

"Did—did we start a fire?" J.T. asked.

"Nah, them bombs are 'cussive, not 'cendiary."

"But, we—we definitely did some damage to the classroom."

"Yeah, I know," Mickey laughed again. "That was really something, huh?"

"But, we could be in big trouble."

"Nah, I doubt it."

"W—whadda you think we should do now? What about tomorrow?"

"Nothing. Absolutely nothing. Nothing but keep our mouths shut. Nobody can prove nothing. Tomorrow, I'll talk to the other guys again. Make sure they're on board."

"I—I don't know. I'm worried. Maybe we should—"

"No, this is the only way," Mickey cut him off. "You've gotta promise."

"I don't know; maybe if we confess—"

"No, you've gotta promise." Mickey interrupted again, then got in J.T.'s face. "If you crack, then all of us will pay the price."

"Yeah, well, okay," J.T. sighed, backing down, "but that don't mean I like it."

"You don't have to like it."

They continued to undress in silence.

"Maybe, we should get on back now." J.T. hesitated after pulling off his shirt.

"Nah, let's go back after dark."

"But, I've got evening chores."

"Yeah, so, what chores?"

"The same as always, milk the cow, slop the hogs and feed the chickens."

"No different than me."

"'Cept my dad gets mad if I do my chores after dark."

"No!" Mickey said firmly, shaking his head. "We need to lay low for a while. Let things cool down."

They were silent for a few moments, then Mickey looked over at J.T. "So, does this count?" he asked, again flashing his trademark, lopsided grin.

"Count for what?"

"Toward setting the record?"

"What record?" J.T. frowned. Sometimes he couldn't follow Mickey at all.

"You know, for the most pranks in a single summer. Judd and Howie's record."

"It's not summer yet," J.T. finally slipped off his Levis, "it has to be for one summer."

"It's pretty damn close to summer. School's out in three more days. I'm goin' to count it. Anyway, it's hot enough for summer."

"Yeah, okay," J.T. shrugged, "I guess we could count it."

"Let's go swimming." Mickey ran, splashing his way into the water.

For nearly an hour, the boys floated, lazily bobbing around the little pool. Inadvertently, when they bumped into each other a water fight would erupt, then end almost as fast, as they drifted apart again. Once Mickey decided to dunk J.T. and he let him without offering a struggle. He was not in the mood for a fight, and he knew for Mickey it was important to show dominance.

Floating on his back, again away from Mickey, J.T. watched the sun slowly sink; its rays becoming more acute, more slanted. Determined photons, however, still managed to fight through the overhead canopy of leaves, creating a mottled, checkered, almost hypnotic pattern on the slowly rotating water.

Mesmerized by nature's light and shadow show, J.T.'s mind, even without his consent, returned to the earlier catastrophe.

When Mickey pulled all those cherry bombs from his pocket, he should have known. He should have turned away and walked to school by himself. But he had not and then it quickly became too late.

Sure, J.T. knew no matter how much he wished for it, he could never go back, but also he couldn't shake the nagging suspicion that regardless of Mickey's casual attitude, this silly prank might very well change their lives forever.

The day had started innocently enough with just his daily morning walk to school.

3

"Hey, John Tobler Kunz, hold up a sec!"

Gritting his teeth, J.T., nevertheless, slowed to a stop. He hated being called by his full and formal name, preferring the more cryptic J.T. It sounded more mature, more sophisticated, and more grown up. Only one person, other than his father in times of anger or annoyance, ever dared call him John Tobler, and he was directly behind him and catching up fast. The only other tag he willingly accepted was 'Jackie', which was his mother's pet name for him.

"Yeah? What do you want?" Not at all trying to hide his disgust, J.T. turned around. No surprise here, it was his best friend, sometimes enemy, and almost constant irritation, Mickey T. Graff. The 'T' in both their names stood for Tobler, so they were related, as were most people in Santa Clara. Their mothers were first cousins, which made them second cousins.

"Hold up, J.T." As Mickey got closer, he intuitively changed to the more favored moniker. "Hold up, I've got something to show you."

"I am holding up." J.T. answered, trying not to show too much interest. Mickey always had something. He was forever trying to suck him into some kind of caper, or scheme, often making him the fall guy.

"Would you look at this?" Mickey said, his voice was suddenly low and confidential.

In spite of himself, J.T. moved in closer. From the pockets of his baggy denim jeans, Mickey fished for, and eventually produced, a handful of red spheres with curved green stems. To J.T., they kinda looked a little like artificial crab apples or even cherries.

"What's that?" J.T. knew he was being drawn in, but now he was trapped.

"Cherry bombs!" Mickey whispered, while glancing over his shoulder.

"They look more like round firecrackers."

"Nah, they're bombs, all right."

"No way. There nothing but a glorified firecracker."

"You wanna see?"

Before he could answer, Mickey pulled out a book of matches, lit the little red bomb's green fuse, then tossed it into a nearby flower bed of irises, not more than two or three feet away.

KA-BOOM!

The flower patch exploded, disintegrating in a lumpy cloud of purple flower petals, ragged green leaves, and chunks of stems.

"Geez!" J.T. exclaimed wide-eyed. "Maybe they are bombs!"

"Whadda I tell you?"

"Where'd you get 'em?"

"They're left over from last Fourth of July." Mickey shrugged. "My older brother ordered them from Wyoming."

"Ordered them?"

"You know from a catalog, in the mail."

"And you're bringing them to school?"

"Yeah, why not? There's no law agin it."

"Yes, there is. Actually, they're illegal in Utah. At least firecrackers are."

"Not if you don't set them off. It's like thinkin' about stealing someone's bike, but if you don't do it, then it's not a crime."

"I don't know about that."

"Well, I do."

"So, if you're not going to set them off," J.T. asked, "then why are you bringin' then to school?"

Mickey answered by breaking into his patented lopsided grin. His bronze freckles bunched on the bridge of his nose, then seemed to slide primarily down the left cheek to meet the corner of his asymmetrically upturned lips. "I don't know; maybe I'll think of somethin'."

"Yeah, well, you can count me out."

They walked in silence for a few more moments before Mickey continued. "Only three more days of school, we ought'a do something great this summer."

"Well, I'm going to help my dad on the farm and I would like…" J.T. hesitated, then blushed a sheepish red.

"Would what?"

"Oh, I—I don't know."

"Yes, you do," Mickey persisted, "tell me."

"Well, I'd like to make a rocket that actually flies."

"You and your rockets. Are you still working on that?"

"Yeah, and I think I've almost got it," J.T. replied.

"Got what?"

"Got the fuel figured out."

"So, what's the problem?"

"I'm still working on the aerodynamics."

"The aero—what?" Mickey asked.

"Trying to get it to fly straight."

"Just make sure you aim it at Moscow," Mickey laughed.

"So, what about you?" J.T. asked. "What's your plans for the summer?"

"I gotta work too—the family fruit stand," Mickey shrugged, "but in spite of our jobs, we still ought'a do somethin' big."

"Like what?"

"Like maybe two pranks a month?" Mickey grinned. "That way we can set the record."

"The record. What record?"

"You know what record, Judd and Howie's record for the most original pranks in a summer. They did a total of five."

"I don't know," J.T. replied, shaking his head. "I don't think we can come up with that many. Nobody can."

"Sure we can, or at least we can have fun trying."

"Yeah, well, let me think on it," J.T. said, slowing his pace. Of the two of them, he was the thinker, the idea man. He usually came up with the plans. Mickey, on the other hand, was the engineer, the foreman. He had a knack for putting a plan into motion, making it happen.

"Okay, you think on it," Mickey agreed, re-pocketing the cherry bombs. "Anyway, we better get going or we'll be late."

"Who cares?" J.T. hated school, not that he wasn't a good student, he was, but he was easily bored. "Anyway, I hear Mister Frei's sick today and we're going to have a substitute."

"Sick? He seemed fine last week."

"I don't know. He's got something nobody wants to talk about." But privately, J.T. hoped it wasn't too bad. He liked Mr. Frei, even though he tended to ride him hard. For some reason, it seemed Mr. Frei had taken on him as his personal reclamation project.

"It might be fun having a substitute teacher." Mickey grinned.

"Substitutes can be mean," J.T. shrugged, "they're like adopting a stray dog, you never know what you're going to get."

Up ahead, the huge brass bell in the school tower began tolling. Unfortunately, the boys were still two blocks away. With the ringing of the bell, J.T. broke into a slow trot. Always competitive, Mickey sprinted a little ahead, then suddenly the race was on. With reckless abandon, they cut through lawns, hurdled hedges, jumped irrigation ditches and dashed across U.S. Highway 91 without stopping or checking for traffic, as they steeple-chased toward the Santa Clara Elementary School.

Constructed out of eighteen-by-eighteen-inch gray cement block, the school was a stark, two-story building located roughly in the center of town and adjacent to the Mormon chapel. The floor plan was simple. Upon entering the double doors, there was a large central foyer, which ran the entire length of the building. Exiting off the foyer were three classrooms, two on the right, one on the left. Each classroom was also a perfect square with two outside and two interior walls. The outer walls each sported three windows or a total of six. Located at the far end of the foyer on the left, beyond the solitary classroom on that side, were two tiny restrooms, a small lunchroom, and the base of a fairly wide staircase. The wooden staircase ascended to a landing, made a right-angle turn, then continued on up to the second floor.

The second floor housed a basketball gymnasium complete with opposing backboards, metal hoops and cotton nets, but it also featured an elevated actor's stage centered just off the north sideline. When school plays were performed, folding chairs were set up on the polished, hardwood gymnasium floor.

Just as the bell ceased pealing, J.T. jerked open the front door and stumbled headlong into the darkened foyer, crashing into a metal folding chair. The resulting collision sent both him and the chair skittering across the floor.

As he struggled to right himself, the overhead lights abruptly turned on and there, scowling down at him, was his teacher/principal, Mr. Jacob Frei. Even from this angle and in this light, Mr. Frei did not look good. His face was thin and sallow, and his cheeks were hollow. As he loomed over J.T., the loose skin of his cheeks drooped, like the jowls of an old dog, and his eyes seemed too big, even though they were deeply recessed in their bony sockets. In the background, behind Mr. Frei, J.T. could hear the subdued snickers of the other students.

Now, with the lights on, J.T. realized the foyer had been set up to show a movie. A projector, perched on a rolling metal stand, was aimed at a white, retractable movie screen positioned at the far end of the foyer. Appropriated from the adjacent classrooms, the student's desk chairs were arranged in horizontal rows, facing the now blank screen.

"J.T.," Mr. Frei said sarcastically while peering over the rims of his round-frame glasses, "you should have let us know you were going to be late; we would have waited."

Sheepishly, J.T. picked himself up from the hardwood floor while Mickey quietly slid into the back row. He could think of nothing to say.

For a full five seconds, Mr. Frei glared down at J.T., then sighed. "Well go on, find a seat. Sometime in the near future, we'll need to talk about this."

As Mr. Frei turned away, J.T. slipped into the empty chair on the back row beside Mickey. At that moment, three tardy sixth-grade girls also slipped through the door and tiptoed in, but no one noticed them.

"Um-m-m—well, it appears we now have a quorum," Mr. Frei said, "so let me start over with the introductions."

"Mister Rudy Popovich of the Atomic Energy Commission is here with us today. First, he will show a short film, then he will say a few words. After that, we will retire to our respective classrooms."

Mr. Frei paused for a moment, eyeing the group, then nodded at a pretty lady seated next to him in the first row. "Oh, also, Miss Stella Miller is here today. Would you please stand, Stella?"

Rising to her feet, Miss Miller smiled nervously as she looked over her shoulder at the rows of students.

"Miss Miller will substitute in my room today," Mr. Frei added, "I will be leaving shortly and won't be back for the rest of the week. So with school ending in three days, I won't see most of you again till next fall—God willing. To the sixth-grade students, who next year will be moving on to Woodward Junior High School in St. George, I wish you all the best and much success. I hope we have prepared you well." He paused for a moment, then continued, "but in my absence, I expect you all to behave." Once again, he looked slowly around the foyer, finally focusing on J.T. and Mickey. Swallowing hard, Mr. Frei seemed to wipe something from first one eye, then the other. Finally he nodded to Mr. Popovich and in a husky voice added, "okay, Rudy, let's try it one more time."

As Popovich got up and began re-threading the celluloid film through the various pins and rollers of the 16 mm Bell & Howell projector, J.T. leaned over to Mickey and whispered, "I told you there was something wrong with Mister Frei."

"Maybe," Mickey nodded, "but did you hear what he said?"

"Yeah, what?"

"He's going to be gone for the whole week!"

"So?"

"Did you see our new teacher? Hubba-hubba-hubba!"

"Yeah," J.T. nodded, "but she's pretty young, probably just out of school."

"Young," Mickey grinned, "that's the way I like 'em."

Suddenly the film started rolling, Mr. Frei flipped off the overhead lights, then quietly slipped out of the foyer, exiting the building through the back door.

Mickey started to say something, but J.T. shushed him; he wanted to concentrate on the film.

It was a black and white film produced by the Atomic Energy Commission (AEC) and explained how vital nuclear research was to the preservation of our country's fragile and presently endangered freedoms. We, the United States, were literally in the race of our lives with the Soviet Union to harness the immense power of the atom. It was deadly serious business. If the Soviets won, undoubtedly, they would dominate the world, a truly bone-chilling thought. As good citizens we had a sacred duty to do our part, and from time to time we might be asked for our help, for our cooperation.

Next, the movie showcased several scenes demonstrating the colossal power of the atom bomb, including a graphic scene of the actual moment of detonation right at ground zero. Almost instantly a shaggy-looking stem formed. This was quickly topped by the signature mushroom cloud, then as a unit it rapidly soared high above the desert floor. The resultant concussive shockwave flattened the walls and shattered the windows of a dummy village the AEC had erected several miles from ground zero, but surprisingly left a mannequin family essentially unharmed. Was there a lesson to be learned in that? J.T. was not sure.

Leaning in close, Mickey covered his mouth with his hand and whispered. "That bomb—it just gave me an idea."

"Sh-s-s-s." J.T. still wanted to watch the film. He was fascinated by science in general and in particular with nuclear physics and ICBM rocketeering.

The movie ended by reassuring the audience atomic research was safe and absolutely vital to our national interests and security. Radiation from each test was and would be continuously monitored, but so far levels were minimal and were not even close to the harmful range. Nobody need to fear these shots and it was each citizen's patriotic duty to cooperate in any way he or she could. The final frames showed a striking image of Old Glory, the Stars and Stripes being whipped by a stiff breeze to a stirring rendition of America the Beautiful.

Suddenly, it was over. Now, only a cone of white light illuminated the screen, accompanied by a rhythmic clack as the full reel continued to rotate with the tail end of the film slapping against a projector post.

"Could somebody hit the lights?" Popovich shouted as he switched off the projector.

As the overhead lights came on, he slapped his knees loudly, stood up and walked to the end of the foyer, standing in front of the blank screen. Subconsciously, he tugged at his salt and pepper goatee as he looked out over his young audience.

"How did you like the film?" he finally asked.

Silence.

Rudy Popovich surveyed the group again, his gaze finally settling on J.T. "You—you there in the back, the fellow who knocked over the chair earlier, what is your name?"

"Uh—uh, J.T., sir—J.T. Kunz."

"Well, what did you think of the film, Mister J.T. Kunz?"

"Uh—me?"

"Yes, you. Stand up and tell us what you thought."

As the rest of the kids twisted around in their chairs, J.T., with his face burning, slowly stood up.

"Well?" Popovich prodded. "Go ahead."

"Uh—uh, frankly," J.T. tried to make his voice deep and more resonant. "I think this stuff is real interesting and—and that's what I want to be when I grow up, a nuclear physicist."

Scattered titters erupted from the group.

"Well, let me tell you what," Mickey muttered, just loud enough to be heard. "I don't like it—not one damn bit."

"What?" Popovich looked sharply at Mickey. "What was that? I didn't quite hear you."

"Oh, nothing," Mickey mumbled, but his scowl said as much or more than his words.

Popovich shrugged, then turned back to J.T. "If you could, would you be willing to help with that nuclear research right now?"

"Yeah—yes, of course."

"Well, today you'll get your chance and so will the rest of you who want to volunteer. All you have to do is wear these little radiation badges for a month," Popovich held up a small object with an attached metal clasp, "then I will come back and pick them up. But you must make sure to wear them everywhere—even when you're at home or when you're outside and when you sleep. The only time you don't have to wear them is when you take a bath. Ha, ha, ha." Rudy paused to laugh at his own joke. "So, how about it, Mister Scientist there in the back row, would you be willing to do that for me?"

"Sure, Mister Popovich," J.T. agreed. "I—I would be honored."

"Well then, come on up here—and all the rest of you who would like to help, line up behind Mister J.T. Kunz."

As the kids fell in line, Rudy opened a small cardboard box containing the badges. Mickey, still scowling, remained rooted in his seat.

As Rudy clipped on the badges, he handed each kid a slip of paper, then gave them a little pat on the back and sent them back to their chairs. When he had finished, he called the room back to order.

"I'll need to pick up these badges in exactly one month. School will be out for the summer by then, but Mr. Frei has graciously allowed us to use this hall next month for a town meeting. I'll pick up the badges at that meeting.

"The sheets of paper I gave you explain this program to your parents and also informs them of the time and day for collection. Be sure you take the note home so your parents can help you remember, and please encourage them to attend the next town meeting with you.

"Now, I will turn the time back to—" Popovich's voice trailed off as he looked for Mr. Frei. Failing to find him, he glanced around the room again, then settled on Miss Stella Miller. "I'll turn the time back to Misses—uh—Miss Stella."

Looking like a deer caught in the headlights, Stella slowly rose from her chair and with her voice quivering announced, "Uh—uh—um, let's all now adjourn to our respective classes."

Mr. Cannon, the first and second grade teacher quickly stood and added, "please take your chairs with you."

Suddenly there was a cacophony of confusion as the assembly broke up. After locating their chairs, J.T. and Mickey headed toward the fifth and six-grade classroom.

A large central aisle divided the room precisely in half, separating the four rows of fifth grade from the four identical rows of the sixth grade. Regardless of the grade, however, each desk had a retractable central drawer, an empty inkwell, which was now obsolete, and a flat writing surface—well mostly flat though the surfaces were often scarred from years of use and abuse. Most desks had more than one set of initials carved into them, as well as a variety of cupid hearts, a scattering of other symbols as well as other assorted words of graffiti.

At the head of the room stood a much larger teacher's desk and directly behind the desk was a wall-to-wall blackboard complete with a chalk tray and felt erasers. Secured high above the blackboard a six-foot-long metal cylinder was attached, housing various pull-down maps, including one of the great state of Utah, another the United States (all 48 states a different color) and finally one of the entire world with all its many countries. On the wall just to the right of the blackboard hung a picture of President Dwight D. Eisenhower, looking slightly uncomfortable in civilian clothes, and to the left, a picture of the very popular governor of the great state of Utah, J. Bracken Lee.

After some initial searching, arguing, and inspecting, each student finally located his or her chair and lugged it back to the appropriate desk.

When the commotion had subsided, Miss Stella Miller rose and stood before her fifth and sixth grade classes. She appeared to be nervous, repeatedly glancing down at her notes. Loudly clearing her throat, she struggled to make eye contact with the students.

"Uh—uh, Mister Frei indicated we should study world geography for an hour, then recess for about a half-hour, then spend the rest of the morning on multiplication tables."

“That’s for the sixth grade,” a sandy haired girl named Jill blurted out, while simultaneously raising her hand. “In the fifth grade we read first, then we do geography while the sixth grade do their times tables.”

“Oh,” Miss Miller again consulted her notes. “Yes, yes, I believe that is correct. So, the fifth grade should take out their readers for an hour, while I teach the sixth-grade world geography.”

As the fifth-grade students opened their readers, Stella consulted her notes one last time.

“Today, the sixth grade will be studying world geography, specifically concentrating on the USSR.” She paused for a moment to see if there were any objections. There appeared to be none. “Okay, then, can—can anyone tell me what the letters U-S-S-R stand for?”

Silence.

“Anyone at all?” She almost sounded desperate.

Finally, Annie Leavitt, a skinny, but pretty brown-haired girl who sat in front of J.T. raised her hand. “United Soviet Socialists Republics.”

“Almost, but not quite right,” Miss Miller replied. “Anyone else?”

Silence. Everyone bowed their head and suddenly seemed fascinated by the graffiti carved into their desks.

“How about you in the back,” Stella’s gaze settled on J.T., “the one who wants to be a scientist. Again, what is your name?”

“Me—uh—J.T.—J.T. Kunz.”

“Oh, yes,” Miss Miller nodded, “now I remember. So, J.T., what does U-S-S-R stand for?”

Blushing, J.T. looked down at his desk, but nevertheless mumbled, “uh—the Union of Soviet Socialist Republics.”

“Very good! Now who can come up here and point out the USSR on the map?” ”

“All I know,” someone whispered, “is they’re the bad guys.”

Annie Leavitt turned around, her brown eyes wide with admiration and whispered, “how’d you know that, J.T.?”

“I don’t know,” he mumbled, still not looking up from his desk.

Meanwhile, no one volunteered for map duty.

“How about you?” Now Stella’s gaze landed directly on Mickey. “Tell us your name, then come up here and show us which country is the USSR.”

Slowly Mickey stood up, scowling. “Mickey Graff,” he muttered, then abruptly sat down again.

“Hey, not so fast, Mister Graff,” Miss Miller smiled patiently. “Come on up and show us where the USSR is. I’ll give you a hint; it’s a very big country.”

Trying to protect Mickey, J.T. quickly raised his hand, but Stella ignored him and continued to focus on Mickey.

After another uncomfortable moment, Mickey grudgingly rose and shuffled to the front of the class. Smiling encouragement, Miss Stella handed him a long stick pointer. For a few moments, Mickey surveyed the map, the pointer circling like a sparrow hawk hunting field mice. Suddenly, he plunked it down right on chocolate brown Tibet.

A chorus of snickers erupted from the class after Stella announced he was indeed pointing at Tibet. "Do you want to try again?"

Looking at his feet, Mickey stubbornly shook his head.

"J.T., you raised your hand earlier," Stella said brightly, "why don't you come up and show the class where the USSR is located."

Now, J.T. didn't want to, but it was too late. It was one thing to save Mickey, quite another to show him up.

"Come on," Miss Miller encouraged, offering the pointer.

As J.T. slowly shuffled to the front of the class, he passed Mickey who was heading back to his chair. He'd seen that look on Mickey's face before and he didn't like it.

Quickly, J.T. grabbed the pointer, plunked it down on the Soviet Union, then without further comment gave the pointer back to Miss Stella, ducking back to his seat. As he passed, Annie briefly looked up, smiled, and touched his hand. By the time he'd found his seat, he was sure his face was as red as ripe tomatoes.

As a grudging concession to the inevitable onset of puberty, the parents of Santa Clara traditionally allowed their children one date after graduating from elementary school. It was usually a movie date and took place at the end of the summer. To further ensure propriety, it was always a group date and always well chaperoned. For the kids, it was an exciting, albeit an awkward and stressful affair. Social and peer pressure required they secure a date, or otherwise be branded as a loser, a social outcast. In many ways, it was a pernicious tradition, but nevertheless it persisted as did the very real pressure to find a date. So far, J.T. had no prospects and had made up his mind he was not going, regardless of the inevitable stigma that would follow him for years, maybe even a lifetime. Anyway, he didn't mind being a recluse.

But now, suddenly both his spirits and his prospects had taken an unexpected turn for the better. Annie seemed interested. She had smiled and touched him. For the first time, he was a man with possibilities.

Most of the rest of the morning was consumed with a lengthy discussion of how the USSR came into being. Stella began with the overthrow of the czars, followed by the Red and White Civil War, then a detailed discussion of the Red Revolution and finally ending with the forced assimilation of the Eastern Bloc of European countries following the end of World War II.

At mid-morning recess, Mickey did not participate in the customary game of dodge ball, even though when the sides were picked he was, as usual, the first chosen. Instead, he spent his time surveying the exterior walls of their classroom, paying particular attention to the open windows. Occasionally, he would stand up on his tiptoes and peer over the windowsill into the classroom, probably at a seated Miss Miller. Preferring not to participate in recess, Miss Miller remained in the classroom, sitting at her desk and reading a novel.

At precisely eleven o'clock, the tower bell rang, calling the students back to class.

Stella announced it was time for the sixth grade to work on multiplication tables, today concentrating on the number eleven. They were expected to learn the product of eleven times every number from one to twelve and furthermore each student must practice these tables until they could do them in their heads, even without using a pencil and paper.

Firmly, Miss Miller jerked down on the world map to unlock it, then let it roll back into the metal housing. Next, she pulled down a map of Utah, color-coded into its twenty-nine counties, and turned her attention to the fifth-graders. Today, it appeared their geography would be the study of the great state of Utah.

By now, late May, it was stifling hot in the classroom. Even with every window open, the students were perspiring like field hands. Most were fanning themselves with anything that would move air: sheets of paper, notebooks, or simply open hands. A couple of the girls had brought folding fans, which looked feminine and seemed to work well. J.T., however, resorted to his math textbook, which did not work as well.

By the noon break, the temperature had soared to well over ninety degrees with the promise of climbing even higher. Rather than joining them in the cafeteria, again Miss Miller remained in the classroom seated at her desk. She munched on a sandwich as she settled back into her novel.

After wolfing down their lunch, most of the boys gathered under the shade of an immense mulberry tree to shoot marbles. The girls congregated under the same huge tree, but on the opposite side and played jacks.

Using a controversial steely as his shooter, Mickey cleaned up at marbles. After he knocked the last of Greg's cat-eyes out of a circle drawn into the dirt, he looked around and issued a challenge. "Anybody else wanna try?"

No one came forward. Playing a competitive game of marbles was one thing, but just giving them away to Mickey with his deadly steely was quite another. With no challengers forthcoming, Mickey settled back against the deeply ribbed trunk of the mulberry tree.

"Me and J.T. are goin' to set the record this summer," he announced loudly, so everyone could hear.

"Record? What record?" Curley asked, still toying with his prized taw.

"Judd and Howie's record," Mickey declared with confidence. "You know the one for the most original pranks in a single summer."

"Can't be done," Alan insisted, shaking his head. Obviously, he felt some loyalty to Judd, his uncle on his mother's side. "Nobody has ever come close."

"D—do ya really think you can?" Greg's eyes were wide with admiration.

"Hey, everyone!" Curley shouted. When all the kids, including the fifth graders and the girls, had gathered around, he continued. "Hey, everyone, Mickey and J.T. are going to break Judd and Howie's record this summer."

A gasp arose from the group.

"Do you really think you can?" Susan Hafen asked breathlessly, moving closer to Mickey.

J.T. knew Mickey had been sweet on her for some time now, ever since the fourth grade, and from the look of admiration on her face, he was pretty sure she felt the same about him.

Eyeing the two of them, J.T. was jealous. He had no one—well, well, except maybe, Annie Leavitt.

"Piece of cake," Mickey declared. "Anyway, what did they ever do that was so great?"

"For starters," Alan retorted, "there was the privy prank. That was a classic."

"We got something even better," Mickey bragged, "don't we, J.T.?"

J.T. cringed, but remained silent.

"What?" someone asked.

"You'll see."

After lunch, Stella instructed the sixth graders to read for the next thirty minutes, Chapter Twelve of their American History book, the chapter dealing with World War II. After that, they would discuss the chapter for a few minutes, then she would give them a quiz on Chapter Eleven from last week, the one dealing with World War I. Thankfully, following the quiz, it would be time for afternoon recess.

World War II was recent history and was the last section in their textbook. D-day, and history in general, intrigued J.T., especially since one of the ally beachheads was christened Utah Beach. And even though it was probably just used as a diversion, still it added a bit of local significance to an otherwise far away event.

At the end of the period, Stella asked for their homework assignments to be turned in on Chapter Eleven, World War I, which of course J.T. did not have. He did not believe in homework. Next, she passed out the quiz on the same subject, which of course he nailed.

For the afternoon recess, Stella once again sent the kids outside to play in the hot May sun, while she again picked up her novel, settling back into her desk chair.

"You want to play kick ball?" someone suggested, though only half-heartedly.

"No!" J.T. replied, heading straight for the shade of the mulberry. "It's too hot."

"How about marbles?" Another fifth grader asked. "It's in the shade."

"That's a kid's game," Mickey snapped.

In just two short hours, J.T. thought suppressing a smile, Mickey had become too old to play marbles. Probably, because no one would play with him.

"You go ahead," Mickey said to the fifth grader, "we've got other things to do."

"Who's we?" J.T. looked closely at Mickey.

"We, is you and me, and Alan and Curley, and Greg and Easy Earl."

"Easy isn't here today," Alan remarked.

"Where is he?" Mickey demanded.

"Home sick," Alan replied, "the mumps, I think."

"The mumps! Isn't he too old for that?"

Alan shrugged.

"Well then, let me tell you what," Mickey looked around, "we need one more. Greg, go see if you can find Weird Willie."

Almost instantly, the boys started grumbling, though no one dared to openly challenge Mickey. That is no one except JT.

"Come on, Mickey, not Weird Willie, he—he's just too weird."

"But we got no choice," Mickey stood firm. "I need six, I need one other person."

"For what?"

"You'll see. Greg, go get him."

Greg frowned, made a circle in the dirt with his shoe, but finally complied.

A few minutes later Greg returned with Weird Willie. Actually, his given name was Wilhelm Adolf Wittwer. To say he was different was a huge understatement. With shaggy unkempt hair, he was slight of build, but nevertheless sported a springy gait, like that of a predatory cat. Physically, he was not all that imposing, except for his eyes. Also like a cat, they were green and ice cold. Furthermore, Willie was a loner. He did not socialize, rarely bathed, or brushed his teeth, and always smelled of garlic. His lips seemed to be too small for his mouth and were unable to completely cover his protuberant teeth. This anomaly created the illusion of a frozen or perpetual grin, or perhaps it was a snarl. But regardless of his slight build, Willie was a bully and possessed a mean streak as wide as the Virgin River in flood. It was rumored he liked to torture cats and dogs as well as other small animals. Other than Mickey, everyone else was afraid of him and preferred to stay as far away as possible.

As Willie joined the group, he immediately singled out J.T., blindsiding him with a fist to the chin. The blow sent him reeling backwards, stumbling to the ground. Picking himself up, J.T. lowered his head and charged, striking Willie squarely in the chest. The impact knocked Willie flat and J.T.'s momentum carried him on top. Now, he was entirely too close, and the smell of garlic was almost unbearable. Gagging, J.T. quickly backed off. Immediately, Mickey stepped in, wedging himself between the two of them.

"Cut it out, you two." Mickey pushed them further apart. "I need you two to be friends, at least for now. Now shake hands."

Reluctantly, J.T. held out his hand. Weird Willie slapped at it.

Excluding the mumps-stricken and absent Easy Earl, this little band was the entire male population of the sixth grade of the Santa Clara Elementary School.

"Come on," Mickey said, and amazingly everyone followed. Mickey had the instincts of a natural leader.

Like the Pied Piper, he led his group to where they could see the outer wall of their classroom, stopping in the shade of a small locust tree. Here he proceeded to lay out his plan.

"I don't know," J.T. frowned, shaking his head. "Somebody could get hurt."

"Nah, ain't nobody goin' a get hurt," Mickey argued. "Just throw 'em in, but not too far."

"We could get in big trouble," Alan added, nervously looking over his shoulder.

"Well, let me tell you what," Mickey declared, "nobody's goin' to know as long as we keep our mouths shut. All the other kids are on the other side of the building at the Mulberry tree. Nobody can prove a thing."

"I'm in." Weird Willie grinned, exposing his caked and yellow teeth. "This is goin' a be fun."

"I—I don't know," Greg muttered, forking a dark lock of Hitler hair out of his eyes.

"He'll do it," Curley added. He was accustomed to making decisions for Greg.

"Well, how about it, J.T.— you and Alan?" Mickey asked. "It's four against two."

"Only if we're careful and nobody gets hurt," J.T. replied, finally yielding to the pressure after a long moment of indecision.

Alan just shrugged his shoulders. "I guess so—if everyone else does."

Nodding, Mickey then proceeded to pass out two cherry bombs to each boy. "Take the two fuses and twist them together like this," he said, demonstrating, then after all five boys had successfully knotted their fuses together, Mickey assigned each of them a window.

“Remember,” Mickey cautioned. “Nobody does nothing till I give the signal.”

In the oppressive afternoon heat, the six boys stealthily advanced to their assigned posts, one under each of the classroom’s six open windows. Contrary to Mickey’s instructions, J.T. stood up on his tiptoes and peeked in. Miss Miller was still seated at her desk, holding an apple in one hand and her book with the other. Apparently totally absorbed in her book, she did not look up.

Mickey chose the north window, near the corner. When everyone was in place, he backed up far enough until he could see the boys in both directions, down both walls.

With the first hand signal, all the boys, including Mickey, fished a stick match out of their pockets. On the second signal, they struck the match on the block cement wall. When all had flame, Mickey gave the third signal, and they all touched the flame to the twisted green fuses.

As the fuses hissed, then started to spit smoke, Mickey quickly gave the final signal, then jumped back to his original position under the corner window.

Like WWII marines heaving grenades at a fortified German bunker, the boys tossed their smoking cherry bombs through the open windows.

KA-BOOM!

4

Even in memory, J.T. still flinched and ducked from imaginary flying debris. In his mind, he could still see the explosion and its aftermath. How much damage had they done? Was Miss Miller okay? What would be the consequences of this prank? He shivered at the thought, then suddenly realized he was also shivering from the cold.

Now fully ousted from his reverie, J.T. looked around for Mickey. He was nowhere to be seen. Had he left without saying anything? Standing up in the shallow end of the pond, he scanned the banks, then spotted Mickey lying in the sun. A half a dozen strokes later, J.T. climbed out of the pond and joined him. In lieu of a towel, he found a similar sunlit patch of grass, flopping down spread-eagle to dry. An afternoon breeze assisted with the drying but fostered the instant eruption of hundreds of goose bumps on his exposed skin.

Meanwhile Mickey got up and wandered around, eventually settling on the gentle curving trunk of a cottonwood tree.

In silence, they watched the sun slowly sink beneath the cottonwood canopy and eventually behind Utah Hill. Suspended high above the western mountains, unsuspecting wisps of cirrus clouds suddenly inflamed to a miner's gold; perhaps, the work of a master alchemist. Within minutes, however, the fluffy gold rifled to a bright cranberry, then faded to a deep purple orchid.

Nature's show calmed J.T. Maybe, everything was going to work out after all.

"Well," Mickey said, standing, "I guess we ought'a go. Them cows of yours ain't goin' to milk themselves."

Nodding, J.T. gathered up his clothes.

After the boys had pulled on their clothes, they carefully picked their way through the dense river foliage toward town. Once they were free of the creek bed, the going got much easier. To save time, however, since they both lived in the northeast section of town, Mickey suggested they forego their usual route, Hafen Lane, and take a shortcut. J.T. instantly agreed; he was already late, too late.

Prying apart the two lower strands of barbed wire, they ducked through the fence, then cut across Emil Gubler's alfalfa field. Even though it was still early in the growing season, late May, Emil's alfalfa was already knee high and flowering. It appeared about ready to cut. As the boys approached the north end of the field, the town's distant streetlights began to wink on.

Their path led straight through old man Rosenkranz's place on the outskirts of Santa Clara and just one block south of the Main Street (Highway 91). J.T. would have preferred to stay away from the Rosenkranz compound, but unfortunately there was no other viable option. To the left of Rosenkranz's was a high unscalable, chain link fence, which housed the gasoline storage tanks of Chevron Oil. To the right was the Leavitt's house with its full acre lot. It did have a scalable backyard fence, but it was also the home of a very large German shepherd with saber-like canines and a fabled bad attitude. Of course, the boys could always detour way back around to Hafen Lane, but that would take them several blocks out of their way and would probably add a full half hour. To J.T. that was not an acceptable alternative since it was getting dark and his evening chores were supposed to be done already. As they got closer to the Rosenkranz compound, the boy's gait progressively slowed, then at his fence they hesitated.

In general, Borch Rosenkranz was something of an enigma to the town folks and a total mystery to the boys. As opposed to nearly everyone else in town, he had not descended from one of the original Swiss immigrant company of 1861, or at least not directly. A year ago, and without advance warning, he'd arrived with his leather suitcases and a steamer trunk. He claimed to be from Switzerland and even insisted he was a distant cousin to the Ruesch's, though old man Johannes Ruesch maintained he'd never heard of him. 'Johnny', however, readily admitted he was somewhat delinquent in completing his church genealogy and the subsequent baptisms of his dead ancestors. He had only traced his family tree back three generations, so technically it was possible they were related, but Johnny seriously doubted it.

Upon his arrival in Santa Clara, Borch quickly negotiated and rented Fritz Ence's old and previously unoccupied house at the southeast edge of town. Some say he simply pulled out his wallet and paid old Fritz (also the town's postmaster) a whole year's rent in U.S. greenbacks. That was hard to believe, but still it was possible. The house was so dilapidated and had no associated irrigation water, so the conventional wisdom was it couldn't have rented for much.

At times, people wondered why Rosenkranz bothered to rent the place; he spent so little time there. He could be seen almost every day, sometimes several times a day, driving through town in his black Ford Deluxe Tudor. He must love automobiles and road trips, as he seemed to be always going to or coming back from somewhere. It was kind of odd since he always went alone (he appeared to have no friends), but perhaps he was visiting the heralded red rock national parks of southern Utah.

But despite his frequent vehicular wanderings, Borch had managed to fix up the place a bit. He'd painted the exterior clapboards an eggshell white and the eves and trim a baby blue. Also, he cleaned up the front yard, planted a patch of lawn and a tiny flower garden. Behind the house, however, he'd not done much, except to build a small service shed from weathered boards that he'd apparently appropriated from someone's old barn. But he had not yet tackled the years of accumulated clutter randomly strewn back of the house. Perhaps, that was next on his list.

Also, old Borch did not mix socially with the rest of the townsfolk. He apparently preferred solitude to the company of the second and third generation Switzers, allegedly his kinfolk. And though he claimed to be Mormon, he did not attend church and seemed to know very little about church history or doctrine. Furthermore, he never attended the Atomic Energy Commission's briefings, nor did he participate in any of the town's holidays or festivals, such as the Fourth of July, Pioneer Day, Easter, or Christmas. The only time he mingled with the residents was when he went to Reber's Mercantile on Main Street to buy groceries, or to the adjacent single room post office to collect his mail from the postmaster (and his landlord), Fritz Ence.

Madge Reber, proprietor of the mercantile, had remarked that when he came into her store she would make him point out what he wanted, because his accent was so thick she could not understand a word he said. She thought his accent was Russian, but other shoppers insisted it was German and some even contended it might be Polish. But whichever language it was, his English was mostly incomprehensible.

J.T. had seen him up close on a couple of occasions and found him to be quite intimidating. He was tall and thin, and his bearing was rigid, almost aristocratic. Though starting to thin on top, his hair was a distinguished silver-gray and closely clipped; his cheeks were lean and hollow, and his face was drawn and gaunt. J.T. couldn't imagine how he could possibly smile. And like a bird of prey, a raptor, his nose had a prominent hook, or beak, and his eyes were a cold, chilly Nordic blue. All in all, he had a stern and unapproachable appearance.

And even his dress was strange. Regardless of the weather, hot or cold, he wore thick woolen and/or leather garments and a hunter green fedora, with a feather wedged in the hatband, was invariably perched on his head.

On the rare occasion, you passed him on the sidewalk, he always reeked of pipe smoke, and he never spoke or nodded. Furthermore, he expected you to move aside. One time when J.T. was concentrating on trying to step on every expansion line, he didn't see Borch coming. Like a highway-construction steamroller, Rosenkranz literally mowed him over, then proceeded on without apology or any attempt to help him up.

Yes, without question, the boys preferred not to go through old man Rosenkranz's place, but it was already dark and of course they were now way overdue for their evening chores.

Years ago, old Fritz Ence had erected a six-foot high board fence around the backyard, but it was not a major obstacle. From past experience, the boys knew there was a loose board near the southwest corner. By rotating it like a pendulum, they could create enough space to crawl through, then they would swing it back vertical.

As previously mentioned, Rosenkranz's (Fritz Ence's) backyard was strewn with a variety of objects, but in the flat gray light of evening it was difficult to identify any of them. Like trying to negotiate an enemy minefield blindfolded, it made for a hazardous crossing. The incandescent light radiating from the windows of the house's back rooms would normally be of some help, but not tonight. Only one room appeared to be lighted, and that was on the west side. As a consequence, it did not offer much backyard illumination. Also of concern, they had to pass right by that solitary west light to get around the house and to Ence Lane, then onto Highway 91 (Main Street), one block further north.

Carefully, they picked a path through the gauntlet of junk, heading roughly for the shaft of light effluxing from the bedroom. When they got closer, they dropped down on all fours to pass unseen under the window. With Mickey leading, as usual, they cautiously inched forward. Up ahead, J.T. saw Mickey drop down and crawl beneath the window.

As J.T. joined him, he glanced up and noted the window was open and the curtains were also drawn. Even though the sun was down it was still hot and apparently Borch Rosenkranz was trying to catch an evening breeze.

At that moment, directly overhead, a shadow flitted by. Instinctively, J.T. crouched even lower, but after the shadow passed he couldn't resist the temptation. Slowly rising to his knees, he peeked through the corner of the window. From the other side of the window, he could see Mickey rising up to do the same.

What a queer sight!

Old Borch Rosenkranz, dressed in a spotless military uniform complete with calf-high black jackboots, gray polo pants, a navy-blue coat with silver buttons and a billed flat hat, stood before a full-length mirror. His ensemble appeared to be a military ceremonial or dress uniform, rather than the more casual field or combat fatigues. Turning first to the left, then the right, Borch seemed to be admiring his reflection in the mirror. Over his left breast were three cornrows of multi-colored ribbons complete with dangling gold or silver medallions. A scarlet red sash, boasting the embroidered image of a block-eagle was draped across his chest and over his right shoulder, like a single bandoleer. Lastly, hanging from a thick leather belt was a jeweled brass scabbard, housing an ornate gold-handled sword.

"Looky at that!" Mickey whispered, wide eyed.

"Yeah," J.T. whispered back.

"What the hell is he doin'?"

"Trying on a uniform—I guess."

"Really?" Mickey said sarcastically, then added, "Why?"

"How should I know?"

"What kind of a uniform?" Mickey asked, his voice still low.

"I don't know," J.T. took another quick peek, "but it's definitely not one of ours."

"I'll bet," Mickey blurted, half-standing, "I'll bet it—it's Russian!"

Instantly, Rosenkranz froze, then slowly turned his head, focusing his cold blue eyes on the open window and the boys. Unsheathing his gold-handled sword, he took a menacing step toward the window, then another.

Mesmerized, the boys froze.

"Raus! Schrecklichen Kinder!" Rosenkranz shouted, then thrust his Degen straight sword through the open window nearly parting Mickey's blonde hair!

5

It was hot! Hot even for this remote finger of the Mohave Desert.

It was the kind of heat that made purple clay parch and crack like thin pond ice, creating a giant jigsaw puzzle in the desiccated earth. The kind of heat that turned semi-arable clay soil into fine sterile powder.

A barefoot crossing of U.S. Highway 91, regardless of foot speed, flirted with the painful prospect of second-degree burns, as well as black tarry feet. Exposed steering wheels baking behind convex windshields became tacky, adhering like Elmer's glue to unprotected hands. Metal gearshift knobs were downright dangerous, heating to temperatures of one hundred and eighty degrees or more. Carelessly discarded Wrigley chewing gum quickly melted, transforming summer sidewalks into gummy minefields.

In this kind of sweltering heat, alfalfa fields first wilted, then died, while the Kunz's nearly moribund peach orchard prematurely shed its brittle leaves, then released shriveled fruit to collect on the hard ground like oversized raisins. Cold blooded horny toads, lizards and Gila monsters scurried from one patch of shade to another, desperately trying to keep their core body temperature down, while freely perspiring warm-blooded humans generally stayed indoors, underground or submerged in the cool waters at the pool or lake.

This kind of heat was difficult for all land dwelling, carbon-based life forms and without question it was too hot to go to school. Even with every window open, classroom temperatures could soar to ninety degrees or more, making the last week of school nearly insufferable.

This year was particularly bad. Nobody, not even the old timers, could remember a spring like this. Standing on dry ditch banks, farmers frowned and cast apprehensive eyes skyward, while everyone else looked for shade. Church meetings were not only used to praise God, but also to petition the Almighty for rain. These supplications were often accompanied with a day of fasting, not only to demonstrate faith, but also to show how desperate the situation was. Skeptics wondered if the Almighty was listening. If he was omnipotent, then he already knew the people were in trouble without being told. So, did he enjoy seeing them beg? If so, that was kind of sadistic. Or perhaps, there was no one up there to hear the prayers.

As J.T. shuffled to school in the early morning heat, as usual he was in no hurry. Sure, he was relieved to be out of the house and the looming specter of his father's belt, but he was not looking forward to what might be waiting for him at school, and facing Miss Stella Miller would be difficult if not downright uncomfortable. Slowing his pace even more, his mind wandered back to the events of last night. Needless to say, it had not been a good night.

~~~

It was a moonless night and well after sundown when J.T. arrived home. First, he went to the pens in back of the house and slopped the hogs, grained the chickens, and gathered the eggs. Being as quiet as possible, he deposited the egg basket on a counter in the service/mud room. Pausing briefly at the kitchen door, he could hear subdued voices on the other side; more than likely his mother and Mary were preparing dinner. After some fumbling in the dark, he didn't dare turn on a light, J.T. finally located the stainless-steel pail and headed out the door again.

As a practical concession to the offensive smell of ripe cow dung with its inevitable swarm of blue bottle flies, the corrals in Santa Clara were located away from the neat row of houses clustered on Main Street. A block north of Highway 91 (Main Street) and at the base of the Red Sand Hill, an entire unpaved lane was dedicated to the housing and care of large animals. When the Swiss colonizers first arrived in the valley, they assigned each family a smaller lot for the construction of a corral in addition to their larger building lot on Main Street. Fortunately, the Kunz's corral lot was close, just a hundred yards or so north of the house.

Carrying his empty pail, J.T. dodged a couple of passing cars as he crossed the highway. Other than the stress of being late for chores, the evening was pleasant enough, warm, but the brutal heat of the day had tempered. A soft gentle breeze carried the mixed barnyard aromas of fresh cow dung and moldy hay.

Even in the light of day, milking Dorey, a huge black and white Holstein, was not easy, but at night it could be tricky, even dangerous. If not hobbled, the ill-tempered bovine would sometimes kick with the force of a mule, sending the unsuspecting milkman flying off his stool. Cussing and grimacing in pain, he would pick himself up and carefully check for broken bones.

Tonight, even after several minutes of frantic searching in the dark, J.T. failed to locate the hock-hobbles. In his hurry to finish with the milking that morning, he must have misplaced them.
~~~

With growing trepidation, he tossed Dorey a flake of hay, mainly to distract her, then standing back as far as he could, he leaned in and quickly washed the udder. Carefully and with no sudden movements, he positioned a three-legged stool just right and gingerly sat down. Wedging the bucket between his knees, he began to squeeze the teats. Slowly he exhaled, so far so good. In the dark he could not see the bottom of the bucket, but the metallic ping as the milk spray echoed off the empty bucket told him when he'd hit the mark.

Slowly the ping was replaced by a rhythmic splash as the bucket began to fill. Subconsciously, J.T. relaxed a little more and settled in. It appeared Dorey had taken the bait. Thankfully, at the moment she seemed more interested in eating than kicking. And anyway, the bucket was already half full. He'd soon be finished.

Then Dorey struck!

It was a direct hit. Her left hind hoof caught J.T. precisely on his floating ribs just below his extended milking arm. The blow sent him cartwheeling sideways, along with the half-full bucket. Ever so briefly he was airborne, then Isaac Newton's gravity prevailed, and he collided with the ground, smashing a fresh cow pie beneath his shoulder blades. In that millisecond, while lying flat on his back, he caught sight of the bucket, also briefly aerial. Almost as if in slow motion, it rotated a half-revolution, then came crashing down, drenching him with foamy milk.

Groaning, J.T. wiped the milk from his eyes, snorted some out of his nose, then took a minute to catch his breath. Gingerly, he stood up. Wincing in pain he grabbed his ribs and sat down again. He attempted to take a full breath and flinched again. After a few seconds, he endeavored to stand one more time. It hurt like Hades, but after another careful exam he was pretty sure nothing was broken.

Finally convinced he would live, J.T. took another minute to examine his clothes. He was a mess! The back of his shirt was caked with a patch of green cow manure and the front of the shirt, as well as his jeans, was soaked with milk, now coated, like a sugar cookie, with dirt and powdered dung.

With a start, J.T. remembered his radiation badge. Thankfully, it was still there, but he couldn't help but wonder if it was okay, or if water (or in this case milk) had somehow deactivated it. Perhaps, he'd already managed to screw up the single greatest research project in American history. Some patriot he was.

Right now, however, J.T. had a more immediate problem. He dare not go face his father, not only was he late, but now with an empty pail. On the other hand, he didn't want to risk Dorey's deadly hoof again. Anyway, he suspected he'd nearly milked her dry. After a few minutes of weighing the alternatives, he finally settled on an another plan. Picking up the pail, he hopped the pole fence and headed for the neighboring corral, the one belonging to Rex 'Red'

Leavitt. His plan was simple; he would get milk from their Guernsey cow.

From occasionally doing chores for Red when he was out of town or otherwise indisposed, J.T. knew the Leavitt cow did not kick and he also knew Red almost always milked her late after he got back from his shift at the Apex copper mine. Sure, J.T. was aware Guernsey milk was richer in cream than Holstein milk, but that was a minor point compared to going home empty-handed. Anyway, probably, hopefully, no one would notice the difference.

Just his luck. Tonight, it appeared the Guernsey had already been milked and try as he might he could only manage a quarter of a bucket. That would have to do. At least, he was not going back completely empty handed.

Returning to the service room, J.T. toweled off as best he could, but the back of his shirt, though no longer caked, still sported a large green stain about the size of a cherry pie. The front of his shirt and Levi's were still soaked, but he managed to brush off most of the dirt. And the smell—oh, well, there was nothing he could do about that.

After straining the particulate matter from the milk, J.T. poured the remainder into a two-quart Mason jar. Unfortunately, the jar was only about half full. He sighed out loud; there was nothing he could do about that either.

Pausing at the kitchen door, he took a few more moments to summon the courage. Finally, he took one last deep, and still a painful breath, quickly rechecked his ribs, then reached for the doorknob.

The entire family, his father, mother, and older sister Mary, was seated around the oval dining table. Seeming somewhat out of place, a white linen tablecloth covered the scarred Formica surface, and the table was set with expensive china. Sporting a yellow poppy flower pattern, J.T. knew his mother loved that ceramic tableware. It was perhaps her only possession, which could be considered a luxury.

As J.T. entered, it was obvious they were just starting the meal. All heads were bowed, and eyes closed while father said grace. From past experience, J.T. knew this usually took a while. Silently and impatiently, he watched, while still clutching his half full Mason jar.

With dark walnut hair, combed straight back, J.T.'s father was a big man, over six feet tall and solid, like a linebacker, with a square jaw and no-nonsense pale blue eyes. In his youth, not only had he played baseball, but also was an amateur boxer, reportedly a good one. Along with his commanding appearance, Mr. Kunz had a knack for giving orders, which he fully expected to be carried out, and they usually were.

J.T.'s mother, on the other hand, was small, thin, and frail. Like wet clothes hanging from a clothesline, her sallow, almost gossamer-like, skin hung slack from her bony skeleton. The only physical traits, which hinted of her Navajo ancestry, were high cheekbones, dark inscrutable eyes, and raven black hair, now thinning and graying. Though J.T. tried not to think about it, his mother, in some ways, was beginning to bear a remarkable resemblance to his teacher, Mr. Frei.

His sister, Mary, by contrast, was the picture of health. She was big-boned, robust, and always looked a bit disheveled. Adding to her tousled appearance was her frizzy dark brown hair, which seemed nearly impossible to tame. Probably because she was older than J.T., she had the irritating habit of telling him what to do. As a matter of fact, they all did.

One member of the family was absent from the table, his older brother Christian. Chris had always been the ideal son, eager to please, willing and ready to work on the farm, responsible for his age, a good student, and an all-state football player. Now, and against their father's wishes, he was somewhere in North Carolina finishing his basic training for the marine corps. The unspoken fear was he would soon ship off to Korea. While Mr. Kunz whole-heartedly agreed in the abstract with the concept of stopping the relentless advance of the godless communists, he just didn't want Chris to be the one to do it.

At last, Father finished grace with a loud amen and was immediately joined by a chorus of seconding amens. Then, almost simultaneously all heads raised.

At first, his father said nothing, didn't even look at J.T.

"Oh, Jackie!" his mother exclaimed, raising a frail hand to cover her mouth. "What happened?"

"Phew!" Mary made a big show of holding her nose.

"Give me the milk," his father growled. Though everyone else ate regular food for supper, Father always had a bowl of broken bread swimming in a pool of warm milk. Years ago, Dr. Hilton had placed him on a bland diet for a stomach ulcer. It was either that, or surgery, the doctor had warned. "Is that all you got?" Mr. Kunz asked, as he unscrewed the lid of the jar, pouring the milk into his bowl.

"I—I spilled most of it," J.T. confessed, which was mostly true.

"That is precisely why," his father meted his words slowly through tightly stretched lips, "that is precisely why I insist you do your chores before dark."

Lowering his eyes, J.T. meekly replied, "Yes, sir."

"Where were you?" Mr. Kunz asked.

"Boy's Pond," J.T. answered, still not looking up, "just kinda lost track of time."

For another long moment, his father said nothing. "Well, go on and get cleaned up. You stink. Then come back and have some dinner."

Thankful for the reprieve, J.T. hurried for the hallway and toward his bedroom. Was he really going to get away with it? Was it possible his father did not know about the cherry bomb fiasco? Maybe this cow disaster was a blessing in disguise—a more immediate, attention-grabbing diversion.

"And when you get back," his father's words seemed to follow him down the hallway, "we'll discuss what happened at school today."

Inwardly, J.T. groaned, his spirits sunk as fast as the flaming-out of a Perseid's meteor. Now, he knew he was not going to get away with it.

Taking his time, he shed his soiled clothes and washed up. He was in a major quandary. He'd promised Mickey he wouldn't tell anyone, and if he did, he'd surely would be labeled a snitch, and get the other boys in trouble. Literally, their fate was in his hands. But on the flipside, he was not a very good liar, particularly to his father, and furthermore he knew lying was a sin. Still unsure of what to do, he pulled on a clean T-shirt and Levi's, then shuffled back toward the kitchen.

As J.T. took his customary seat opposite Mary, he noted his father was scowling down at his bowl of broken bread and milk. Quickly, he looked away and began loading his plate with pork steak, mashed potatoes with gravy and string beans. The lingering aroma of hot pork grease and flour gravy made his stomach grumble.

"You think you got enough?" Mary said sarcastically, while eyeing J.T.'s heaping plate.

"Mind your own business."

Finally, Father looked up from his bowl, focusing on J.T. "This is not Holstein milk," he declared. "It's much too rich."

J.T. remained silent. What could he say?

"John Tobler Kunz," his father said sternly, "do you want to tell me where you got it?"

Swallowing hard, J.T. knew there was no way to fib his way out of this one. "Red Leavitt's Guernsey cow."

"You mind filling in some of the details?"

"Well," J.T. stammered, then decided on the truth. "Well, in the dark I couldn't find the hobbles, and Dorey kicked, and I spilled the—"

"After dinner," his father cut him off, "I want you to go find my—"

"Oh, for heaven's sakes, John," J.T.'s mother interrupted, "don't you think he's a little old for the belt?"

"Not if he behaves like this," his father replied, glaring at J.T., then at Mrs. Kunz, then back to J.T. "Okay, now I know about the milk, so tell me what happened at school today?"

"Nothing," J.T. replied, staring at his mostly untouched plate, "nothing that I know of."

"That's not what I hear." His father's face was hard as Pine Valley granite.

"W—well, I guess some of the kids threw cherry bombs into the classroom," J.T. finally acknowledged, still not taking his eyes off his food.

"You have anything to do with that?"

"Nah—no. I was playing rubbers with Mickey and the other guys."

"This whole thing sounds like a Mickey Graff prank."

"N—nah, he's not as bad as you think."

"Look at me," Mr. Kunz barked, "when I'm talking to you. John Tobler, you better not be lying to me, or I will get my belt and believe me it won't be pleasant."

Swallowing hard, J.T. nodded, then tried to change the conversation. "Was Borch, you know Mister Rosenkranz, ever in the army?"

"I don't know," his father shrugged, spooning up another mouthful of soggy bread. "Why?"

"Oh, tonight on the way home we just happened to see him wearing a military uniform. It wasn't one of ours."

Suddenly, his father seemed more interested. "Not one of ours, you say? So, what did it look like?"

Thankful for the diversion, J.T. described the uniform in detail, at least the details he could remember, then he asked, "does it sound like any you've ever seen?"

"Russian!" his father declared without hesitation. "It has to be Russ—."

"Oh, John," Mrs. Kunz interrupted, "you don't know that for sure."

"It's all starting to make sense now," Mr. Kunz's eyes narrowed, "I've heard some things."

"John, those are just rumors," Mrs. Kunz insisted.

"What rumors?" Mary looked puzzled. "I'm not getting any of this."

"Well," Mr. Kunz began, after glancing sideways at his wife, "old Fritz Ence down at the post office has told me some things."

"What things?" Mary asked.

"Well, according to Fritz Ence, once ole Borch Rosenkranz got a letter addressed to Boris Romanoff, but with his address, and took it home."

"So?" Mary forked up another piece of pork.

"So," Father continued, "he never returned it as a wrong address."

"Really, John," Mrs. Kunz sighed, "what does that prove?"

"For starters, it doesn't take a genius to figure out Rosenkranz is probably just an alias for Romanoff, and Borch is the same for Boris. Anyway, nobody but the Russians would name their kids Boris. It's like John or James over here."

"Don't you think that's, uh—uh," Mrs. Kunz searched for the right words, "that's grasping at straws?"

"H-u-m-p-f," Mr. Kunz snorted. "Absolutely not."

"So," J.T. asked wide-eyed, "what are you going to do about it?"

"Well, for now, nothing. But I want you to keep a close eye on Comrade

Boris Romanoff. If you see him do anything suspicious, let me know. Maybe, at the next town meeting, I might even talk to that government man, Rudy Popovich, about it."

Mrs. Kunz frowned and shook her head. "Don't you think you're overreacting just a little, John?"

"No!" he snapped. "There's definitely something not right about him. He claims to be Swiss, but nobody's ever heard of him, not even his supposed relative, Johnny Reusch."

Mrs. Kunz didn't have a rebuttal, or at least one she wanted to share. Soon it became quiet, each Kunz immersed in their own thoughts.

A Russian! J.T. thought between bites, and not in Berlin, London, or Paris, but right here in little Santa Clara, Utah!

"Tomorrow," Mr. Kunz finally broke the silence, "I have to go on my produce run to Panaca and Pioche. I'll be gone till Sunday, so here's your work schedule for the week." Pausing, he looked J.T., then Mary in the eye. "While I'm gone, Mary, I need you to finish hoeing the tomatoes and cantaloupes, and also, I'll need ten lugs of cherries for next week's deliveries. You can help too, J.T."

"But John," Mrs. Kunz objected, "we talked about this, I need Mary's help around the house."

Mr. Kunz didn't answer right away, but finally seemed to notice how frail his wife had become. "Yeah, okay, Anita," he nodded his head, "J.T., you do the hoeing and pick the cherries. You're old enough now. Chris pretty much ran the farm by himself when he was your age."

But I'm not Chris, J.T. thought bitterly, and I hate the farm but kept his mouth shut.

"On the Monday after I get back, we'll need to haul a load of cows up to the summer range. School will be out by then, so maybe we can go up as a family, kind of a mini-vacation, and watch them government boys fire off one of them bombs. I don't know which one it is, but there's one on Tuesday and it supposed to be bigger than ever."

"Shot Able," J.T. replied.

"I'm not sure I'll feel like going, John," Mrs. Kunz stood to clear the dishes. "It's such a long, rough road and you are planning on spending the night, aren't you?"

"It's up to you. I just thought maybe…" Mr. Kunz never finished his thought.

Actually, J.T. thought his mother didn't look so good. He was worried about her, even though she steadfastly maintained she was okay. Nothing a little rest wouldn't cure.

~~~

Suddenly, a horn blared!

Instinctively, J.T. jumped back. The speeding Chevy passed so close he could smell the gasoline fumes and feel the whip of hot air as the car passed.

Now completely shaken out of his musings, J.T. realized he was crossing Highway 91 and had almost gotten struck by a car, probably another California tourist on the way to visit Utah's national parks. All of the sycamore trees lining the street made it difficult to see the oncoming cars, but this time he knew it wasn't the sycamores; he wasn't paying attention. But, geez, that was too close!

But maybe—maybe—that was it! The trees and the California car had given him an idea for a future prank. He'd have to run it by Mickey. Perhaps, they really could break Judd and Howie's record after all.

In the distance, the school bell pealed and J.T. quickened his stride. He didn't want to be late, not today. With what was probably waiting, he didn't want to attract more attention to himself.

"Hey, hold up, John Tobler."

Cringing, J.T. slowed up, but did not bother turning around. He knew who it was.

Running the last dozen or so yards, Mickey joined him, then matched his stride step for step. "Did you tell anyone?"

"No. Did you?"

"Of course not."

With Mickey at his side, J.T. continued to hurry toward the school.

"So, what do you think goin' to happen today?" Mickey asked.

"How should I know?" J.T. kicked a pebble straight ahead, trying to keep it within his projected path, "but I'm sure Miss Miller is going to be real mad."

"At least Mister Frei won't be there."

"I hope there wasn't too much damage."

"There wasn't," Mickey replied confidently, "just the maps, maybe some damaged books and a broken window."

"Somebody'll still have to pay."

"The school district will. They have lots of money."

"Well, I hope so," J.T. caught up with and booted the pebble again, "cause I sure don't have that kind of money."

The two boys walked in silence for a few moments. J.T. was still trying to imagine what they faced when they walked through the school doors.

Finally, Mickey broke the silence. "Your dad mad last night?"

"Yes."

"You get a belting?"
~~~

"Nah," J.T. shook his head, "but he did tell me something very interesting about old man Rosenkranz."

"What?"

"His real name is not Borch Rosenkranz; it's Boris Romanoff!"

"Seriously," Mickey's eyes widened, "that means he's Russian!"

"I guess so."

"I knew it."

"No, you didn't," J.T. retorted, then added, "so, why do you think he's trying to hide it?"

"Hide what?"

"That he's Russian?"

"That's not so hard to figure." Mickey nodded his head with conviction. "This is the closest town to the test site at Yucca Flats. He's keeping an eye on it for Mother Russia."

"You mean, he's a spy?" J.T. raised an eyebrow. "In the movies spies are much younger."

"Movies are not real, J.T.," Mickey said. "Actually, this way it's pretty damn smart. It's all part of their disguise. Nobody would ever suspect an old man."

A cold shiver raced down J.T.'s spine. Just the thought of a Russian spy right here in Santa Clara, Utah gave him the willies. How long before they heard the clack of Russian tanks rumbling down Highway 91or the tramp of Russian jackboots on the local sidewalks?

"Hey, hold up, you guys!"

Turning around, J.T. saw Weird Willie Wittwer hurrying to catch them. "Let's run," he whispered to Mickey, but it was too late. Willie had already wedged himself between J.T. and Mickey.

"What do ya think goin' a happen?" Willie said, grinning. His protruding buck teeth prevented his lips from fully closing, creating the illusion of a perpetual grin, or maybe a grimace. It was hard to tell for sure.

"Nothin'," Mickey declared, "nothin' goin' to happen if nobody talks. They can have their suspicions all they want, but nobody'll be able to prove a thing."

"But what if they do find out?" Willie asked.

"Personally," J.T. replied, "I think they would make us pay for the damages and that could be a lot."

"Maybe for you two, but it would be nothing for me," Willie boasted.

"Oh, yeah? What you talking about, Willie?" J.T. knew, if possible, Willie's parents were even poorer than his.

"Me and my cousin from Saint George," suddenly Willie's voice was low and conspiratorial, "have summer jobs lined up and the pay is great."

"Which cousin?" Mickey asked, rolling his eyes.

"Leonard. You know, Lenny Weeks."

Mickey protested. "But he's in high school!"

"Yeah, and he just got his driver's license too," Willie said, perhaps with a smile.

"I heard he was in reform school," J.T. said, kicking the pebble forward again.

"Nah, that was last year," Willie shook his head, "he's out now."

"So, what you guys goin' to do," Mickey asked suspiciously, "that'll make you that much money?"

"I can't say—I promised Lenny. But I can tell you it will be plenty, even enough for me to buy a car."

J.T. insisted, "nobody around here is going to pay you that kind of money."

"I didn't say it was around here," Willie said slyly, shrugging his shoulders, "now did I?"

"Then where?" Mickey asked.

"Well, I guess I can tell you this much," Willie looked over his shoulder to make sure they were alone, "it's way up Goldstrike Road, up by Flattop and Windy. And that's all I'm goin' a say about it."

"Buy a car, my butt," Mickey snorted. "You're not old enough to drive anyway."

"There's plenty of places around here a guy can drive if he wanted."

"Like where?" J.T. asked.

"Like any of the dirt roads," Willie replied. "I'll bet you drive the truck on your farm."

By then, they'd arrived at the school. Mickey opened the front door to let them in. Quickly, they crossed the now empty foyer, then paused at their classroom door. As an implicit understanding of their bond of silence, they looked each other in the eye and took a collective deep breath. Then Mickey pushed the door open.

Surprisingly, the room looked pretty good. Everything had been cleaned up. Gone were the glass shards and the chunks of plaster ripped from the wall. The random book and paper debris had been swept up and the brackets and the metal cylinder housing the maps had also been removed. Lastly, the broken window was temporarily covered and taped with a cardboard cutout, apparently while waiting on a glazier from St. George.

Also absent was Miss Stella Miller. In her place, a tall man, who J.T. did not recognize, was standing in front of the class. In spite of what promised to be another hot day, he was fully clothed in a three-piece olive-green suit, a long-sleeve white shirt with a pencil thin black tie. Prematurely balding, he was only partially successful in combing his long hair over the large bald spot on his crown. Balanced on his Romanesque nose was a pair of wire-rimmed bifocals, and a no-nonsense scowl emanated from both his gray eyes and his angular face.

As the boys entered, he turned to face them, planting both hands firmly on his boney hips.

"You're late!"

The boys froze in mid-stride.

"Well," he continued, "don't stand there like Roman statues. Take a seat and be quick about it."

Without a word, all three boys complied.

Scowling, he slowly scanned from right to left, sixth to fifth grade, then he spoke.

"My name is Superintendent Bob Hartley," the tall man said, addressing the class, "Miss Stella Miller won't be here today, in fact she won't be back at all. Unfortunately, she resigned yesterday, completely forsaking her teaching career. She told me it was too much like being in combat and that's not why she chose teaching in the first place."

Superintendent Hartley paused for a moment to again eye both classes. "Now why in the world would she say something like that?" he asked, pretending to be bewildered.

Instantly, J.T. was suffocating in a deep pool of guilt. He couldn't breathe. Were they responsible for all that? Had they destroyed Miss Stella's teaching career? When he had thought about what possibly could happen on this day, he had never considered that option. Somehow, he'd thought Miss Miller would be back and would be hopping mad. They would apologize, she would forgive them and everything would get back to normal.

"Well, believe you me, I am going to get to the bottom of this," Hartley continued. "This morning I'm going to interview everyone in this classroom. We'll start with the first desk on the first row," he tapped the desk with his hand, "then we'll move down that row till it is finished, then start up here with the first desk, another tap, on the second row and so on, and so on. I have set up a command center up in the second-floor gymnasium. As soon as one student returns, the next one will immediately leave their desk and come upstairs. Is that understood?" he asked, glaring down at the students.

Once again, everyone seemed intent on studying the graffiti chiseled into their desktops. No one wanted to make eye contact with his laser-like daggers.

"While I'm conducting these interviews, the rest of you take out your history books, that would be American history for the sixth grade and Utah history for the fifth, and study them. You know what chapters you are on. There will be a test at the end of the day and if you know what's good for you, you'd better pass it."

As Superintendent Hartley turned to leave, he again tapped the desk of

Corrine Ence, in the first chair. Meekly, she got up and followed him upstairs.

Pulling out his American history book, J.T. did not immediately open it. Instead, he stared at the cover while calculating the order the six of them, the six perpetrators, would be interviewed. First would be Alan, then Curley. After Curley would be Mickey and after that it would be his turn. He would be followed by Greg and last would be Weird Willie Wittwer.

The morning dragged on with agonizing slowness. As each successive student left for his/her interview, J.T.'s anxiety ratcheted up another notch. Within the hour, his face had drained of blood, and he was diaphoretic (and not just from the ambient heat). By midmorning, add to those symptoms, nausea and a pounding, kettledrum headache. Nervously, he wiped the beads of perspiration from his brow, then eyed the wall clock again—probably for the hundredth time—still not opening his history book.

When Alan returned, he looked visibly shaken. Nevertheless, he glanced at Mickey and gave a silent nod, which J.T. interpreted as, I'm good; I told him nothing.

When Curley strutted back from his interview, he shrugged, then brazenly signaled Mickey with two thumbs up. Then it was Mickey's turn.

A swaggering Mickey left the classroom, then later returned the same way. Loudly he proclaimed, "a piece of cake."

Next, was Annie Leavitt, seated directly in front of J.T. In what seemed like no time at all she returned to her desk and sat down, briefly glancing back and smiling at J.T.

Now it was his turn. Swallowing hard, J.T. set down the book he wasn't reading, glanced over at Mickey, then stumbled toward the door. As he passed Annie Leavitt, she reached out and squeezed his hand. This time he was too worried to blush. Like a man headed for the gallows, he slowly climbed the wooden staircase to the second-floor gymnasium, then briefly hesitated at the open door.

"Come on in," Superintendent Hartley growled, impatiently pointing to an empty chair. "I don't have all day."

Hartley's interrogation room was furnished with just the basics: two high-backed wooden chairs separated by a small, square, oaken table, probably appropriated from the lunchroom. Sure, they were in the big gymnasium with abundant light and open windows, but just the starkness of the occasion was intimidating. Doing as told, J.T. shuffled in, sat down, immediately concentrating on his shoes.

Sitting opposite of him, Hartley shuffled through a small stack of papers, then peered over his wire-rimmed glasses. "Name?"

"Huh?"

"Name? What's your name?"

"Uh—uh—J.T. Kunz, sir." J.T. tried hard to keep his voice level and not cracking.

Hartley again reshuffled his papers. "Would that be the same as John Tobler Kunz?" he asked with just a trace of sarcasm.

"Yes sir, but I go by J.T."

"Well, now, Mister John Tobler Kunz," Hartley continued, ignoring the preferred moniker, "why don't you tell me all about the firecracker incident of yesterday?"

"Uh, they were cherr—" J.T. abruptly caught himself. Had he already spilled the beans? He'd almost told Superintendent Hartley they were not firecrackers, but cherry bombs. Sure, now he knew there was a big difference, but it wasn't his job to correct Hartley. "Those were—uh—uh—it was just noise to me," he finally said lamely. "I was playing rubbers with the other boys on the other side of the building."

"What's rubbers?" Hartley asked suspiciously.

"Huh? Oh—it's a game where we make shooters by cutting up of old inner tubes, then you choose sides. It's kinda like playing war."

"Okay, I guess. Who are the other boys," Hartley picked up a pen and began to write, "that were playing rubbers? I want their names."

"Uh—Mickey, Curley, Alan, Greg and Weird—uh—Willie Wittwer."

"What about Earl Jaussi? Isn't he in your class?"

"Easy—uh—Earl was home sick with the mumps. Still is, I think."

"I see. So do you have any idea who did this firecracker stunt, Mister John Tobler Kunz?" Hartley's gaze was both cold and penetrating.

"No—no sir, not really," J.T. mumbled, looking down at his feet again.

"Well, just by the process of elimination, I think I do," Hartley continued. "Or at least, I have a pretty good idea. Do you want to hear my theory?"

J.T. really didn't want to hear it, but he nodded yes anyway.

"I sincerely doubt girls would do something like this, they're usually not into explosives, so that eliminates half of the class. I also doubt the fifth graders would have the balls—uh—I mean the guts to pull off something like this, so that eliminates half of those left.

"So, Mister J.T., who does that leave? Well, I'll tell you who, just the sixth-grade boys. And by my count, there are seven sixth grade boys, but yesterday only six were present at school. So that means some of you six had to be involved—at least one or two, and maybe all six. Perhaps, it's time you come clean with me, Mister John Tobler Kunz. If you do, it will go easier on you, I'll see to it."

Again J.T. swallowed hard. This was just as tough—no—actually it was harder than he'd imagined. But there was no way he could let the others down. He couldn't, wouldn't be the snitch. Not today.

"S—superintendent Hartley," he struggled to look him in the eye, "I really don't know anything about it."

"You'd better not be lying to me, John Tobler Kunz." Hartley locked eyes with him again, this time for a full five seconds. "Okay—go on, now get out of here."

When J.T. returned to the classroom, he did not feel triumphant like Mickey and Curley, instead he felt sick. Stumbling past Mickey, he mumbled he'd kept his promise, then sat down, lowering his head onto his desktop. Telling little lies nearly always made him nauseous, telling big lies made him sick.

Somewhere out of the corner of his eye he sensed when Greg left and was a bit more conscious of when he returned. Also, he was faintly aware when Weird Willie departed, but he really didn't care. He was too busy nursing his own guilty conscience and continued rolling waves of nausea.

In a few minutes, maybe even a half hour, Willie returned accompanied by Superintendent Hartley. With Willie standing directly in front of him, Hartley rested his knobby, arthritic hands on Willie's shoulders, then called the class to order.

Willie's countenance was hard for J.T. to read. He decided it was not the face of pride, or steadfastness, or even satisfaction, but it was more like his usual perverse grin. Grin of what? For what? Maybe revenge.

"Mister Wilhelm Wittwer," Superintendent Hartley began after he'd gotten their attention, "has done his civic duty today and has told me everything—what happened and who the perpetrators were.

"I must commend Mister Wittwer on his honesty, courage, and forthrightness, while at the same time I must tell you how disappointed I am with the rest of you. And you know who you are. Not only for what you did to poor Miss Stella Miller, but then having the temerity to lie to my face about it." Pausing, he slowly shook his baldhead; the hair flap over the bald spot flipped and now hung over his left ear.

"It sometimes makes me wonder," he continued, "it makes me worry about this younger generation. What will happen to this country, even this world, when you are finally in charge? It will eventually happen, and it truly gives me pause. God help us!

"Anyway, Wilhelm you may take your seat now. In my book, you are a real hero and to be commended. You had the courage to tell the truth in spite of overwhelming peer pressure, that is the mettle, the stuff of heroes." Reaching up he not so discreetly flipped the flap of hair back over the bald spot.

As Weird Willie strutted back to his seat, Superintendent Hartley's face suddenly turned dark, like an approaching thunderstorm.

"So, right now," his voice suddenly dropping a decibel lower and becoming more menacing, "so, right now I need Alan Heinke, Charles Reber,

Gregory Gubler, Michael Graff and John Tobler Kunz to follow me back upstairs."

Maybe it was because they were in shock, but at first no one moved.

Right now!" he bellowed.

6

Hooray!

At last school was over. They'd taken their final exams and turned in their textbooks. With mixed emotions, J.T. walked out of the front door. He had some good memories, some bad, but in general he had been happy at the Santa Clara Elementary School. He was, however, also more than happy to leave the drama of the last few days behind. Still, it was a bittersweet moment. He would never again return to this school, at least not as a student.

Unfortunately, his graduation was not a foregone conclusion. It was contingent on his successful completion of a few (actually quite a few) outstanding homework assignments and the payment of his share of the damages from the cherry bomb disaster, but more than likely he would move on. He suspected they, the principal, and teachers of Santa Clara Elementary, didn't want him to stay for another year any more than he did.

After completing the sixth grade, Santa Clara students were bussed five miles to the larger city of St. George and Woodward Junior High School for the seventh through the tenth grades. Eleventh and twelfth grades were sent one block away to Dixie High School, which also shared its campus with Dixie Junior College, a tricky, awkward, and sometimes contentious marriage.

To J.T.'s dismay, Miss Stella Miller did not return to finish the school year and rather than hiring another substitute for the three remaining days, Superintendent Hartley finished the year as their teacher.

As a teacher, Hartley was both exceptionally boring and incredibly uninspiring. Rather than concentrating on the curriculum, he seemed determined to teach them discipline. In his repertoire, he had no jokes, no motivating anecdotes and certainly no encouraging smiles or pats on the back. Furthermore, he did not seem to be opposed to publicly berating a student or even throwing felt erasers at misbehavers, and it was not too surprising he was particularly hard on the Cherry Bomb Six, as they had become known. Actually, it had been reduced to the Cherry Bomb Five as Weird Willie was now treated like a teenage hero, a paradigm of virtue. In class discussions, regardless of the topic, Hartley invariably called on the five bombers with the hard questions. Queries to which J.T. usually knew the answer, but for which Mickey and the others often floundered and badly. Typically, any didactic session ended with a sermon, a lengthy discourse on morality, specifically the timeless virtue of honesty and/or the equally timeless principal of the golden rule.

Thankfully, however, that was all over now except for earning enough money to pay for the damages. The unfinished homework assignments were nothing. He could finish them in a day or two at most, if and when he set his mind to it.

Tomorrow he would begin hoeing his father's melon patch and start earning reparation money, but today he felt he deserved a day off. His father was gone for the rest of the week with his weekly produce trucking business; his mother was not feeling well and was spending the day in her bedroom, and Mary had a yearbook signing party at the Woodward Junior High School. What that all meant for J.T. was he had the day to himself and was planning to use it to work on his rocket.

Well, actually, he didn't have it completely off. They did have their regular field water turn, which meant he still had to flood irrigate the old Loren Reber piece. Fortunately, even though late winter and early spring had been dry, lately they'd received enough rain (maybe as an answer to the church-faithful's prayers), coupled with an early winter good snowpack, meant there should be adequate irrigation water. What J.T.'s job amounted to was going down to the field every couple of hours or so to divert the water onto the next section of alfalfa. Other than that, the field pretty much watered itself.

Santa Clara's irrigation system was essentially the same in the 1950's as when the Swiss pioneers designed and constructed it in the early 1860's. Half of a mile upstream above the town, a concrete dam diverted the water away from the Santa Clara River into a series of canals. There were two main, but totally separate systems of canals: one for the field water and one for the lot water. Lot water was used for lawns and personal gardens within the town itself and the field water was exclusively for irrigating the outlying farms. Each family was allocated both lot and field water, and the watering turns rotated from family to family on a weekly basis. The lot water share was usually no more than a couple of hours, but the field water allotment was often much more, depending on how much land the farmer owned. For the Kunz's, the field water turn was usually eighteen hours.

Once the water arrived via the main canal to the field, header dams diverted the stream from the main canal into smaller feeder ditches and from there it was distributed down each individual field row. In the blistering heat of summer, any row of alfalfa, which did not receive water on a weekly basis, quickly withered and died. It was critical, therefore, to make sure the water got down every single row.

Gophers, with their incredible maze of tunnels, were a constant problem. When they dug a tunnel, water in a nearby furrow could instantly disappear, leaving the downstream portion of the row dry. When Mr. Kunz got back from his produce route, he invariably drove down to the fields for inspection, to make sure everything got watered.

This time of year, however, late May to early June, there was usually a big stream of water coming off the Pine Valley Mountains from spring snow melt, and unlike the dry months of July or August, getting the entire field watered was not much of a problem. In fact, there was almost always water left over and J.T. frequently diverted the water back into the main canal early. Also, in early summer, it was prudent to not use the whole stream due to the risk of erosion. A half stream would usually do. Therefore, J.T. could often split the stream and water two sections simultaneously.

Today, even though it was a little risky, J.T. planned to use the whole stream on each section, thereby ensuring it would all get watered in a shorter period of time and without him having to stay there to nurse it down each furrow.

The Loren Reber piece had substantial gradient from top to bottom. This was both good and bad. The bad, it could potentially be a recipe for disaster: a lot of water combined with a lot of slope equaled erosion. The good, the field would surely get watered and between turns he should have time to work on his rocket. Something he'd wanted to do for a long time.

From reading the Encyclopedia Britannica, J.T. had learned the formula for gunpowder: 75% potassium nitrate, 10% sulfur and 15% charcoal. Obtaining potassium nitrate was easy; it was common field fertilizer. Sulfur he procured from his starter chemistry set that he'd received as a Christmas present, and he obtained charcoal by simply burning, then pulverizing scrap wood.

The Kunz's basement was small, consisting of a crowded food storage room complete with shelves of canned fruits and vegetables, a small bathroom, an even smaller furnace room and a spare bedroom. It was the spare room which J.T. had appropriated for his chemistry lab. On the west side of the room, opposite the bed and under the window well, he'd positioned an old plank table as a workbench. Today, as usual, it was cluttered with an array of lab equipment: test tubes, graduated beakers, Florence flasks, glass tubing, a variety of rubber stoppers, metal crucibles, an alcohol Bunsen burner and a ceramic mortar and pestle. Adjacent to the wall was an assortment of corked bottles containing a variety of powdered and/or liquid chemicals, and lastly a light-reflecting microscope was positioned directly under the window to catch the direct light of the afternoon sun.

After getting the water started on the first section of the Loren Reber piece, J.T. headed downstairs to his lab. The first thing he did was to place his burnt wood in the mortar and with the pestle he ground it into a finely powdered charcoal. When sufficiently milled, he placed the charcoal on his balance scales and weighed out precisely 1.5 ounces. Next, he weighted 7.5 ounces of fertilizer (potassium nitrate) and then 1.0 ounce of sulfur for a total of 10 ounces. Using a little metal spatula, he thoroughly blended all three elements together into a homogeneous gray pile.

Next, J.T. spooned away a small amount for testing. There was no point in filling his rocket full of powder if it didn't burn properly. From his impressive collection of matchbooks, he selected one from the Flamingo Hotel in Las Vegas (its cover sported a scantily clad lady suggestively hiding behind a large pink flamingo feather). Looking at the cover, J.T. couldn't help but wonder what was behind the fan-like feather. Sighing, he struck the match and dropped it onto the test pile.

For a full second it sputtered, then fizzed, then fumed. Suddenly, it sparked like a lightning bolt. A millisecond after that, it flashed across a small powder trail J.T. had inadvertently dragged and left behind when he'd separated the test pile from the larger pile.

ZO-O-O-S-H!

When the big pile ignited, it instantly produced a billowing cloud of black smoke. Almost immediately, the smoke filled the bedroom, then pushed out into the hall.

Not only was the smoke dense, it also was caustic, and smelled of rotten-eggs and burning nitrates. Coughing, J.T. had to drop to the floor to breathe. Through the nearly opaque cloud, he saw his worktable was on fire! As he watched, the flames leaped from the bench to the window drapes, also catching them on fire. Now, not only was he danger of losing his entire chemistry set, but he was in real danger of burning down the house.

Jumping up, he ripped down the drapes, throwing them down on the still blazing table. Next, he snatched the comforter from the bed, throwing it over the flames, then bellyflopping down on it. Through the comforter, he could feel the trapped heat on his chest and abdomen and feared any moment the comforter would also burst into flames.

Thankfully, it did not. Slowly, things began to cool. After a couple of minutes, J.T. climbed down off the table and cautiously lifted up one corner of the comforter. No live flames. It appeared the table fire was out.

To be absolutely sure, he removed the comforter, looking for residual hot sparks and also to assess the damage. Fortunately, the loss was not that great. There was some black singe and chemical burn on the table, and the drapes and comforter were pretty much destroyed, but thankfully there was just minor damage to his chemistry set and his light microscope was totally unscathed

The bedroom itself, however, was still churning and boiling with smoke.

J.T.'s eyes burned and watered and his throat and nose felt raw and irritated. Suddenly, he was hit with another paroxysm of coughing. When that subsided, he noticed not only was the black current making its way out into the hall, but it was also ballooning up the stairwell.

That would never do! Slamming the bedroom door shut, he struggled to open the window above the worktable. Finally, he succeeded, allowing the smoke to billow out the window and to slowly be replaced by untainted air. At least now he could breathe again.

But what about all the smoke working upstairs? And his mother? He didn't want her to breathe that stuff, particularly when she was not feeling well. Furthermore, that would require a detailed explanation where the smoke came from, and he would prefer she did not know what had just happened and how close he'd come to burning down the house.

Racing up the stairs to the service room, he opened the door to the outside, then sprinting across the kitchen, he quickly closed the hallway door, thereby, hopefully, isolating the kitchen and service room from the rest of the house. Now he'd done all he could. Wiping the sweat from his forehead, he sank down onto a kitchen chair and watched the black smoke filter out of the service room door.

Once he was satisfied the smoke had cleared, J.T. decided he'd better check on his mother. Opening the kitchen door, he stepped into the hall, then quickly closed the door behind him. With some trepidation, he then headed down the hallway to his mother's bedroom.

"Oh, hi, Jackie," his mother said brightly as he cautiously opened her door. With all the windows closed and the drapes drawn, the room was hot and dark, and had a definite melancholic quality.

"How you feeling, Mom?" J.T. asked, crossing the room next to her bed.

"Okay," she smiled, "just a little bit tired. I'll be better tomorrow."

"You need anything?"

"No," she smiled again and grasped his hand, "but thanks for asking. You're such a good boy, Jackie."

J.T. gulped, but said nothing. If she only knew...

He hated to be called Jackie, his mother's pet name. To him, that sounded much too childish, too juvenile. He much preferred the more mature moniker of J.T., but he wasn't going to make an issue of it, not with his sick mother.

"Well," J.T. said after a few seconds, "I've got to be going. It's time to change the field water."

Mrs. Kunz patted his hand, then released it. "Go ahead and tend to your chores. We're so lucky to have you here to help."

Nodding, he started to walk away.

"You smell something burning?" his mother asked, sniffing the air.

J.T. hesitated for a moment. "I was toasting some bread. Must have burnt it a little." Immediately, he felt remorse rise, like bile, in his throat. He was getting way too good at lying.

Nodding, Mrs. Kunz smiled, then collapsed back on the bed.

Still regretting his most recent lie, J.T. climbed onto the Massey-Ferguson tractor and headed down the Vineyard Road. When he arrived at the old Loren Reber piece, a quick survey told him that this section was completely watered. Not only were all rows watered, but there was standing water everywhere. It had ponded about two to three inches deep on the field and was now pouring off the lower end, completely filling the wastewater channel. From there, it roared down a steep bank, then back into the Santa Clara River.

Sprinting down the bank of the main canal, J.T. stopped at the next feeder ditch, tearing down the dam blocking the water's access to it. Quickly, he then transferred those boards to the main canal, stacking them up against a concrete header. After positioning a canvas tarp over the boards to make the dam watertight, he then shoveled mud around the periphery to seal the canvas and hold it in place. Now all he had to do was hurry back upstream and remove that diversion dam in the main canal, transferring those boards over to the side to block access to the watered section's feeder ditch. Completing that maneuver effectively blocked any more water from entering the flooded section, allowing the water to flow down to the next diversion dam, the one he'd just erected, and onto a new section of field.

Man, that was close, he thought as he frantically worked the dams, too close! Another thirty minutes and the south end of the field would have washed away. Taking out a handkerchief, J.T. wiped the sweat from his forehead. In the future, he would need to be more vigilant, keep a closer eye on things.

With the changing of the water complete, J.T. jumped back on the Massey-Ferguson and headed back home. It was still early, and he had high hopes of launching his rocket today.

Back in the basement, J.T. set about making another batch of gunpowder. The formula he had used seemed okay; it certainly had burned good, almost too good. He'd almost burned down the house!

When he had mixed an acceptable pile of granular-gray powder, he retrieved his rocket from its hiding place under the bed. It was a sleek looking bird, silver bullet in shape, with a twelve-inch body made from lightweight aluminum pipe. The cone, also constructed from aluminum, had been soldered to the top of the rocket. This, J.T. knew, was a potential weak point. He worried whether his solder would hold when exposed to the intense heat of burning gunpowder. Soldering aluminum was tricky at best, requiring a special solder and admittedly he was not very good at it.

For the engine, he had simply crimped down the bottom of the aluminum tube, constricting it from one inch in diameter to less than half an inch. Lastly, he glued on three fins, carved from model airplane wood, spacing equal distance around the bottom of the fuselage. This was another potential weak point. Would the glue melt with the heat of combustion and the wooden fins simply drop off or burn? Without fins, it would be hard to get the rocket to fly straight.

Using a teaspoon, J.T. carefully scooped up the gunpowder, transferring it to a little funnel he'd wedged into the crimped aperture at the bottom of the rocket. When he had the body, the fuselage, completely full, he removed the funnel and inserted a short length of dynamite fuse, working it deep into the gunpowder. Lastly, he ripped up newspaper, wadding it and packing it tightly into the aperture at the end of the fuselage. This, of course, was designed to fix and hold the fuse and the gunpowder in position.

After one final inspection, J.T. decided he was ready for his long-anticipated test flight, but first he needed to go down to the Loren Reber piece and change the water one more time.

He was early this time and had to wait an agonizing thirty minutes for the section to completely water. Finally, he diverted the water down to the next section and raced home.

When he got back to the house, it was still early afternoon. Maybe, he could catch Mickey at home. Surely, Mickey would want to be a part of this historic event. When he picked up the phone, however, he heard the all too familiar babble of voices.

Like most people in Santa Clara, the Kunz's were on a party line, and he had to wait for old Ella Leavitt to get off the phone. He knew it was her by the way she whispered when she spoke, like everything was a secret. He also recognized the second voice. Obviously, Ella was trading gossip with Lola Frei. He waited and waited. Just when he was going the break in and tell Ella he needed the line, it was an emergency, she hung up. He then had the operator ring Mickey's number.

Indeed, Mickey seemed excited and agreed to come, saying he didn't start his shift at the fruit stand till three o'clock. They agreed to meet on the Red Sand Hill in thirty minutes.

Gathering all his rocket paraphernalia, including the Flamingo book of matches, in an empty flour sack. J.T. quickly crossed the tarry asphalt of Highway 91. Hurrying past the corrals, he climbed the Red Sand Hill, a two-hundred-foot bluff composed of volcanic blue clay capped with a thick carpet of red sand, often two to three feet deep.

Once on top of the hill, the red sand stretched north for a mile or more, all the way to its apparent origin, a huge bulwark of fractured and deeply eroded, red sandstone cliffs that ringed the valley to the north. Vegetation on top of the hill was sparse, consisting of a scattering of purple sagebrush, rabbit brush, black brush, and Mormon Tea. Interspersed with these bushes was a few larger plants, mainly thorn trees and spindly creosote.

Previously, J.T. had scouted the area and selected a location fairly devoid of flammable vegetation for his launch site. Off to one side, there was a natural hollow in the sand. Over this swell, he'd excavated a bunker and roofed it with old cedar posts and scrap pine boards, leaving a small glassless window for viewing. On top of the boards, he shoveled a thin layer of sand, making the bunker nearly invisible to the casual passerby. With the bunker now completed, J.T. felt he'd created a safe command center from which to launch and observe the flight.

Today, as the command center was already finished, J.T. just had some minor housekeeping chores. He removed a few old, but combustible tumbleweeds, then just as he was smoothing out the sand in the launch area, Mickey arrived, carrying a .22 rifle. As usual, and as opposed to J.T., he was right on time.

"What you doing?" J.T. asked, eyeing the pump action rifle. He had one just like it at home.

"Hunting rabbits on the way." Mickey propped the gun against the forked branch of a thorn bush.

"Get anything?"

"Nah, but I just missed an ole jack above Tobler's. Did you bring your gun?"

"Don't have time today," J.T. replied, shaking his head. "I've got the field water. I only have time for this, then I've got to run and change the water."

"So, this time, do you think it will work?"

"Yeah," J.T. nodded, then immediately tempered his answer, "I don't know, maybe."

"What you using for fuel?"

"Gunpowder."

"Damn," Mickey's eyes widened with amazement, "where'd you get it?"

"Made it."

"Damn! Does it work?"

"Almost burned down my house."

"Damn! Let's get it loaded."

"It's already loaded." J.T. showed Mickey the rocket.

"Wow, it's a beauty," Mickey whistled softly as he rotated the little silver bird in his hands. "It ought to go at least a couple hundred feet. Maybe more."

"I sure hope so."

"This looks even better than the last one," Mickey commented, handing back the rocket.

"Well, let's get 'er on the launch pad," J.T. said. "I've only got about thirty minutes."

From his flour sack, J.T. produced a small square platform constructed of pinewood. It had four squat legs, which he firmly anchored into the sand, some forty feet from the observation bunker, then he attached the vertical rocker arm. Next, he balanced the aluminum rocket on the platform, positioning it directly over a small hole bored in the floor. Through that hole, he threaded the dynamite fuse, angling it to the left so it could be easily lighted from below, then steadied the rocket with the rocker arm.

When all was ready, he advised Mickey to head for the bunker, then fished the flamingo book of matches from his pants pocket. With his hand poised to strike the match, he paused, looked skyward, uttered a silent prayer, then he struck the match. Just as he lowered it to touch the fuse a puff of wind snuffed it out.

This only served to heighten the tension. Taking a deep breath, he knelt in the sand closer to the platform, then struck a second match, quickly cupping his hands. The flame flickered, then burned strong. Ever so slowly, he lowered the match under the platform and toward the waiting dynamite fuse.

At first the fuse fizzed, then smoked, then flashed!

Pivoting, J.T. dove for the bunker.

Through the small window, the boys followed the progress as the fuse burned upward. Spitting sparks as it went, it left a spiral of smoke as it rapidly shot upward through the platform, aperture and into the base of the rocket.

Suddenly, the fuel in the fuselage caught fire and black smoke billowed from the aperture. The rapidly expanding gases from the combusting gunpowder created a powerful thrust as they were forced to escape through the crimped aperture. First, the silver bird shuddered, then slowly, almost majestically, began to rise above the platform—one—two—three feet!

The expelled black smoke bounced off the platform, then mushroomed upward, instantly enveloping the silver bird.

KA-BOOM!

An ear-shattering explosion suddenly shook the bunker; red sand trickled down from the ceiling between the pine boards.

Flinching, the boys ducked below window level, but recovered quickly, peeking out again. For a millisecond, a residual of the fireball was visible, then it was replaced by a cloud of black smoke. A couple of seconds after that, the smoke disengaged from the wounded craft, as it continued to drift upward. The rocket, however, did not follow. Abruptly, it ceased its ascent, shuddered a death rattle, then plummeted back to the earth, like a shotgunned mallard.

Stunned by the disaster, the boys were speechless.

Finally, J.T. sighed out loud. "Come on," his voice was laden with disappointment, "let's go see what happened."

Scrambling out of the bunker, the boys shuffled toward the fallen rocket. Leaning over, J.T. reached down to pick it up.

"Ye-ow!" Instantly, he dropped it. "Geez, it's hot!" Inserting his fingers in his mouth, he got them wet, then blew on them. Within seconds, telltale white blisters, heralding a second-degree burn, appeared on his right thumb and index finger.

Kneeling in the sand, the boys visually examined the downed silver bird; this time taking care not to touch it.

The first thing J.T. noticed was the soldered cone had indeed held, but the glued wooden fins had not. Apparently, as he had feared, the glue melted with the heat of combustion and the fell off. But on the other hand, being finless shouldn't have made the rocket explode. Using his foot, J.T. rolled the aluminum craft over.

"Here's the problem," J.T. used a creosote stick to point, "there's a crack here in the fuselage."

"The what?" Mickey asked.

"The fuselage." J.T. pointed again with the stick. "It's an aeronautical term. Means the body of the aircraft."

"Sometimes, I wish you would just talk plain English," Mickey said, frowning. "So, that means there was a weak spot in the metal."

"Nyet, nein, mein Freund, das ist nicht das Problem."

Startled, the boys nearly jumped out of their sneakers. Coming from directly behind them, the voice was heavy with a foreign accent.

Whirling around, they were suddenly face-to-face with none other than old Borch Rosenkranz, or Boris Romanoff, or whoever he was. His dress was as foreign as his tongue. Under a dark brown leather vest, he wore a long-sleeved, ruffled white shirt tucked into hunter green knee-length leather pants. On top of his head perched a matching green fedora with a feather wedged in its hatband. In his left hand, Rosenkranz or Romanoff held an ornately carved walking stick capped with an polished brass knob.

"Mein Gottes ist es heiss," Borch took off his fedora, using it to fan his face.

"What?" J.T. asked, with a mixture of confusion and fear.

"It es heiss," Borch pointed skyward, "the Sonne."

J.T. followed the angle of his finger. "Oh, yeah," he nodded, "it is hot."

"Vas ist da problem?" Borch used his Black Forest walking stick to point at the rocket.

"Huh?" J.T. frowned. "Oh, the problem, I can't get it to fly." He used his hands to demonstrate. "At first, I couldn't get enough thrust, then when I got the right fuel, the fuselage couldn't stand the strain. It split apart."

Nodding, Borch leaned over to pick up the fallen rocket.

"It—it's hot!" J.T. reached out to stop him.

Quickly, withdrawing his hand, Borch more cautiously tapped it with the tip of his finger. Satisfied it had sufficiently cooled, he picked it up and slowly rotated it in his large sinewy hands. Grunting, he handed it over to J.T.

"Vhat did you use for fuel?"

"Gunpowder."

"Oh, Schießpulver. Wie behieltest Du es darin?"

"What?" J.T. asked.

"Wie—uh—how Du sie keep es in?" Rosenkranz asked in broken English, but used the rocket to demonstrate his words.

"Oh, newspaper for wadding." J.T. gathered up a couple of pieces of extruded paper, handing them to Rosenkranz.

"Wie, uh—how did sie—uh—ignite es?"

"Dynamite fuse."

Borch was silent for a moment. "Vell, here's the problem. This ist a Bombe—uh—a bomb. Es blows up." He flung his hands in apart for emphasis. "Sie need—uh—to steuern, uh, control the burn. Vhat sie really need is a Rakete-Motor und besser kraftstoff."

"Huh?" J.T. shook his head.

"A motor."

"How do I do that?"

"Vell for starters," Borch's replied, "sie need some kind—uh—a schießpulver—uh— fuel delivery system, so es don't—" he flung his hands apart up again, "blows up. And sie need better—uh—Motor. Sie needs to Verankerung—uh—fix—uh—a metal brushing, one mit a small hole. Needs more thrust. For fuel, try to—uh—mix a small amount of powdered aluminum mit schießpulver—uh—gunpowder, or even caxap—uh—zucker wird tun."

"Zucker?" Mickey asked.

"Uh—how do sie say mit English?" Borch bowed his graying head in thought. "Sugar—sugar vorks zehr gut."

"How much sugar?" J.T. asked. "Or aluminum?"

"Klien—uh—not much," Borch turned to leave. "Experiment mit it."

"Mister Rosenkranz," Mickey said, as Borch walked away.

"Ja." Borch turned around again.

"How do you know so much about rockets?"

"Ich made paketa—uh—raketen," Borch explained, "very much time ago." He swung his walking stick down to the ground and stiffly marched away.

With mouths agape, the boys watched Borch's back as he trudged to the edge of the Red Sand Hill.

"Geez," J.T. blurted. "I had no idea he was so smart."

"Damn," Mickey laughed, "I had no idea he could talk. Could you understand him?"

"Yeah, some," J.T. gathered up his launch pad and broken rocket. "Actually, he had some pretty good ideas."

"Paketa and schießpulver?" Mickey stumbled over the words. "What language is that?"

"I don't know," J.T. shrugged. "Either Russian or German or both."

"So do you think he worked for the Russians on their rockets?"

"Or maybe the Germans. They had rockets too at the end of World War Two."

"But your dad said his real name was Boris Romanoff. That's not German."

"Yeah, I know," J.T. nodded, but right now he felt like giving Borch the benefit of the doubt.

"I wonder what he's doing here in Santa Clara?"

"Maybe, it's just like he told everyone," J.T. replied. "Maybe, he's retired and he came here cause he's related to old man Ruesch and over the years he'd heard stories about our Swiss colony and how great a place it is."

"Santa Clara! A great place?" Mickey laughed. "You've got to be kiddin'. Who would come here if they didn't have to?"

"It's possible."

"Or maybe," Mickey lowered his voice to a conspiratorial whisper, "he really is a Russian spy and all that stuff is just a cover."

"A cover for what?" J.T. asked, slinging the flour sack over his shoulder.

"Geez," Mickey replied, "what do you think? So, we don't know he's a spy."

"Or maybe he just reads a lot," J.T. said, "like me."

"Or maybe he really is a rocket expert," Mickey countered, "and that's why the Russkies recruited him for this job in America."

Both boys were silent for a moment, each lost in similar thoughts, as they watched Borch Rosenkranz (or Boris Romanoff) disappear down the hill. First his legs vanished from view, then his pelvis, then his back and eventually all that was visible was the green fedora with its signature hatband feather.

When Borch was out totally of sight, Mickey smacked his lips. "Man, I'm dry. Did you bring any water?"

"Water? No. Water!" J.T. turned white as desert alkali. "Geez! In all the excitement, I forgot about the water."

"It's okay," Mickey replied, "I'm not that thirsty."

"No, the field water! I've got the field water."

"Oh, how long since you turned it?"

J.T. checked his wristwatch. "About two hours, maybe a little more. I've gotta go." Pivoting, he left Mickey on a full gallop.

"Are you," Mickey shouted after him, "goin' to try the rocket again?"

J.T. didn't answer him. With reckless abandon, he sprinted down the Red Sand Hill, dashed across Highway 91 and leaped onto the Massey-Ferguson. Grinding the tractor into fourth gear, he accelerated down Vineyard Road as fast as the old machine would go. As he roared the intersection with Highway 91, he caught up with Borch Rosenkranz who was just getting into his black Ford he'd parked at the base of the hill. J.T. waved at his new friend, but Rosenkranz didn't acknowledge. Maybe, he didn't recognize him.

Seven minutes later, J.T. steered the tractor across the railroad-tie bridge, spanning the main irrigation canal, which signaled the entrance into the Kunz's fields. Jumping off the tractor, he squeezed through the barbwire gate, then raced through the peach orchard, heading straight for the Loren Reber piece.

As he hurtled the orchard fence, he got his first full view of the field. Actually, it didn't look much like a field at all, but more like a photo he'd seen of the African savannah during flood season. Not only was the section watered, but now the entire field appeared to be a lake. The alfalfa plants were totally submerged with only an occasional flowering purple head peeking above the water.

Like a man possessed, J.T. ripped down the diverting dam, allowing the water to again rush down the main canal. He then transferred the boards back to the secondary header, blocking the water from entering the feeder canal and onto the field. Lastly, he reapplied the canvas with a layer of sealing mud.

With heart pounding against his chest, he forced himself to stop and slow his breathing. He'd done all that he could. Now he had to wade to the bottom of the field and assess the damage. Hopefully, the erosion wasn't too bad. If the collector and wastewater canals had held and done their jobs, transversely channeling the excess water off the field and down to the Santa Clara Creek, then damage shouldn't be too bad.

Staying to the high ground by the fence line, J.T. worked his way south, down to the far end of the field.

Suddenly he stopped; his jaw dropped! He'd never seen anything like this.

7

THE SOUTHERN UTAH HAMLET OF SANTA CLARA WAS COLONIZED IN 1861 when Brigham Young, then president of the Church of Jesus Christ of Latter-day Saints (the Mormons), called a small band of Swiss immigrants to settle on the banks of the Santa Clara River. For their new religion, these unsuspecting, but intrepid converts forsook their beloved Switzerland, with its verdant meadows, flowing streams and snowcapped Alps, for the unknown and unseen deserts of the great American southwest. One can only imagine their shock when they finally arrived in southern Utah after the long journey across the Atlantic Ocean and the Great Plains. Here they found almost no green, but rather a lot of sand and rock. Instead of tall pine forests, they found towering sandstone bluffs; instead of flowing streams, they found ancient black lava flows; and instead of green grassy hills, they found hills of purple clay.

The Santa Clara soil was shallow and poor, primarily purple clay or red sand, and the native flora was sparse, consisting of varied colonies of cacti, clumps of creosote bushes and stunted blue sage or spiny hopsage. The entire valley was served by a single source of water, the diminutive Santa Clara River.

All surnames of this band of zealous pioneers were traditional Swiss: Ence, Frei, Graff, Gubler, Hafen, Leavitt, Reber, Stucki, Staheli and Tobler and even now those families make up a substantial portion of the population.

Apparently, Brigham's Young's motives for settling southern Utah were twofold. First, this new settlement would provide, hopefully, a profitable re-supply station for caravans traveling the Old Spanish Trail, as they were about to cross the forbidding Mojave Desert on their way to southern California. And, these new settlements would further define and solidify the southwestern boundary of Young's new kingdom, the Territory of Deseret.

Brigham's second reason for colonizing southern Utah was both practical and personal. After having recently been driven from their homes in Illinois, coupled with the latest skirmishes with the Federal Government (Johnson's War), Young had dreams of making this new territory self-sufficient, perhaps even independent of the United States. He hoped the warmer climate would be conducive to growing cotton, which the colonists heretofore had imported from the southern states. Cotton was essential for clothing the burgeoning number of saints (Mormons) who arrived almost daily from the eastern sections of the United States and Europe. Furthermore, cotton was not always available or easily transported the fifteen hundred miles from the true Dixie (the southern tier of states), especially with the Civil War brewing.

Immediately on their arrival in the valley, the Swiss settlers divided up the land. By drawing straws, each family was assigned a building lot, a corral (barn) lot and a tract of land to farm. The building lots were located adjacent to the main road and hence the town of Santa Clara was born. Within the town itself, the northern most row of smaller blocks, the ones right next to the Red Sand Hill, were reserved for individual family corrals. The larger acreage for fields, the farm plots, were a bit further from town and scattered throughout the remainder of the valley.

Not only were canals constructed to supply the farms, but also ditches were dug down either side of Main Street. These municipal ditches were used to irrigate the vegetable gardens, usually located at the rear of each building lot, and they also served as a source of potable water for the town. At daybreak, the settlers would draw their day's supply of drinking water from the community canals, then an hour later the livestock would be turned loose to drink their fill from those same ditches.

Though Brigham Young wanted to grow cotton in the new colonies, that endeavor was met with limited success. Unfortunately, the fiber was short and of poor quality, and after the civil war ended, it was almost impossible to sell southern Utah cotton on the open market. But regardless of the marginal success of cotton, the area forever became known as Utah's Dixie.

Nevertheless, the struggling pioneers did find the climate more favorable to growing fruit, specifically peaches, apricots, apples, cherries, pears, and grapes, ostensibly for the making of the sacramental wine. And due to the long growing season, a variety of melons could also be cultivated, including cantaloupes, watermelons, honeydews, and casabas.

Eventually, however, alfalfa became king. With the failure of cotton as a cash crop, most pioneers turned to raising alfalfa hay and cattle. Throughout Washington County and even northern Arizona and eastern Nevada, they homesteaded large tracks of land, often thousands of acres, for their growing herds. Obviously, the high country was used for the summer range and the warmer desert for winter. Typically, the winter desert ranges were a poor graze, often requiring the rancher to supplement the sparse winter forage with alfalfa from the fields. As a rule of thumb, one full square mile of desert graze was needed to support one cow for the winter.

It was up to the Kunz's summer range high on Utah Hill, straddling the

Utah/Nevada border, they were now headed. John Kunz Senior, of course, was behind the wheel of the 1950 International flatbed truck. Sardined next to him on the bench seat was J.T., then Mary, and lastly Mrs. Kunz hugged the passenger door and window. Wedged into metal slots on the truck's flatbed were eight-foot-high stock racks, presently corralling some twenty head of bawling cows and one dun quarter horse. Like most of the area ranchers, the Kunz's herd was exclusively Herefords. Rust colored with white faces, they had a reputation of being hardy, gaining weight rapidly and producing sizeable hindquarters ideal for the premium cuts.

After leaving Santa Clara, John Kunz followed Highway 91 west across the Shivwits Indian Reservation. About a mile past the reservation boundary, he turned right onto Pahcoon Road, a dusty washboard track, which eventually wound its way up to the summit of Utah Hill. Though the distance was not great, only about twenty-five miles, the trip usually took a couple of hours or more, due to poor road conditions and the remarkably uneven terrain.

"So, what the hell happened to the Loren Reber piece?" Mr. Kunz growled above the whine of the overloaded and straining V-8 engine.

"Uh—uh," J.T. squirmed uncomfortably next to his father. "There was just too much water and it kinda got away from me."

"What the hell were you doing?" Mr. Kunz jammed the gearshift down into third, preparing for a steep decline. "Why weren't you keeping an eye on it?"

"I—I thought I was," J.T. replied, dodging the floor gearshift which was dangerously positioned between his knees.

"That's not what I asked." Mr. Kunz's eyes were focused on the road, but a permanent scowl graced his face. "I asked you what you were doing?"

"Uh—uh—between turns, I was working on my rocket."

"I'm going to destroy that damn thing," Mr. Kunz declared. "Bet you turned the whole stream on it, didn't you?"

"Uh—uh."

"Damn it, answer me!"

"Uh—yes, sir."

"You know better than that!"

"Yes, sir."

Though his father was silent for a minute, J.T. could still feel him fuming. "Well, I'm going to have to get a Cat in there to level it out again, then re-furrow and replant. Now, it won't produce good hay for a couple more years."

J.T. gulped. "I—I'm really sorry."

"Sorry won't do it this time, Mister. I'm giving you the bill and I expect to be paid every cent in full."

A tense silence settled over the cab. It was so quiet J.T. could hear himself breathe, even above the drone of the over-worked engine. Subconsciously, he knew he was hyperventilating; he tried to slow his breathing down.

Finally, Mr. Kunz spoke again. "So, when's the meeting?" he asked, his eyes still focused straight ahead at the constantly changing road conditions.

Nobody answered.

"I'm talking to you, J.T.!" Mr. Kunz snapped, as he braked down, steering the flatbed around a hairpin curve.

"Uh—what meeting?" Quickly, J.T. glanced sideways up at his father.

"You know what meeting," Mr. Kunz stepped down on the accelerator again as he double-clutched and shifted back into fourth, "the one with you boys, Superintendent Hartley and Miss Miller."

"Uh—I think—it's next Wednesday." J.T. squirmed to find a comfortable position. His buttocks were still raw from the belting of last night.

"Where?"

"School district offices in St. George."

"How you goin' to get there?" Mr. Kunz braked again, shifting down as they reached the crest of the ridge and started downhill once again. "I'm goin' to be gone on my produce run."

"I'll take him, John," Mrs. Kunz sighed.

"You sure you're going to feel up to it, Anita?" Mr. Kunz asked, concern abruptly replacing the perpetual scowl on his face.

"I'm okay," Mrs. Kunz cranked the window open a little more. "Anyway, I've got a doctor's appointment the same day. We'll kill two birds with—"

"Will you need to have the money by then?" Mr. Kunz interrupted.

Silence.

"I'm still talking to you, John Tobler."

"Uh—no, sir, not till school starts in the fall." J.T. tried sitting on his hands. That definitely was more comfortable.

"So, then, why the meeting?"

"Uh—uh, I guess, to apologize to Miss Miller."

"Well, I'm not giving you the twenty dollars," Mr. Kunz said flatly. "You're going to have to earn it. I'll pay you fifteen cents for every row of tomatoes and cantaloupes you hoe and ten cents for every lug of fruit you pick."

"What about hauling hay?" J.T. knew there would be plenty of that.

"Ten cents an hour and that's five cents more than you're worth."

J.T. thought about trying to argue, to barter up the wages, but thought better of it.

In the ensuing silence, J.T. did the mental calculations. It took approximately one hour to hoe each row and about thirty minutes to pick a lug of fruit. At that rate, it would take roughly one hundred plus hours of labor to get the twenty dollars to pay off his share of the school's damages. After that, he still had to make money for next year's school clothes and spending money. Plus—plus, he didn't know for sure if his father was serious about him paying for the damage to the Loren Reber piece. If he was, that would take a lifetime.

"And," Mr. Kunz continued, "if you think last night was bad, if you ever do anything like that again—"

He didn't finish the sentence. He didn't have to; his meaning was clear.

Again, J.T. squirmed on the bench seat. The whole scene last night was a nightmare. Though he'd not said it out loud, silently he'd vowed if his father ever tried that again, he would fight back. His days of passive submission were over. He was too old to meekly bend over and be belted. Anyway, he was almost as tall as his father right now.

Kunz's summer range was defined and bounded by a four-strand barbwire and cedar post fence. The eastern boundary started right at the summit and extended about a half-mile down the western slope, so about a third of it was in the state of Nevada and two-thirds in Utah. It was good graze, particularly after a wet spring. Native grasses, mainly blue grama, but also some guyetta, squirrel tail and rice grass, thrived after good-snow winters. In the sunny areas, the grass tended to be more sparse, dried, and turned brown earlier, but in shaded areas, the thickets of Utah junipers, piñons, or Gamble oak, it grew thicker and remained green till mid-summer. The west sloping land was ribbed with countless drainage ravines and arroyos, providing natural windbreaks and some shade for the livestock, but making fall roundups difficult at best, often requiring a variety of expletives to complete the job.

Also, the summit made an excellent place to view the detonations at the new Yucca Flats facility. As the crow flies, it was roughly eighty miles away with no intervening high country. This usually provided spectacular viewing. From this distance, you could not see the signatory mushroom cloud, but you could see the blinding flash illuminating the entire western sky, feel the ground rumble and shake beneath your feet and hear the sonic boom echoing off the canyon walls. An hour or so later, often the pink and glowing remnants of the dissipated mushroom cloud would drift by.

As Mr. Kunz pulled up to the barbwire gate, J.T. noticed a brown and white paint horse tied to a nearby juniper. Propped up on one side of the tree was a 30/30 carbine and on the other the shaded profile of a man seated on the ground. With his Stetson pulled forward over his eyes, the man's head rested back against the ribbed tree trunk. At first glance, he appeared to be sleeping.

Mr. Kunz groaned out loud. "Who invited him?"

"I did," Mrs. Kunz replied, her delicate jaw thrust forward and her black eyes defiant and unflinching. "He's my cousin."

"Yeah, I know," Mr. Kunz growled, "but I thought we'd make this a family outing."

"He is family," Mrs. Kunz said curtly.

Though she grew up in Kanab, Utah, Anita Kunz was half Navajo. Her father, Levi Judd, an Indian art and artifacts dealer, had met Anita's mother, J.T.'s grandmother, when she worked at the Gray Coyote Trading Post near Kayenta on the northwest corner of the Navajo Reservation. After a brief courtship followed by a temple marriage, the newlyweds moved to Kanab and started a business, the Kanab Fruit, and Vegetable Emporium. Shortly thereafter, a daughter was born, J.T.'s mother, Anita Judd. It was at the Emporium, while delivering fruit, young John Kunz first met and fell in love with the dark-eyed beauty.

After their marriage, the couple moved to Santa Clara. Mrs. Kunz raised three kids, kept the house, canned the fruit and vegetables and helped some with the farm chores. Though Mr. Kunz had long ago given up his Kanab route, he continued to supplement the farm income by supplying the southern Nevada mining towns of Pioche, Ely and Ruth with fresh fruit and produce. These things they could not grow due to their higher elevation, colder climate, and shorter growing season.

The man sleeping under the juniper tree was Smokey Grayman, Mrs. Kunz's first cousin on her mother's side and J.T.'s first cousin once removed.

Quickly, the trailing dust cloud caught up as the flatbed slowed to a stop, engulfing them in a swirling, powdery fog. When the cloud cleared, J.T. saw Smokey was now on his feet and stomping out a cigarette. Apparently, he had not been asleep after all. Reaching down, he snatched up a brown pint bottle, sequestering it inside his leather jacket. Slapping the dust from his shirt and pants, he repositioned his black, flat-brimmed reservation hat on his head. As he walked toward the flatbed International, the conchos of his hatband sparkled, like silvery rhinestones in the bright morning sun.

As he grudgingly rolled down the window, John Kunz's scowl deepened further.

"Yaa' eh t'eeh," Smokey greeted them. His picket fence smile was courtesy of poor dental hygiene and several missing teeth.

"How many times do I have to tell you," Mr. Kunz snapped, "no Injun talk around the kids. I don't want them speakin' nothin' but American."

"Yaa' eh t'eeh," Smokey repeated, still grinning, "is American, native American." He almost looked comical with his black-graying braided hair, round face, and absent teeth. "Hi, Anita," he added, looking past Mr. Kunz.

"Hi, Samuel," Mrs. Kunz smiled warmly and reached across Mr. Kunz for his hand. "Glad you could make it."

"And I don't want no smokin' and drinkin' around the kids," Mr. Kunz continued, swatting a pesky gray fly away from his ear.

"Okay," Smokey nodded, but his smile had already started to fade.

"Anyway, I thought you were Mormon," Mr. Kunz added, unable to keep the disgust out of his voice.

"I am."

"Mormons don't smoke or drink."

"In this life you can be many things. Being one thing doesn't keep you from being another."

"I'll never understand you people." Mr. Kunz shook his head. "Yeah, sure, you can be many things, but not all at once. It's like being pregnant, either you are or you're—"

"John," Mrs. Kunz leaned over J.T. and jabbed his ribs, "watch your language."

"Uh—maybe that's nct a good example. Well, it's like—uh—like being dead. You're either alive or you're dead, but you can't be both, at least not at the same time. It's the same with religion, either you're Mormon or you're not."

"Why not take the best of all things? Biligaana or Dinetah, what difference does it make? There's good in everything."

"Well, obviously you don't understand the gospel of Jesus Christ, or you'd wouldn't make stupid statements like that," Mr. Kunz said. "If you want to get into heaven, you walk the straight and narrow. And which road you take, makes a hell-uv-a lot of diff—"

Mrs. Kunz jabbed him again.

"Anyway, the way is straight and the road is narrow," Mr. Kunz continued, "and most people don't make it. There's only one road that leads to heaven, and that's through the teachings of Joseph Smith and the atonement of Jesus the—"

"Oh, John," Mrs. Kunz interrupted, "settle down. Remember your ulcer."

"So, let's get one thing straight right now." Mr. Kunz's voice grew more shrill and louder. "I don't want no smokin', drinkin', cussin', or talkin' Injun around the kids."

"You already said that." Now Smokey seemed to struggle with keeping a neutral face. "I just want to hunt deer and see Anita and the kids, that's all."

"It's not deer season - oh—oh, that's right, you people don't need a license, do you?"

"No, not on government land. So, where do you want to camp?" Smokey asked in an obvious attempt to change the subject.

No answer.

Again J.T. shifted his weight on the bench seat; the silence was growing uncomfortable.

"Over by the spring," Mr. Kunz finally said. "And don't you be takin' that flat area right in front of the spring. That's for me and Anita's tent."

"I'll get the gate for you," Smokey shrugged, turning he walked away.

After unloading the cows and the quarter horse, they set up camp by the spring, the only standing water for miles and the lone source of water for the Kunz's entire BLM lease. The spring seeped out of the foot of a gray limestone cliff, forming a shallow pool, which overflowed into a Lilliputian-size creek. Not only was the creek small, but it was also short lived. It rushed down the hill for about two hundred yards or so before seeping back into the porous earth. Ringing the pool and stream, however, was abundant riparian flora: river reeds, coyote, and white willows and behind the willows, Gulliver-size sagebrush. A little further back from the water, towering cottonwoods, twenty-foot junipers and robust piñons flourished.

As expected, a layered ecosystem of fauna had also evolved around this little oasis. Herbivores such as mice, rabbits, squirrels, and mule deer struggled for existence with their niche-matched carnivores, gray foxes, desert coyotes, red-tailed hawks, and mountain lions.

After Smokey had opened the gate, Mr. Kunz drove through, then backed up to a loading dock, surrounded by a circle corral, both constructed of juniper logs. After J.T. removed a rear section of the sideboards, they unloaded the bawling Herefords, immediately turning them loose, but corralling the Dun gelding.

With the help of J.T. and Mary, Mr. Kunz erected an old army canvas tent on the level ground in front of the spring. After the big tent was staked, J.T. and Mary chose locations for their smaller pup tents. Several yards away Smokey found a spot under a low canopy of piñons to throw down his canvas tarp and sleeping bag. While the family searched for firewood, Smokey announced he was going deer hunting. Taking his 30/30 carbine with him, he mounted his paint and disappeared, heading north into the pygmy forest.

After they had accumulated a sizeable stack of wood, Mr. Kunz, as was his custom, gave them their work assignments for the afternoon. Mrs. Kunz and Mary would start the fire and began preparation for the evening meal. He, Mr. Kunz, would walk along the western boundary to check the integrity of that fence line. J.T. would mount the dun and ride the far north line over by Dead Man's Point, also checking for breaks in the wire. Drifting winter snow and thunder/windstorms, Mr. Kunz reminded them, were experts at destroying fences.

First, J.T. collected his fence-mending supplies: slip-joint pliers, a coil of barb wire, a splice of baling wire, and a claw hammer, along with a handful of fencing staples. After that, he saddled the tall, sixteen-hands dun, christened Casey. Probably without realizing it, his father had given him the one task he really enjoyed; to him anything that involved riding a horse was not a chore. He'd fed and grained Casey from a colt and helped some with his training. Casey was his baby.

After struggling with the heavy Carl Darr saddle, J.T. bridled Casey. When he had him ready, he looked for his usual rock for mounting, then decided this year he didn't need it. He'd grown at least three inches since using it last year. By raising his foot as high as he could, he managed to plant his left boot in the stirrup, then grasping the saddle horn for leverage, he stepped up, swinging his right leg over the cantle. Nudging Casey with his boot heel, they headed north.

The terrain was remarkably rough and broken. J.T.'s path took him over several arroyos and finally to a high, west-facing bench. From here, J.T. imagined he could see most of southern Nevada and even into California. Like a series of ocean waves queuing to come ashore, he could see successive rows of purple mountain ranges, also apparently queued, but instead of separated by wave troughs, they were separated by dry desert valleys. The distant mountains and valleys were all part of the great Mojave Desert, and the view was nothing short of spectacular.

At the edge of the bench, J.T. picked up the north-boundary fence, then headed east, looking for downed strands, or breaks in the wire. Occasionally, it was necessary for him to dismount and staple up a fallen strand or splice a broken section of wire.

From the northwest corner, the fence line crossed the jumbled terrain for about a mile, then headed straight up a box canyon. J.T. let Casey pick his way up the wash, still closely following the fence line. As he worked up the canyon, the walls gradually got steeper and narrower, and the rimrock got higher. The canyon, J.T. knew, abruptly ended in about a quarter mile at the face of a granite cliff. At the mouth of the canyon, the fence terminated, then resumed on top of the cliff. The north wall effectively served as a fence, so he really didn't need to ride the canyon, but it was a scenic ride and well worth the short detour.

When J.T. got to the cliff, he would have to backtrack, as there was no direct trail to the crest from the canyon floor. Back at the entrance, he would have to locate an old prospector's trail, which did snake its way to the top. Once on the summit, he would continue to ride the fence line until he reached the eastern boundary.

Relaxing in the saddle, J.T. soaked up the sun and the ambiance. It was a perfect early June day. There was a slight breeze, no clouds and the temperature was hovering in the mid-70's. It was the kind of day that made you forget your troubles. At this moment, out here in nature, everything seemed okay. In the comfortable silence, J.T. continued up the canyon. The only sounds came from the clomp of Casey's rhythmic gait and/or the occasional grate of steel horseshoes scraping across sandstone.

As Casey picked his way up the wash, J.T. worked on a problem that had baffled him for some time, specifically rocket fuel and rocket motors. Over the last few months, he'd been working on the fuel to power his rocket and had thought gunpowder was the answer, but after the recent failed attempt on the

Red Sand Hill he was not so sure. Borch Rosenkranz, or Boris Romanoff, or whomever he was, had suggested adding a bit of powdered aluminum or sugar to the mixture and certainly that was worth a try. He'd probably use sugar as it was more abundant and easier to get. All he needed now was some time to do the experiments and figure out the best proportions.

Also, Borch had hinted he needed a better motor. He'd done enough reading to understand the basics of rocket engines. When the fuel ignited, the rapidly expanding gases from combustion had to escape somewhere. If the aperture at the bottom of the rocket was sufficiently small, the escaping gases would thrust the rocket forward, the same force that propelled an over-inflated balloon when released. The problem, however, was how to dramatically reduce the outlet of the fuselage (the aluminum pipe) and still preserve the aerodynamic properties. If the motor, i.e., the reduced rear aperture, was not machined perfectly round, the rocket would veer off and crash. Mr. Rosenkranz had suggested soldering a metal brushing, or at least that's what J.T. thought he'd said. A metal brushing might work, but would the solder hold? Maybe, as it did on the cone with his recent failed attempt. And more than likely, he'd have to do the same with the fins. Instead of using wood, fashion them out of sheet aluminum and solder them to the fuselage. But he still worried about his ability to solder aluminum; it was a little tricky. In frustration, J.T. sighed out loud. What he really needed was more time to work on the project.

Also, there was the problem of explosion. Somehow, he had to work out a system, so all the fuel didn't ignite at once. Like Borch had said, he needed some kind of fuel delivery system. Perhaps, a two-chambered fuselage might work, one chamber for storage and another for the burning of fuel.

Taking off his ball cap, J.T. scratched his head. Once again, it boiled down to time. He needed more free time to experiment and design these things. However, with all his newly accumulated and substantial debt, plus the added responsibility of running the family farm, his free time would be at a premium.

Next his thoughts turned to Weird Willie Wittwer. Plain and simple, Willie was a skunk. Not only had he turned them in to Superintendent Hartley, but he had shamelessly lied about his own involvement. Hartley thought he was a saint, but J.T. and Mickey knew otherwise. J.T. was working on a fitting punishment for Willie and with any luck it might also qualify as another original prank, thereby moving him and Mickey a little closer to the record. Also, ever since his close call with the California tourist, when he'd almost been hit on the way to school, he'd been developing an idea for another prank. Soon, he'd run it by Mickey for his approval. But if he could keep coming up with ideas, they might just do it, beat the unbeatable record of the immortal Judd and Howie.

Lastly, his thoughts turned to a more pleasant subject, Annie Leavitt. No, she would not qualify as a Hollywood beauty, she was more of a tomboy, but she was cute enough with her freckled face and sandy hair. And, if he wasn't reading her wrong, J.T. was pretty sure she liked him. The first date night was coming up in a couple of months and until now he'd had absolutely no prospects, no one he even dared ask. He'd felt like a nerd, the town leper, a social outcast, but now maybe he had possibilities. In spite of himself, he broke into a full-toothed grin.

As J.T. nudged Casey up the wash, he noticed several crows aloft, or were they ravens, or possibly turkey vultures? Whatever they were, the black birds were carving lazy spirals in the azure sky, but other than that everything was quiet, almost too quiet. From the height of the walls, he knew they were almost to the end of the canyon. Up ahead, he could see where the sandy wash curved around a huge pillar of granite, then disappeared. As they approached it, J.T. pretty much let Casey choose his own path around the massive rock. The breeze had picked up some, now blowing down the canyon and directly into his face.

Abruptly, Casey stopped! His ears shot forward and the muscles of his shoulders tensed. He seemed nervous and edgy. Using his boot heels, J.T. gently nudged his flanks. Reluctantly, Casey moved forward.

As soon as they rounded the granite pillar, J.T. saw the cougar. She was crouched over a fresh kill, probably a young doe, feasting with her two newborn cubs. Sporting a beautiful harvest gold coat, she was big and rangy. Like a toned athlete, her muscle bundles were well defined and rippled when she moved. When she looked up, J.T. noted with alarm, her face was smeared with fresh red blood.

On seeing him, the cougar pivoted to escape, but the vertical cliff blocked her escape. Turning back around, she faced J.T. Baring her bloody fangs, she emitted a low, guttural sound. Very nervous now, Casey wanted to bolt, but J.T. held him back. Still determined to get away, Casey danced and scooted sideways. Somehow in all the confusion, they, J.T. and Casey, ended up between the mother and her cubs.

That's when she attacked! In two swift and graceful bounds, she was on J.T.

Terrified, Casey reared, his hooves pawing the air, then whirling, he fled back down the canyon.

Clinging to the saddle horn, J.T. had managed to stay in the saddle when Casey reared, but the sudden three-hundred-and-sixty-degree pivot unseated him. Tumbling sideways out of the saddle, he collided with the canyon wall, then crumpled on the sandy wash. Rolling over, he clutched his injured ribs, groaning and gasping for air. The pain was excruciating! From the pain or shock or both, his vision blurred and his mind fogged over. He struggled to remain conscious.

Somehow through the gossamer thin veil of semi-consciousness, he saw the cat charge. In two balletic leaps, she was on him. Instinctively, he raised his hands to protect his face, then rolled to his left, uninjured side, curling up into the fetal position. Closing his eyes, he mumbled an abbreviated prayer to God, while hoping he wasn't too busy.

So, was this going to be it? Was this to be his last day on earth? The nineth of June, nineteen hundred and fifty-two, and just a couple of days before his fourteenth birthday?

Was this the day he was going to die?

8

KA-BOOM!

A single gunshot rang out, reverberating off the sheer canyon walls, then echoing up-canyon to the granite cliff, then back again. Instantly, the huge cat crumpled, falling on top of J.T. Her enormous weight made breathing difficult and further intensified the pain from his damaged ribs. Though the chest pain was intense, it was rapidly becoming secondary to the need for oxygen. Like a drowning man, he fought for air, but couldn't draw a breath. He needed to move the cat, but even with the added adrenaline, fueled by hypoxia and panic, he still couldn't budge her.

Abruptly, the big cat was jerked from him.

Almost instantly, he could breathe again and with the weight off his chest the pain began to recede, though not completely. Forcing open his eyes, the first thing he saw was the flat-brimmed reservation hat; next a row of tobacco-stained teeth with some missing came into view and lastly, he recognized the leathery brown face of Smokey Grayman.

"Yaa' eh t'eeh, Jack," he pushed the flat-brimmed hat back on his head and extended a gnarled brown hand. "This, my little shił naa'aash, is not a good day to die."

At first, J.T. said nothing. He had not yet accumulated enough air to speak, but he did accept the proffered hand, then winced as he got up.

"Are you okay," Smokey helped him dust him off, "my little cousin?"

Still taking only half-breaths due to the rib pain, J.T. simply nodded.

"Then help me load up this cat."

J.T. tried, but wasn't much help and even needed Smokey's assistance to remount Casey. And even though he'd only ridden a couple miles from camp, the ride back seemed more like forty. Each step of Casey's triggered a spasm of pain and trotting was out of the question.

When they arrived back at camp, Smokey led his paint, with the big cat roped across the saddle, straight to the grove of junipers where he'd previously unrolled his sleeping bag.

J.T. nudged Casey back to the pole corral, while keeping an eye on Smokey as he untied the ropes securing the cougar. After lifting her from the saddle, he used the same rope to string her up, hind paws first, to a high branch of a nearby juniper. Next, employing his bone-handled knife, he made an incision from the top of the cat's chest all the way down to her pubic bone. Once he found the correct plane, right under the subcutaneous fatty layer but above the fascial plane and muscle bundles, he began to systematically remove the hide.

This all was too much for Mr. Kunz. Dropping an armful of wood by the blazing fire, he walked over to Smokey. J.T. inched closer, straining to hear the conversation.

"What ya doing, Smokey?"

"Skinnin' a cat." Smokey paused to strike a match, then touched it to a Marlboro.

"What you going to do with the hide?" Mr. Kunz asked, waving off the offending smoke.

"Sell it"—Smokey took another drag from his cigarette—"A big cat like this could bring fifty—maybe a hundred dollars."

"Where'd you get it?"

"Over at the box canyon." Smokey fell silent as he continued to work. He was never one for small talk.

"Did you see, J.T.?" Mr. Kunz asked, then quickly added, "put out that damn cigarette."

"Yeah," Smokey nodded toward the corral while taking one last drag, "he's over there."

J.T. tried to wave, but just the movement of raising his arm made him groan in pain and clutch his right side. Turning back to his horse, he struggled to remove the heavy Carl Darr saddle.

Leaving the cat half-skinned, Smokey sheathed his knife and hurried over to help. Apparently still puzzled, Mr. Kunz tagged along, his frown deepening.

"What happened?" he asked J.T.

"Well—uh," J.T. stuttered. "Well, I guess Smokey saved my life."

"Maybe," Mr. Kunz said, his eyes narrowing, "you'd better explain."

For the next five minutes, J.T. recounted the entire episode, then finished by saying, "it's a good thing Smokey was there, or I'd be the one that's dead."

"The cat was trapped in the canyon with her cubs," Smokey explained, "Casey was dancing and sidestepping and somehow he got between the cat and her cubs. She was just trying to protect her young."

For once, Mr. Kunz was speechless.

It was obvious to J.T. his father didn't know what to do. On the one hand, he didn't care at all for Smokey, but on the other hand Smokey had just saved his son's life.

"What were you doing over that way," he finally asked, "following the boy?"

"Yeah," Smokey shrugged as he walked back to the cat, "that and hunting deer."

"Come and get it!" Mrs. Kunz called from the campfire.

As they started for the campfire, J.T. searched his shirt pocket. "Oh, no!" he exclaimed.

"What?" his father asked.

"I—I lost my radiation badge."

"That's no big deal," Mr. Kunz growled. "That research is a waste of time anyway. We all know we're not getting enough radiation from those Shots to harm a cricket."

"But—but I promised Mister Popovich—"

"Half the kids'll lose their badges," Mr. Kunz predicted, "before the month's out."

"Where do you think you lost it?" Smokey asked.

"Probably over where the cougar attacked," J.T. said after a moment's thought, "that's where Casey threw me."

"Forget it," Mr. Kunz growled. "Your mother and Mary have dinner ready."

"But…" J.T. objected. Apparently, however, the conversation was over as Mr. Kunz had already turned and walked away.

As the campers neared the campfire, they were greeted with the mixed aroma of Dutch oven steak and sizzling onions and potatoes. The odor made J.T.'s stomach churn. Until that moment he hadn't realized how hungry he was.

Mrs. Kunz and Mary had cooked the evening meal entirely in cast iron Dutch ovens and were just now removing the lids to inspect the food. Declaring it was done, Mrs. Kunz instructed each camper, except for Mr. Kunz, to grab a metal plate, then Mary would serve up the food.

Not taking a plate with the others, Mr. Kunz began rummaging through the camp gear.

"Anita, I don't see my bowl and there's no milk."

"Oh," Mrs. Kunz sighed, "John, I forgot to pack it. I guess you'll just have to eat what everybody else does."

"But my ulcer," Mr. Kunz grumbled. "The doctor said—"

"One meal's not going to hurt your stomach," Mrs. Kunz said sharply, turning away. "Anyway, I don't think that bland diet's doing your ulcer any good."

"It's better than an operation."

"Yeah, maybe," Mrs. Kunz said doubtfully, offering him a metal plate.

After a few more moments of fussing, Mr. Kunz grudgingly took a tray, got his food, and settled down on a rock. At first, he picked at his food, like it was a suspect foreign dish, then after a couple of minutes he wolfed it down, like a bear coming out of a long winter's hibernation.

As dusk gathered, any residual light fled the camp, like a war-weary refugee. In silence, the five of them munched, watched the fire pop and hiss, and occasionally shoot geysers of ash and sparks high into the night sky.

"So, what time do we have to get up?" Mary finally asked, breaking the hypnotic silence.

"The test is at 5:00 a.m.," Mr. Kunz replied. "So, let's get up at four-thirty. We can have some hot Postum before we go over to see the shot, then we'll eat breakfast later."

"Geez," Mary grumbled, "four-thirty! What's the big deal, anyway? I've seen Shots before."

"Not like this one," J.T. said.

"Oh, yeah," Mary said, "what's so special about this one?"

"This one," J.T. replied, his eyes aglow with excitement, "is called Shot Able. It's the first one of the new Operation Ranger series, and it's supposed to be even bigger than those used on Nagasaki and Hiroshima."

"What's Nagasaki and Hiroshima?" Mary asked, badly mispronouncing the names.

"Cities in Japan," J.T. replied, "we bombed them to end World War Two."

"Oh," Mary said, looking unconvinced, then added, "and how would you know that?"

"Cause, I read a lot."

"Anyway, it should be quite a show," Mr. Kunz said, rejoining the conversation. "Mary, it'll be well worth getting up for. This is literally history in the making."

"Well, I don't like it," Mrs. Kunz mumbled, glancing down at her plate. As usual, rather than eating, she played with her food. Presently, she had just rotated the sliced potatoes and with a chunk of meat.

"Why not?" Mr. Kunz asked.

Before she could answer, Smokey jumped in. "Old coyote, the trickster, is always out there and waiting," Smokey paused, looking out into the vast blackness of night, then barely above a whisper he added, "coyotes and skinwalkers — this is the work of the chindis."

In spite of warmth of the summer night and the nearby campfire, J.T. felt a cold shiver creep up his spine. He knew enough Navajo folklore to know the significance of skinwalkers and chindis.

"What the hell's a chindis?" Mr. Kunz asked, wiping his plate clean with a soda biscuit.

"They're evil ghosts, sometimes they come as coyotes, sometimes not," Mrs. Kunz said softly. "They're shape-shifters."

"That's all poppycock," Mr. Kunz snorted. "The whole idea of ghosts is totally absurd. I can't believe half-intelligent, grown men could believe in that stuff."

"Is it any more ridiculous than the Joseph Smith story?" Smokey asked. Standing, he stoked the fire with a long stick, then stared intently into the black night. "He saw ghosts too."

"No, he didn't!" Mr. Kunz snapped, raising his voice a few decibels. "He saw angels. Big damn difference."

"What's the difference?" Smokey asked, as he resumed stirring the fire.

"That comment," Mr. Kunz said, "is so ludicrous, I don't know where to start with an answer."

"Ghosts and angels are not that different," Smokey continued, "they're both spirits without bodies, and they're both not of this world."

"But—but," Mr. Kunz fumed, "angels do good things; they're sent from God."

Smokey was silent for moment, then asked, "so, why do they call Lucifer the Fallen Angel?"

"Well—well, that's different, he—"

Mrs. Kunz interrupted. "Will you two please stop it."

In spite of his cousin Anita's request, Smokey continued to murmur. "They're here right now." Smokey turned away from the fire, his dark eyes scoured the impenetrable night. "They're gathering right now. The chindis are waiting and watching."

"That's enough of that kind of talk," Mr. Kunz snapped. "You'll scare the kids. Don't you have to finish with that cat? You can take a lantern."

Needless to say, J.T. did not sleep at all well that night. He wasn't sure if it was the constant reliving of his near-death encounter with the cougar, the excitement of the upcoming Shot, or Smokey's eerie prediction of the gathering chindis. Perhaps, it was all three, but regardless, he barely closed his eyes, making for a very long night.

The next morning his father was up early, trying to re-kindle the fire and make hot Postum. Joining him, J.T. offered to help. Mr. Kunz handed him the stick matches and a wadded-up sheet of newspaper. In a couple of minutes, J.T. had a fire blazing. Not waiting for it to burn down to coals, Mr. Kunz placed a pot of water directly on the flames. Out of the corner of his eye, J.T. noted that Smokey had a similar, but smaller fire over by the cedar trees, but rather than hot Postum, J.T. suspected he was heating up a pot of coffee.

They, father and son, while waiting for the water to boil, stared at the fire in comfortable silence. In the unique tranquility offered by the predawn, J.T. felt a rare sense of belonging, of family. This was how it had been since the beginning of time, father and son bonding around a campfire.

After a couple of minutes, Mr. Kunz sighed loudly, ending the moment. "I sure wish Chris was here. In his last letter he said he would be shipping off to Korea any day. Might even be there now."

Though the spell had been broken. J.T. did not immediately reply, but continued to gaze at the dying flames. It had always been, even now, about Chris. Chris the marine, Chris the football player, Chris the firstborn, Chris the farmhand, Chris the favorite son.

"Well, it's four forty-five," Mr. Kunz abruptly announced, leaning close to the fire to check his wristwatch, "time to wake the girls."

Neither Mrs. Kunz nor Mary, seemed particularly happy about the hour, but both dutifully crawled out of their sleeping bags and accepted a metal mug of hot Postum.

With John Kunz leading, each of the Kunz's carried their mugs of hot Postum, and Smokey trailed behind with his forbidden mug of coffee. In the faint glow of the Milky Way, they carefully worked their way, following a game trail to the natural bench. From here, there was nothing to block their view to the west and Yucca Flats was just ninety miles away.

Turning back to the east, J.T. noted a precocious smudge of predawn pink had just appeared on the star-speckled canvas of black. Returning to the west, he saw the canvas remained unchanged, a dappled but constant celestial black. They didn't have to wait long, however, for all that to change.

At exactly 5:01 a.m., like a sudden cosmic event, a blinding flash exploded on the western horizon. The intense light forced the campers to throw up an arm to protect their eyes.

Seconds later, they heard a low rumble, seemingly coming from deep within the earth itself. Beginning far to the west, it rolled toward them, like a subterranean tsunami. Rapidly growing in intensity, it sounded like the roar of an onrushing locomotive. Suddenly, the earth beneath them began to tremble, then shake, then roll. Casting their eyes downward, they warily surveyed the ground, fearing it might actually split open and swallow them.

Over at the camp, Casey and Smokey's paint whinnied loudly and lunged against their picket ropes. Breaking free, a terrified Casey bolted eastward, trying to get away from the shaking earth.

Immediately following the quake, supersonic sound waves battered their ears. Recoiling in pain, the campers doubled over, quickly moving their arms from their eyes to cover their ears. The shock waves quickly swept over them, echoing off the granite cliffs and canyon walls, like salvos of cannon fire.

To the west, the intense white light had already begun to fade, but a single cirrus cloud lingered in the fast-fading light. Suddenly, it seemed to catch fire and begin to glow, not campfire orange, but rather a scintillating, neon pink.

To J.T., the entire spectacle was both amazing and a bit surreal. In fact, it was so bizarre, it could possibly qualify as an apparition, or a harbinger, or even one of Smokey's chindis.

Then as quickly as it began, it was over. Transfixed, the campers did not immediately turn back to camp. In the paralytic aftermath, each seemed deeply immersed in his or her own thoughts.

"Wow!" Mary finally exclaimed. "That really was worth getting up for."

"Kinda makes you proud to be an American," Mr. Kunz said, solemnly placing his right hand over his heart.

"I don't feel so good," Mrs. Kunz added. She looked pale and immediately started coughing.

"I—I'm going to work on those someday," J.T.'s said, his eyes still wide with wonder; apparently already forgetting about the chindis, "that's what I want to be, a nuclear physicist."

"Walk lightly on the land; especially when Mother Earth is full and pregnant," Smokey mumbled, then added, "that pink cloud was Soaring Hawk, sending us a warning from the Great Spirit."

"You mean from God." Mr. Kunz corrected, "from Jehovah."

"Tis one and the same," Smokey replied, fumbling in his shirt pocket for a Marlboro. "It's a warning from the Great One."

"Oh, come on, Smokey," Mr. Kunz dropped his hand from his heart, "don't you think you're being a little over-dramatic."

"No, no, this is no good," Smokey paused to light his cigarette, coughed loudly, then continued, "tis the mischief of the skinwalkers, yee naaldlooshii, dressed in the skins of the sly coyote. No good comes of this."

"That's enough of that kind of talk," Mr. Kunz snapped, "you'll scare the kids. Come on, let's go get some breakfast." He started to walk away, then turned back. "And Smokey, put out that damn cigarette. I told you no smokin' around the kids." Mr. Kunz took a couple more steps then turned around once again. "Oh, and no more of that hocus-pocus, pagan stuff."

As they walked the short distance back to camp, the eastern sky rifled from pink to purple, to blazing orange, making it easier to see the game trail. And though the sun had yet to make its appearance, it, nevertheless, hurled a battery of photons upwards, piercing the night sky, creating a golden corona. In the distance, J.T. could make out the crimson/white spires of Zion National Park, now backlighted by the rising sun. The craggy purple peaks of the Pine Valley Mountains would be next in Helios' spotlight, and lastly Utah Hill. Mother Nature, it appeared, was trying hard to not be outdone by the recent man-made spectacular.

Back in camp, J.T. stirred the coals back to life, added more wood, then Mrs. Kunz and Mary set about preparing breakfast. It looked as though they were going to have fresh ham, scrambled eggs, and leftover Dutch oven potatoes. Soon the aroma of frying ham and browning onions permeated the camp. With his stomach grumbling, J.T. found a seat on a piñon log and waited, though impatiently.

Suddenly, the sky darkened!

A roiling, black cloud drifted overhead, blotting out the morning sun. Then without warning, it began to hail, not frozen water, but the dark cloud began spitting out pea-sized particles. Seconds later, it turned to a feathery gray ash.

"What the heck?" Mr. Kunz muttered, looking up at the maverick cloud.

J.T. caught a tiny particle in his open palm. "Ye-ow, it's hot!" Immediately, he shook it from his hand.

"Maybe," Mr. Kunz suggested, "this is what's left of the mushroom cloud."

"What about the hail?" J.T. asked, as a punctate second-degree burn appeared on his right hand.

Mr. Kunz thought about it for a second. "It's probably leftover from incinerated cedar and piñon trees."

"No, it's more than that," Smokey said, frowning, "the sky's raining down coyote dung and the chindis are dancing up there." He pointed up at the cloud, then ducked under a piñon.

In eerie silence, they watched it transition from hail-like particles to snow-like flakes.

"It's kind of pretty." Mary snatched a flake. "Kinda like dirty snow."

"This is not just incinerated trees," Mrs. Kunz declared, her face creased with worry, "it's fallout radiation! Mary, J.T., get in the truck now!"

The weird snowfall lasted for less than ten minutes, then just as quickly as it began, it ended. As the slanted morning rays again fought through the thinning black cloud, the campers settled down for breakfast.

Famished, J.T. wolfed down the ham and eggs and surprisingly Mr. Kunz did not complain about there being no bread or milk.

The moment breakfast was over, Smokey saddled his paint and without saying a word, rode out of the camp, heading north.

"Who put a burr under his saddle?" Mr. Kunz asked, as he watched him ride off.

"Doesn't mean anything," Mrs. Kunz replied. "Samuel's not big on farewells."

"Well," Mr. Kunz shrugged, "let's saddle up Casey and go finish riding the fence, and check on the cows. Then we'll plan on heading home by early afternoon."

“No, John,” Mrs. Kunz said firmly. “I don’t feel so good. Let’s pack up and go home now.”

“But we really ought to check on the cattle before—”

“The cattle are fine,” she cut him off. “You just unloaded them yesterday. We’re going home.” Turning, she began gathering up the breakfast dishes.

“But,” Mr. Kunz continued objected, “we haven’t rode the whole fence line since—”

“Now!” Mrs. Kunz interrupted again. “We’re going home now.”

An hour later, and in spite of Mr. Kunz’s repeated objections, they were ready to go. All the camping gear, along with Casey, was stowed in the back of the flatbed. As Mr. Kunz doused the campfire with a bucket of spring water, Smokey rode back into camp. Dismounting, he tied the paint to a piñon, then walked over to J.T.

“Here’s your radiation badge, shił naa’aash,” Smokey said, pressing the badge into J.T.’s hand. “But I do want to know what the biligaana fathers find out with these things.”

“Me too,” J.T. replied, then added, “thanks a lot, Smokey.”

“Samuel, do you want to ride with us?” Mrs. Kunz asked. “We could load your paint in the back with Casey.”

Scowling, Mr. Kunz started to object, then bit his lip.

“No,” Smokey shook his head. “I still need deer meat, but you can take this cat hide back. I’ll pick it up in a few days. I’ve already salted and started to dry it, so when you get home you can start soaking it.” Pausing, he picked a burlap bag and handed to Mr. Kunz. “Chop up the brain, it’s in the bag, mix it in the water, then add the pelt. I’ll be back by then to do the rest.”

“Haven’t you heard of salt and alum?” Mr. Kunz asked sarcastically. “Works better and is a heck-of-a-lot less messy.”

“Do it the Indian way,” Smokey said firmly, “use the brain.” Remounting, he rode over the cedar hill, again heading north.

Shaking his head in disgust, Mr. Kunz tossed the burlap bag in the back of the flatbed with Casey, then growled, “if we’re going, let’s go.”

They rode back to Santa Clara mostly in silence. Looking exhausted, Mrs. Kunz leaned her head against the window, closed her eyes and appeared to doze. Also uncharacteristically subdued, Mary appeared to be lost in her own thoughts, but J.T. was worried—worried about his mother. Lately, she never seemed to feel good; she had lost a lot of weight and her skin looked kind of yellow. He couldn’t help but think she was beginning to resemble the scarecrow they planted in the garden every year along with the corn and tomatoes.

A minute later, Mrs. Kunz’s dark eyes fluttered open. When she saw J.T. staring at her, she smiled, reached across Mary, and patted his hand. After that, he felt a little better.

Still holding her hand, he asked, "why does Smokey take such an interest in me?"

"Well," his mother said, "of course, he is your cousin, but also you share the same birthday. You were born on the same day. Samuel thinks that's an omen."

"Everything," Mr. Kunz mumbled, "is an omen to him."

"Really," J.T. said, "the very same day?"

"The very same day, Jackie," Mrs. Kunz confirmed, ignoring her husband, "just twenty-five years later. He considers himself your Godfather."

"I just wish he didn't have to go everywhere with us," Mr. Kunz complained. "Either that, or clean himself up, and quit that smoking and drinking."

"I think he's—uh—what's the word? I think," Mary added, "he's quite colorful."

"Yes, Samuel's all right," Mrs. Kunz said, as she leaned her head back against the window. "He has a heart of gold."

J.T. couldn't help but notice how in the last few weeks her raven hair had grayed and thinned considerably. Now, he could literally see the paleness of her scalp.

Once again silence settled over the cab. Mrs. Kunz dozed and Mr. Kunz seemed totally absorbed in negotiating the steep hills, the horseshoe-curves, and the teeth-rattling washboard of Pahcoon Road.

Suddenly, a horn blared behind them, shattering the short-lived tranquility. Half-turning, J.T. peered over his shoulder through the rear window. Behind them, and only occasionally visible in their trailing dust plume, was a vehicle, probably a car. Even though the car also had to be at least partially blinded by the swirling dust, it was following close, too close! J.T. wondered how the driver could see anything.

The horn blared again. This time a long-sustained blast, then the vehicle surged forward, trying to pass on the left. The road was much too narrow, and the automobile had to back off. Once again engulfed in dust, the driver leaned on the horn.

"What the hell!" Mr. Kunz cussed, his face now flushed with anger. "What the hell is his problem?"

"He trying to pass," J.T. said.

"Really, J.T.? I didn't know that," Mr. Kunz said sarcastically. "Well, I'll teach that son-of-a-bitch a lesson!"

"John," Mrs. Kunz said, now fully awake, "watch your language."

Abruptly, John Kunz stomped on the brakes; the on-rushing auto nearly collided with the flatbed. At the last instant, the driver also slammed on the brakes, swerved hard to the right, missing them by mere inches.

“Oh, for heaven’s sakes, John,” Mrs. Kunz said sternly. “Why don’t you just pull over and let him pass?”

Indeed, Mr. Kunz s did slow down, but every time the vehicle tried to pass, he veered in front of it, blocking its progress. One time when the sedan surged forward, there was the telltale screech of metal on metal, then the car backed off.

“Please, John,” Mrs. Kunz pleaded, reaching over J.T. and Mary, to grab his arm, “it’s not worth it. Just let him pass.”

“D—daddy,” Mary sobbed, “I’m scared.”

“Okay, okay,” Mr. Kunz finally relented, “but I’m going to talk to that son-of-a—uh—uh—that son-of-a-gun. Give him a piece of my mind.”

Slowing down even more, Mr. Kunz searched for a wide spot to pull over. None was immediately available, but with the slower speed the trailing dust cloud settled some and J.T. got a better look at the vehicle. Indeed, it was a car, probably dark brown or black with a single occupant.

At last, up ahead, where the road crossed a dry wash, there was a flat sandy area. Braking again, Mr. Kunz pulled over to the right, then threw open the door and jumped out. Waving his arms above his head, he was ready for a confrontation.

Seeing his opening, however, the auto accelerated.

Realizing the car was not going to stop, Mr. Kunz dove headfirst off the side of the road, as the automobile roared by. Immediately, it accelerated even more, once again generating a towering plume of dust. Through the trailing cloud, J.T. could not see the driver or his car, but could see his father struggling back to his feet, then he too was engulfed in the gritty maelstrom. A few seconds later, the dust cloud drifted over the hill and out of sight.

About ready to explode, Mr. Kunz took out a handkerchief and wiped the grit from his face, then while trying to blink the sand out of his eyes, he climbed back into the cab.

“Judas H. Priest!” he shouted, his angry blue eyes still fixed on the receding plume. “Do you know who that was?”

9

Groaning, J.T. stood up, then slowly arched his spine backwards, trying to stretch out the sheepshank knot in his lumbar muscles. Covering one eye with his hand, he squinted with the other eye at the blazing sun. From its height in the summer sky, almost directly overhead, and its considerable production of heat, well over a hundred degrees, J.T. reckoned it had to be close to noon. For further confirmation, he checked his shadow. There was almost none. On his right side, as he faced south, his shadow was nearly totally eclipsed with just a thin rim of his head and shoulder projected on the ground. Now shading both eyes with his cupped hands, he redirected his attention, looking down the furrow. He had at least another twenty yards, or so, to go, maybe even a little more. Sighing, he bent over once again, grabbed a fledgling pigweed sprout, pulling it out by the roots. He'd finish this row, he decided, then take a break for lunch.

All morning he had been weeding his father's cantaloupe patch. The entire field was just short of three acres, though it seemed more like a two-hundred-acre farm in California's famed Imperial Valley. But regardless of its size, it was a big job for just one worker. And even though the rows were harrowed a spacious four-foot wide, melon vines needed a lot of room to grow, there was still over sixty furrows with each an impossible four hundred feet long. Not only did J.T. have to hoe the burgeoning early-summer weeds, but he also had to lift each melon, no matter how small, out of the furrows to the safety of the dry bank. The reason for this, his father had explained, was to keep the melon from rotting. If soaked when irrigating and left in the furrows in the hot sun, they would rot in a matter of days.

It was hot and tedious work. He'd been working since dawn, but all he had to show for his efforts were three and three-quarters rows. At ten cents a row, he'd made nearly a whopping forty cents. Big deal! That only left him nineteen dollars and sixty cents to go. At this rate, he'd be dead long before he earned the twenty dollars to pay for his share of the school room damages. And that didn't include the bill his father had threatened to serve him with for flooding the Loren Reber piece. Unfortunately, the unruly, unsupervised water had eroded away most of the southern quarter of the field, washing away the topsoil and leaving a series of deeply eroded gullies. During their mandatory inspection, J.T. had watched as his father scrambled down into one of those gullies and almost completely disappear from sight.

Shortly after that, his father had hired Sam Hirschi, who owned a D-5 Cat, to come and doze and re-level the field, then they'd re-furrowed and replanted. Of course, all of that cost money, money they couldn't afford. And that didn't include the loss of revenue from the field; there would be very little alfalfa produced from that field this year. Adding it all up, J.T. could not even imagine, if you included the loss of revenue, what the final bill might be. More than likely he would be an indentured servant for the rest of his life.

Scowling in frustration, J.T. picked up the hoe and hacked furiously at a robust colony of ragweed, totally destroying them. Somehow that made him feel better.

His father had pretty much mapped out his entire summer. For early summer, the month of June, there would be, of course, these fields to hoe, then corn, cherries, and apricots to pick and the first cut of hay to haul. Mid-summer brought more weeds, but also the first tomatoes, cantaloupes, and early cling peaches to pick, and once again hay to haul. Late summer was dedicated mainly to the harvest of apples, peaches, and the last of the tomatoes and cantaloupes. Also, at the end of summer, there would be the fourth and the fifth, the last cut of hay to haul. It went without saying all these crops needed to be irrigated throughout the entire summer season, one painstaking furrow at a time. And obviously, no more unattended flood irrigation.

On the days he was home, his father would help, especially with the heavy work like hauling hay, but that still left plenty for J.T. to do when he was gone. At times, J.T. wished Chris (who he hadn't always gotten along with) had not joined the marines and was here to do his share of the work.

As he hacked away at the weeds, J.T. did the math in his head. At ten cents a row, or fifteen cents a lug, or the same fifteen cents for an hour of labor, depending on what he was doing, it would take him roughly one hundred and seventy hours to earn twenty dollars. Assuming eight hours a day, that was over twenty days. After that, he would still have to earn money for his school clothes and any movies or entertainment money he might need for the upcoming school year. Sighing out loud, J.T. shook his head and silently hoped his father was not serious about him paying for the damages to the Loren Reber piece.

After Chris had departed for the marines, these field assignments were supposed to be divided equally between him and Mary, but lately it was just him. With his mother not feeling well, Mary was forced to assume more and more of the household chores, but—but those chores were indoors, in the shade! Somehow J.T. did not think that was a fair division of labor, but what could he do? Unfortunately, he was not asked his opinion or given a vote or a say on the matter.

Before Mr. Kunz left on his produce run, each Wednesday he would tape a list of chores on the kitchen cabinet; things he expected to be done by the time he returned early on Sunday morning. His father always got back in time for church, you could count on it, and he always checked to make sure the work got done. You could count on that too.

Mr. Kunz didn't specify what had to be done on each day, but rather what needed to be done for the entire four-and-one-half day period he was gone. This, of course, gave J.T. a little latitude, a bit of wiggle room. He could pretty much arrange his days the way he wanted as long as the work got done by Sunday, and it damn well better get done. His father, as J.T. very well knew, was not opposed to corporal punishment, especially for liars or slackers.

Mentally switching gears, J.T. thought about the recent trip to Utah Hill and his near-death experience with the cougar. There was no question he owed his life to Smokey Grayman and he was thankful—sort of. Personally, he liked Smokey, it was just, well it was—it was that Smokey was always hanging around and J.T. really didn't want Mickey and the other guys to know he was part Indian. He knew what they, and most Santa Clara people, thought of Indians. Almost instantly he was ashamed of himself and mentally tried to change topics once again as he continued down the row. He settled on the ride home from Utah Hill.

So, according to his father, the sedan that was trying to pass, and almost ran him over on the shoulder of Pahcoon Road, was none other than Borch Rosenkranz, or Boris Romanoff, or whomever he was. J.T. couldn't imagine what he was doing up there. Maybe like them, he was up there to watch Shot Able. If so, why? Was it just harmless, tourist-like curiosity? Or was it something more sinister? And why was he in such a big hurry? Knowing he would not be able to come up with any answers, J.T. lowered his head and murdered another pigweed. That felt good!

Today, he decided he would work till noon, then take the rest of the day off. It was just too hot to work in the afternoon and anyway he'd arranged to meet Mickey later to work on their summer pranks. After all, it was already mid-June and they had only one prank to their credit. Though J.T. was a little hesitant to count the cherry bomb fiasco, Mickey had insisted, but even counting that if they were going to beat Judd and Howie's record of five, they'd better get more pranks in the pipeline.

In his mind, J.T. had envisioned two separate pranks and he was anxious to see if they would actually work. For one, he and Mickey would construct an apparatus right out of the history books, but then they would have to wait for the right opportunity to set it in motion. The other prank, they might very well implement tonight.

At last, J.T. finished the row, placing the final little striped melon safely out of the furrow and onto the bank. Slowly, he straightened his stiff back, wiped the sweat from his brow and gulped down the last of his water from a two-quart Mason jar. Before leaving, he concealed the hoe in a thick clump of Johnson grass at the top of the field along the ditch bank, then headed for the Massey Ferguson.

At his age, nearly fourteen, he was not allowed to drive automobiles, or trucks, except on private property, but he was permitted to drive a tractor, even in town, which in his mind was the only positive thing about farming. Even if he passed the Highway Patrol on Main Street (U.S. Highway 91), they always turned a blind eye. On Sunday afternoons, he and his friends, Mickey, Alan, Curley, Greg and Easy, would sometimes gather outside Irene's general store for tractor drag races down the relatively straight Vineyard Road, which he usually won. Smooth shifting, not raw speed, he'd discovered, was the key to victory.

With some determined coaxing, J.T. started the old tractor. After grinding through the gears, he offered the Massy-Ferguson more gas, then started down the Vineyard Road for the mile and a half trip back to the house.

When he arrived home, all drapes and window shades were pulled, but even at that the house was hot, quiet, and of course gloomy. No one was in the kitchen or living room. J.T. searched the remainder of the house for his sister, but Mary was nowhere to be found. His mother, however, was lying on her bed, her withered arm flopped across her face.

"Oh, hi, Jackie," she said, her face lighting up when she saw him in the doorway.

"Are you okay, Mom?"

"Yes, just a little tired. How did the hoeing go?"

"Okay, four rows. Where's Mary?"

"She's gone to a church campout. You know, the annual M.I.A. girls' outing up at Pine Valley. She'll be back tomorrow."

"Oh, yeah, I forgot," he turned to leave, then turned back, "do you need anything?"

"No, I'm fine, Jackie," Anita Kunz repeated. Sitting up, she rested her back against the old white pine headboard. "Come on over here," she patted the bed next to her, "I want to talk to you for a minute."

"Mom," J.T. blurted, "I am really sorry about Miss Miller. I won't—"

"That," she interrupted him, "is not what I want to talk about." She patted the bed again.

Now he was worried, but he did as instructed and sat down beside her.

There was a moment of silence.

After taking a deep, but labored breath, his mother began, "you know your father loves you, don't you?"

Silently, J.T. breathed a sigh of relief when he realized the direction the conversation was headed. "Sometimes I wonder."

"Well, he does, but I must admit, I don't think he understands you. You're not at all like Chris, with all the pranks and all the trouble you get into."

"Yeah, I know," J.T. mumbled. "I think maybe I try on purpose not to be like Chris."

"Yes, I suspect you do," she forced a weary smile, "but, I guess the thing your father has the most trouble with is that you are smart. He knows you'll never stay here on the farm and that you'll never be satisfied with living here in Santa Clara, and frankly I don't think he knows how to handle it."

"Chris is smart too. He always got A's. I don't."

"It's not the same kind of smart. You are motivated by different things—for example, the rockets."

They lapsed into silence again, then she added, "how did it go the other day?"

"Huh?"

"The other day when the house filled up with smoke," she smiled again, "did it fly?"

J.T. gulped. How did she know? "Nah," he shook his head, "but I'm still working on it."

"You'll get it."

"I sure hope so."

More silence.

"Go easy on the pranks this summer. Make sure nobody gets hurt."

"Okay."

She patted his hand. "If you ever learn how to channel all that creative energy into something constructive," her dark eyes glowed with pride, "you're really going be something, do something worthwhile in this…" Her voice trailed off.

A tear collected in the corner of J.T.'s eye as he held his mother's hand.

"There may be some tough times ahead," she continued after another moment, "but you'll be fine. Remember your father does love you, Smokey is a good and loyal friend and that you should always stay true to God and the church."

"Yes, mother." J.T. blinked away a tear.

"And you should go on a mission. Your father would like that."

"Yes, Mother."

"Now," she said more brightly, "do you want me to fix you a sandwich?"

"No," he patted her hand again. "I can do it. You should rest, but I could fix you one."

"No thanks." She smiled wearily, then lying back on the bed closed her eyes again.

From homemade bread, leftover roast beef, sliced tomatoes, lettuce, and mayonnaise, J.T. fixed himself a sandwich. Barely taking time to chew it, he washed it down with a glass of cold milk. Hurriedly, he washed and dried the glass and plate, then went outside.

From his father's workshop, he grabbed a spool of heavy cotton thread and a couple of large straight needles, the kind used to sew up burlap bags full of potatoes or onions. After stowing the materials in a flour sac, he headed across Highway 91, then onto the corrals, one short block away. When he arrived, Mickey was already there, sitting on a pile of hay and whittling on a short piece of white river willow.

"Damn," Mickey complained, but did not look up, "it's hot!"

"Mickey, you really shouldn't cuss. The church forbids it."

"So? What do I care what the church forbids?"

"So, don't do it," J.T. said then changed the subject. "What are you making?"

"A flute," Mickey replied, still concentrating on his work.

"How does it work?"

"It's simple. You loosen up this collar of bark so it can slide over the wood, then you cut a wedge and a channel for the air to go. When you blow on this end, while sliding the collar up and down, it changes the pitch."

Finishing up, he demonstrated by playing several random notes. It did indeed sound good, at least to J.T.'s untrained ear.

"Play something."

"Nah, I don't know no music," Mickey declined, pocketing the flute. "So, what we goin' to do today?"

"Did you bring the stuff?"

"Yeah, sure." Mickey produced a burlap bag. Reaching in, he extracted an old long-sleeve flannel shirt, a pair of tattered Levis, worn-out sneakers, a faded Yankees ball cap, and a punctured and utterly useless kickball.

"Good," J.T. nodded, "that should work."

"So, what are we goin' to do?"

"Make a mannequin."

"Make a man-a-what?" Mickey frowned, shaking his head.

"A mannequin. You know, a dummy."

"Ain't Santa Clara got enough dummies?"

Smiling in spite of himself, J.T. said, "you know what I mean."

"And what, may I ask, are we goin' to do with this man—this manny—uh—this dummy?"

"You'll see when it's time," J.T. replied vaguely, "but this one's going to be good."

"So, when will it be time?" Mickey looked dubious, as he stared at the raw materials.

"Tonight, after dark. We'll meet on Main Street."

"Well, what we going to do till dark? Making this manne—uh—dummy won't take that long."

"I've got another project we can work on," J.T. took out a needle and cotton thread, "not here, but down at the fort."

"I thought maybe we could go skiing?"

At first J.T. didn't comment as he tried to match the bottom of the shirt to the top of the pants.

When J.T. didn't answer, Mickey continued, "we could make ski's outta them wooden barrel slats and bindings outta strips of inner tubes, then we could go down that gravel hill. You know, the steep one over behind Reber's."

Silently, J.T. shook his head and started to sew.

"Maybe, we could even count it as a prank."

Again, J.T. shook his head. "First of all, it isn't a prank. And second of all, it isn't original. We did that last year. Remember all the skin we lost?"

"Oh, yeah," Mickey nodded.

For the next hour, the boys busied themselves sewing the sneakers to the bottom of the pant legs, the shirt tails to the waistband of the Levi's and finally they stitched the long sleeves of the shirt closed. After the sewing was completed, they stuffed the connected clothes full of straw, filling out the chest, abdomen, arms, and legs. Then as the piece de résistance, they sutured, which wasn't easy, the old kickball to the collar of the shirt and the Yankee baseball cap to the top of the kickball. When finished, the boys slowly circled and inspected their work from every angle.

"What we goin' call him?" Mickey asked.

"Huh?"

"Yeah," Mickey added, "what's his name?"

"I don't know," J.T. answered, "how about Manny."

"Manny, what?"

"Huh?"

"He needs a last name."

J.T. thought about it for a couple of seconds. "How about Manny Quinn?

"But that's a Mexican name."

"So?"

"So, it don't look much like a Mexican," Mickey commented, "or a white man either for that matter."

"It should be good enough, especially after dark," J.T. replied. "Let's leave it for now and go on down to the creek."

"Good enough for what?" Mickey asked, frowning.

"You'll see," J.T. grinned, heading for the barn door.

As they waited for a break in the steady stream of summer tourist traffic, crossing Main Street (Highway 91) this time of year was never easy. A '51

Chevy hatchback, painted cherry red, skidded to a stop in front of them, spraying a Gatlin gun of gravel. Jumping backward, they scrambled to get out of the way. As the Chevy screeched to a full stop, the boys checked for injuries.

Abruptly, the passenger door opened, revealing expensive tuck-and-roll upholstery and Weird Willie Wittwer.

"You guys wanna go for a ride?" Willie asked, climbing out of the car. He brushed a lock of red hair out of his green eyes.

Ignoring the invitation, Mickey immediately got in his face. "Hey, Mister, I've got a bone to pick with you."

"Why?" Willie seemed to feign ignorance. "What?"

"You know what." Mickey got up close, eye-to-eye with Willie. "What you told old man Hartley at school the other day?"

"Didn't tell him nothin'."

"Then why'd he call you a hero?" J.T. asked, joining in.

"I—I don't know."

"And, how did he know it was us that did the cherry bombs?" Mickey demanded.

"H—how should I know?" Willie replied, standing his ground. "Probably just guessed, like everyone else."

"Do you have to go to Saint George next Wednesday" Mickey demanded, "and apologize to Miss Miller?"

"And pay twenty dollars in damages?" J.T. added.

"Well, if I did," Willie replied, "I could do it easy."

"No, you couldn't." Mickey shook his head. "No way you have that kind of money."

"I could make that much," Willie bragged, "in a single day."

"Doing what?"

"Can't tell you."

"No jobs around here pays that much," J.T. insisted. "I doubt my dad even makes that much."

"You just gotta know the right people," Weird Willie replied with a cagy grin.

"Yeah," Mickey said, "then why don't you pay for me and J.T.?"

"I could if I wanted to, but I don't want to." Willie gave Mickey a little shove. "Now get outta my face."

"You're nothin' but a damn liar and a snitch." Immediately, Mickey scooted back in front of Willie.

"Am not!" Willie pushed Mickey even harder.

For a moment, Mickey glared at Willie, then exploded. With his left hand, he pushed Willie back just far enough he could throw a full haymaker with his right.

Stumbling backwards, Willie didn't see the blow coming. Mickey's fist collided with Willie's jaw, cartwheeling him sideways. Immediately, Willie's feet tangled and he crashed to the ground; sharp roadside gravel ripping small divots out of his exposed skin. Before he could get up, Mickey was on him. Straddling Willie, he raised a hammer fist to strike.

Suddenly, the driver's door opened and a Mister Leonard Weeks, jumped out. Lenny, already in junior high school, was a head taller, thirty pounds heavier and already possessed the testosterone-sculpted muscles of a man. Sporting a buzz haircut, he had shifty brown eyes and a scruffy mustache. He wore faded blue jeans with the belt loops removed and the waistband folded over, but his trademark was a pack of cigarettes was rolled up in the sleeve of his white t-shirt.

Grabbing Mickey by the collar, Lenny jerked him off Willie, then spun him around. With a flurry of rabbit punches, he pounded Mickey's abdomen. When Mickey doubled over in pain, Lenny's uppercut caught him flush on the jaw, knocking him backwards. Stumbling and flailing, Mickey struggled to remain upright.

Seeing Mickey's plight, J.T. quickly joined the fray. Leaping onto Lenny's back, he clung like a house cat on a screen door. With his open hand, he slapped at Lenny's face. Groaning, Leonard clutched at his right ear, then heaved J.T. off, as easily if he were tossing that the same screen cat from his back.

By then, however, Mickey had recovered enough to return to the fray. As Mickey danced around Lenny, both fists raised, J.T. struggled back to his feet.

Lowering his head, J.T. charged. It wasn't Lenny, however, he slammed into, but instead a newly resurrected Weird Willie who had inadvertently stepped into his path. That was fine by J.T. Trying hard to ignore Willie's garlic breath, J.T. bulldozed him to the ground. Unfortunately, that was to be the last of his and Mickey's small victories.

The rest of battle probably didn't last more than five minutes, though it seemed like hours. By the time it was over, both J.T. and Mickey lay in a bloody tangle alongside Highway 91. Mickey was bleeding from the corner of his mouth, J.T. from his nose, and both were covered with multiple raspberry bruises and striated abrasions. It was hard to know exactly which wounds had been inflicted by Lenny and Willie and which were courtesy of the roadside gravel.

During the brief, but furious roadside brawl, a continuous line of California tourists passed by. Though they looked horrified, even mortified, none stopped. Perhaps they thought this sort of thing was commonplace in southern Utah's corner of the wild west.

Groaning, Mickey and J.T. rolled over, getting further away from the highway traffic, then watched the Chevy hatchback pull out of sight, instantly blending into the constant stream of traffic. Using each other for support, the boys struggled to their feet.

"You okay?" Mickey asked, spitting blood from his mouth.

"Y—yeah." J.T. mumbled. His voice had a distinct nasal twang, secondary to pinching his nose in an attempt to stop the bleeding.

"I guess we sure showed them." Mickey managed a lopsided grin.

"Yeah," J.T. said, then added without conviction, "I doubt they'll mess with us again."

Mickey spat more blood. "We gotta do something about that Willie."

"We will," J.T. nodded once again, "I've got a plan." After taking a few more seconds to inspect his injuries, he continued, "you still feel like going down to the creek?"

"Yeah, why not," Mickey nodded. "I'm okay, just a couple of scratches. My cat's done worse."

On the way to the Santa Clara River, the boys faced the same dilemma they encountered the other night. They either had to cut through Borch Rosenkranz's property or take the long detour around the fuel storage yard.

Before deciding, they surveyed Borch's compound from a safe distance. Everything seemed quiet. J.T. noted the dark sedan, which had passed them yesterday on Pahcoon Road, was now conspicuously absent. The driveway was empty. It appeared Borch Rosenkranz, or Boris Romanoff, or whomever he was, was not home. It should be safe enough to pass through his property on the way to the creek.

Boldly, the boys headed straight down the gravel driveway. Their path took them past the very same window they'd seen the uniformed Rosenkranz admiring himself in the mirror. Not able to resist, the boys quickly glanced in, but today the window was closed and the room appeared to be vacant. And they could not see the military uniform, the sword, or hat of the other night.

Continuing into the backyard, they passed a pine board shed. Apparently, in the gloom of the other night, they had not noticed it. Constructed of old barnwood, it was roughly 8 by 8 feet in size, had no windows and a single door, secured by a steel padlock.

Giving it only a cursory inspection, they bypassed the shed and continued on into the backyard. Fifteen feet past the shed, J.T. noted something else they had not seen the other night, a tall, metal pole. It was at least twenty-feet high and was anchored by a concrete base and stabilized by three, equally spaced guy-wires. It looked a bit like a flagpole, but without the ropes, pulleys, or a flag.

"I never noticed this the other night." J.T. nodded at the pole.

"It was dark."

"I know, but I think it's new."

"Why?"

"Look at the base," J.T. replied.

"So?"

J.T. dropped to his knees, running his hand over the square base. "The concrete is still gray, not white."

"So?"

"It's new concrete, not yet cured." After a bit more inspection, J.T. asked, "so, what is it?"

"I don't know," Mickey replied, walking around the tall aluminum rod. "Maybe it's an antenna, or something."

J.T. frowned. "It doesn't look like any T.V. antenna I've ever seen." Although Santa Clara did not yet have television, St. George did. And he'd seen those weirdly branched antennas, which looked kinda like leafless, aluminum trees, bolted to the roofs.

"No, not television," Mickey shook his head, "but radio. You know, one of them high-powered radios; the ones you can talk to other people with."

"Oh, you mean a shortwave radio. Yeah," J.T. nodded, "I hear you can call anywhere in the world with them."

For a few moments, the boys studied the strange pole, then Mickey bent over and examined the square concrete base, raking his fingers through the dirt around it.

"Well, looky here!" he exclaimed. "There's a wire coming from it."

By jerking upward, the two boys excavated the wire and traced it back to the board shed where it disappeared under the baseboard. Squinting, Mickey put an eye to a crack between the board slats, but said he couldn't see anything.

"Boy, I'd love to know what's in there," he said, circling the shed and checking every board to see if all were secure. Finally, he found one missing a couple of nails at the base. If they pulled hard, they could bend and rotate the board just enough to peek in. While J.T. pulled, Mickey got down on his hands and knees.

A moment later, he whistled. "Well, would you look at that!"

"What?" J.T. pushed Mickey aside. "You pull." Dropping down, he positioned himself in front of the small portal. "Wow!"

Inside he could see an electronic instrument resting on an old plank table. It had perforated, gunmetal gray casing, glowing vacuum tubes and a myriad of electrical wires. At the base of the casing, red and green indicator lights flashed on and off. Directly in front of the flashing lights, was a gooseneck microphone mounted on a small wooden platform. The only furniture in the room, other than the table, was a solitary armchair.

"That's a shortwave radio," J.T. declared, backing away.

"So, why do you think old Borch Rosenkranz would have somethin' like that?" Mickey asked, his eyes narrowing with suspicion.

"How should I know?" J.T. shrugged. He was still willing to give Mr. Rosenkranz the benefit of the doubt after his help with the rocket. "Maybe, it's just a hobby."

"Yeah, maybe, but spies use th—"

Suddenly, they heard the sound of a combustion engine, followed by the crunch of gravel as a car pulled into the driveway. Cautiously, the boy's peaked around the corner of the shed. It was the black Ford sedan!

Without stopping to take a second look, they whirled and zigzagged through the littered backyard all the way to the board fence. Behind them, they heard the car door slam, followed by the pounding of footsteps on the hard ground.

"Mach Halt Ihr Schweine Hund!"

Glancing over his shoulder, J.T. could see Borch was coming after them. And—and he was moving fast!

10

J.T. WANTED TO STOP AND SAY, 'HEY, MISTER ROSENKRANZ, IT'S ME, THE rocket kid', but instead he ran even faster.

With his longer legs, Rosenkranz was gaining on them.

Quickly, they located the loose board on the back fence. Mickey jerked it sideways. It didn't move, then aided by adrenaline, he yanked even harder, creating a small window. As the boys scrabbled through the fence, they collided with each other; the hole was not big enough for both at the same time. Backing off, J.T. let Mickey squeeze through first, then with his heart pounding, he wriggled through. Without looking back, they raced across Emil Gubler's alfalfa field for the thick vegetation of the Santa Clara River.

For the entire Santa Clara Valley, the riverbank was the only place teeming with natural vegetation. Dense stands of stink willows, groves of sapling cottonwoods, coyote willows, white willows, and skunk bushes made great cover to escape the charging Borch Rosenkranz, and it also made an ideal location for a hideout. It was for this secret retreat the boys were now headed.

As they fought through the tangle of foliage, they periodically checked over their shoulders to see if old Rosenkranz was still coming. He was not, or at least as best they could tell he was not. But with the limited visibility allowed by the thick riparian foliage, it was hard to say for sure.

Chris, J.T.'s older brother, had started construction of the hideout several years ago, but it was J.T. and Mickey who had finished it and made it into something special.

Built in the classic manner of the old-west stockade, its floorplan was roughly a square, with four large cottonwood trees anchoring the corners. Connecting each anchor tree were two parallel 2x4 studs, one nailed approximately two feet off the ground and the other about five feet higher. To this framework, eight-foot tall, piked stink willow poles were nailed, then small observation square portholes were cut into each of the four walls. Lastly, short cross planks were nailed up the corrugated trunk of one of the cottonwoods, thereby making a crude stairway up to the higher limbs. The purpose of this arboreal stairway was twofold: a route for quick escapes, if necessary, and to serve as an observation station or a spotting tower.

Sequestered deep in this thicket of stink willows and cottonwood saplings, the fort was hard to find, unless you knew the path, and very few people did. The end result was a surprisingly solid structure, which was also difficult to find; in other words, a perfect hideout.

Over the years, J.T. and Mickey appropriated a number of items for their hideout including additional boards, nails, hinges, metal scraps, an assortment of small tools for the occasional repair, and they had even collected a small quantity of canned goods and bottled water in the event of an emergency, such as a war with Russia. It was Mickey's opinion the Russians were on the verge of bombing and/or invading us. It could happen any day.

After running all the way from the Rosenkranz compound, the boys arrived at the fort winded. Once safely inside the structure, they slammed the door shut and locked it by inserting a 2x4 plank across three iron rungs, one anchored on the door and two on the opposing jambs. Breathing heavily, they flopped onto the earthen floor. All was quiet except for their gasping for air, and a nearby squawking tree squirrel.

"Damn!" Mickey exclaimed, between gasps for air. "That—was—close."

"D—do—you think," J.T. croaked, "he—followed—us?"

"No way," Mickey shook his head, but nevertheless got up and looked through a porthole to the east. "Nobody can find this place."

"I—I sure hope not." J.T. also struggled to his feet and peered out and identical porthole to the north.

"So, what do you think of him now?" Mickey asked.

"What?"

"So," Mickey repeated his question, "what do you think of Boris now?"

"I don't know," J.T. frowned and shook his head. With this recent development, he was beginning to change his mind. "What did he call us?"

"Swine, I think," Mickey laughed nervously, then added, "nobody uses that word."

"I guess he does," J.T. replied, "and I think he meant it as an insult."

"Ya think?" Mickey said sarcastically.

"Why didn't he call us pigs or hogs?"

""I don't know," Mickey replied crossly. "Maybe swine is more of a Russkie word."

"Do you think he knows we were snooping around?"

"Yeah, probably, but who cares? What can he do?"

"He can call the sheriff," J.T. replied, "and have us arrested for trespassing."

"Do you really think a spy is going to want law enforcement poking around?"

"Well, if he is a spy..." J.T.'s voice trailed off.

"Well, there is no 'if' about it; he is. So, what?"

"Well then…" J.T. still did not finished his thought.

"What?"

"Well, in the movies, you know what spies do to people who find them out?"

"What?" Mickey demanded again.

"You know," J.T.'s voice dropped to barely a whisper, "usually they do it at night, with something real quiet, like a dagger or a piano wire, or they just put a hand over your mouth and break your neck."

"Yeah, well if he tries that, I'll be ready," Mickey declared, then after a moment he added, "do—do you really think we're in danger?"

"I—I don't know. All I'm saying is we'd better watch our backs. If he is a spy, he's not going to let two kids ruin his whole operation."

"I wouldn't put anything past them damn commies." Mickey spat out the words like they were rancid milk. "They've got no conscience."

"How could they?" J.T. asked, then added, "They don't even believe in God or church."

"I know," Mickey nodded, then shrugged, "but I don't much like church either."

They sat in silence for a few more minutes, then J.T. systematically re-checked, looking out of every porthole. All was quiet, even the loud tree squirrel had quit squawking.

"Well," J.T. sighed, "all's clear. Let's get going, we've got work to do."

"What work?" Mickey got up and dusted off, but nevertheless looked relieved they had something to do other than worrying about being the target of Soviet spies.

"We're going to build some English stocks."

"What?"

"You know, English stocks. Remember the picture in our European history book of the man locked in a wooden stock? All you could see was the top of his head and his hands poking through the boards. You know, it was during the Renaissance Period."

"No," Mickey shook his head, "I didn't do very good in history."

"Well, anyway, it's easy. You just take two heavy planks and carve out holes in them for the neck and both wrists, then you lock people in it for punishment. You can throw rotten eggs or tomatoes at them and they can't move and can't get away. They just have to take it."

"Why?"

"Why, what?"

"Why are we building that?"

"Why do you think?" J.T. replied.

"I'm sure I don't know."

"Three words, Weird Willie Wittwer."

Breaking into a full grin, Mickey's freckles bunched over the bridge of his nose. "Then what are we waiting for?" he said, grabbing a board.

For the next two hours, the boys worked on the project. First, they selected two appropriately thick boards, 2 x 10 inch. In the middle in both planks, they sawed semicircular holes, one larger central hole for the neck and two smaller lateral ones for the wrists. Next, they nailed the lower board to two suitably spaced cottonwood trees, then attached the upper board with a hinge on one end and a leather strap for locking the boards on the other. When they were finished, J.T. backed off to inspect the final product. Rotating the upper plank on its hinge, he brought it down again flush against the lower board. All the holes lined up perfectly. Mechanically and theoretically, it seemed to work fine.

"Climb in," J.T. nodded toward the stocks. "Let's see if they work."

"I don't know," Mickey hesitated. "It's your idea, you should have the honor."

J.T. shrugged. "Okay, but no funny stuff."

"What are you talking about?"

"You know very well what I'm talking about. You promise to let me out?"

"Yeah, of course," Mickey agreed, his face immobile as a mask.

J.T. hesitated for a couple more seconds, then stepped forward. "Okay, let's give it a try."

Like a man placing his head on a chopping block, J.T. stretched his neck across the larger half-circle of the lower plank, then placed both wrists in the smaller holes. Involuntarily, he cringed as Mickey rotated the heavy top plank down, banging it across the back of his neck and wrists. Nothing pinched! It was a perfect fit. Next, Mickey secured the leather-locking strap to the bottom board.

"Okay, now try to get out."

"You're serious?"

"Sure, let's test it. We need to see if it will hold Weird Willie."

For the next couple of minutes, J.T. heaved, squirmed, pushed, and pulled, but to no avail. The planks held fast. No way could he break free and he was a little bigger than Willie.

"Well, John Tobler, I gotta go," Mickey grinned, "time to do my chores. See you later." He turned and headed for the path.

"Wait!"

Mickey turned around. "This is payback for when you locked me in the rabbit pens."

"What are you talking about?"

"You remember, maybe five years ago. We were playing cowboys and Indians?"

"W—what?"

"Yeah, we were the Indians and were going to ambush the wagon train."

"So," J.T. was confused, "What's that got to do with anything?"

"You told me to hide in the rabbit pens."

"Yeah, so?"

"So, you locked me in the rabbit pens and wouldn't let me out. Remember?"

"Uh—I guess so, but that was when we were kids."

"How 'bout an apology?"

"You're not serious?"

"Try me."

"I—I'm sorry, Mickey."

"Sorry about what?"

"I—I'm sorry I locked you in the rabbit pens!" J.T. shouted at Mickey's receding back.

Then Mickey was gone. There was absolute silence. The only sounds came from the pounding of J.T.'s heart and the rasping of air flowing in and out of his lungs. As he fought back a growing wave of hysteria, he silently chided himself; he should have known better than to trust Mickey T. Graff.

Then just as he was about to give in to panic, Mickey was back, grinning from ear to ear. As he released the locking strap, he commented, "works pretty damn good, huh?"

"That wasn't funny."

"I can't wait to get Weird Willie in this."

"We will," J.T. agreed, as he examined his abraded wrists, "he's got it coming."

After admiring the stocks for a couple more seconds, J.T. said, "we best get going. I still have evening chores to do."

"Me too," Mickey replied, heading for the path.

"After dinner," J.T. continued, "when it's dark, we'll meet at the old schoolhouse."

"Okay," Mickey led the way out of the thicket, "you goin' to tell me what we'll be doing?"

"All I'm going to say this one ought to be better than Judd and Howie's outhouse prank."

"Really!" Mickey seemed impressed."That was a classic, and this'll be number two."

After chores and another roast beef sandwich, Mary was not yet home, his father was still on his produce run and his mother was still in her bedroom, J.T. headed for the barn. He slung Manny Quinn over his shoulder and headed for the school.

By then, sun had grown weary of trying to hold off a determined moon and had collapsed behind Utah Hill. In its dying wake, it'd left a stunning afterglow. Almost immediately, the fading sunlight was replaced by the softer, silvery luminescence of the rising moon. In the twilit sky, cave bats, soaring like miniature P-51 Mustangs, were already out, dive bombing and dogfighting, while invisible Mormon crickets tuned up their bowstrings.

On purpose, J.T. avoided the busy Main Street. Instead, he took Corral Street to directly north of the schoolhouse, then simply headed south for another block. When he arrived, Mickey was already sitting on the schoolhouse steps.

"Did you bring it?"

"Yeah, of course." J.T. rotated Manny Quinn forward, so Mickey could see him in the fast-fading light. "Did you bring the catsup?"

"Of course." Mickey fished the glass bottle from his back pocket. "So, what's goin' to happen now?"

Sitting down beside Mickey, for the next five minutes J.T. laid out his plan. With each new detail, Mickey's eyes got wider. When he finally finished, Mickey whistled. "Wow! That is better than Judd and Howie."

"This looks like as good a place as any," J.T. said, gesturing up at the arboreal canopy created by the giant sycamore trees. "Right here, it looks like the branches go all the way across the highway."

"And the light's about right too," Mickey added, pointing at the streetlights spaced approximately every two hundred feet. "Just enough light that we can see what we're doing, but still not enough for them to see us."

"And there's going to be a full moon."

"Probably. We should go about halfway," Mickey pointed again, "between those two streetlights."

"Well," J.T. slapped his knees, then stood up, "let's get going." He grabbed the mannequin, then asked, "what's the traffic been like?"

"Been pretty steady, but lately, with the sun going down, it's slowed down a bit."

"Just this week," J.T. observed, "the traffic has doubled."

"California schools must be out."

"Where do you suppose they're all going?" J.T. nodded at the near-steady stream of headlights passing by.

"I don't know. Maybe the national parks, like Zion's, Bryce or the Grand Canyon."

"At least it's good for your fruit stand business."

"Yeah," Mickey agreed, "we've been real busy."

"And," J.T. continued, "it gives us someplace to sell our extra fruit."

"Yeah, and my dad says he'll take all you can give us."

For a few more moments, the boys watched the car headlights go by.

"Nobody's going the speed limit," Mickey commented.

"At night they almost never do," J.T. said as a sleek, bi-finned, red and white Mercury flashed by, "but actually it's better for us. Gives them less time to react."

"Well, John Tobler," Mickey walked away, "let's do it."

J.T. started to correct him, but what was the use? Mickey already knew he favored the moniker J.T.

Instead, he retaliated. "I'm coming, Michael Tobler."

Taking the straw dummy and the catsup with them, the boys crossed Highway 91, stopping at the base of a giant sycamore tree. Mickey boosted J.T. up to the first crotch, then he reached down and pulled up Manny Quinn. After locating a resting place for the dummy, he extended an arm downward, helping Mickey up. When Mickey was aboard, they climbed even higher, taking Manny Quinn with them. A couple of seconds later and two forks higher, they came to a solid branch, growing out over the highway.

Carefully, they inched out onto the branch. It groaned and sagged a bit under their weight, but nevertheless held. They continued to scoot outward until they were directly over the eastbound lane, the one coming from California and heading toward St. George.

This seemed to J.T. to be an ideal spot, as here two opposing branches met and even overlapped for three or four feet. The upper branch, originating from the sycamore on the far side of the highway, was a foot higher, forming a natural backrest. Carefully, the boys sat down on the lower branch, rested their backs against the higher one, while dangling their feet out into space. Of more importance than comfort, however, this spot provided a stationary platform from which to operate.

"Okay," J.T. nodded, "go ahead and douse Manny."

Fishing the catsup bottle from his hip pocket, Mickey unscrewed the cap, liberally splashing Manny with the red tomato sauce. "Don't look much like blood," he observed, dabbing a finger, and tasting it.

"Maybe not up close," J.T. also dipped a finger, "but at a distance it'll do."

"If you say so," Mickey still looked unconvinced as he recapped the catsup, "but let's give it a try."

Quickly, J.T. placed a restraining hand across Mickey and Manny. "We have to wait for the right time."

"There's no time better than right now."

“No,” J.T. shook his head, “We need a single car, one by itself, and one with California plates.”

“What difference does it make?”

“First, we don’t want to cause an accident and second, we don’t want to do it to anybody we know.”

J.T. readjusted his position on the perch, draping an arm around Manny Quinn. Now he was sitting with one arm around the mannequin and the other looped securely around the top branch. On the other side of the dummy, Mickey followed suit.

“Yeah, okay,” Mickey nodded his agreement. “Just tell me when.”

Looking back over their shoulders, the boys watched the line of approaching headlights. In the poor light, they could not see the classic black and gold California license plates until the vehicles were almost directly under them, giving them little time to react. Patiently, they waited for the right conditions, a solitary car with California plates. Five minutes went by, then ten, then fifteen.

By his constant fidgeting, J.T. could tell Mickey was getting impatient. J.T. was worried he would do something rash, but still he waited.

Suddenly, there it was, almost directly under them and coming fast. The car was a black and white Buick with its trademark row of vents (nostrils) running down both sides of the hood.

Quickly, Mickey positioned Manny Quinn.

“Now!” J.T. said.

Letting go, Mickey dropped Manny directly in front of the California Buick. It was a perfect shot. Manny Quinn flopped on the road just ten feet in front of the on-rushing car.

With no time to react, the Buick thumped over the mannequin twice, front and rear tires, then slammed on the brakes!

For a few seconds, nothing more happened. J.T. supposed the driver was trying to compose him or herself while checking things out through his rearview mirror. Finally, the door creaked open and a large, lumberjack of a man, complete with a full beard and a flannel shirt, struggled out of the car. Pausing, he peered back intently at the mannequin. Still, he hesitated, then apparently made up his mind, and hurried toward the still body. Kneeling, he dropped an ear to its chest and groped for the carotid artery.

“Shit!” he exclaimed, then stood up, still holding onto the dummy in his huge paw. Carefully, he put his fingers to his mouth.

“God damn it!” He shouted again, wiping his hands on Manny’s jeans. Looking like he was about to explode, he scanned the area, three hundred and sixty degrees, then scanned it again.

"Damn kids," he cussed again. Flinging Manny to the ground, he stomped back to his car. At the Buick, he turned around one more time, glaring up at the tree canopy.

Quickly, J.T. and Mickey shrunk further back into the deep shadows of the sycamore leaves.

"You little sons-a-bitches," Paul Bunyan bellowed out into the night, while shaking his hammer fist, "by damn, you'll pay for this." He surveyed the area one last time, then climbed back into his Buick and slammed the door. Spinning his tires, he roared off, leaving the night air saturated with the caustic smell of burning rubber.

"Wow!" Mickey exclaimed. "That was really something."

"I—I don't know," J.T. stammered. He wasn't sure what he'd expected, maybe even a small chuckle at their ingenuity, but certainly not this. "May—maybe we'd better stop."

"What? No way. That was great."

"But he got awfully mad."

"What'd you expect?" Mickey said, laughing. "At least he didn't call us swine."

"But he called us sons-a—you know what."

"Oh, you mean sons-a-bitches," Mickey said, still grinning.

"But—but, I didn't think he'd get that mad."

"What did you think? That he'd laugh and say, 'hey, fellows, that was a good one'."

"I don't know, but maybe this is not such a great idea after all."

"It's a classic," Mickey insisted, "just like Judd and Howie's outhouse prank only better. Let's do it three more times."

"Nah. I don't think so."

"Two more."

"No."

"Then one."

"Okay, one more," J.T. finally gave in, "then we'll quit."

"Deal," Mickey agreed, then quickly upped the ante, "okay, then it's two more times."

Under his breath, J.T. mumbled something inaudible.

Carefully, they descended out of the tree and retrieved the mannequin before more cars came by and totally destroyed it. In the amber glow of the incandescent streetlight, they inspected Manny Quinn. Other that a three-inch rip in his shirt, he seemed no worse for wear. After fluffing him out again, Mickey applied fresh catsup. Taking Manny with them, the boys scrambled back up the sycamore tree crawling out to their same two-limb perch.

As before, they cranked their heads at the sound of every approaching engine, waiting for the right car and the right time. By now, the traffic had thinned considerably, and it took less than ten minutes for a solitary California car to approach. It was a boxy, light brown Plymouth sedan.

Again, at precisely the right moment, Mickey dropped Manny Quinn. Once again, there were two distinct thumps as the car thudded over it, after which the Plymouth screeched to a stop. As before, for a few seconds nothing happened. Finally, the headlights turned off and the engine killed. Cautiously, the door cracked open and the driver emerged. The metal rims of her spectacles glinted in the moonlight as she looked back at the body. Wearing a knee-length, yellow sun dress, she appeared to be visibly shaken. At first, she seemed indecisive, staring back at the crumpled body, then she took a couple of tentative steps toward it. Stopping, she hesitated one more time, anxiously looking back at her vehicle.

Finally, she made up her mind. Pivoting around, she hustled back to her car, climbed in and softly closed the door. Starting the engine, and without turning on her headlights, she steered the Plymouth down the highway. Quietly, almost stealthily, the car rolled east, until seconds later it disappeared around a turn.

"Damn!" Mickey exclaimed, wide-eyed. "What was that?"

"I—I think," J.T. stammered, "that—that's what the cops call a hit and run."

"But isn't that a crime?"

"Yeah, and it's a bad one, a felony, I think."

"Damn," Mickey repeated, shaking his head, "that just goes to show, you never know about people."

Suddenly, J.T. felt a shiver raced up his spine. What they were doing was probably a crime too. "Let's get out of here. This is way too dangerous."

"Nah, it's just getting interestin'. Let's see what the next guy does."

"No," J.T. shook his head, "we may have crossed a line already."

"What line? Nobody got hurt and we agreed on three."

"No, you agreed on three."

"Oh, come on," Mickey said, climbing down from the tree, "we spent a lot of time building that dummy."

"Not that much time."

"One more and we'll quit, I promise."

Ten minutes later and after much convincing, J.T. reluctantly climbed back in position with the dummy; Manny Quinn was seated between them. Fresh catsup had been applied.

"I'll be the lookout this time," Mickey suggested, "you throw the dummy."

"No," J.T. shook his head, "no way. I'm done. You'll have to do both."

By then, the traffic had thinned out significantly, sometimes thirty seconds or more passed between cars. Again J.T. could tell Mickey was getting impatient; he squirmed and cussed every time the wrong car went by.

"Now!" he finally shouted and dropped Manny Quinn in front of an on-coming dark Ford sedan.

Once again, they heard the signature thump, thump, and the screech of tires as the Ford came to a stop. The moment the door opened, however, J.T. realized Mickey had made a huge mistake. The license plate was not the classic black and gold of California, but rather the blue and white of Utah. He started to reprimand Mickey, but Mickey shushed him, putting a finger to his lips, as the man was getting out of the sedan.

He was a tall, thin man, wearing a green corduroy jacket over a white ruffled shirt, which was smartly tucked into short leather pants. On his head perched a dark green Fedora sporting a feather in the hatband.

"It's Mister Rosenkranz!" J.T. whispered, as Borch approached the dummy.

"What the hell is he doing out so late?" Mickey whispered back.

"I don't know, but—"

Suddenly, J.T. was interrupted by the distant wailing of police sirens. The thick curtain of sycamore leaves prevented him from seeing the cars, but he could clearly hear the sirens, which got louder by the second. Moments later, the rhythmic strobe of red lights flashed through gaps in the sycamore leaves.

At first, Rosenkranz hesitated, seemed paralyzed.

Looking down the highway from their higher vantage point, J.T. counted two, no three cruisers headed their way. That must be the entire night shift of both the St. George Police Department and the Washington County Sheriff's Office.

Abruptly, Borch Rosenkranz whirled and raced back to his sedan. Clamoring inside, he slammed the door and whipped the Ford around, then roared back down the highway to the west, the same direction from which he'd just come.

"What the hell?" Mickey arched an eyebrow.

Also confused, J.T. turned and watched Rosenkranz's rapidly receding taillights.

"I think," Mickey nudged J.T. back into the presence, while pointing at the cruisers, "I think maybe we better get the hell outta here."

seconds or more passed between cars. Again J.T. could tell Mickey was getting impatient: he squirmed and cussed every time the wrong car went by.

"Now!" he finally shouted and dropped Manny Quinn in front of an oncoming dark Ford sedan.

Once again, they heard the signature thump, thump, and the screech of tires as the Ford came to a stop. The moment the door opened, however, J.T. realized Mickey had made a huge mistake. The license plate was not the classic black and gold of California but rather the blue and white of Utah. He started to reprimand Mickey, but Mickey shushed him, putting a finger to his lips as the man was getting out of the sedan.

He was a tall, thin man, wearing a green corduroy jacket over a white ruffled shirt, which was smartly tucked into short leather pants. On his head perched a dark green Fedora, sporting a feather in the hatband.

"It's Mister Rosenkrantz!" J.T. whispered, as Burch approached the dummy.

"What the hell is he doing out so late?" Mickey whispered back.

"I don't know, but—"

Suddenly, J.T. was interrupted by the distant wailing of police sirens. The thick curtain of sycamore leaves prevented him from seeing the cars, but he could clearly hear the sirens, which got louder by the second. Moments later, the rhythmic strobe of red lights flashed through gaps in the sycamore leaves.

At first, Rosenkrantz hesitated, seemed paralyzed.

Looking down the highway from their higher vantage point, J.T. counted two and three cruisers headed their way. That must be the entire night shift of both the St. George Police Department and the Washington County Sheriff's Office.

Abruptly, Rosenkrantz whirled and raced back to his sedan. Clambering inside, he slammed the door and whipped the Ford around, then roared back down the highway to the west, the same direction from which he'd just come.

"What the hell?" Mickey yanked on J.T.'s sleeve.

Also confused, J.T. turned and watched Rosenkrantz's rapidly receding taillights.

"Hurry," Mickey nudged J.T. back into the brambles while pointing at the cruisers. "I think maybe we better get the hell outta here."

11

Town bell is a team sport played by both sexes and in the United States seems to be unique to the small southern Utah town of Santa Clara. Though its origin is somewhat obscure, most historians believe its roots date back centuries to the rural villages of Switzerland.

Played exclusively at night, the rules have evolved over the years, each generation adding, subtracting, or tweaking the rules, but the basics have remained fairly constant. Lots are drawn, two opposing sides are chosen, then one team is awarded custody of the prized bell, a common cowbell. While in their possession, that team must ring the bell three times under every designated, lighted street corner. If the person possessing the bell is touched, or tagged, by any member of the opposing team, that team immediately loses custody of the bell. Obviously, the bell team is most visible, most vulnerable, when ringing under the streetlights. The winning team is the first to ring the bell under every corner streetlight in the prescribed area, usually a total of ten lights, and has undisputed ownership of the bell after the last ring.

Some commonly employed strategies include splitting up the team, so the opposing team doesn't know which squad has the bell, or who to follow. While in the act of ringing under a streetlight, forming an impenetrable scrum to protect the player (the bell). And not ringing at consecutive blocks, but at random streetlights, so opposing team cannot anticipate the next ring, thereby lessening the chances of a strategic ambush. Of course, all this is done under the relative obscurity of night.

And it goes without saying, town bell is normally a summer game. By tacit approval of the town elders, the games are allowed to commence only after school has adjourned for the year, after which games are tentatively scheduled for each Wednesday night with the variable starting time of dusk. Why dusk? By nightfall most of the day's work has been completed and of course it's a little cooler. So, on Wednesdays, almost like magic, when the sun goes down players begin to appear from every corner of town, congregating at the old schoolhouse. Teams are chosen, the bell assigned by drawing lots and play begins. Play ends when one team has rung the bell at each of all assigned street corners. Often the game can continue for hours, but on the other hand, sometimes it can be as short as thirty or forty minutes.

Tonight, was to be this summer's first gathering of town bell and J.T. could hardly wait (he loved town bell), but at the moment he had other, more pressing problems.

Why more pressing? Right now, he and his mother were sitting in the waiting room of Superintendent Robert T. Hartley at the school district offices in St. George. Following this meeting, they were scheduled to go to Dr. Hilton's office where his mother had an eleven o'clock appointment.

Anxiously, J.T. glanced up at the moon-shaped wall clock, affixed next to a rectangular picture of the ever-popular Utah Governor, J. Bracken Lee. Unlike the moon, however, this circular body sported a white face with black Roman numerals. Long spear-shaped hands clearly pointed out the time, now 10:05 a.m.

Superintendent Hartley was late!

The big question, was why? Was something else going on? Maybe, they, Hartley and the county authorities, had decided to charge them with a crime after all—criminal mischief or maybe even assault. Or perhaps, they had decided to ban them from ever again attending school within the boundaries of the Washington County School District. The next closest district was Iron County, some fifty miles away, but it might as well be a thousand. J.T. had absolutely no way to get there. Or perhaps, they were recalculating the damages and now instead of twenty dollars, he owed forty or even fifty. Like an indentured servant straight from his seventeenth century, early American history book, he might have to work forever just to pay them off.

The black spear-hand jerked forward again. Now it was 10:11 a.m. and in spite of the heat, J.T. broke out into a cold sweat. Anxiously, he looked around for a way to escape, but realistically he knew he couldn't run. Well, he could, but what would that accomplish? No, figuratively, if not literally, he was trapped!

Abruptly, the door opened and like a desert microburst, Superintendent Hartley blew in, the overhead florescent lights reflecting brightly off his baldhead. Forcing a tight smile, he shook Mrs. Kunz's hand, then he scowled down at J.T.

"Follow me," he said curtly, "Miss Miller is waiting."

J.T. took a deep breath, then like a man being led to his execution, followed his mother, who followed Mr. Hartley into the room.

Wearing a floral, lemon-yellow sundress, Miss Miller was seated on an unpadded wooden chair in front of Hartley's intimidating, Victorian office desk. As they entered, she nibbled nervously on her lower lip, then briefly glanced in their direction.

Suddenly, J.T. realized how young she was. Miss Miller didn't appear to be a whole lot older than his sister Mary. Undoubtedly, the substitute position at the Santa Clara Elementary was her first professional job. Instantly, J.T. felt terrible.

Looking every bit the commander-in-chief, Superintendent Hartley took charge. "Well, John Tobler," he said sternly, looming over him, "do you have anything to say?"

"Uh—uh," J.T. stammered, glancing down at his shoes. "Misses—uh—Miss Miller, I—uh—I'm very sorry."

Appearing to be close to tears, Miss Miller continued to bite her lower lip, but said nothing. The silence rapidly expanded until it became painful and begged to be filled with something—anything—but still no one spoke.

"Uh—uh," J.T. continued, searching for something else to say, "uh—I hope you stay in teaching. You are a good teacher."

Like the breaking of a thunderstorm, tears suddenly began to flow. Sobbing, Miss Miller reached over and patted J.T.'s hand, then stood up. "Excuse me," she sobbed, then fled from the room.

"Okay," Mr. Hartley sighed, walking from behind to the front of his desk. "Okay, I guess that will have to do. Understandably, she's very upset."

J.T. said nothing. What could he say? Mere words were inadequate, seemed almost inappropriate right now.

"I hope you have learned something from this unfortunate affair, young man."

"Yes, sir," J.T. mumbled, still eyeing his shoes.

"What?" Hartley asked sternly.

"Huh?" J.T. glanced up at the glaring face.

"Tell me exactly what you have learned."

"Uh—uh—I guess—not to make girls cry," J.T. blurted without thinking.

"What?" Hartley thundered, planting both hands on his boney hips. "You mean to tell me that is all you've learned? Then, Mister Kunz, you've missed the whole point."

"W—what point?" Involuntarily, J.T. backed up a step further away from the incensed Hartley.

"There is much more wrong here than just making girls cry."

"W—what?" "J.T. looked at his mother for help, but she too looked perplexed.

Hartley continued to loom over J.T.

Finally, he said, "well, why don't you take some time and think about it, then this fall when you bring in your share of the damage money, you can also turn in a three-hundred-word essay on what lessons you've learned from that firecracker fiasco."

Cringing, J.T. backed up another step and even Mrs. Kunz seemed stunned by the outburst.

"I'm serious," Mr. Hartley snapped.

"O—okay," J.T. stuttered. What else could he say?

"Well then," Hartley continued after another long and painful moment, "go on then; we're done here."

Mrs. Kunz started to say something, then changed her mind and ushered J.T. toward the door.

As they walked back through the waiting room, J.T. saw Mickey and his mother had arrived and were sitting in the very same chairs they'd earlier vacated. Grinning, Mickey gave him a two-thumbs-up. Ducking his head, J.T. didn't respond.

"How did it go?" Mickey whispered as J.T. walked by.

Shaking his head, J.T. just kept going. Right now he did not feel like talking to Mickey or anyone else for that matter.

In silence, they drove the half dozen blocks to Dr. Hilton's office. J.T. was still stinging from the confrontation in Hartley's office and was thankful for the quiet.

Located at the corner of 100 South and 300 East, Dr. James Hilton's office was nearly in the geographic center of St. George. Sequestered in a residential neighborhood, it was several blocks north of the McGregor Hospital. The clinic, a single story, L-shaped structure, had a flat roof and was constructed with pottery brown brick. Neatly landscaped, it boasted large, arching pecan trees and a manicured bluegrass lawn. Towering cypress trees were posted at the corners of the building and neatly trimmed Japanese box shrubs filled in the rest of the perimeter. Clearly visible on top of the flat roof were two squat metal boxes with slotted panels, signaling the welcome presence of swamp coolers, apparently one for each wing. With no dedicated parking, patients were required to park on the street, then had to dash through the sweltering heat to the clinic entrance and the waiting air conditioning.

"Well, come on, J.T.," Mrs. Kunz sighed, turning off the engine. Without the benefit of movement, no air circulated through the open windows. Almost immediately, the Plymouth's convex windshield became a magnifying glass for light and heat.

"I'll wait here," J.T. replied stubbornly.

"I don't know how long I'll be."

"I don't feel like being around people right now."

"They have air conditioning and Boy's Life magazines."

"They do?"

For proof, Mrs. Kunz pointed to the swamp coolers on the roof. "You'll die of a heat stroke out here."

"Okay," J.T. grudgingly gave in, "but I'm not talking to anybody."

"I'm sure everyone will be disappointed."

The air conditioning, J.T. had to admit, did feel good after sitting in the oven-like car.

After checking in at the reception window, his mother apologized profusely for being five minutes late, then they found two empty chairs near the back of the waiting room.

Meanwhile, J.T. rummaged through a wall-mounted magazine rack until he found an old issue of BOY'S LIFE, then sat down directly under an air conditioning vent. Even though the air conditioners were going full blast, he couldn't help but notice the room still reeked of rubbing alcohol and/or other strong disinfectants. The caustic odors of doctor's offices always made him queasy. The smell, as much as the torture they inflicted, he decided, was the reason people hated to go to the doctor.

As was his habit, J.T. noted the time, 11:07 a.m. The next time he checked, it was 11:30 a.m. When he finished with his magazine, 11:45 a.m. Finally, at 12:06 p.m. the front door flew open and in rushed Dr. Hilton, his white lab coat tails flaring.

"Sorry, folks," he mumbled, as he hurried through the waiting room, "an emergency C-section."

"What's a C-section?" J.T. asked his mother.

"Surgery."

"What kind of surgery?"

"Abdominal surgery."

"For an appendix?"

"Something like that," she said vaguely.

After another thirty minutes, the receptionist finally announced, "Missus Anita Kunz," and a white-frocked, white-capped nurse escorted her back to an exam room.

Again, rummaging through the magazine rack, J.T. found a fairly recent issue of *Time* magazine. He thumbed through the magazine, finally settling on an article that featured the fledgling American nuclear program and the newly completed test center at Yucca Flats, Nevada. Because of money constraints and time concerns, President Harry Truman had recently relocated the National Test Center from the Pacific Marshall Islands to the deserts of Nevada.

The paramount problem facing us, according to the article, the Soviet Union had already acquired the atomic bomb, probably stolen from us, and was now working on a potentially more powerful weapon, called a hydrogen or H-bomb. It was feared the Russians were on the verge of a major breakthrough, a fully operational H-bomb, which could be miniaturized small enough to mount on an ICBM (Intercontinental Ballistic Missile.) If true, this would surely tip the already teetering Cold War balance scales in favor of the Soviet Union. However, Mr. Rudolph (Rudy) Popovich of the Atomic Energy Commission had assured the TIME reporter his agency was doing everything they could to win this most critical race. Many more tests were scheduled at the new Nevada Test Center, almost one a month, to keep us competitive and hopefully win the H-bomb race. In his opinion, Mr. Popovich went on to say, it was only a matter of time till the Russians, or us, or perhaps both countries would have this incredibly powerful weapon. And the H-bomb could/would certainly be a game-changer.

It was well after one o'clock when Mrs. Kunz emerged from the exam room. Setting down his magazine, J.T. looked up and once again noted how pale she looked. Her gaunt face seemed even more drawn and her normally inscrutable black eyes, seemed suddenly more readable, almost forlorn. Or was it depressed?

As she motioned to J.T. to follow, she seemed preoccupied, then without waiting for him to catch up, she headed out the clinic door.

"What's wrong?" he asked once they were back in the car. After sitting in the sun for nearly two hours, it was Death Valley hot, well over a hundred and twenty degrees.

"Oh, nothing," Mrs. Kunz replied vaguely, not looking at J.T.

"Come on, Mother. You've not felt good for months."

"It's just a summer cold. They're always the worst."

"What did Doc Hilton say?"

"Nothing much," she shrugged.

"He must have said something."

She glanced sideways at J.T., then after a moment added, "uh—he wants me to go to Salt Lake City to see a specialist."

"A specialist? What kind of a specialist?"

For a few more seconds, Mrs. Kunz said nothing. "Well, I guess you're old enough," she finally said, "he wants me to see an oncologist."

"What's an oncologist?"

"A cancer specialist."

"A cancer specialist," J.T. repeated, mostly to himself. "Do you have cancer?"

"It seems so."

"What kind of cancer?"

"You know," Mrs. Kunz replied, then hesitated, seemingly searching for the right words. "You know, down there."

J.T. didn't know exactly what 'down there' meant, but he had a vague idea. "Why Salt Lake City? Is it that bad?"

"I'm not sure. Doctor Hilton said in Salt Lake they could run more tests and maybe start some treatments."

"What kind of treatments?"

"Again, I'm not sure." Mrs. Kunz replied again, turning the ignition key. "Probably surgery or cobalt radiation or both."

"Does Father know?"

"No, not everything," his mother replied, as she stomped on the clutch pedal and ground the gears. "I'll tell him on Sunday when he gets back. I didn't know for sure myself until today."

"They'll be able to cure it," J.T. declared with more confidence than he felt. "They've made some great strides in medical science lately."

"Yes, Jackie—I'm sure that's true."

"No, really, they can do some amazing things."

"Yes, I'm sure they can, but nevertheless I think I'll have the elders come by and give me a priesthood blessing," Mrs. Kunz said as she steered the car onto Highway 91 and headed west toward Santa Clara, "and maybe I'll even have Smokey perform a Navajo Sing, the blessing way. He's a shaman, a yataalii, you know."

Yes, J.T. did know, but he didn't understand why his mother insisted on clinging to the old Navajo ways, particularly when she'd joined the church as a child. Apparently, there were some things not even baptism by immersion could wash away.

"It wouldn't hurt," Mrs. Kunz added, as the Plymouth crossed the Halfway Wash, "to cover all my bases."

Frowning, J.T. glanced over at his mother. "I don't know about Smokey; Father won't be happy."

"Then I'll do it when he's not around."

With growing anxiety, J.T. listened to the sound of hot air whistling through the half-open windows as they drove the rest of the way in silence.

Cancer!

Like polio, just the word itself struck the fear of God into J.T. Even though he had no formal medical training, he knew very few cancers could be cured, at least not medically. Covertly glancing over at his mother, he tried to fight back a surging wave of panic.

But cures through the power of the priesthood, by the laying-on-of-hands, were well documented, at least by word of mouth, and were even commonplace. Everyone in Santa Clara knew someone, who knew someone, that was cured by the laying-on-of-hands. They talked about it all the time in fast and testimony meeting. All that was needed, other than the priesthood and the physical act of laying-on-of-hands, was a little faith, probably a lot of faith.

As soon as they rounded the gentle curve in the highway, a block from their house, J.T. spotted the sheriff's cruiser, parked right out front. As his mother pulled the car into their driveway, Sheriff Evan Meecham struggled to get his massive frame out of his back and white patrol car. His mother parked the Plymouth, then they scurried to the shade of the front porch and waited for the sheriff.

As the sheriff shuffled toward them, J.T. noted he had a .357 Magnum tightly belted under his overflowing abdomen. Beads of perspiration dotted his forehead and the slack skin of his face and abdomen jiggled with every step. Everything about him looked incongruous for a lawman, except for his eyes; they were a calculating, no-nonsense, azure blue. Slightly out of breath, the sheriff lumbered up the porch steps, a white flour sack slung over his right shoulder.

"Afternoon, Missus Kunz," he removed his billed sheriff's hat to expose closely cropped, clay brown hair, graying at the temples.

"Afternoon, Sheriff," Anita Kunz replied, "what can we do for you, Evan?"

"If you don't mind, I'd like to talk with John.," Sheriff Evan Meecham replied, replacing his hat. He then fished a wadded handkerchief from his rear pant pocket and mopped the perspiration from his forehead.

"About what?"

"About last night," Meecham said, then quickly added, "Ma'am, this is official business."

Mrs. Kunz considered this for a second, and shrugged her thin shoulders. "Then come inside, Evan. It's too hot out here."

With Mrs. Kunz leading, they trailed inside to the living room, then everyone located a seat. Immediately, J.T. grabbed the mint green, overstuffed chair positioned under the air conditioning vent, the coolest place in the house. Mrs. Kunz sat in an identical chair on the opposite side of the living room, leaving Sheriff Meecham no other option than the gold-leaf-pattern sofa. Grunting, he sat down, placing the white flour sack beside his bulging thigh.

With no knickknacks, photographs, or wall art, the living room was a fairly spartan. The only thing that could be interpreted as a fashion accessory was a ship clock on the mantel positioned directly over a smoke-smudged fireplace. Even though the room was clean and neat, all the furniture was a decade out of style and the carpet, a faded beige, was worn threadbare, particularly in the high traffic areas.

"Would you like some lemonade, Evan?" Anita Kunz asked, then added, "I don't think I've ever seen it so hot this early in June."

"Yes, Ma'am, it is hot," Meecham agreed, again mopping his forehead, then added, "lemonade would be great."

As Mrs. Kunz rose to leave, the sheriff leaned toward J.T. "Son, I want to talk to you about last—"

"I'll thank you, Sheriff," Mrs. Kunz interrupted, "not to interrogate my son while I'm out of the room. I'll be back in a minute."

In the minutes that followed, J.T. couldn't decide which would have been worse, fielding Sheriff Meecham's probing questions by himself or the uncomfortable silence of waiting for his mother to return. Every time he looked up, the sheriff's pale blue eyes were boring a hole right through him, but still the sheriff said nothing.

In spite of the air conditioning, J.T. broke out in a cold sweat. Thankfully, a few minutes later his mother arrived with three frosty tumblers on a silver metal tray. Starting with the sheriff, she passed out glasses, then filled them with lemonade.

"Now," she sat down again, "what were you saying, Evan?"

"Well," Meecham took a long-sustained gulp of lemonade, "um, that's good!"

As he tipped the tumbler again, J.T. could hear the ice cubes clink against the glass, then Meecham smacked his lips and started in. "I just want to know where John was last night."

"Why?" Mrs. Kunz asked, not giving her son a chance to answer.

"Well, last night we had some trouble over here in Santa Clara, right here on Main Street. It seems some kids thought it would be funny to make a dummy of straw and toss it in front of passing cars. You know, tourists from California."

"Was anyone hurt?" Mrs. Kunz asked, giving J.T. a quick glance.

"No, but we've got some mighty angry motorists," the sheriff said. "Even had one lady thinking she'd killed someone. After getting all the way to Cedar City, her conscience got the best of her and she turned around, drove back to Saint George and gave herself up. She was literally a basket case."

"I see," Anita Kunz said frowning, then carefully measuring her words, she added, "that is terrible, but where's the crime if nobody was hurt?"

"Yeah, nobody was hurt," Meecham agreed, finishing his lemonade. "You got any more of this?" He held up his tumbler.

Mrs. Kunz poured him another glass, then the sheriff continued, "yeah, nobody was hurt, at least not physically, but that don't mean it wasn't a crime. You should've saw that poor lady who thought she'd killed somebody. Talk about mental anguish. Yeah, this is a crime all right and it's called criminal mischief."

"Is that a misdemeanor?" Mrs. Kunz asked, still frowning.

"Yeah, that's right," the sheriff nodded, "but it ought'ta be more. Anyways, it's a Class C misdemeanor, punishable by a fine of one hundred dollars and up to six months in jail."

"I see," Anita Kunz said, rotating her still untouched glass in her hands. "What makes you think Jackie had anything to do with this?"

J.T. cringed. He hated to be called Jackie, particularly in public, even if it was his mother.

"Been asking around," Sheriff Meecham replied, "and two names kept surfacin', John T. Kunz and Michael T. Graff. Also, I heard through the grapevine some nonsense about trying to break a record for the most pranks in a summer. Anyways, most people think it was probably them two, or if not, they know who it was."

"Do you have any evidence," Mrs. Kunz asked, "other than rumors?"

"Just this," Meecham fumbled for the flour sack at his side, then fished out a bottle of catsup and an old sneaker. "Found these things at the crime scene."

In silence, the three of them stared at the eight-ounce, half-empty bottle of catsup and the scuffed white, right-foot sneaker.

After a moment, the sheriff continued, "is this your catsup bottle, Missus Kunz?"

"Good heavens, sheriff!" Mrs. Kunz shook her head. "Everybody in town has a bottle like that."

"Well, it don't matter, I've already lifted fingerprints off'n it." For a few long seconds, Sheriff Meecham toyed with the glass bottle.

"Well," Mrs. Kunz asked, "what did they show?"

"Huh," the sheriff replaced the catsup bottle back into the flour sack. "What did what show?"

"Oh, good heavens, Evan," Mrs. Kunz exclaimed, "the fingerprints!"

"Oh, we had to send 'em to Salt Lake City."

"So, what happens when you get them back?"

"What?" Meecham looked puzzled.

"My guess," Mrs. Kunz continued, "is they won't match any of fingerprints they already have on file in Salt Lake."

"So?"

"So, then what?"

"Oh, if they find identifiable prints, then we'll get your boy, John, here, and Mickey Graff to come in and we'll fingerprint them too."

"And I suppose," Mrs. Kunz said, "those fingerprints will then also have to be forwarded to Salt Lake City."

The sheriff nodded.

"Seems like a real inefficient way of doing things," Mrs. Kunz remarked, "all this back and forth to Salt Lake."

"Well, that where the crime lab is."

"So, what if the boys don't want to be fingerprinted?"

"Then we'll issue a warrant for their arrest."

"I see," Anita Kunz replied, again quickly glancing sideways at J.T. "Anything else, Sheriff?"

"As a matter of fact, there is, Misses Kunz," the sheriff said, holding up the sneaker. "This your shoe, John Junior?"

Seemingly lost in thought, J.T. didn't immediately answer."

"Well, John?" The sheriff waited for an answer.

"Uh—uh, I go by J.T."

"J.T., huh?" the sheriff shrugged. "Okay, J.T., is this your shoe?"

"Uh—uh." J.T. stammered. It wasn't his, but he knew it was Mickey's. "Nah—no," he glanced down at the almost identical sneakers he was wearing. "See, I've got mine on."

"So, do you know whose shoe this is, John, uh—I mean J.T.?"

"It could be anyone's."

"That's not what I asked," Meecham insisted, "I said do you—"

"He said no!" Anita Kunz snapped. "Please don't badger my son, Sheriff."

Mrs. Kunz and the sheriff locked eyes again.

"Well, if you don't mind," Sheriff Meecham said, turning back to J.T., "I want to hear it from him. J.T. Did you have anything to do with that fiasco last night?"

"Uh," J.T. gulped, looking down at his shoes again. This wasn't just about him. If it was, he would confess, but now if he did, that would also implicate Mickey. "Uh," he managed to look the sheriff in the eye, "uh—no. I spent the whole evening here, down in the basement working on my rocket."

The sheriff glanced over at Mrs. Kunz for confirmation.

"I don't know," she shrugged her frail shoulders, "I wasn't feeling good last night and didn't leave my bedroom. Mary's on a church camping trip and John's on his produce run."

"I see," Meecham struggled to get upright, then handed his empty tumbler back to Mrs. Kunz. "Well, anyways, I hope you will understand," he his blue eyes again seemed to bore right through J.T., "if I tell you I'm not convinced."

"Well, I hope you'll understand," Mrs. Kunz's black eyes hardened to obsidian, "I will stand by my son."

Once again, they locked eyes.

"Well then, let me say this much," Meecham finally glanced away, "this is bad business, real bad. It's bad for tourism; it's bad for the economy, and that's how this county pays its bills."

"I agree," Mrs. Kunz replied, again being careful with her words, "it is very bad and I sincerely hope it will never happen again."

"Yeah, okay, but before I go, I'd like to give J.T. a little bit of free advice." Meecham said, then apparently waited for permission.

Mrs. Kunz shrugged a silent consent, but still the sheriff waited.

"O—okay," J.T. finally croaked after a few more uncomfortable moments.

"Mark my words," Evan Meecham said solemnly, "someday these stupid pranks are goin' to get you into serious trouble, son. Maybe even get you into prison."

J.T. gulped, but said nothing.

Meecham gave J.T. one final glance, shook his head, then shuffled toward the door. Here he paused. "And you can mark my words," his voice now low and almost threatening, "we're going to catch 'em; whoever they are."

12

"Jackie, I'm a little tired," Mrs. Kunz sighed, as they watched Sheriff Meecham's broad backside disappear as he closed the door, "I'm going to lie down." She started for the hall, then turned back. "You know, the sheriff gave you some pretty good advice." She gave him a pointed look, then weaved down the hall toward her bedroom.

Fighting back a wave of guilt and another of remorse, J.T. got up and wandered around the house. Maybe they were going too far with these pranks. Criminal mischief! Six months in jail! And a one hundred dollar fine! Almost like a compulsive gambler, his debts kept climbing. First the school fiasco, then the damaged Loren Reber piece and now this, the possibility of a one hundred dollar fine for criminal mischief. At the rate he was making money, he'd never be able to pay off the one hundred dollars, and everything else, not in one hundred years, particularly if he was in prison. As far as he knew, they didn't pay you to sit in prison and he knew his dad would never come up with a penny for bail. Not for this. Not when he already owed him at least a hundred dollars for the Loren Reber piece. Undoubtedly, he'd let him rot in jail. I might just as well pack my bags now, J.T. told himself, then go turn myself in.

Whoa, slow down! Don't jump to conclusions. More than likely Sheriff Meecham didn't have anything solid. He was just using scare tactics. Otherwise, he and Mickey would already be in custody. Well, J.T. thought with a nervous laugh, he had to give the sheriff credit; if he was trying to scare him, he'd done a pretty good job.

Sighing, J.T. glanced up at the ship clock on the mantle; it was only 3:06 p.m. Even though it was well over a hundred degrees outside, he might just as well go down to the field and hoe a couple more rows of cantaloupes. Heaven knows, he could use the money and the physical labor might help take his mind off his problems. And, he still had about five hours to kill before the season's first game of town bell.

Grabbing a half-gallon Mason jar, he filled it with ice and water, then wrapped it with old newspaper for insulation. Planning ahead for later tonight, he grabbed old, and probably rotten eggs from the fridge (it seemed nobody in the Kunz household cooked anymore), placing them in a burlap bag he salvaged from the granary. Being careful not to touch anything made of metal, J.T. used a fold of the same burlap bag to start and shift the Massey-Ferguson, then he headed down the Vineyard Road. As he drove, heat waves shimmered up from the hot asphalt, then like a desert mirage, they constantly receded in front of him.

Out in the field, the heat was nearly overpowering. Frequently, J.T. had to stop and rest in the shade of a huge Bartlett pear tree. He noted with some satisfaction his hands were already developing thick, protective calluses. After gulping down more water, he headed back to the field and the seemingly endless rows of cantaloupes.

With the temperature approaching one hundred and four degrees, J.T. struggled to reach his goal of two more rows. When he'd finally finished, he had one more job to do before heading home. Putting them in the burlap bag, he harvested a few overripe tomatoes and decaying cantaloupes, adding them to the rotten eggs he'd brought from the house. Slinging the bag over his shoulder, he hauled it down toward the river.

It was not far, as the crow flies, to the fort. Once there, he stowed the sack inside the fort, and though it was a relief to be in the shade of the huge cottonwoods, he did not tarry. Hurriedly, he retraced his steps back to the vineyard field and the waiting Massey-Ferguson tractor.

As he drove and bounced home, J.T. noted the sun was almost touching the sawtooth, purple shoulder of Utah Hill. He'd have to hurry if he was going to make tonight's game. In the fast-fading light, he rushed through his evening chores. After milking Dorey (this time he found the hobbles), he ran the milk through a strainer and was just putting the milk in the fridge, when Mary walked in. Dropping her sleeping bag and dirty clothes on the floor, and without acknowledging J.T., she headed straight for the fridge.

"Who ate all the roast beef?" she asked, pushing J.T. aside and rummaging through the fridge.

"I did. There was nothing else."

"Well, I'm starving. What am I supposed to eat?"

"There's bread and milk, or cereal, or you could break down and cook something."

"Don't even go there, J.T.," Mary hissed. "I do three times the work around here that you do."

"Oh, yeah, I haven't seen you in the fields all summer."

"That doesn't mean I—"

"That's enough," Mrs. Kunz said wearily. She was standing in the doorway, wrapped in her faded turquoise robe. "I'm so sorry," she added, bursting into tears, "I know this has been hard on both of you."

Instantly, J.T. felt like a first-class heel. With tears now welling in his eyes, he announced he was going out to play town bell, then as an apparent peace offering he asked Mary if she wanted to come. Also biting her lip, she shook her head and quietly informed J.T. that she was too old for town bell. Nodding, he quickly turned away. Wiping a tear from his eye, he headed out the service door.

As usual, the gathering place was the front steps of the Santa Clara Elementary School, the very same place J.T. had met Mickey the night before for the ill-fated mannequin caper. A silver corona had just appeared on the eastern horizon, heralding the coming of not only a full moon, but what was forecast in the paper to be a super moon. It was a good night for town bell.

By the time J.T. arrived, a sizeable crowd had already gathered and it looked as if they were getting ready to choose up sides.

Out of the corner of his eye, J.T. spied Annie Leavitt. Tonight, she was standing close to Curley, real close, maybe even holding hands. Immediately, his spirits plummeted and he tried to stay as far away from her and Curley as possible. In a matter of seconds, his prospects for a late summer date vanished, like irrigation water down a gopher hole. Now he had no date options. Circling the group, he finally settled on a spot where he couldn't see her or Curley. If she was that fickle, Curley could have her. He really didn't care.

As a minor consolation, it appeared he wasn't the only one being jilted. Susan Hafen, the pretty blonde Mickey was sweet on, looked like she couldn't get enough of Easy Earl. And like J.T., Mickey also acted like he could care less, but J.T. knew differently. Mickey must be as upset as him, and like was J.T. pretending he didn't care.

No big surprise here, Mickey was elected as one captain and big Easy Earl the other. Earl had the first pick. He looked at J.T., hesitated, then chose Curley. Now it was Mickey's turn. Grinning mischievously, he looked directly at Alan, paused for dramatic effect, then called out, "John Tobler." Glaring at him, J.T. joined Mickey, but he just grinned back at him.

Ignoring Mickey's antics, J.T. whispered, "you've got to pick Weird Willie."

"Why," Mickey whispered back, "he the worst player."

"It's part of the plan."

With his next pick, Easy Earl selected Susan, and in spite to J.T.'s urging, with his next pick Mickey took Greg.

After that, each captain alternated picks until everyone was chosen, that is everyone except Weird Willie Wittwer. As luck would have it, the last pick fell to Mickey, and as a consequence he had no choice.

"Weird Willie," he called out, without enthusiasm.

As opposed to Mickey, J.T. was happy Weird Willie was on their team. In fact, his plan depended on it.

Since Easy Earl had first pick, by the rules Mickey's team got first possession of the cowbell, a decided advantage.

However, just as the teams were about to separate, a '51 cherry-red, hatchback Chevy screeched to a stop, scattering players, like bowling pins. Tinted dark windows prevented seeing inside, but nevertheless Easy Earl and a couple of the bigger boys doubled their fists and took a threatening step toward the hatchback. Slowly, the driver rolled down his window.

Instantly, J.T. recognized the car, then as the window came down, he saw the trademark pack of cigarettes rolled up in the sleeve of the T-shirt. It was none other than Leonard Weeks, Weird Willie's older cousin from St. George.

"Hey, Willie!" Lenny shouted through the open window. After taking on last drag, he tossed out a glowing cigarette butt at the circle of players, then added, "we've gotta talk!"

"A—about what?" Willie answered, shrinking back a step, fear lacquered across his ferret-like face.

"You know what," Lenny barked, leaning an elbow out the window. "They know about us!"

"No-o-o," Willie retreated further into the knot of players. "I—I don't want nothin' to do with it no more."

"Don't you think it's a little late for that?"

"L—leave me alone or I'll tell."

"Get in the car, now!" Lenny hissed. "Don't you understand? They're coming for us."

"No-o-o," Willie shook his head, "and you can't make me."

"Didn't you hear what I said?" Lenny quickly glanced over his shoulder. "They're coming for us!"

"No—no, I don't want nothing to do with it," Willie insisted, hiding behind big Easy Earl. "I'm out!"

"You can't get out."

"Yes—yes, I can."

"Okay, Willie, don't say I didn't warn you; now it's outta my hands." Shaking his head, Lenny rolled up the window, stomped on the accelerator and roared down the highway, spraying loose gravel.

"Trouble in paradise?" Mickey asked sarcastically, looking at Willie, then added, "what the hell was that all about?"

"Oh, nothing," Willie shrugged, quickly regaining his composure, "just a little business disagreement. That's all."

"Sounds like more than that to me," J.T. added.

"Nothing I can't handle," Weird Willie replied. "Are we goin' a play or not?"

"Okay," Mickey jangled the bell indicating the start of the game, "your business is your business."

As per the rules, Easy Earl's team gave Mickey's squad five minutes to plan strategy before disappearing into the night with the bell. By now the moon had risen well above the eastern horizon. With its appearance, the gray, indistinct light of dusk turned more silvery, more hoary. Now, the only real darkness was in the moon shadows.

"Huddle up." Mickey barked, gathering his team. "Here's what we're goin' to—"

"I wanna a be captain," Willie interrupted, before Mickey could utter another word. "It shouldn't always be Mickey."

"No way," Mickey shook his head. "I was elected captain." The rest of the team quickly agreed. Though Willie didn't look happy, there was nothing he could do about it.

Mickey mapped out a brilliant strategy. First, they would divide into two squads so the opposing team would not know which one had the bell. At each ringing (under a corner streetlight) the two groups would meet to protect the cowbell, then exchange possession of the bell with the other squad, and go their separate ways, only to meet again for the next ringing. The bell ringing would occur precisely every fifteen minutes at the street corners, but not in regular sequence, but randomly. First would be Frei Lane, next Stucki Lane, then Gubler Lane and so on until all ten light poles were rung. Lastly, as prescribed by the rules, they would finish with the streetlight right here in front of the schoolhouse.

"Any questions?" Mickey asked.

"Why can't I be captain?" Willie tried one more time.

Ignoring him, Mickey divided the team into two squads. He, J.T. and Weird Willie would make up one crew. The remaining four team players would make up the second group with Greg being in charge. Initially, Mickey's squad would head east; Greg's would go west. As a final gesture, Mickey handed Greg a whistle and he kept one for himself.

"If one squad needs the help of the other, blow the whistle twice," Mickey instructed. "If you just want to check on the position of the other squad, blow once. Understood?"

"Is that legal?" J.T. frowned.

"As far as I know," Mickey grinned, "nobody's ever used whistles before, so how could it be illegal? There ain't no rules agin it."

J.T. was unconvinced. "Just seems like an unfair advantage."

"There is no such thing as an unfair advantage in town bell," Mickey insisted. "Okay, now, does everyone know their assignments? Then, let's go."

Everything went according to Mickey's plan for the first hour. They rang the bell at Frei Lane, exchanged possession, then disappeared into the night without ever seeing the opposing team. Also, all went well at Stucki Lane and Gubler Lane, the ringing and exchange were again executed seamlessly with no opposition. However, when the two squads rendezvoused at Tobler Lane they were ambushed.

As Mickey raised the cowbell high above his head and started the ring, the opposing team suddenly materialized out of the moon shadows.

Shrieking a primordial battle cry, they rushed the bell from all four directions. Mickey's team quickly circled, forming a protective scrum around him and the bell, but in doing so they inadvertently trapped themselves. There was no easy escape; they were completely surrounded.

Players of Easy Earl's squad tried multiple frontal assaults, rushing and lunging at the bell, but each time Mickey's scrum held, rebuffing them. In desperation, big Easy decided to try it himself. First, he plunged straight into the scrum, but was repelled. Changing tactics, he circled Mickey's team looking for an opening, a weakness in their human ramparts, then he spied Weird Willie Wittwer. Abruptly he stopped, then like Babe Ruth pointing the direction of his famous home run, Easy Earl leveled a finger at Willie. Lowering his head, he charged. Right before impact, Willie abruptly vacated his position, leaving an opening to the bell. Like a blitzing linebacker, Easy Earl went through the line, hit Mickey, slamming him to the ground. The impact dislodged the bell, sending it skittering and clanging across the asphalt.

Almost as quickly as it had begun, the battle was over. The bell scooted right to Susan. Reaching down, she picked it up, then Mickey's team had to watch helplessly as Earl's team took full advantage of their free five minutes for planning strategy. After huddling, Earl's squad disappeared into the night, taking the coveted cowbell with them.

J.T. was both furious and bewildered. Furious that Willie had betrayed them, but he was even more bewildered at Annie Leavitt's behavior. During all the chaos, she had brushed up against him, then seemed to linger. Was that purely by accident? He didn't think so. But on the other hand, it was hard to figure. She was with Curley, but leaning up against him, and once again he'd felt the electricity of her touch. He knew there was a word for girls like that, but at the moment he couldn't think of it. So, he settled on fickle, but that didn't seem quite strong enough. He had to admit, however, that brief contact with her did make him feel better. There was no question about it, he told himself, he was still in the running, despite the handsome Curley Reber.

"Well, at least we're still ahead four, zip," Weird Willie said, rejoining the group as though nothing happened.

"What the hell was that?" Mickey demanded, getting in his face.

"W—what?" Willie asked, retreating before his enraged captain.

"You just stepped aside and let him in!"

"If you think that I'd take a bullet for you," Willie snorted, "you'd be dead and wrong."

"Come on guys," Greg joined in, "they're getting away."

"You're really something, Willie Wittwer," Mickey declared, shaking his head.

Gathering the team together, Mickey hurriedly updated their game plan. They would keep the same squads; Greg's would go back to Frei Lane and wait to see if Easy Earl's team showed up there. Mickey's squad would head over to Gubler Lane and wait there. Easy's team would eventually have to show up at both places. If either squad spotted Easy Earl's team, they notify the other squad with three short bursts on the whistle.

Five minutes later, Mickey, J.T. and Weird Willie arrived at Gubler Lane and found adequate hiding places in the rapidly shrinking moon shadows. Patiently, they waited for nearly twenty minutes, but nobody from Easy's team showed up.

"Well," Mickey sighed, standing up, "let's go see what's happening."

"Maybe," J.T. said vaguely, "maybe this would be a good time to do that other thing."

"What other thing?" Mickey asked, frowning.

Weird Willie immediately joined in. "Yeah, what other thing?"

"You know," J.T. said vaguely, "a change of strategy."

"That's what we're doin'." Mickey still looked confused. "What are you talkin' about?"

"Well, you know, perhaps we should circle back to the other end of town, but head down by the creek so no one sees us."

"By the creek?" Mickey asked, confused. "But that's kind of out of our way."

"You know," J.T. covertly nudged Mickey with his elbow, "by way of the stocks."

"Oh, yeah!" Mickey smiled and nodded. "You mean down by the river stocks."

"Stocks?" Willie asked, now it was his turn to look puzzled. "What stocks?"

"Uh—uh, that's short for stockyard," J.T. replied, struggling to come up with an answer. "We'll take the shortcut over by Gubler's stockyard."

"Shortcut," Willie frowned, then added, "but that's the long way around."

"But that way nobody'll see us," Mickey insisted, "and, it's shorter than you think."

"Are you sure you guys know what you're doing?"

"Yes, sure we do," Mickey answered, suppressing a smile, "and we'd better get goin'."

Their circuitous path again took them right past Borch Rosenkranz's place. However, before stepping on his property, they paused to reconnoiter. Even from a full fifty yards away, it was easy to see the compound in the bright light of the full moon. There were no lights on in the house and no car in the driveway. Nevertheless, they continued to watch the house for another full minute. Nothing stirred. Finally Mickey nodded and the boys started down the driveway.

At the window, J.T. couldn't help but peek in again. Even though the drapes were open, the room was dark and he couldn't see anything. They continued down the gravel driveway into the backyard. Here, Mickey paused at the wooden shed, then went straight to the loose slat. Dropping to his knees, he rotated it a couple of inches and looked in.

"Damn, it's gone!"

"What's gone?" J.T. pushed Mickey aside, positioning his eye next to the slit. Inside, there was total darkness, no blinking red and green lights, and no glowing vacuum tubes.

"Maybe he just turned it off."

Walking around to the back side of the shed, Mickey dropped down on his knees and began searching. Aided by the bright moonlight, he rapidly found the cord from the antenna, then followed it to the shed. Gently, he gave it a tug. Offering almost no resistance, the cord slid out from under the baseboard. Mickey looked closely at the end, but J.T. could tell it had been disconnected, not cut.

"It's gone all right," Mickey held up the end of the cord. "This wasn't plugged into nothin'."

"What are you guys talking about?" Weird Willie asked, pushing in closer.

"Why?" J.T. asked, ignoring Willie. "Why would it be gone?"

"Maybe, when he saw us snooping around the other day," Mickey theorized, "he moved it into the house."

"Or maybe, he's getting ready to move his whole operation," J.T. added, "move to another location, or even go back to Mother Russia. Maybe his work here is done."

"What," Willie asked impatiently, "are you guys talking about?"

"I'd sure hate to see him get away with it," Mickey replied, still ignoring Willie.

"I'll bet he's got a whole suitcase of data he's taking back with him," J.T. added. "Hard data that can't be sent over the airwaves."

"Sometime, maybe we ought'ta go in there," Mickey nodded toward the dark house, "and look around. Maybe we can get some proof before he leaves."

"Yeah, " J.T. agreed, "if he hasn't already left."

"I'm going to tell," Willie suddenly blurted. "Tomorrow, I'm going to tell Mister Rosenkranz you've been spying on him and you're going to break into his house."

"Willie, I swear!" Mickey blurted, raising a fist. "Don't you ever get tired of tellin' on people?"

"Nah," Willie grinned, "not with you two. I kinda like it."

Mickey shook his head. "Someday, you'll get yours."

"Maybe, sooner than you think," J.T. added.

"Do you think I'm afraid of you two clod farmers?" Willie sneered. "With my money and connections, I could make you disappear anytime I want."

"Yeah, right," J.T. laughed.

"Well, we best get goin'," Mickey dropped the black antenna cord, "if we're goin' to win this game of town bell."

As they headed south through the littered backyard, they heard the drone of an approaching automobile. Suddenly, headlights beams bounced off the ground, then projected on the fence.

"Damn it," Mickey exclaimed, "he's coming!" Pivoting, he sprinted for the fence.

As he ran, J.T. could almost feel the beams of light strike his back, but without question he could see his silhouette outlined on the board fence.

Arriving at the fence, and with hands shaking, J.T. rotated the loose board, allowing the other two to scrambled through. Once on the other side, Mickey did the same for him. Then without looking back, they raced across Gubler's alfalfa field.

"Do you think he saw us?" J.T. gasped, after they'd crossed the field and slowed to a walk.

"No, probably not," Mickey replied, looking over his shoulder, "but damn that was close."

Also turning back to scan the moonlit field, J.T. saw the loose board rotate again. "Hurry," he exclaimed, pointing, "he's coming!"

"Well," Willie taunted, not moving, "I'm going to stay here and tell Mister Rosenkranz."

"Will you shut up, Willie," Mickey snapped. Grabbing him by the arm, he jerked him around, then half-dragged him toward the dense foliage of the riverbed.

Ten minutes later, just as the boys approached the stink willow thicket surrounding the fort, they heard a twig crack directly behind them. Whirling around, they anxiously scoured the surrounding brush and willows, expecting Borch Rosenkranz to appear. But there was nothing. A little further on, they heard another noise. This time not a twig, but it sounded like an animal pushing through thick foliage. Again, they stopped, held their collective breaths and waited. Once again, nothing materialized.

"Deer live down here year around," Mickey said nervously, "even in the summer. I've seen 'em here before."

"Yeah, that must be it." J.T. forced a laugh as they turned back to the trail.

But surprisingly, now it was Weird Willie who seemed most shaken by the unexplained night sounds. "Y—you guys sure there's nothing out there," he stammered, wiping perspiration from his forehead.

"What you afraid of?" J.T. asked with more bravado than he felt. "Your buddy, Lenny Weeks?"

"N—nah," Willie laughed nervously. "No, not him."

"He seemed pretty mad," Mickey added, then taunted, "maybe he's comin' for you."

"L—let's get out of here." Willie mumbled, then started walking ahead.

"You don't know where you're goin'." Mickey grabbed and stopped him. "Let me lead."

In an edgy, jittery silence, they continued on; the full moon lighting the way.

A couple of minutes later, J.T. recognized the familiar skunk bush thicket right before the clearing. Here Mickey paused, telling Willie they had to pass by the hideout and they couldn't let him see it, as he was not yet a member of the stockade clan. Removing his white tee shirt, Mickey used it to blindfold Willie. At first, Willie protested, but Mickey explained this was also a test of his obedience and loyalty. If he passed the test, they would consider giving him a coveted clan membership and free access to the fort. Reluctantly, Willie agreed, confessing he'd heard rumors of the fort and had even tried to find it a time or two.

Again, with Mickey leading, they guided a blindfolded Weird Willie through the thicket, crawling on hands and knees. When they were directly in front of the newly constructed stocks, Mickey paused, looking at J.T. for help.

"Uh—uh, this is a real tricky area," J.T. said, thinking fast. "You'll just have to trust me to guide you through it."

"O—okay," Willie stuttered.

J.T. could tell Willie was getting nervous and at any moment he might jerk off the blindfold. "We are almost there," he reassured. "Now give me your hands, stand up and I'll help you get through."

When Willie stood up and offered his hands, J.T. guided his wrists in the two lateral notches of the lower board.

"Good, now keep them there for a minute," he said, "this is the tricky part. You're going to have to duck your head to get through. Let me help you."

Carefully, J.T. steered Weird Willie's neck to the larger central notch. When he had Willie's neck and wrists in exactly the right position, he nodded to Mickey.

Slamming down the upper board, Mickey quickly secured the locking straps!

At first, Willie seemed confused and offered no resistance, but when Mickey jerked off the blindfold, he immediately realized his predicament. Heaving and hurling, he threw his body forward, backward and sideways, trying to break free, but the stocks held tight. Fueled by high-octane adrenaline, he tried again and again, but could not break the hinge or the locking mechanism. Breathing hard, he finally collapsed, his weight supported by his arms and neck. However, once he caught his breath again, he started cursing.

J.T. was shocked! Half of the words, he'd never heard before. Later, he would ask Mickey what they meant.

"Let's see if we can shut that foul mouth of yours," J.T. said, disappearing inside the fort. A moment later, he returned with the burlap bag and showed the contents to Mickey.

"Yeah, okay, let's do it," Mickey nodded, "let's shut him up."

Grinning, he picked up a rotten egg, hurling it at Willie. It was a perfect opening pitch, striking Willie on the forehead right between the eyes. As the slimy, ochre yolk oozed down Willie's face, the distinctive odor of sulfur gas permeated the compound.

Not to be outdone, J.T. picked up an overripe tomato and hurled it. Another direct hit. It was like shooting fish in a barrel!

For the next three minutes, Mickey and J.T. pelted an increasingly enraged Weird Willie with rotting tomatoes, mushy cantaloupes and putrid eggs.

After they'd run out of ammunition, the boys inched in for a closer examination. Looking like a modern art collage, Willie's face and hair was splattered with pulpy red tomatoes, gooey orange cantaloupes and slimy yellow eggs. Shards of alabaster eggshells added contrast and texture. And in spite of Willie's continued fury, J.T. and Mickey couldn't help but laugh.

"That's for ratting us out to Superintendent Hartley," Mickey declared, searching the burlap bag for more ammunition. There was none.

"And for the unfair fight the other day with Lenny," J.T. added.

"And," Mickey continued, throwing the empty sack at Willie, "if you think this was bad, then you better not go talkin' to old Borch Rosenkranz."

"You sons-of-bitches," Willie snarled, "you are in big trouble now and don't even know it. I know some people."

"Sure, you do," Mickey laughed.

Motioning to J.T., Mickey led him out of earshot. "I'm kinda afraid to let him go now."

"Why?"

"Can't you tell; he's in a rage right now. No tellin' what he'll do."

"Like what?"

"Well, like pick up a stick and beat us, or stab us in the back with it, or when we're not lookin', run off and tell Borch."

"We gotta let him out some time," J.T. replied.

"What if we just left him?"

"You mean forever?"

"Yeah, who would ever know?"

"You can't be serious!"

"Why not? He deserves it."

"He would die!" J.T. protested. "That's why not."

"Yeah, yeah, I know; I was just kidding," Mickey laughed nervously, "but let's give him some time to cool off. We've still got a game of town bell to win. Let's go finish the game, then we'll come back and let him go."

"Okay, I guess," J.T. frowned as they walked back toward Willie, "Yeah I guess that would be okay."

Once back at the stocks, Mickey winked at J.T., then turned to Willie. "We'll be back in the morning to let you go." Abruptly, he turned and walked away.

Instantly, Weird Willie stopped cursing. His countenance morphed from anger to fear. "You—you're not really going to leave me, are you? Not all night?"

"Just watch us," Mickey shouted over his shoulder.

They'd crawled partway through the skunk bush thicket, well out of earshot of Willie, before J.T. stopped Mickey. "You're not really planning to leave him all night, are you?"

"Nah," Mickey grinned mischievously, "of course not. I just want him to worry a little. Like I said, as soon as town bell is over, we'll come back."

As they continued through the thicket and surrounding stink willows, once again J.T. thought he heard a rustling in the bushes. This time, however, he shrugged it off. After all it was a full moon and undoubtably the animal kingdom was on the prowl.

When they reached the highway, Mickey blew a short blast on his whistle. From only a block away came an answering blast. The other squad must be over at Stucki Lane. With Mickey in the lead, they sprinted the short distance to the streetlight. When they arrived, Greg's squad had surrounded, as best they could with just four players, Easy Earl, and the coveted bell.

"Where you been?" Greg demanded, then not waiting for an answer quickly brought them up to date. Easy's team had just one more lighted corner to ring, the one in front of the school, and the game would be over. For the moment, they had Easy's team contained, but couldn't hold them long. So far, they had not been able to tag the bell; it was too well protected by Easy's larger team.

With the addition of Mickey and J.T., however, they had the other team better surrounded and to J.T., it looked like they were headed for another defensive scrum.

Suddenly, whirling and diving, Greg tried to breech the opposing scrum, but was easily repelled. Then slowly, like a Jurassic raptor, Mickey circled, looking for an opening. He feigned an attack, but that opening quickly closed. Backing off, he continued to circle.

Suddenly, Easy Earl, accompanied by two blockers, broke out of the pack. The lead blockers bowled over two of Mickey's team, Greg and Alan, then Easy Earl, clutching the bell like a halfback, sprinted for the goal line, the streetlight in front of the school.

Mickey, immediately recognized the danger, started in hot pursuit. It looked like it would be close, real close! Would Easy Earl get the last ring, or would Mickey tag him?

The other players, of both sides, followed as fast as they could. Everyone wanted to see the dramatic climax.

By the time Easy Earl got to the streetlight, he had a ten-yard lead on Mickey. Raising the bell well above his head, he rang it once—then twice.

Mickey lunged for him!

But just before Mickey tagged Easy's pant leg, Earl rang the bell a third time—clang—clang—clang!

Suddenly, the game was over.

A triumphant Earl held the bell, like a state championship trophy, high above his head as the rest of his team gathered around him and cheered. Grudgingly, Mickey congratulated Earl and the opposing players all shook hands. As a last order of business, they agreed to meet again next Wednesday and do it all over again.

It was a bitter pill to swallow, but Earl and his team would keep possession of the prized bell for an entire week.

"Where's Weird Willie?" Greg asked as the group began to break up.

"I don't know," Mickey looked around. "I thought he was with you."

"No," Greg replied, shaking his head, "he was never with us. I thought he was with you."

"Then he must've gone home," Mickey shrugged, turning away.

Hanging back, J.T. and Mickey watched the players disperse. With renewed frustration, J.T. noted Curley appeared to be walking Annie home. Suddenly, he was depressed again. There was no way he could compete with Curley. Sure, he was smarter than Curley, but Curley was better looking and a better athlete. It wasn't even close. Girls, he knew, or at least assumed, always chose looks and muscles over smarts.

Anyway, he couldn't worry about Annie right now, they still had to go back down to the creek and release Weird Willie.

"Come on, Mickey," he said glumly, "let's go."

Staring straight ahead, Mickey didn't answer. Apparently, he hadn't heard J.T.

"Mickey, let's go," J.T. repeated a little louder.

Still, Mickey did not answer.

Scooting to the left around a couple of departing players, J.T. got a better look at what had captured Mickey's attention. Up ahead, Easy Earl and Susan were walking, hand-in-hand down Main Street.

"Come, on, Mickey," J.T. draped an arm around his friend and cousin's shoulder, "she's not the only fish in the pond."

"I know, I know," Mickey mumbled, "but right now it looks like all of the good fish have been caught."

"Yeah, I know what you mean," J.T. nodded toward Curley and Annie. "Anyway, we still have to go let Weird Willie out."

Mickey hesitated, his eyes still focused on Easy and Susan. "I can't go right now, I've gotta get home and do my chores."

J.T. arched an eyebrow. "You haven't done them yet?" That was kind of hard to believe.

"Nah," Mickey shrugged, still not looking at J.T. "I was up on the Red Sand Hill hunting rabbits. It got dark on me and I didn't want to miss town bell."

"My dad would kick my butt if I did my chores this late."

"So would mine, but my parents are gone to Fillmore to a cousin's wedding," Mickey replied vaguely, "they left me behind to take care of the chores."

"We can't leave Willie there all night."

"I wouldn't care if we left him there forever."

"Oh, come on, Mickey."

"All right, all right. Give me an hour, then I'll pick you up at your place."

"I don't know," J.T. replied doubtfully, "maybe, I should go down there right now and let him go."

"Do you really want to do that?" Mickey asked. "What if he's still angry? You want to tackle him all by yourself?"

J.T. considered this for a moment. "Well, don't knock on the door, just tap on my bedroom window."

"I know the routine," Mickey mumbled. Turning, he hurried down Main Street.

As promised, Mickey did tap on J.T.'s window, but in was more like an hour and a half later. With the moon now directly overhead, it was nearly midnight when the two friends headed back toward the Santa Clara Creek and their hideout. Once again, to save time, they went through Rosenkranz's property, but even though the dark sedan was parked in the driveway, everything was dark and quiet. Undoubtedly, Borch was sleeping. This time, they crossed his property without incident and ten minutes later, they passed through the circling stink willows and crawled through the familiar skunk bush thicket.

At the edge of the thicket, Mickey abruptly stopped and stood up. After negotiating the last tangle of brush, J.T. joined him.

Without uttering a single word, Mickey grabbed J.T.'s shoulder and pointed!

13

It had been two days since town bell and once again J.T. was hard at work, weeding the seemingly endless cantaloupe patch. Today, however, he was making good progress. Already, he was half done with his weekly assignment and his father would not be back till Sunday, still two full days away. And already his prospective paycheck had ballooned to a whopping six dollars and twenty-five cents! That only left him thirteen dollars and seventy-five cents remaining.

With that somewhat depressing realization, his spirits began to plummet. Would he ever make enough money? Probably. It was only the end of June and there was still plenty of work left to do, but the required twenty dollars was still a long way off. Sighing, he wiped the sweat from his brow, then viciously attacked a clump of Johnson grass. This weed was hard to kill, as its red roots ran incredibly deep, but he dug even deeper.

His fourteenth birthday had been—well, if he was being strictly honest, it had been sort of a bust, a major letdown. What he'd asked for, and hoped for, was an advanced chemistry set to augment his beginner set (he was already running low on sulfur for rocket fuel), but what he got was much more practical: high-top, leather work shoes. Of course, he knew his mother didn't feel good enough to go out and do much shopping and considering all his recent screw ups, he suspected his father wasn't feeling all that generous. On opening the gift, he'd attempted to fake a smile of appreciation, but was not entirely successful. Trying hard to make the day somewhat special, his mother had assigned Mary to bake him a cake. After deciding on a pound cake, she immediately overbaked it, so it didn't rise. Even with the benefit of thick, powdered-sugar frosting, it was tough as shoe leather, a fitting symbol for the entire day.

J.T. was just starting down row sixteen when he spied Mickey headed his way. As usual Mickey was not wearing a shirt, apparently working on his tan. By the end of the summer Mickey always had the best tan of any of the boys, a deep copper bronze, almost charcoal brown. If you were to place him next to Smokey Grayman, J.T. suspected Mickey would be darker. Leaning back on his hoe handle, J.T. watched Mickey's erratic progress as he jumped over the rows of cantaloupes.

"Did you hear?" Mickey asked breathlessly.

"Hear what?"

"Weird Willie's not home yet."

"How do you know that?" J.T. was always skeptical of Mickey's facts.

"Annie told me."

"How does Annie know?" Just the sound of her name made J.T.'s heart race.

"She heard it from Curley?"

"Oh, and how does Curley know?" Of course, she'd heard it from Curley. Already J.T. was getting tired of this game. All he wanted to know was if the rumor had any basis, not that Annie had been talking to Curley.

"He heard it from Easy Earl."

"Okay, I give up. How does Easy Earl know?"

"Well," Mickey grinned. "Easy lives next to the Wittwer's and I guess Misses Wittwer asked him yesterday and again this morning if he'd seen Willie."

J.T. knew Mickey loved this game, and unfortunately he couldn't help but play along. "What did Easy say?"

"Nothing, 'cept that he'd played town bell with us, but he didn't see him leave and hasn't seen him since."

"So where do they think he is?"

"Nobody knows for sure," Mickey replied, "but Easy also told Misses Wittwer about that weird thing with Lenny Weeks. You know how he drove up all angry and yellin'. Now they think maybe he's with Lenny. I guess they've taken off all night before."

"Doing what?"

"Nobody knows for sure. But everybody thinks it's probably somethin' illegal."

"Like what?" J.T. asked frowning. This was all news to him.

"Like I said, nobody knows, but it's rumored they might be poachin' deer."

"Deer?" J.T. repeated. He was even more puzzled now.

"Yeah, deer."

"There's no market for deer meat. Half the people in town have fresh deer meat in their freezers right now."

"It's not the meat; it's the antlers they're after," Mickey insisted, "and the bigger the better."

"Why?"

"Sell 'em to the Orientals and from what I hear they pay big bucks for 'em."

"Antlers?" J.T. shook his head. "I still don't get it."

"They take all kind of antlers, deer, elk and moose, even the shed ones, but they like the fresh ones."

"For what? To mount?"

"No. They grind 'em up and make something called an appro-dees-si-ack."

"What the heck's that?" J.T. knew he was one of the smartest kids in town, but this conversation was going right over his head.

"I don't know," Mickey confessed, "probably somethin' to do with medicine or somethin'."

"So," J.T. frowned, "they're just going to wait for him to come home?"

"Nah, Misses Wittwer's really worried this time. She's talked to the sheriff, and I guess if Willie hasn't returned by this evening, they're going to organize a search party."

"Well, one thing's for sure," J.T. said, "he didn't break out of the stocks by himself. Somebody had to let him out."

"Why do you say that?" Mickey asked, swatting at a pesky mosquito.

"For one thing, the leather locking strap was undone, not ripped off, and for another, the top plank was neatly removed."

"Maybe it was Lenny Weeks."

"Maybe," J.T. agreed, "but how would he have known where Willie was? And nobody, and especially nobody from Saint George knows where that fort is."

"Maybe, he followed us. Remember we heard somethin' in the bushes."

"Oh, yeah, maybe—but I'm still not convinced. It's hard to track someone in the dark. You have to stay real close, or you'd lose them. We should've seen something."

"Remember it was a full moon," Mickey reminded. "I still think he could've followed us."

"Yeah, okay, maybe," J.T. conceded. "I guess it is possible."

"Well, it sure wasn't ghosts," Mickey laughed. "Somebody had to let him out."

J.T. didn't answer, but silently thought of another possibility. After they'd finished with town bell, Mickey claimed he had to go home to do chores before they let Willie out. To J.T., at the time that sounded a bit bogus, and it still did. If Mickey's parents really were gone, then he could do chores anytime. So, what difference would it have made if he'd done them an hour later and after they'd let Willie go. Either way, he'd still be doing them in the dark. It just didn't add up. Had Mickey slipped back down there and let Willie go, or done something else to him, then returned to town and knocked on his bedroom window? If so, why? Why would he do that? None of this made any sense. But regardless of what was the truth, J.T. couldn't shake a nagging feeling that Mickey wasn't coming clean.

With a big swing of his hoe, he decapitated another fledgling tumbleweed before answering. "Yeah, I guess it was Lenny. He probably did follow us."

"So, what you goin' to do now?" Mickey asked.

"Hoe as long as I can. Why?"

"I thought maybe we should drop by old man Rosenkranz's place and see if he's left town. Maybe he left behind some clues."

"He was still there last night."

"Yeah, but remember, the shortwave radio was gone," Mickey argued. "I still think he's packin' up, getting ready to leave. Maybe he already has."

"I've got to finish my rows," J.T. said, locating his spare hoe in the ditch bank weeds, "but if you help me do two more rows, then I'd have the time to go and check out Mister Rosenkranz's place."

"Deal," Mickey readily agreed, accepting the hoe.

Inwardly, J.T. smiled; this was like receiving free money, getting Mickey to do a row. "Race you," he challenged, "and you have to get every weed."

For the next hour, there was very little conversation as the boys furiously hoed down parallel rows. Like Olympic swimmers in adjacent lanes, they stroked, chopped, and sliced their way toward the finish line. At first, J.T. forged ahead, then as Mickey got into a groove, he surged in the lead. Now, as the boys neared the finish line, a mere twenty feet away, it was a dead heat.

There's no way, J.T. silently vowed, he was going to let a fruit stand clerk out-hoe him, particularly since he'd already developed a layer of protective hand calluses and had a couple of weeks to master his technique. Clenching his jaw in determination, he bent even lower and set a frenetic pace, but Mickey hung with him. With a last second burst of adrenaline, J.T. hacked across the finish line. However, with his last stroke he barely missed a ragweed sprout; instead, slicing through the stem root of a neighboring cantaloupe plant.

"Damn!" he exclaimed. The fledgling plant was already wilting in the hot midday sun.

"Wow!" Mickey feigned surprise. "I didn't think you cussed."

"I don't," J.T. groaned, "but my father's going to kill me."

"He'll never know; you just as well throw it away. Get rid of the evidence."

"I hope you're right." J.T. picked up the dying plant, already drooping like a dead octopus, and deposited it in the thick weeds along the ditch bank.

"Your dad won't even notice."

"He notices everything."

"Well, there's nothin' we can do about it now," Mickey shrugged, "let's head over to the Rosenkranz's place."

"Before we do," J.T. said, as he hid both hoes in the same weed patch, "let's make a quick detour to the fort. I want to look around in the light of day; see if we can figure out how Willie got out. It'll only take a few minutes and it's kinda on our way anyway."

As he spoke, J.T. eyed Mickey closely, looking for hesitation or reluctance, some kind of a clue he might be involved.

"Okay by me," Mickey replied, readily agreeing on the plan.

Ten minutes later the boys crawled through the skunk bush thicket and into the little clearing of the fort and stocks. Even in the light of day nothing seemed terribly amiss. The leather hinge connecting the two opposing planks was still secure and the locking strap was still firmly nailed to the upper board. There was simply no way Willie, with head and wrists locked in the stocks, could reach it. And since the leather was not torn or ripped from the plank, it was obvious he did not escape by himself. Somebody must have unlatched it. There simply was no other explanation.

With heads bowed, the boys began systematically searching the little clearing. There was enough ground cover, fallen leaves, clumps of grama grass and downed twigs, they were unable to find identifiable footprints, but with the determination of blood hounds they continued to search, extending outward in ever widening circles.

"Well, looky here!" Mickey suddenly exclaimed, reaching down, and picking up a small object.

Quickly, J.T. joined him. "What you got?"

"A bullet." Mickey rotated it in his fingers.

"A shell?"

"No, it's intact, unfired."

"What kind?" J.T. asked.

"Rifle, probably."

"What kind of rifle?"

"Don't know."

"Let me see it." J.T. extended his hand, accepting the cartridge from Mickey.

He took a few moments to study it, looking at it from every angle. It was unusual because there were no markings of any kind on the brass cylinder or butt end. Without comment, J.T. disappeared into the fort, returning with an old metal measuring tape.

After taking some preliminary measurements, he finally spoke. "Well, it's a central fire, cause the primer's right in the center. It has a ballistic tip for long-range shooting and measures exactly three-tenths-of-an-inch in diameter."

"So?"

"So, it's a thirty/thirty."

"You sure about that?"

"Pretty sure," J.T. nodded. "It's a thirty/thirty, or something pretty darn close."

"Boy, that narrows it down a lot," Mickey said sarcastically, "almost everyone in Utah owns a thirty/thirty."

"Yeah, but not everyone shoots a ballistic tip bullet with a casing that has no markings."

"Where did you learn all that, anyway?" Mickey asked, taking the bullet back.

"I've been studying. The science of ballistics and rocketeering are pretty closely related."

"How so?"

"Well, they both use propellants, like gunpowder, for thrust; the range depends on the kind of powder and how much you use; and the distance depends on the angle of fire or the trajectory."

"So," Mickey asked, again rotating the bullet in his fingers, "why do you think there are no markings?"

"Ain't it obvious? Somebody didn't want it traced." J.T. snatched the bullet back, examining it again. He didn't find anything new.

"Who?" Mickey asked, arching an eyebrow. "Who would want to use bullets that can't be traced?"

"I suppose anyone that commits a crime with a gun."

"Maybe, like them Russkie spies," Mickey blurted, "and their assassins!"

"Yeah, maybe," J.T. agreed, "but a few minutes ago we were talking about deer antlers and poachers? I don't suppose they'd want their bullets traced either."

"Lenny Weeks!" Mickey blurted. "It has to be Lenny Weeks' bullet."

"Yeah," J.T. nodded, "he probably lost it crawling through the brush."

"Or a branch scraped it from his ammo belt," Mickey added. "So, it must've been Lenny who let out Weird Willie."

"Not necessarily," again J.T. eyed Mickey closely. "It's possible Willie was already gone by the time Lenny got here."

"What you talkin' about? That's makin' it more complicated than it has to be."

"All I'm saying," J.T. shrugged, "is this bullet doesn't necessarily prove anything."

"Well, I say it does!" Mickey argued. "It says Lenny Weeks!"

"Probably, but all I'm saying is Lenny isn't the only one in southern Utah that carries around thirty/thirties and bullets."

"Yeah, well anyway, I still say it was Lenny. That makes the most sense."

Privately, J.T. wondered if Mickey wasn't protesting too loudly. It almost seemed as if he was trying too hard to pin this on Lenny.

"Anyway," Mickey grabbed the bullet back and shoved it in his pants pocket, "let's head on over to the Rosenkranz place."

"What you going to do with the bullet?" J.T. asked, falling in step behind Mickey.

"Well, if we ever get a chance to look at Lenny's rifle or ammo belt, we can compare bullets and tell for sure."

"How we going to do that?"

Instead of answering, Mickey dropped down on all fours and began crawling back through the skunk bush thicket.

Once free of the thicket, the boys again cut across old man Gubler's alfalfa field and within minutes were back at Rosenkranz's wooden slat fence. After rotating the loose board counterclockwise, they both peered in. From the fence, they could see the now empty shortwave radio shack and its aluminum antenna, the back rooms of the house and part of the driveway. There was no sign of the Ford sedan, at least from this vantage point, but it could still be parked in that portion of the driveway that was not visible. Patiently, they waited another five minutes and looked in again. Still nothing stirred.

"Let's go as far as the shack," Mickey suggested. "From there we can tell for sure if the driveway's clear."

They crawled through the fence, then bending low dashed forward, not stopping until they were safely behind the shack. Once again, they looked through the crack between the boards, and once again the shed appeared to be empty, no shortwave radio. Hugging the wall, they worked around to the northwest corner. From there, they still could not be seen from the house, but had a good view of the entire driveway. No dark Ford sedan.

After looking around one last time, they sprinted to the house, flattening out against the south wall. Motioning with his hands, Mickey indicated they should separate and circle the house. J.T. was to head to the east and Mickey to the west. Stealthily, the boys worked around the entire perimeter, peeking in every window, and checking every door. After each had completed their half circle, they rendezvoused at the north wall.

"See anythin'?" Mickey whispered.

"Nope."

"You think he's gone?"

"Yeah," J.T. replied, "at least for now."

"How do you want to do this?"

"Well, there's a window on the east side that's not locked," J.T. replied, "but it's up pretty high."

"You try raisin' it?"

J.T. nodded his head. "It'll raise."

"Well then, let's go do it." Mickey nodded. "You lead."

Staying close to the house, they circled back to the east side, the side opposite the driveway. J.T. went directly to the high window, then reaching up as far as he could, on tiptoes, pushed upward. The window groaned, then grudgingly raised another couple of inches. Mickey, being a little taller, tried and raised it a couple more inches. Then, by grabbing hold of the windowsill, Mickey pulled himself up waist high. Reaching through the half-open window, he parted the curtains.

"It's a bathroom," he announced.

"Can you get in?"

"If you give me a boost." Mickey balanced a forearm resting on the sill, then used his other hand to raise the window even higher.

Getting down on hands and knees, J.T. worked his shoulders under Mickey's feet, giving him something solid to stand on. Now that he was able to stand, Mickey used that platform to climb over the sill and into the bathroom. Immediately, he returned, leaning out the window as far as he could. Locking arms with J.T., and grunting with exertion, Mickey arched backward for maximum leverage and pulled. Simultaneously, J.T. used his feet to scramble up and into the room.

The bathroom smelled sterile, aseptic, like a mixture of Ajax cleaner and chlorine bleach. A quick survey told them there was nothing of interest in there. With Mickey leading the way, the boys left the bathroom and turned left down the hall. Even though it was early afternoon, the drapes were still drawn, leaving the house somewhat dark, but as an added bonus it remained surprisingly cool.

The hallway led directly to the kitchen. At first glance, nothing appeared amiss here, either. No food or clutter on the counters and no dirty dishes stacked in the sink. Opening the refrigerator, J.T. noted it was empty except for a basket of eggs, a pound of bacon and a quart of milk. Also, the cupboards were bare except for the clean dishes and the usual cooking pots and pans. In the pantry, there was a small collection of canned goods, mostly sauerkraut and chicken and dumplings, and on the top shelf was a small selection of wine in green-glass bottles, sporting official winery labels, not in plain Mason jars like J.T. had seen in his grandfather's root cellar.

There was nothing here that would indicate anyone had used the kitchen recently, but on the other hand there were no moving boxes or bags, nothing to indicate Rosenkranz had moved or was planning to move. Moreover, there was nothing incriminating, no spy paraphernalia or assassin tools (like guns, daggers, or piano wires), no shortwave radio or folders of data. Nothing to indicate any espionage might be going on. All in all, it was a pretty normal-looking kitchen.

Returning to the hall, the boys headed in the opposite direction. They passed the bathroom, then ducked into the first small room off to the left. It appeared to be a bedroom that had been converted to a study. In the center of the room sat an old, scarred pine desk and behind that an equally damaged bookcase, jammed full of books. Picking up a volume, J.T. noted there was no dust on the cover. He flipped it open, but couldn't read a word. It was written in a foreign language. A quick survey showed all the books were foreign works except for one volume titled, Learning English. It had both foreign and English words.

To the right and behind the desk was a stacked, three-drawer file cabinet. Opening the top drawer, J.T. rifled through the folders. At first glance, the filing system was puzzling, certainly not alphabetic. For example, the file he presently held was labeled, Able – Tag Eins. The next folder was labeled, Able – Tag Zwei, then Able – Tag Drei, etc. In the next drawer was a series of folders marked Easy, again labeled: Tag Ein, Tag Zwei, Tag Drei, etc. and drawer number three was stamped as Charlie. Each manila file contained standard 8 1/2 by 11-inch papers and each individual paper was divided into three longitudinal columns, containing only numbers. There was no written text.

Somewhere, J.T. knew, he'd heard those names before, but exactly where, he couldn't quite place. And he doubted this Easy had anything to do with his friend Easy Earl Jaussi. Puzzled, he shook his head; Able, Easy and Charlie—what did it all mean?

"Well, looky, here," Mickey suddenly broke the silence. He had been combing through the desk drawers.

"What?" J.T. replied, looking up from the Charlie, Tag Drei, manila folder. As with the others, each sheet was divided into three columns of numbers.

Reaching into the drawer, Mickey hauled out a rectangular, box-like instrument with an attached, insulated cord, protected by a long coil of spring-like wire. Looking a lot like a hand-held microphone, the terminal end of that cord boasted a wand-like instrument covered with a perforated metal screen.

"What is this?" Mickey held it high.

Setting down the manila file, J.T. accepted the instrument. Looking it over, he noted on the rectangular, box-like body there was a toggle switch. He flipped it on and instantly the device started clicking. As J.T. moved the wand closer to the window, it clicked faster. When he moved away from the window, it slowed down again.

"This," J.T. finally concluded, "is what is called a Geiger counter. It measures radiation."

"Oh, yeah!" Mickey's eyes widened. "Why would old Borch have one of them?"

"I don't know," J.T. shrugged, replacing the instrument back in the desk drawer.

"Well, I bet'cha I know," Mickey exclaimed, then added, "ain't it obvious?"

"Why obvious?"

"It's for spying," he replied, his voice barely above a whisper. "He's checking radiation levels for the Russians."

Suddenly, it dawned on J.T. where he'd heard the names, Able, Easy and Charlie. They were the names given to the atomic tests; the most recent series of Shots detonated at Yucca Flats! The sheets of paper in the folders, though they were labeled in a foreign language, were probably for each day following the Shot. And the three columns of figures were the amounts of radiation measured in rads and recorded three times a day, probably morning, noon and evening. And that explained where Borch was going on his frequent trips out of town.

"L—let's get out of here!" J.T. said, not able to completely stop a shiver. Suddenly, he realized they might be in way over their heads.

"Why? What's wrong?"

"We've seen enough, let's go."

"You going to take that folder?" Mickey nodded at the file J.T. had set on the desk.

"Nah, I don't think so. He'll miss it; know we've been here."

"Nah, there's dozens of them; I don't think he'll miss one, at least not right away."

"Even if that is true, why? Why take it?"

"It's evidence. We need to let everyone know what he's been up to. It's our duty as Americans."

Sighing, J.T. wedged the file in the waistband of his Levi's, then pulled his t-shirt over it.

Once again, they were back in the hallway and in spite of his objections, Mickey turned right and followed the hall to its end. Cautiously, Mickey opened the door and peeked in. It was another bedroom, but this one apparently was used as a bedroom.

The master bedroom was dominated by a mahogany-frame, queen bed with four corner posts and a matching mahogany headboard. Spread across the bed was an olive-green comforter, which had been perfectly smoothed out, not a single wrinkle showing. Against the wall at the foot of the bed stood a four-drawer matching armoire, topped with a double-wing mirror. As with the other rooms, there was absolutely no clutter and opposed to J.T.'s bedroom, there were no dirty clothes carpeting the floor.

To the left of the armoire was a door, apparently leading to a walk-in closet and just to the right of the bed was a two-by-two foot window overlooking the driveway. With a start, J.T. realized this was the very same window they'd peeked in that night and seen Borch Rosenkranz admiring himself in the mirror.

"This is the room," he whispered.

"I know." Mickey nodded.

"I can't tell if he's still living here. Everything's so neat."

"Let's check the closet for clothes," Mickey gestured at the closet door, "if he's gone, the clothes will be gone too."

With J.T. at his heels, he opened the door and together they peered in. It was a fairly large room, considering how small the bedroom was, but as opposed to the bedroom, it was windowless. In the poor light, J.T. saw virtually nothing until his eyes accommodated, then he noted indeed the closet was filled with clothes.

There were two parallel pipe crossbars, one approximately six-feet from the floor and the other two-feet lower. Hanging from the top pipe bar were dark suit coats with their companion pants and on the lower bar hung the long-sleeve shirts. Conspicuously absent, however, was any evidence of the usual work clothes, such as blue jeans or denim shirts. Lastly, there was a gentleman's corduroy-hunting jacket (sporting leather patches at the elbows), long and short leather pants, and an assortment of suspenders.

On the top row, next to the dark suits, hung a military uniform. The coat was navy-blue, draped with a red sash and flaunting three cornrows of metals with ribbons. Below this, on the lower bar, were the matching gray polo pants. Without question, this was the same uniform they'd seen Borch wearing that night!

"Hey, what's this?" Mickey exclaimed, as he lifted the uniform from the rack.

After removing the uniform, he had partially exposed a couple of articles tacked to the back wall. Reaching up, Mickey separated the remaining suits, the metal hangers grating as they slid across the pipe crossbar.

In the resultant portal, the boys saw a triangular pennant and a small silk flag, both tacked to the back wall. Each of the items featured a magnificent spread-wing block eagle, clutching a circle or hoop in its talons. Under the hoop, a foreign phrase was cross-stitched.

Suddenly outside in the driveway, there was the hum of a combustion engine accompanied with the sound of crunching gravel. Quickly, the boys left the closet, shut the door, then on hands and knees crawled over to the window. Parting the curtains a crack, they peeked out.

The black sedan slowed to a stop in the driveway, then the driver's door opened and out climbed old Borch Rosenkranz. He was dressed in his trademark brown leather pants, a green corduroy-hunting jacket, and a dark fedora. Groaning, he arched backwards, then immediately glanced over his shoulder, as though he was worried someone might have followed. Slowly and deliberately, he looked to his right and to his left. After a couple of seconds, he repeated the maneuver one more time. Apparently now fully satisfied, he walked around to the rear of the car and used his key to open the trunk.

At that moment, the passenger door opened, and a second man climbed out. Built solid, like a college linebacker, he was as tall as Borch, but opposed to Rosenkranz he was dressed like an American. Instead of a fedora with a feather, he wore a sweat-stained, gray Stetson, and instead of leather pants and a corduroy jacket, he was dressed in patched blue jeans, a faded denim shirt, and scuffed riding boots.

Also, stretching, he groaned out loud, as though it had been a long trip, then he also took a minute to survey the entire compound. Apparently when satisfied, he slammed the car door, then walked around to the trunk, joining Rosenkranz.

With seemingly great effort, they lifted a sizeable bundle from the trunk. It looked to be roughly six feet long, wrapped in a white canvas and tightly bound with hemp cord. Borch grabbed hold of one end and the cowboy the other, then shuffling, they lugged the bundle around the car, clearly headed for the wooden shack. The bundle was bulky and unwieldly, and the apparent weight of it required Borch and the cowboy to take a couple of rest stops. Then after repositioning their grip, they picked up the bundle again and shuffled forward.

As Borch and the cowboy rounded the corner of the house, they were no longer in the line of sight of the bedroom or the boys. Curiosity instantly trumped caution and the boys hurried back to the kitchen. Here they parted the venetian blinds just in time to see Borch unlock the shed, then re-pocket the key. This time, however, rather than lifting the heavy object, both men grabbed hold of the same end and dragged the canvas-wrapped bundle into the shed and out of sight.

"What the hell!" Mickey exclaimed, dropping the venetian blind, and turning to J.T. "What in the hell was that?"

14

"What the hell was that?" Mickey repeated, when J.T. didn't immediately answer.

"I—I don't know," J.T. stammered.

"To me," Mickey volunteered, still staring out the window, "it looks like they're tryin' to hide a body."

"You don't know that for sure," J.T. countered, "it could be anything."

"Like what?"

Before he could answer, Borch and the cowboy exited the shed. After pausing to relock the door, they again looked over their shoulders, then headed straight for the kitchen door.

"We've gotta get out of here!" Mickey blurted, bolting for the hallway. J.T. followed close behind.

As they rounded the corner and slid into the bathroom, J.T. heard the kitchen door open, then slam shut. Without a moment's hesitation, Mickey dove headfirst through the open window, then like a trained paratrooper executed a textbook tuck and roll landing.

Following Mickey's lead, J.T. also vaulted through the window, however he had not seen, and did not duplicate, Mickey's perfect landing. Like an amateur springboard diver, he dove through the window, then belly-flopped on the hard ground, his momentum carrying him forward another a foot or two.

With the air knocked out of him, J.T. fought to remain conscious. Through the gathering fog, he knew his ribs were throbbing (the same ribs he'd injured on Utah Hill and the same ones Dorey, their milk cow, had hammered), but the more immediate problem was air, or the lack thereof. Struggling to his knees, he sucked in air like an asthmatic.

"Come on," Mickey urged, "we gotta get outta here."

With Mickey's help, J.T. struggled to his feet, then the two of them limped as fast as they could out of the Rosenkranz compound and onto Highway 91.

When J.T. got home, he carefully re-examined his ribs in the mirror, decided more than likely nothing was broken, then he hid the pilfered Rosenkranz file in the service room. After that, he set about doing his evening chores.

It was just after 7:00 p.m. when he returned to the house. Still nursing his sore ribs, he carried the pail of milk using the arm from his uninjured side and a basket of eggs with the other. As he stepped through the kitchen door, he collided with an out-rushing Mary. Half of the milk slopped from the bucket and the basket of eggs crashed to the floor. The result was a messy mosaic of white milk, yellow egg yolk and white eggshell shards. Surprisingly, a couple of yolks remained intact, floating on a slimy puddle of albumin, like yellow water lilies in an alpine pond.

"Geez, J.T.! Would you watch where you're going," Mary exclaimed, quickly checking her dress for splatter.

"You ran into me," J.T. groaned, clutching his sore ribs.

"Well, get out of my way," Mary growled. "I'm in a hurry."

J.T. refused to move. "Somebody's got to clean up this mess."

"You do it," Mary said, skirting around him. "I've gotta go."

"Then it'll be here," J.T. gestured at the mess, "when you get back."

"Geez," J.T., quit being such a brat. I've got to pick up Brenda and I'm already late."

"Where you going?"

"To the movies in St. George."

"Which movie?"

"Why does it matter?" Mary snapped.

"Just curious."

"Gone With the Wind," she said, "starring Vivien Leigh and Clark Gable."

"Is it a western?"

"No!"

"Then it's probably no good."

"How would you know?" Mary said derisively.

"Why don't you see High Noon with Randolph Scott? I hear it's at the Gaiety."

"Don't you ever watch anything but westerns?"

Instead of answering, J.T. changed the subject. "How you getting there?"

"Mother said I could take the Plymouth." Mary held up the keys as proof, then as she pushed past him, she added, "and clean up this mess, will you?"

J.T. was envious. It would be two more long years before he was able to drive, at least legally, not that he didn't drive now. From driving the flatbed in the fields and the tractor on the highway, he was probably already as good a driver as Mary. "What's for dinner?" he shouted at her receding back.

"Nothing." She turned back around. "Mother didn't want anything and I'm on a diet."

"What am I supposed to do?"

"Well, you could break down and cook something or make a sandwich."

"There's no roast beef left."

"Well, there's always tuna fish." Mary opened the door to the service room. "All you have to do is open a can. Even you can do that."

Grumbling to himself, J.T. decided maybe Mary was right; he was being a brat. Grabbing a broom and dustpan from the closet, he began sweeping, but all he managed to do was stir the collage and streak it across the linoleum. Pausing, he studied the problem. If you removed the shards, he decided, it looked like he could make an omelet. Maybe he should scoop some into a fry—.

"Oh, I almost forgot to tell you," Mary burst back into the room, "Sheriff Meecham came by a couple of hours ago."

"So?" J.T. asked, trying to sound casual.

"He wanted to talk to you about Willie Wittwer, but when I told him you wasn't here he told me to tell you they were organizing a search party tonight at the elementary school."

"Oh," silently, J.T. breathed a sigh of relief, "okay, what time?"

Mary glanced up at the wall clock. "In a little over an hour, at nine o'clock."

"Okay."

"Are you going?"

"I don't know. Why?"

"It's just the sheriff made it sound important for you to be there," Mary replied, then before disappearing again she added, "try using a mop and water."

Making a face at her that she didn't see, J.T. returned to his cleaning. He was still ticked off at Mary. You'd think if he spent all day working in the fields, the least she could do would be to fix some dinner. Since she didn't have to work the fields anymore, her job was supposed to be household duties, and in his humble opinion, fixing dinner was a household duty—diet or no diet.

Ten minutes later, J.T. finished sweeping, mopping, and cleaning. Rather than make an omelet, he disposed of the mosaic goo into the wastebasket, then took the wastebasket outside and dumped it. He then washed off the mop, broom, and wastebasket. Finally, after all that he had a moment to think.

So, why did the sheriff specifically want him in the search party? Want him enough to come by and extend a personal invitation—or perhaps that was more like an official order. Had he also extended the same invitation to Mickey? Could he have possibly heard about the English stocks? Should he go?

Yes, he decided, probably he should go, but he wasn't going without

Mickey. He wasn't about to face the sheriff by himself. While still trying figure the sheriff's motives, he picked up the phone. Surprisingly, the party line was open and he got Mickey on the first ring. Hopefully, that was a good omen.

Of course, Mickey argued it made more sense to just go straight to Borch Rosenkranz's shed, but J.T. contended it would look too suspicious if they didn't show up for the search party, at least at the beginning. For once, J.T. prevailed and Mickey agreed to join him.

After hanging up the phone, J.T. fixed a dill pickle and mayonnaise tuna fish sandwich, topped with lettuce and a slice of tomato, then washed it down with a glass of cold milk. When finished, he glanced up at the clock, deciding he still had time to check on his mother before heading over to the school.

His mother seemed a little better and her mood a little brighter. Or maybe it was just that the curtains were drawn open and the room was brighter. Out of the west-facing window, J.T. could see the sun was rapidly aging. Rather than blazing a fiery yellow, it glowed a burnt orange, like the embers of a dying campfire. Somewhere out there, even further to the west, behind Utah Hill, this very same sun was setting on Yucca Flats, Nevada. And possibly at this moment, the AEC workers were busy preparing for another Shot. This one would undoubtedly be bigger and more magnificent than the last one. They always were.

Turning from the window, J.T. focused on his mother. Superficially, at least, she seemed more happy, more optimistic than she'd been in a long time.

After he'd sat down beside her and grasped her hand, she informed him she had arranged for her cousin, Smokey Grayman, who was a trained yataalii, to come and perform a traditional Navajo Sing, the blessing way. The blessing way, she explained, was a five-day event, very traditional and very beautiful. And after that, she'd arranged for the Elders to come by on Sunday to give her a priesthood blessing, the laying-on-of-hands for healing the sick. Sighing with satisfaction, she affectionately patted J.T.'s hand, seemingly to assure him everything was going to be all right.

For his part, J.T. had mixed emotions. Yes, he was happy his mother was feeling better, but he was not so excited about Smokey's traditional Navajo Sing. On the other hand, what could it hurt? Maybe, hopefully, nothing. To his way of thinking, however, it was just a little inconsistent, and probably unnecessary. If the Mormons had the one and only true church, then maybe God might even be offended with his mother giving Smokey's pagan ritual equal billing with his own Melchizedek priesthood. Historically, at least in the Old Testament, God was a jealous god and was easily offended. Just look at the ten commandments. And if the Bible was even close to being correct, an offended God was a very scary thing. You could end up as a pillar of salt, or in the belly of a fish, or worse.

Anyway, it was out of his hands. But he was happy that the prospect of these two healing ceremonies had raised his mother spirits. As he kissed her goodbye on the forehead, he told her he was going to join a search party looking for Willie Wittwer. Of course, she then made him fill in the details, which he did, minus the part about locking Willie in the stocks.

After leaving his mother's bedroom, J.T. briefly looked for a flashlight, couldn't find one, finally gave up and headed for the Santa Clara Elementary School.

Shortly after nine o'clock, J.T. stood in the center of the growing crowd; those who had answered the sheriff's call to search for Willie Wittwer. And even though the sun had disappeared thirty minutes ago, the thermometer still flirted with one hundred degrees. The group was noisy and restless, milling about like penned livestock at the cattle auction. With no breeze, coupled with the oppressive heat, the dominant smell was perspiration along with its running companion, stale body odor.

Like sprouting barley seeds, J.T. felt the insidious kernels of claustrophobia begin to take root and grow. He hated tight quarters and he really hated big crowds. Just as he was about ready to flee, he felt someone slip in next to him. Even without looking, he knew it was his cousin, Mickey T. Graff. At least for the moment, it took his mind off his growing agoraphobia.

"So, John Tobler," Mickey said, "looks like he hasn't turned up yet."

J.T. refused to answer. Not after being called John Tobler.

A moment later, Mickey amended his statement. "So, J.T., Willie still hasn't turned up yet?"

"Guess not," J.T. finally responded, looking Mickey in the eye. He still could not shake his nagging suspicions of Mickey and the inexplicable hour delay in releasing Willie.

"Have they talked to Lenny Weeks?"

"Well," J.T. sighed, "as best I can tell there are two versions."

Silence.

"Would you mind telling me what they are?"

"Well, one story, Lenny has denied everything, for whatever that's worth. He says the only time he saw Willie that night was when he drove up right before we started playing town bell."

"And the other story?"

"Well, the other version is that Lenny is also missing."

"Which one do you believe?"

"I don't know," J.T. replied, "but I think most people here are going with the first one."

"Well, I don't know nothin' about Lenny or his story," Mickey whispered, "but I have a pretty good idea where Willie is."

An involuntary shiver ran down J.T.'s spine. "You don't know that for sure."

"You saw it too. Right now, he's in Rosenkranz's shed!"

J.T. started to argue, but at that moment Sheriff Meecham lumbered up to the top step, positioned himself in front of the school's large double doors, then faced the crowd. Loudly, he cleared his throat, then patted down the air, like he was trying to compress it.

"May I have your attention!" he said loudly, waited for a couple of seconds, then said even more loudly, "Please, may I have your attention!

Like a hot combustion engine after the ignition has been turned off, the crowd noise continued to sputter and backfire, then finally, and almost grudgingly, died down.

"Anyways," the sheriff began, "I'm sure by now you know the reason we are here is to search for Willie Wittwer. And I'm sure some of you are wonderin' why we waited for nighttime to begin the search."

"Yeah!" someone shouted from the middle of the crowd. "Makes no damn sense."

"The reason, of course," the sheriff continued, undeterred, "is he's not officially, at least accordin' to the law, a missing person until he's been gone for forty-eight hours. I know I might be fudgin' a little bit, but Willie disappeared approximately forty-eight hours ago. Now he's legally a missing person and I can officially marshal the resources of the county and state to look for him. There's still enough moon left, so we should be able to do a pretty decent search. If we don't find anythin' tonight, we'll reconvene right here at eight o'clock sharp tomorrow." He paused for a breath.

"Willie was last seen playin' that bell game on Wednesday night. According to his mother he has gone missin' overnight before, but never for two nights in a row. Needless to say, she is very worried. Also, Missus Wittwer has told me Willie has been spendin' a lot of time on Utah Hill. She says she doesn't know why, but in law enforcement we have been aware of that situation for some time now and have been investigatin'. At the moment, I am not at liberty to divulge the details of that investigation, but suffice it to say it might possibly be linked to Willie's disappearance." The sheriff paused again to let the crowd digest this information.

"Deer antlers," a person on the first step shouted. "I hear it's all about deer antlers."

Ignoring him, the sheriff continued. "Tonight, we'll divide up into groups of three or four. Those with cars, I'm going to send over toward Utah Hill. Those of you without cars will search right here around Santa Clara, the town itself, the Red Hill, the fields, and the creek bed." Meecham paused and looked over the crowd, waiting for any objections.

Surprisingly, there were none.

"Okay, then, I'll assign those with cars first. By raise of hands, how many brought cars?"

"I brought a pickup," a man shouted from the middle of the crowd. "Does that count?"

Looking mildly annoyed, Meecham nodded his head, then added, "Okay, those with vehicles raise their hands.

Four or five hands went up.

"All right, then," the sheriff continued, "Cecil, you take another guy and search up Pahcoon Road all the way to the to the top of Utah Hill. Joseph, take three or four guys and go up toward Gunlock, then search the Goldstrike Road and Slaughter Creek area. Fritz, head on over to the Shivwit Indian Reservation and search that area and the hills around there - you know all the way up to the Lost Dutchman Mine. Edmond, you take your group up the Apex Mine Road and search all that area south of the highway. And Syd, take a couple of guys and go over by Motaqua and the Beaver Dam Creek area."

Silently, those groups nodded their assent.

"Okay, now for you without cars. Jake, Theron, Cecil, and Lamont, I want you guys to head up the search here in town—oh, and Hafe, you probably shouldn't be drivin' either. Jake, take Curley and Alan and his group, and search the east side of town. Look everywhere, woodsheds, corrals, ditches, weed patches and granaries. You know, everywhere. Nothin's off limits. There's no such thing as trespassin' tonight. Theron, take three or four kids and do the same on the west side. Lamont, I want you take charge of Greg and Earl and that bunch standin' over there. Your assignment is the fields south of town. Cecil, you take a couple of kids and check out the Red Sand Hill, and Hafe, you take J.T. and Mickey and search the creek bed. From what I hear, those boys know that area better than most."

For an almost unheard second time, all parties nodded their agreement.

"Okay, any questions?"

There were a few procedural questions and scattered mumbles from the crowd, but no one openly protested their assignments.

"Okay, then, I need to talk to J.T. and Mickey for a minute." The sheriff paused once again for air. "Other than that, the rest of you can get going."

The sheriff watched the groups disperse, then motioned to J.T. and Mickey to join him on the top step. "Hafe, give us a minute. I need to talk to these boys."

Hafe Hafen nodded and sat down on the bottom step.

"Anyways," Sheriff Meecham began after the others had faded into the non-descript gray of dusk, "do you two know anythin' about Willie's disappearance?" The sheriff locked eyes first with J.T., then with Mickey.

"No," Mickey answered quickly, the brazenly asked, "why?"

"Well, as best I can tell, you two were the last to see him before he disappeared."

"What about Lenny Weeks?" J.T. blurted. "Have you talked to him?"

"Nah, I haven't been able to talk to him yet, but other people have already told me about the incident before that bell game started. And I also know Willie was on your team."

"So," Mickey said stubbornly, "it's not like we wanted him."

"Yeah, well why don't you tell me about the last time you saw him."

To J.T., the sheriff's persistent probing was a little unnerving, but Mickey seemed unfazed.

"Yeah," Mickey nodded and shrugged, "yeah, sure, Weird—uh—I mean Willie was on our team. He was with us for, I don't know, maybe an hour or so, then he just up and disappears. He's weird like that."

"What time was that?" Meecham asked.

"I can't say exactly when," Mickey continued, "I don't have a watch."

"And exactly where," the sheriff asked, "was the last place you saw him?"

"Maybe Stucki Lane," Mickey replied, but I don't know for sure. One minute he was with us, the next minute he wasn't."

The sheriff looked at J.T. for confirmation.

Gulping, J.T. nodded, but kept his mouth shut. Mickey was certainly better at lying than he was.

"Well, okay," Meecham locked eyes with them one last time. "Okay, then go on with Hafe, and search the creek bottom." Turning to Hafe, he said more loudly, "if you find anythin' call my office in Saint George. They'll know how to get in touch with me."

As the boys turned to leave, the sheriff added, his voice suddenly hard as Pine Valley granite. "And don't think for a California minute I've forgotten about that dummy, hit-and-run fiasco. The fingerprints should be back any day. We've got some mighty upset people and they're demandin' somethin' be done."

Without another word, the two boys turned and followed Hafe into the strangely silent night. It was that eerie sliver of time wedged between the dying of the sun and the birth of the moon. The nocturnal animals had not yet started to stir and the diurnal animals had already sought refuge for the night. Even the crickets hadn't started up yet.

As they walked down the highway (Main Street), J.T.'s mind turned to the task ahead. Suddenly, he was hit with a jab of conscience. Had their English stocks somehow backfired, resulting in something bad happening to Willie? He surely hoped not, but there was something in Borch's shed. Maybe Sheriff Meecham had been right all along about their pranks, that someday, someone would get hurt. Also, he wondered if the sheriff was just blowing smoke about the dummy incident or was he close to arresting them? Perhaps, they were already in big trouble. It was certainly beginning to look like Edgar Allen Poe's proverbial walls were closing in on them.

They had walked about a block down Highway 91 and were adjacent to Alfred "Hafe" Hafen's house when he stopped and huddled for a conference. As Hafe leaned in, J.T. caught a whiff of his breath. It reeked of fermented grapes, probably gewürztraminer. Tying hard not go gag, he held his breath and backed up a step.

"Phew!" Mickey exclaimed, not being at all subtle, as he pinched his nose.

Hafe ignored him. "You two don't really need me fur this," he paused to exhale more fermented fumes, "do ya?"

"What?" J.T. asked, retreating another step. He wasn't sure he'd heard Hafe correctly.

"You two know that bloody crick a hell-uv-a-lot better than me." Hafe paused to rub his bleary eyes. "I don't see how I can be of much help. Anyway, I got some pressin' business."

Mickey winked a J.T. "Pressin' business, huh?"

"Yeah," Hafe nodded at his house, then added, "look real good now and if you find anything let me know and I'll call the sheriff."

"Sure thing, Hafe." Mickey winked at J.T. again.

Amused, the boys watched Hafe weave towards his house.

When Hafe was out of earshot, Mickey turned more serious. "So, do you think he knows anything?"

"Hafe? No, why?"

"No, not Hafe," Mickey said, "the sheriff. Do you think he knows?""

"You mean about the stocks?"

"Yeah, and about Manny Quinn."

"Nah," J.T. replied, but did not feel at all confident. "I don't know. Maybe."

"Well, I don't think so, "Mickey countered, shaking his head. "He was just blowin' smoke up our—"

"Still," J.T. cut him off, "there's enough smoke to make me nervous."

"Not me," Mickey laughed.

In the obscure light, J.T. could barely make out Mickey's face, but he thought in spite of all the bluster, he looked a little worried.

"Well," J.T. sighed, "come on, let's go search the creek."

"The creek," Mickey refused to move, "why the creek?"

"Cause that's what the sheriff told us to do."

"That's a total waste of time and you know it. My money is on Borch's shed. We should go there."

"I don't know," J.T. replied, shaking his head, "the Rosenkranz place gives me the willies."

"Ha, ha," Mickey laughed coarsely, "the willies, that's a good one. You mean the Weird Willies, don't you?"

"You know what I meant."

"Well, it probably does have the willies, at least one of them."

"Anyway," J.T. added, "I think Mister Rosenkranz knows we've been snooping around.

"So? Why wander around the creek all night looking for Willie when we already know where he is. Makes no damn sense."

"If we are going to that," J.T. argued, "we should've told the sheriff earlier, then he could have brought the whole search party down to Rosenkranz's."

"There was no way to do that," Mickey replied, "without incriminating us."

"Why do you say that?"

"We'd have to tell him how we know," Mickey said. "No, it's better for us to just happen to find Willie, then go get the sheriff."

"We don't even know for sure that's Willie," J.T. argued. "And if it is, we could end up like—like that."

"Not if we're careful," Mickey insisted. Abruptly changing directions, he headed straight for the Rosenkranz compound.

As J.T. watched him go, he debated whether to follow him or head down to the creek. But the thought of searching the creek by himself at night, also gave him the willies. Sighing out loud, he hurried to catch up with Mickey.

By the time they arrived at the Rosenkranz place it was totally dark with only a hint of the fast-fading crimson on the western horizon. Simultaneously, to the east, however, there was an emerging corona, the promise of a nearly full moon.

With Mickey leading, they pressed on, but J.T. couldn't shake the feeling they were headed for disaster. When he saw incandescent lights radiating from the house, however, his mood improved. Obviously, someone was home so they would have to abandon this half-baked idea. With Rosenkranz at home, it clearly was too dangerous.

As they got closer, J.T. could tell the light was coming from the bedroom adjacent to the driveway, the very same bedroom they were in earlier. The dark sedan, partially illuminated by the window light, was parked in the driveway.

"I—I don't think we should do this right now," J.T. whispered nervously. "Looks like Mister Rosenkranz is home."

"But we gotta know. The Sheriff's gotta know. Missus Wittwer has gotta know."

"But what if he catches us?"

"Then we'll run like hell. No way he can keep up with us, particularly in the dark."

"I don't know," J.T. continued to argue, but Mickey had already forged ahead.

Reluctantly, J.T. followed as Mickey carefully picked his way through the gloom. Staying low, he crept past the sedan, keeping the car between him and the window, then headed straight for the board shack. Also staying low, J.T. followed close behind.

At the shed, Mickey flattened out against the weathered boards, then slid around the corner to the far side, now, as it was with the car, the shed was between them and the house. Dropping to his knees, Mickey rotated the loose board to the maximum, which was approximately three inches, then he peeked in. After a moment he backed off, motioning for J.T. to look.

"You see anything?" Mickey whispered.

"I don't know," J.T. replied, still looking in. "It's hard to say for sure, but it almost looks like there might be something hanging from the—"

"That's the body," Mickey blurted, cutting him off. "We gotta get in there and make sure."

"How are we going to do that?"

Mickey pondered the problem for a few seconds before answering. "Why don't we both grab hold of this loose board, then when I give the signal, we'll jerk backwards. Maybe we can break it loose."

J.T. nodded.

As Mickey had suggested, both boys crouched down and grabbed hold of the lower edge of the loose board. When Mickey gave the signal, they used their thighs for leverage and heaved backwards. The board creaked and grudgingly gave another inch.

On closer examination, the lower row of rusty nails had backed out a little, but the others held fast. On Mickey's signal, they tried again. This time the board bowed and creaked, but gave no more space. They tried one more time and a few more nails popped. Now the aperture was nearly a foot wide, but try as they might, they could get no more. Without a crowbar or an axe, it looked like that was all they were going to get.

"Okay," Mickey gave the board one last futile tug, "go on, J.T., and try to squeeze through. I'll hold it open."

No—no way, not me," J.T. backed off, the blood draining from his face. "I'll pull. You go."

"Think about it," Mickey reasoned, "you're smaller than me. And you know very well I'd never make it through that hole. You've gotta go."

For a moment, J.T. contemplated the conundrum. On one hand, he really didn't want to go in there. Bodies made him squeamish, and dead bodies that had been murdered were even worse, not that he'd ever seen a murdered body before. On the other hand, what Mickey said was true. Mickey would never fit through that small hole and just maybe he could.

Finally, J.T. took a deep breath and nodded his agreement. As Mickey got into position, he dropped down to his belly. On the count of three, Mickey heaved back and J.T. started wriggling through the hole. However, even with his smaller frame, it was still tight as a glove. As he squeezed further into the opening, the side boards grudgingly gave a little, bowing inward as he wedged forward.

Determined, he strained and pushed on, but as he inched forward the boards raked against his rib cage. Gritting his teeth, he advanced another inch. That suddenly freed his ribs, but the side boards, acting like an over-stretched spring, abruptly snapped back into position, locking across the hollow of his flanks. Now, as he tried to advance, the boards hung up on the bony shelf of his pelvis.

Fueled by fear, he lunged forward again, but the boards held fast. Next, he tried to back up, but now the boards hung up on the shelf of his ribcage. He couldn't backup either. Like the jaws of an industrial vise, the boards gripped his flanks. Once again, he tried to go forward, but he couldn't gain an inch. He was trapped!

Terror rose in his throat like bile. He'd always been a little claustrophobic, but now with his head in the cave-like darkness and not being able to move, it—it was almost like being in a coffin, like being buried alive!

With a surge of adrenaline, J.T. lunged forward again. He could feel the soft skin on his hips abrade, but still the boards held tight. Now, he could feel something even more ominous, the trickle of warm blood dripping down his flanks.

"Turn sideways!" Mickey shouted, pulling at the board even harder.

Somehow, Mickey's words penetrated his fog of terror and J.T. rotated his body.

"Now push forward with your feet."

Flexing slightly at the knee, J.T. dug his lower foot into the dirt, then pushed as hard as he could. It was awkward, but somehow he generated enough force to pop free.

In the dark, he tried to examine his wounds. Though he couldn't see anything, he suspected, hoped, they were superficial. Bringing a finger up to his lips, he licked and tasted. It was salty, like blood—his blood!

"What'a ya see?" Mickey whispered from outside the shed.

"N—nothing, nothing yet," J.T.'s voice quivered like a banjo string. "G—give me a minute."

Inside the shed, the darkness was nearly absolute. He really couldn't see a thing, but he could smell. Sniffing, like a bird dog, he tried to sort out the odors. Yes, there was the unquestionable odor of blood, old blood, not necessarily his, and—and something else. What was it? Oh, yeah, he knew that smell, the odor of a newly plowed field.

Mimicking a blind person, J.T. stood up, extended his arms, then shuffled toward what he thought was the center of the shack. After two tentative steps, he tripped, falling face first onto the ground.

What had tripped him? Still on all fours, he explored the area with his hands. In a roughly semi-circle, he patted the area, then he found it. Picking up a fresh clod, he crumbled it, then slowly exhaled. What had tripped him was nothing more than a low mound of freshly turned earth. No bodies here! Using his shirt tail, he wiped the beads of sweat from his brow, then stood up again. Again with hands and arms fully extended, he took another step, then another.

Suddenly, he collided with something rigid. The impact caused the object to swing away from him, then like a pendulum it swung back, smacking him a second time.

In the tomb-like darkness, he couldn't see what it was, but used his hands to steady it, then with heart pounding, began exploring.

On cursory, tactile examination, it appeared to be the same bundle they'd earlier seen Rosenkranz and the cowboy lug from the car. But other than that, J.T. wasn't sure what it was. He inspected it again, this time more slowly. Hanging by hemp rope from a ceiling crossbeam, it seemed to be fairly solid, roughly six feet tall and wrapped in heavy canvas.

"You find anything?" Mickey whispered.

"Y—yeah, it—it's hanging right in front of me.

"Hangin'?"

"You know, the bundle."

"What bundle?"

"Geez, the one Rosenkranz and the cowboy took out of the trunk."

"Oh, yeah, is it Willie?"

"I—I don't know. I'm afraid to look."

"Come on, J.T., you've gotta do it."

J.T. was silent for a few seconds. "Okay, Mickey, but g—give me a minute."

With hands trembling, J.T. continued his examination. The bundle was about as tall as him, maybe a little taller, and probably weighed about as much, maybe a little more. Through the thick canvas, it was hard to determine the exact shape. It might be his imagination, but—but it kinda did feel like a body!

After a few more seconds, J.T. traced the rope circling the bundle to its securing knots. Patiently, he worked to untie them. Finally, he jerked the rope free. Without the circling ropes, the canvas slowly slid away.

At that exact second, the near-full moon made its promised appearance. Finally topping the sandstone mesa in Zion National Park, a vanguard moonbeam fought through the gloom of dusk, squeezing through an inch-wide slot between the shack boards. Now the dangling object, like a solo actor spotlighted on a darkened stage, was partially illuminated by the narrow slit of light.

Gasping, J.T. dropped the hemp cord, then as he staggered backward, he again tripped over the dirt mound, landing hard on his backside.

15

ALMOST IMPERCEPTIBLY, THE MOON INCHED UPWARD AND THE VANGUARD beam shifted from the slot between boards, again plunging J.T. into total darkness.

Breathing deeply, J.T. managed to calm himself, then with jaw firmly set, he crawled back over the mound. When he thought he was close, he stood up again, reaching out and touching it. What was this? Oh, this had to be its back.

Instantly, he recoiled!

Even without the benefit of light, he recognized the distinctive feel of marbled fat and taut muscle bundles. That could only mean one thing: this body had been skinned!

Unsuccessfully, he tried to stave off a shudder, then another. When he stopped shaking, he took a deep breath and reached out again, determined to examine the body. Though no longer warm, the object had the unmistakable contours and texture of flesh. Walking his fingers upward, he located the chest. On one side, he discovered a fist-size hole and on the opposite side a companion, but smaller, silver-dollar cavity. Undoubtedly, these were entrance and exit wounds and the cause of death. Considering the location and angle of the two wounds, more than likely he or she was shot right through the heart. At least, they died fast.

Mustering up the courage he didn't think he had, J.T. reached up, searching for the face, specifically the teeth and nose. He wanted to avoid the eyes.

Unexpectedly, there was facial hair—a lot of hair! Wait a sec, what was this? It—it felt like a snout! Sure, Willie had protuberant teeth, but nothing like this.

A snout with thick facial hair?

Stepping back, J.T. grabbed hold of the body, swinging it sideways until he had it positioned in a new slit of moonlight.

Though only fourteen, he'd seen this sort of thing many times before. For there, hanging in the rectangular slit of moonlight, was not Weird Willie

Wittwer; it was not even human. No, hanging there from an overhead rafter was a recently deceased, cleaned, and skinned carcass of a male mule deer. A four-point buck!

Suddenly, over at the house, the porch light flipped on. Now, instead of just an occasional moonbeam, bright incandescent light filtered through the cracks of the shed.

Was someone coming? Like the mother cougar on Utah Hill (the one Smokey had killed), J.T. felt trapped. Figuratively speaking, his back was up against a granite cliff. Stumbling over the floor dirt mound for a third time, J.T. scooted to the wall facing the house. Pushing his face against the boards, he peeked through a crack. At that moment, the kitchen door opened and the tall man, wearing a cowboy hat, stepped onto the porch. As best J.T. could tell, he was the same guy who'd earlier helped Borch drag the bundled deer carcass into the shack.

Not knowing what else to do, J.T. continued to watch. A moment later Borch Rosenkranz joined the cowboy on the landing.

So, old Borch had company tonight! That surprised J.T. Exactly why that surprised him, he wasn't sure, except conversing with Rosenkranz was such a chore and there was no second car in the driveway. Also, Borch had always been a loner; he never had company. At least none J.T. had ever seen.

Their voices sounded loud and angry, as if they were arguing. The overhead porch light, as well as the fully emerging moon, provided enough illumination for J.T. to study their body language. At the moment, the cowboy was repeatedly shaking his head, as he was apparently listening to Borch. Finally, Rosenkranz paused, and the cowboy started in. He raised his voice another octave, and like a maestro conducting a symphony orchestra, punctuated his sentences with exaggerated hand gestures. Placing his ear right on the crack, J.T. strained to hear the conversation. He couldn't make out every word, but he did catch a few phrases.

"—too damn much," the cowboy snapped, his face turning red. "You—friggin' kidding—no way."

"Ja, ja—long way—technische Arbeit—," Borch replied, as usual mixing languages.

"But—already got—dynamite—" The cowboy took off his hat, angrily slapping it against his thigh— "All—got to do—"

"—and gefährliche Arbeit—how do you say—uh—dangerous—," Rosenkranz countered. "Es ist vorth—uh—some—uh—something."

"We—agreement," the cowboy jabbed Borch's chest with an index finger, then pointed to his own chest, "you and me."

"Vell—dinge ändern sich—uh, tings change." Borch countered, folding his arms across his chest in what appeared to be an act of defiance.

"You—other benefits—" The cowboy pointed directly at J.T. and the shed.

Instinctively, J.T. backed away, dropping low on the ground.

"—nyet— nicht sehr viel—"

"Goddamn you, you Russian Kraut—five hundred—that's—all." The cowboy again jabbed at Borch's chest with a stiff finger.

Continuing with their argument, and almost like it was choreographed, the two men stepped off the landing and onto the driveway, never missing a beat. The cowboy continued to do most of the talking, but Borch seemed to be holding his own. Suddenly, the cowboy stopped talking, turned, and looked directly at J.T.

Burrowing even lower, J.T. froze; he didn't dare even draw a full breath. Had the cowboy seen him?

No, no way. Not in the darkened, tomb-of-a-shed. Nevertheless, the cowboy took a step in his direction.

Scrambling to his feet, J.T. started for the exit portal. Immediately, he collided with the hanging carcass, sending it swaying. Dodging the backswing, he started forward again, then stumbled over the low mound of dirt again. Silently cussing at his stupidity, that was the fourth time, he picked himself up and crawled for the outlet.

"Mickey!" he whispered urgently.

No answer.

"M-i-c-k-e-y!"

Still no answer. Had Mickey seen them coming and split? If so, J.T. was trapped like a mouse in a nearly empty grain barrel! Without Mickey's help, there was no way he could get back through that hole.

"Mickey!" he shouted, as loud as he dared, then waited for someone to come. He'd shouted loud enough, so it could be either Borch, the cowboy, or Mickey who showed up.

Suddenly, there was a rustling just outside of the shed! Sure enough, someone was coming! Now he could distinctly hear the fall of footsteps. Once that door opened, there was no place to hide! Shaking with fear, J.T. retreated a few steps back toward the center of the shed and tried to hide behind the carcass.

"Yeah, whadda you want?" Mickey whispered, leaning low and peeking through the hole.

"W—where were you?"

"Takin' a leak. Whadda you think?"

"T—they're coming!"

"Coming where?"

"From the house, on the other side of the shed."

"What did you find?"

"Didn't you hear me?" J.T. snapped. "They're coming!"

"Who's they?"

"Doesn't matter. We've got to go. Now!"

"Okay, okay," Mickey replied, then apparently positioned himself to apply the needed leverage.

"Pull!" J.T. whispered urgently, "I'm coming through."

Using his legs, Mickey heaved backward on the board. Turning sideways and oblivious to personal injury, J.T. frantically wormed through the aperture, but not without inflicting more superficial flesh wounds.

"Let's get out of here!" J.T. blurted.

As the two boys turned to run, twin light beams suddenly spotlighted the ground a few yards in front of them. Dodging the light beams, they bolted toward the back of the compound. A second later they heard a combustion engine start up and the crunch of gravel as the dark sedan backed out of the driveway.

"Wait a sec," Mickey said, grabbing J.T.'s arm and slowing him down. "They're not comin'; they're goin'."

"What?"

"They're leavin'."

"Geez! That was close," J.T. exhaled loudly, as they slowed to a walk. "I guess they didn't see us after all."

"Nah," Mickey shrugged, "and it really wasn't that close. So, whadda you find? Weird Willie?"

"No."

"No? What?"

"Deer meat."

"Deer meat?"

"Yeah, just a buck hanging from his antlers," J.T. explained. "They're probably aging him and will cut him up in a day or two."

"How many points?"

"Geez, Mickey, what does it matter?"

"I just what to know how big it is."

"I don't know; probably a four-point."

"Poached?"

"What do you think? This time of year."

"It's not right," Mickey exclaimed, sounding outraged, "him poachin' our deer."

"Why?"

"Why? He's not even American."

"Well," J.T. shrugged, "I guess he's becoming Americanized. Now, he is just like everyone else in town."

"Yeah, I guess," Mickey shook his head in disgust, "but it's still not right. If he's goin' to poach, he should do it over in Russia, poach Russian deer."

"Or maybe poach Russian reindeer."

"Huh?"

"Oh, nothing," J.T. said, "anyway, he had someone else in the house."

"Who?"

"That same guy with the cowboy hat."

"He's another spy," Mickey declared.

"Maybe—but I don't think so. He looked real American and—and they were fighting."

"What makes you think he was American?"

"The cowboy hat and boots."

"Geez, J.T., don't you think Russians can buy cowboy hats and boots? It's all part of their disguise."

"Yeah, maybe, I don't know," J.T. hesitated, "but he spoke good English."

"What did he say?"

"I don't know for sure, but I think they were arguing about money."

"Money. Why money?"

"I don't know," J.T. replied as they began crossing Gubler's alfalfa field, "but it sounded like the cowboy was trying to hire Borch for something and they were fighting about wages."

"Hire for what?"

"I don't know. It makes no sense."

"I still think," Mickey insisted, "it all has somethin' to do with spying."

"I don't know," J.T. shook his head, "but you could be right."

"Damn right, I am right."

Well, anyway, let's go down to the creek and do like Sheriff Meecham said and see if we can find Weird Willie."

"Did you tie everythin' back up?" Mickey suddenly asked as they approached the ribbon of dense foliage flanking the creek.

"What?"

"Did you tie things back up? You know, the canvas."

"You mean around the deer?"

"Of course, around the deer."

"No."

"You didn't?" Mickey looked surprised.

"No, I just said I didn't?"

"You should have. We should go back and do that while they're gone."

"No!"

"They'll know someone was in there."

"I don't care; I'm not going back." Stubbornly, J.T. stood his ground. This was the hill he was willing to die on. "No, it hurts too much. I'm not going back into that shed."

"Did you see the shortwave radio?"

"Huh? Uh—uh, I don't know." J.T. thought about it for moment. "No, I don't think so."

"Did you look?"

"No, but if it was there, I would have bumped into it or seen all those electronic lights."

"Some investigator you are. We should go back."

"For the last time, I said, I'm not going back!"

"Fine," Mickey shrugged, "you don't need to throw a hissy fit."

"I didn't."

"Yes, you did," Mickey insisted, then added, "anyway, we'll start at the fort, then we'll work our way upstream to Boy's Pond, then on up to the diversion dam."

"Okay," J.T. agreed. Anything was fine, except going back into the shed.

The moon was now well above the horizon. With its bright light, plus crossing familiar terrain, it was not difficult for the boys to find their way. At the fort they stopped and searched the area once again. Nothing had changed. Nothing within, or around the fort had been disturbed. Systematically, they widened their search, crawling through thickets of skunk bushes and dense stands of river and stink willows. There was no sign of Weird Willie and no new evidence.

Convinced Willie was not in the immediate area, Mickey suggested they separate and head upstream. He assigned J.T. to work the south bank and he would canvas the north.

J.T. started to argue, but Mickey had already disappeared into a thicket of skunk bush. Unfortunately, this meant he had to cross the creek to get to the south bank.

With the mountain snow runoff long gone, combined with the hot July weather, and most of the water being diverted upstream for irrigation, the flow in the creek was not much more than a trickle. Nevertheless, J.T. still managed to get his feet wet. Jumping from one slick, river-polished rock to the next, he slipped, splashing into an ankle-deep pool. Silently, he cussed Mickey. Why was he always the boss? And why did he always let him?

Slowly, the boys worked upstream, staying roughly even with each other. They checked behind every large boulder, every eroded hollow in the riverbank, every downed tree and every thicket of skunk bushes or stand of live oak. As J.T. worked upstream, he occasionally caught a glimpse of Mickey on the north bank, briefly spotlighted in the bright moonlight.

Somewhat surprising to J.T., Mickey seemed to being doing a thorough job, checking everything and anything that could possibly hide a body. It was not something he would have expected if Mickey was somehow involved in Willie's disappearance. That was comforting, but other than that, J.T. found the night-search a bit unnerving. There was the usual background cacophony of night creatures, but the only other sounds came from the occasional crack of a twig he'd stepped on, or swish of bushes as he pushed through them. Though the night creatures were active, it seemed too quiet!

Just before they got to Boy's Pond, Mickey motioned for him to wade back across the creek. It would take both of them to search the tangle of foliage around the swimming hole. This time J.T. was careful not to slip, but it really didn't matter, his feet were already wet.

They were approximately fifty yards from the pond, when Mickey gave the sign to halt. Using hand signals, he indicated he would circle east around the pond and J.T. should work around to the west. They would meet somewhere on the north bank.

On hands and knees, J.T. crawled through a remarkably thick growth of Dixie live oak. Its serrated leaves abraded and sliced his exposed skin. Up ahead he could smell the familiar musky odor of cattails and pond moss, growing in the waters of Boy's Pond. He struggled forward another couple of yards. Now through a portal in the branches, he could see a small portion of the pond, the bright moonlight dancing off the standing ripples generated by the whirlpool. From this angle, however, he could not actually see the whirlpool. Blocking his line of sight was a thick stand of river willows.

He inched closer. Now he could see the whirlpool. There seemed to be a clump of trash, probably a collection of leaves and twigs, or driftwood, that had accumulated and now spiraled in the dark water. Silently, it floated by, highlighted in the hoary moonlight.

At last fighting free of the knot of willows, J.T. stood up and walked closer. Pausing, he concentrated on the floating tangle of trash. There was something odd about that heap, trapped there in the circling waters. Picking up a willow stick, he edged closer until he was standing right on the bank. Using the stick as a probe, he poked at the trash, but couldn't quite reach it. Discarding the willow, he looked for something longer. Off the bank and to the right he spied a downed stink will pole, maybe twelve feet in length. That ought'a work.

Back on the bank, J.T. again probed at the floating island of trash. Part of it was quite solid, maybe a hunk of driftwood. He prodded and pushed at it again. As the large chunk of driftwood rocked away, it separated slightly from the other debris.

Dropping his stink pole, J.T. stumbled back down the bank.

T—that was not trash! At least not all of it.

For there, bobbing, like a buoy, in the silvery moonlight was not driftwood, but a human a body! Floating face down, it slowly spiraled in the dark waters of Boy's Pond.

"Mickey!" he shouted. "M-i-c-k-e-y!"

While he waited for Mickey, J.T. worked around the water's edge, eyeing the slowly orbiting body. It was a macabre scene, but nonetheless was totally captivating. Though it bobbed up and down, and angled this way and that, the body never left the magnetic grip of the whirlpool.

After completing one revolution, like a planet in a cosmic solar system, it silently started another. Usually, it would lead with its head, but would occasionally rotate on its axis, lead with its feet, then after a bit, it would slowly rotate back again. But in spite of the occasional change in polarity, it never altered from its prone position. All that was visible was the back of the head, both shoulder blades, the hump of the upper back and rounded curves of the buttocks. Apparently, the arms and legs dangled below the surface of the water. From the short hair, slim hips, and general body shape, it appeared to be a man. Lastly, J.T. noted, the man was wearing a white T-shirt and faded blue jeans.

Somehow, it was both fascinating and surreal at the same time. As with a Hollywood horror movie, you really don't want to watch the gore, but nevertheless with one eye, you still peek.

"So, what you got?"

J.T. nearly jumped out of his goose-pimpled skin. Turning, he saw Mickey standing directly behind him, peering over his shoulder.

"A body," J.T. whispered. Picking up the long pole again, he pointed.

"Weird Willie," Mickey said. "Looks like we've finally found Weird Willie."

"Yeah, maybe, I guess." J.T. looked closely at Mickey, again trying to read his face. In spite of his earlier, careful searching, he was still not convinced Mickey was totally blameless in this whole sordid affair.

"Whadda ya mean, maybe?" Mickey asked, walking to the water's edge for a better look. "Nobody else is missin'. Of course, it's Willie."

"It—it's just that he looks so different."

"Dead bodies always do."

Privately, J.T. wondered how Mickey had become such an authority on dead bodies, but out loud he asked, "I—I wonder how he died?"

"He drowned," Mickey declared with certainty. "Ain't it obvious?"

"But," J.T. shook his head, "Willie was a pretty good swimmer."

"It could have happened anyway," Mickey argued, "if he was running in the dark, tripped and fell into the pond."

"Running from what?"

"Hell, I don't know, John Tobler," Mickey snapped, "probably from whoever let him out of the stocks."

"But Willie was a pretty good swimmer," J.T. said again.

"Well, he could've tripped, hit his head, then tumbled into the pond."

"Yeah, I guess so," J.T. nodded, then added, "or, he could've died somewhere else, then they tossed his body into the pond."

Mickey thought about it. "Yeah, I suppose that's possible too. Anyway," he grabbed J.T.'s long pole, "we can't leave him in there."

Patiently, Mickey waited for the body to complete the far arc of its revolution, negotiate the turn, and begin its near arc. When the body was as close as it would get, Mickey reached out with the pole and hooked the shirt. But as he pulled the body against the current, it submerged briefly, then the current ripped it away. Once again, the corpse floated free, immediately returning to its original orbit.

"You're goin' to have to go in and get him," Mickey declared, withdrawing the sink pole.

"Me? You go."

"You're already wet," Mickey argued, "plus you're a better swimmer than me."

"Why is it always me?" J.T. refused to move.

"Hey, I can't help it if you took the Red Cross swimmin' class last year."

"What's that got to do with anything?"

"Didn't they teach you how to rescue another swimmer. You know how to swim with one hand, using the other to hold onto a drowning person?"

"Yeah."

Mickey nodded at the body. "So, go get him."

This was all true. He was a better swimmer and could swim with one hand. Mumbling to himself, J.T. stripped off his T-shirt, quickly checked to make sure he still had his radiation badge. He took that off too, then pulled down his Levi's and finally removed his already wet sneakers and socks. Sure, he was a better swimmer, but he was tired of having to do all the dirty work, like crawling into Borch Rosenkranz's shack or slogging to the far side of the creek and getting his feet wet. And now this!

Smiling, Mickey shrugged his shoulders as if to say, 'hey, man, it's out of my hands. You can't argue with logic.'

J.T. circled the bank, from that section overlooking the whirlpool to the shallow end of the pond. Tentatively, he put a big toe into the water. At least, it was tepid, semi-warm. As he eased all the way in, he could feel the mud squish between his toes. The bottom quickly dropped off and within a couple of steps he was already up to his chin. Layering out, he employed the American crawl, silently gliding through the water.

In just five or six strokes, he was there. Almost insidiously, the circular current latched onto him and without his consent, he also started to orbit. Not attempting to fight it, J.T. began treading water, while trying to decide where to grab hold of the corpse. He'd never touched a dead body before, the deer didn't count, and he really didn't want to do it now.

Finally, he decided he would not touch the body itself, but instead would grab the shirt. After a couple more strokes he caught up with the corpse and with his left hand snatched a handful of t-shirt. Turning to his side, he began stroking with his right hand. Almost immediately, the body rotated sideways to the current. This increased the drag, like a tugboat trying to tow a barge up the Mississippi crossways to the current. To put it simply, it was not hydrodynamic, and try as he might, he could not get the body out of the grip of the whirlpool.

Finally giving up, he let go and treaded water once again. With some consternation, he realized there was only one workable solution. To keep the body from going sideways, he had to grab hold of one polar end or the other. Gritting his teeth, he swam forward again, grabbed a handful of the corpse's thick black hair, praying it would not pull out, then started kicking and side-stroking.

It worked!

With this technique the body did not turn crossways to the current. It took a half-dozen short, powerful strokes to break the grip of the whirlpool and after another half-dozen strokes to reach the shallow end. Now, with his toes firmly planted in the slimy mud, he stood up and worked through the reeds and the knee-high water, dragging the body behind him.

Meanwhile, Mickey watched the proceedings from the safety of the high and dry bank. "Turn him over," Mickey ordered, standing above J.T.

Incredulous, J.T. looked up at Mickey and shook his head. "No!"

"Go on, do it."

Still J.T. did not budge. He really didn't want to see Weird Willie's face, the yellow buck teeth, the ghostly white skin, the cunning green eyes, now glassed over with death.

"Go on, we gotta know for sure."

Mustering all his courage, J.T. reached across the corpse's back, grabbing the opposite shoulder. It felt heavy and waterlogged. Using all his strength, he pulled up on the shoulder, while simultaneously pushing down on the hip. Slowly, the corpse rotated upward and toward him. When it was nearly perpendicular, he lost his grip.

Promptly, the body splashed face down again. Thinking fast, J.T. grabbed a fistful of t-shirt before it could float away.

"Try it again," Mickey commanded from on high.

J.T. answered with a dirty look, but nevertheless complied. After securing a better grip, he tried again. Slowly, he rotated the shoulder out of the water to the vertical position, then lost his grip once again. This time, however, the corpse had turned far enough past perpendicular that it flopped forward, not backward, smacking against J.T.

"That," J.T. cried, looking down, then stumbling backward, "that's not Weird Willie!"

16

"THEN WHO IS IT?" MICKEY ASKED, STEPPING FORWARD AND BENDING down to get a better look.

"See," J.T. pointed, "there's still a pack of cigarettes rolled in his sleeve."

"So?" Mickey inched forward to the water's edge.

"So, that—that's Lenny Weeks!"

"Grab him!" Mickey shouted as the body began ebbing back to deep water. "Don't let him get away." Snatching the stink willow pole, Mickey used it to pin and draw the corpse up against the bank. "Come on, J.T., help me get him out of the water."

Wading chest-deep into the water, J.T. pushed the body upward and forward. Standing on the dry bank, Mickey grabbed an arm and a leg. Together, they managed to push and drag the corpse through the cattails and onto dry ground.

The silvery moonlight seemed to add a surreal sheen to Lenny's prune-wrinkled skin, highlighting the angular ridges of his cheeks and nose. His mouth was gapping open in the shape of an 'O.' But it was more than the color and texture of the skin, and the open mouth that upset J.T., it was his facial expression. The death mask frozen on Lenny's face was anything but serene; it was one of shock! One of horror!

Certainly, all of that was disturbing enough, but it was Lenny's eyes that really gave J.T. the creeps. Even though they were wide open and unblinking, they nevertheless seemed capable of focusing. And—and, they seemed as if they were following him. Every time he looked at Lenny, his eyes were staring back at him! It was more than uncanny; it was downright unnerving. To put a stop to it, J.T. sidestepped until Mickey was interposed between him and the body. However, when Mickey moved, there they were again, Lenny's cold blue eyes. Consequently, J.T. tried to match Mickey's movements.

Finally, he turned his back to the body and stepped in front of Mickey. "L—let's get out of here."

"What's your hurry? It's not like Lenny needs a doctor."

"But we—we need to get the sheriff."

"We will, but I want to check a few things out first." Mickey knelt down on the bank and began examining the body.

"You're not a detective." J.T. tugged on his arm. "We better leave that stuff to the authorities."

"Don't see no gunshot wound," Mickey said, ignoring J.T. and continuing his investigation. "Yeah, looks like he probably drowned."

"Maybe, but look at him," J.T. forced himself to look at the body, but still stood at least ten feet away. "It looks like he's been in a fight."

"Why do you say that?"

"All the scrapes and bruises."

"Probably hit his head when he fell in."

"No," J.T. argued, "they can't all be from a fall. They're everywhere, particularly on the face, neck and back of the head. A fall wouldn't do that."

"Maybe we did that the other day in our fight."

"Nah, we hardly touched him," J.T. shuffled a bit closer, "anyway, those are fresh."

"How do you know that?"

"No scabs."

"Oh. Well maybe he got them cuts and bruises floating in the pond, you know, bumping into the bank, and logs, and things."

"I don't think so," J.T. shook his head. "These are awful red. They must've happened before death when he was still able to bleed."

"How do you know all that stuff?"

"I read a lot. Let's go!"

"Maybe," Mickey said, trying to duplicate J.T.'s powers of observation, "he has some broken bones."

"So, what if he does? What does that prove that we don't already know?"

"I just think it's interestin'," Mickey replied, "tryin' to figure out what happened."

"Come on, Mickey, let's go."

"Okay," Mickey said, but nevertheless bent down, unrolled the t-shirt sleeve, retrieving the pack of Camels. Turning the pack upside down, he shook out the contents. "Looks like they've all disintegrated."

"So?"

"So," Mickey theorized, "that tells us somethin' about how long the body's been in the water."

"Not really," J.T. argued, "it only takes minutes for cigarettes in water to turn to mush. Let's go."

"Okay, okay, but let's go through his pockets first."

Systematically, Mickey searched every pocket. There was nothing, not even a wallet in the back pockets. In the right front pocket, however, there was some loose change, two quarters, a nickel and three pennies, and from the front left pocket Mickey extracted a couple of brass objects that glinted in the moonlight, like fool's gold.

"What's that?" J.T. asked. As usual, he was being drawn in against his will.

"Bullets, two of 'em," Mickey replied, slowing rotating the brass cylinders in the bright moonlight, "rifle bullets with absolutely no markings on them."

"What!" J.T. edged in closer. "Let me see."

Forgetting his squeamishness, J.T. crossed the remaining few feet and stood right over Lenny's corpse. Snatching one of the bullets, he held it up, slowly rotating it. Sure enough, it looked identical to the bullet they'd found earlier at the fort. It sported a central fire primer, a ballistic tip and absolutely no caliber or manufacturer markings.

"You still got that other bullet?" J.T. asked. "The one we found by the stocks?"

After fishing in his pockets for a couple of seconds, Mickey produced the cartridge. Holding the two side by side, J.T. compared the casings. They appeared to be identical.

"So, now what do you think?" Mickey asked.

"I—I honestly don't know," J.T. replied, frowning, "but it looks like," he held up the first bullet as a prop, "that Lenny must have been at the fort and lost this bullet crawling through the bushes. So, I guess it's possible it was Lenny who let Willie out."

With a sideways glance, J.T. eyed Mickey as he continued to work through this new information. Yes, this latest revelation (that Lenny must have been down at the stocks) almost let Mickey off the hook, but not entirely. He still had not accounted, at least to J.T.'s satisfaction, for those couple of hours after town bell when he allegedly had to go home and do chores before they released Willie. But J.T. had to admit, this new evidence made it look more and more like it was Lenny who had let Willie out. However, being skeptical by nature, J.T. decided to still keep the book open on Mickey T. Graff, at least until those lost two hours were accounted for.

"It's more than possible," Mickey declared, "it was Lenny."

"Then, who killed Lenny?"

"Well, think about it," Mickey replied, "if it was Lenny who let Willie out, then we know Willie was probably one of the last people to see him alive, so it stands to reason—"

"Nah," J.T. cut him off, "I can see where you're going with that, but it couldn't have been Weird Willie. Look at the way Lenny was beat up. Willie could never do that."

"But we saw them arguing at town bell."

"That doesn't mean anything. You and me fight all the time, but you don't go and murder me."

"That don't mean," Mickey quipped with a lopsided grin, "that I wouldn't like to."

"But you don't."

"Well, maybe, Willie surprised him. Got the jump on him, then he might be able to do some real damage."

J.T. shook his head again. "Nah, I don't think so; Willie wouldn't have the guts."

"So, if not Willie, then who?" Suddenly Mickey looked nervous. After quickly glancing over his shoulder, he added, "but Willie's got to be tied into this in some way."

"Lenny was such a nice guy," J.T. said, sarcastically, "he probably has a lot of enemies. Some we don't even know."

Mickey shook his head. "Why drive all the way up to the Beryl Farms to hunt pheasants, when there's plenty in your own hay field?"

"Is that your way of saying, you still think it's Weird Willie?"

"All I'm saying, why look for other suspects, when you already have one?"

"I'm still not buying it."

"Wait till all the investigatin' is over, you'll see."

"Speaking of investigation," J.T. turned from the body, "let's go get the sheriff. Let's let the professionals figure it out."

"Okay, okay," Mickey finally relented. Snatching the bullets back from J.T., he re-pocketed all three bullets.

"Hey, don't you think you ought to leave those for evidence?"

"But we might need them."

"Need them for what? You've got to leave some evidence for the sheriff."

Fishing the three bullets from his pocket, Mickey selected one and put it back in Lenny's pants pocket. Defiantly, he stuffed the other two back into his own pocket.

"Okay, let's go."

With Mickey leading, they backtracked to the fort, then crawled through the thicket of skunk bushes, heading north toward the school.

"Hold up," J.T. yelled at Mickey. Something glinting in the moonlight had caught his eye. Something they'd missed earlier. Probably another bullet. Reaching through the skunk bushes, he picked it up. Holding it up to the light, he rotated it with his fingers.

"What you got?"

"Looks like a ring," J.T. answered, continuing his examination. The ring had a thick gold band, and a flat square face, which was also framed with gold. Around the periphery of the face were several tiny red stones, probably rubies, and inside the square, a small block eagle was engraved. The eagle had spread wings and clutched a leafy ring, perhaps a wreath, in its talons.

"Looks expensive," Mickey commented, snatching the ring.

"I think that eagle means something," J.T. added. "It's a symbol, not just a decoration."

"Maybe it's a ring for a club, like the Elks or Lions. They have animal symbols."

"Maybe," J.T. nodded, "or maybe it's the symbol for a country."

"Yeah," Mickey agreed, "like we have a bald eagle, don't we?"

"But ours looks different. You got a dollar bill?"

"Yeah, I think so, I just got paid at the fruit stand." Mickey searched his pockets until he finally produced a single dollar bill.

"Wow," J.T. arched an eyebrow. "Fruit stand work pays a heck-of-a-lot better than farm work."

"That's two day's work," Mickey admitted.

Nevertheless, J.T. was impressed, if not envious. He never had that much money to just carry around in his pocket. All his money went into a Mason jar to pay for his massive and recently accrued debts.

"Let me see it." J.T. grabbed the money, turning it over. "See, our eagle has arrows and a scroll in its talons, this one has a wreath."

"So?"

"So, I don't know for sure," J.T. replied, pocketing the dollar, "but I don't think it's one of ours. Let's go get the sheriff."

"Hey, John Tobler, I want that dollar back!"

Sheepishly, J.T. returned the paper bearing the image of George Washington.

When they arrived back at the school, nobody was there. After leaving the school, they deliberately avoided Hafe Hafen's place, instead opting for Mickey's house. Picking up the phone, thankfully at this hour no one was on the party line, Mickey asked the operator to connect him to the sheriff's office. On the very first ring, Sheriff Meecham picked up.

"Where's Hafe?" he immediately asked.

"I don't know, probably home," Mickey replied, then went on to explain Hafe's absence. Finally, he got around to telling the sheriff about the body.

"I was afraid of somethin' like that," Meecham muttered. "I'll be right over."

It was thirty minutes before the boys heard the cruiser pull up at Mickey's house and by the time they'd finished with the sheriff, they had to personally guide him to the crime scene, it was after twelve o'clock. Thankfully, after finishing his initial inspection, the sheriff sent the boys home, but instructed them they were to be in his office at 3:00 p.m. tomorrow to give official depositions. Whatever that meant.

Sheriff Meecham offered to have Deputy Fowler give them a ride, but the boys could see they were busy, so they informed the sheriff they could walk. It would be almost as fast anyway.

On Main Street, they said goodnight and parted. Dead tired, J.T. headed for home. As he approached the house, he noticed that during his three-or-four-hour absence, several khaki-green tents had been erected in their backyard. Constructed from oiled canvas, they appeared to be heavyweight, military tents. The larger tent had a conical roof with a central opening. Through that porthole, black smoke, imbued with a steady stream of live sparks, drifted skyward into the moon-lit night.

Like most people in Santa Clara, the Kunz's had a large backyard, over an acre, but now it seemed congested. And all those tents were set up in what was supposed to be their vegetable garden. Father would be furious!

What the heck's going on, J.T. wondered, a bit irritated. Had the U.S. Army or the National Guard decided to billet soldiers in their backyard? If so, why? Was this just training, the so-called war games, or were the Russians really coming? Thoroughly confused and now a bit concerned, he avoided the tents and headed straight for the backdoor.

As he opened the door to the service room, J.T. noted a light was still on in the kitchen. Upon entering, he was greeted with the distinct smell of oil-processed, canned tuna fish. Seated at the dining table, Mary was munching on a tuna fish sandwich. The empty and still reeking tuna can, the very one J.T. had opened earlier, was still resting on the counter.

"Are the Russians coming?"

"Huh?"

"Why's the army here?" J.T. jerked his thumb in the direction of the tents.

"Huh?"

"There's tents out back.""

"Yeah, so?"

"So, are the Russians coming?"

"The Russians," Mary laughed, "that's just Smokey and the clan. They're doing a Sing for mother tonight and tomorrow."

"Oh, yeah, I forgot," J.T. mumbled, "but I thought those Sings were a five-day affair."

"They are," Mary replied, taking another bite of her sandwich.

"Well, father's going to be home day after tomorrow and I can guarantee he won't be happy."

"They're supposed to be gone by then." Mary wiped her face with a kitchen towel. "They did the first three days on the reservation. It's supposed to end Sunday at dawn."

"Geez," J.T. sighed, "I sure hope my friends don't see this."

"Why?"

"Why what?"

"Why don't you want your friends to see it?"

"Because, I don't," J.T. snapped, turning, and heading for his bedroom. Halfway there, he stopped and turned around again. "Mary, could you drive me over to the sheriff's office tomorrow at three?"

"Why?"

"Because Father's gone and it looks like Mother's going to be tied up with this Smokey thing."

"No, I mean why do you have to go to the sheriff's office?"

"Oh, we found a body tonight and I have to give an official deposition."

"Oh, my God!" Mary exclaimed, now suddenly interested. "Only if you tell me all about it." She tucked her legs under her and settled in.

For the next five minutes, J.T. filled in the details, purposefully leaving out the parts relating to Borch Rosenkranz, the deer hanging in the shed and the locking of Weird Willie in the stocks. No point going into all that. After he'd finished, Mary grudgingly agreed to drive, but only if he first okayed it with Mother.

Deliberately trying to end the discussion on dead bodies, J.T. asked, "so, how was the movie?"

"Oh, Clark Gable was dreamy."

"Yeah, I'll bet." Barely able to keep his eyes open, J.T. once again stumbled down the hall toward his bedroom.

"Hey, J.T.!" Mary called after him.

"Yeah." He turned around again.

"You're not in trouble, are you?"

"Nah," J.T. answered with more conviction than he felt. "It's nothing to do with me. Me and Mickey helped with the search for Willie and happened to find the body. That's all. Why?"

"It just seems like you're always into something."

"Nah, not this time."

"Okay, but you better be careful; Father's getting a little tired of your shenanigans."

Shrugging, J.T. turned around again and for the third time headed for his bedroom.

Opening a window for ventilation, he flopped down on his twin bed. Next to him, not five feet away was an identical bed, which belonged to his brother, Chris, now in the marines and just deployed to Korea. Chris's bed was directly under the air conditioning vent, while J.T.'s was next to the window. Usually, Chris had the better location, particularly in the summer, but this year it didn't make much difference. With his mother being sick, they hadn't used the swamp cooler that much. She said the cool, damp air made her bones ache.

Though exhausted, J.T. didn't immediately fall asleep. He couldn't help but think of Smokey's Sing and why his mother thought it was necessary. Was she really that sick? Was she actually going to die? It was all pretty scary stuff. What would happen to them if she did? Would they stay together as a family? They weren't much of a family unit now, with Chris away in the marines, his father gone on the truck most of the time and his mother pretty much bedfast. And Mary was old enough that she could, and probably would, get married or go away to school next year. If his mother did die, that would leave only him and Father. That was like trying to mix communism with democracy or like mixing nitric acid with glycerin! Sighing, he tried to push these disturbing thoughts from his head.

Unfortunately, in lieu of thinking about his family, he switched to the equally unsettling thoughts of this extremely odd day. So, where was Weird Willie? Did Mickey have anything to do with his disappearance? Who killed Lenny Weeks? And why? Was Willie dead too? Had they, he, and Mickey, somehow, though unwittingly, contributed to this horrific chain of events by simply locking Weird Willie in the stocks? He couldn't shake the nagging feeling they had, and try as he might, he couldn't erase the mental picture of the whirlpool and the silently rotating body.

Through the open window, he heard a guttural chant begin accompanied by the rhythmic beat of a pot drum. To J.T., the whole Smokey Sing/ritual was more than a little disturbing. Being Mormon, how could his mother believe in such a thing? It was primitive and aboriginal, and certainly nonsensical. What was next, pins and voodoo dolls, or feathered shamans with maracas or witch doctors wearing jaguar furs? Who could possibly believe in the healing power of chants and drums when they, the Mormons, had consecrated oil and the laying on of hands? They had the authentic and the real healing power of God's own holy priesthood. The two things, Smokey's Sing, and the laying-on-of-hands, were not even comparable.

Closing his eyes, J.T. tried to block it all out, but it was impossible. Finally, he gave up and concentrated on the chant, but unfortunately it was in Navajo. He knew a few Navajo words, but not many, and even though he didn't understand the words, it did have a soothing, almost hypnotic quality. After listening for a few minutes, J.T.'s eyelids drooped, then shut, and he drifted off to the ancient beat of a pot drum.

For a while, his mind wandered aimlessly, bouncing along with the beat, then suddenly, and inexplicably, he was back at Boy's Pond. This time, however, it was different. The pond seemed hazy, vague, almost ethereal, like an old silent movie. And also, like an old movie, there was no color; everything was in black and white noir and metered down to exaggerated slow motion. As the silvery moonlight rippled off the water, scores of bangled nymphs rose from the turbid water. Then ever so slowly, the moonlight started to rotate, spinning in unison with the waters of the whirlpool, like light being drawn into a black hole. At first, the moonlight simply circled, then it was abruptly sucked into the whirlpool's spinning vortex. And suddenly, there he was in that same light, spiraling downward toward the waters of the whirlpool! The pull was intense, like he was trapped in the force field of a super magnet.

Once inside the whirlpool, J.T. noted not only was the light circling, but it also strobed, like the lights of a police car. The constant flashing made his eyes hurt. Soon, trash, twigs and logs were also caught up, joining him in the aquatic merry-go-round. He batted them away, but they always circled back, slamming up against him, again and again.

Abruptly, he saw a body floating above him, also trapped in the gravitational pull. Face down, the corpse silently circled, and circled, but with each orbit it sunk lower and deeper into the vortex. Kicking hard and breast-stroking, J.T. tried to swim away, but somehow the body ended up on top of him. Frantic now, he tried to swim up, or down, but the centripetal force was too great. He was trapped! Like the body, he couldn't leave the whirlpool. As they circled, the body continued to bump against him. He tried to push it away, then as the vortex became tighter, they became entangled. Now, he could see the face!

Perspiring, J.T. willed himself out of the circling vortex and back to consciousness. Sitting on the edge of the bed, he used the bedsheet to wipe the sweat from his face. He forced himself to get up and walk around to make sure he wouldn't return to the dream. At last, fully awake, he noted he was hyperventilating and his hands were shaking. By counting respirations, he managed to slow his breathing, then headed for the bathroom.

By now the vestiges of the nightmare were fading fast, like valley fog on a sunny morning, but in his mind's eye he could still see the face of the bloodless corpse. No, it was not the face of Lenny Weeks, or even Weird Willie Wittwer staring back at him, but—but it was his own face!

What was he supposed to draw from that? Silently, he laughed at his runaway paranoia. Everyone knew dreams were totally nonsensical. Didn't they?

Still shaking, J.T. returned to the bedroom, staring out the open window. Somewhat less bright now, the moon was well on its downward arc, heading for Utah Hill, perhaps even their ranch or the National Testing Site at Yucca Flats. In the backyard, the chanting and pounding of the pot drum still coursed on the night's airwaves and the plume of smoke, still embedded with glowing embers, spiraled up from the hole in the roof of the big tent.

This could go on all night, J.T. thought glumly. Oh, well, anything was better than returning to the nightmare. Flopping back onto the bed, he concentrated on the drums and the chant and though he was determined to stay awake, once again he got caught up in the ancient rhythm—

"Jackie, Jackie, wake up."

He knew someone was shaking him, but they seemed far away.

"Jackie!"

"Huh?" Rubbing his eyes, he returned to semi-consciousness, while deciding he must have fallen asleep after all.

"Jackie, wake up. I want to show you something."

Sitting up, he finally managed to pry open his matted lashes.

"What!"

Recoiling and shrinking back into his bed, J.T. forced his eyes shut. It had to be another dream.

But for conformation, he warily cracked open an eye again.

It was still there. This was no dream!

Even though he was now fully awake, the apparition remained. A coal black face with alabaster eyes and teeth hoovered directly over him.

"Oh, this," his mother laughed, touching her face, "this is nothing to worry about. It's just part of the blessing way ceremony." She reached for J.T.'s hand.

Relaxing a little, J.T. took a closer look. Indeed, the charcoal-smeared ghoul was his mother.

"It's campfire soot," she explained. "It makes me invisible to the evil spirits who have put my body out of balance; you know, caused the cancer sickness. In the morning, I will wash it off, symbolizing my body and spirit's return to hozro."

"Well," J.T. said, finally accepting her hand, "it looks pretty scary."

"I know," she laughed again. "Get dressed. I've cooked breakfast, then I want to show you something." Again, she smiled behind her sooty mask, then turned and hurried from the bedroom.

As J.T. struggled out of bed, he glanced out of the window. Campfire smoke still waffled up from the main tent, but thankfully the drums and chanting had ceased. Turning from the window, he shuffled over to the dresser and started picking through his clothes.

His mother was surely in a good mood today; she'd even fixed breakfast! The first in a long time. That was a strong indication she was feeling better. Grudgingly, J.T. had to admit this metamorphosis could be the result of Smokey's blessing way, but the real question was, would it last? Somewhere he'd read about the placebo effect and that's what this had to be—the placebo effect. But whatever it was, for now its impact on his mother was undeniable. So, even though it was a pagan ritual, it seemed to have produced good results. How could that be bad? As he dressed, J.T. tried to reconcile this with his Mormon teachings.

Breakfast consisted of fry bread, ham, and eggs sunny side up. Mary was not yet up, so J.T. ate by himself. He was starved and quickly wolfed down two helpings and was starting for a third, when his mother stopped him.

"You need to save some for Mary," she admonished, removing the platter, and placing it in the oven to keep it warm.

"Aren't you going to eat?"

"I had some while cooking." His mother smiled as she flitted about.

She always said that, but J.T. knew her snacks while cooking consisted of a half-of-a-bite here and quarter-of-a-bite there, but not enough calories to provide sufficient fuel for daily activities or to maintain body weight.

"Mother, is it okay if Mary drives—" J.T. stopped in mid-sentence. No point in worrying his mother about the events of yesterday, the finding of a dead body. Not when she seemed so happy today.

"What?" His mother turned from the oven.

"Oh, nothing." J.T. replied vaguely, He'd already decided he would fib to Mary that she had given her consent to drive him.

"You finished?" His mother asked as she washed the greasy fry pan.

"Yeah." J.T. took his plate and silverware to the sink. "Thanks, Mom that was great. I'll do the dishes."

"No," his mother grabbed his hand, "I'll do them later, but right now I want to show you something."

With his mother leading, they exited the house and made a beeline for the tents. Now J.T. could see they were probably army surplus tents. His mother stopped at the main tent. The entry flap was drawn and tied. Inside, J.T. could see last night's fire had already been resurrected, once again smoke drifted up through the central portal.

Ducking his head, he entered, following his mother. It was spacious inside and looked like it could easily seat twenty-to-thirty people around a central firepit. Even though it was still early, with no circulating air, it was stuffy inside and the canvas reeked of oil, body odor and the pitchy aroma of burning pinewood.

It took a minute for J.T.'s eyes to accommodate, after which he could make out the slim silhouette of Smokey Grayman. Sitting cross-legged, he was working on a series of complex pictures, a total of ten, positioned roughly in a circle around the central firepit.

"These are sand paintings," his mother explained, and indeed the pictures were constructed from different shades of sand. "Samuel, why don't you tell J.T. what they signify."

Grinning, and exposing his missing teeth, Smokey motioned for J.T. to come closer. Gesturing at the appropriate painting as he told the story, Smokey explained how the Holy People resolved the problem caused by the troublesome remains of death. In sequence, the elaborate paintings showed how the Hero Twins, in their quest to rid the Dinetah (the Navajo) of its fiends, had decided Old Man Death must be spared. And hence, that's how we got the complete circle of life, from birth to death.

After finishing with his explanation, Smokey once again resumed working on the last painting in the creation series.

"It's beautiful," J.T. exclaimed after they'd exited the tent. And it was.

"Yes," his mother agreed. "Samuel does an exceptionally good job."

"So does this go on all day?" J.T. asked, trying hard not to be negative, but he really didn't want his friends to see this.

"Yes, but today, it's mainly chants and more sand painting," his mother explained as they walked toward the house. "You don't have to attend that, but I would like to have both you and Mary here for the finale, the sunrise ceremony in the morning. It's very beautiful."

"Okay," J.T. agreed. He kissed his mother's blackened cheek, then as he turned away, he covertly tried to wipe the black smudge from his lips.

Almost by habit, since he didn't own a wristwatch, J.T. glanced up at the sun. It appeared to be ready to crest over the lofty spires of Zion National Park. It was still early, but he had chores to do and weeds to hoe. Since he didn't have to be to the sheriff's office until 3:00 p.m., he could still get a lot done. Sighing, he grabbed the stainless-steel pail from the service room, then started across the already warm asphalt of Highway 91. He might just as well get started early; it looked like it was going to be another blistering day.

By one-thirty, J.T. had finished two more rows of cantaloupes. He hid his hoe in the ditch bank weeds, then hopped on the tractor and headed for the house. In spite of the oppressive heat of early July, there was still chanting coming from the big tent, but none of the Sing's participants were visible. They all must be in that tent, that oven-of-a-tent!

Taking care not to interrupt, he circled around the tents and hurried into the house through the service door. Inside the house, it was not exactly cool either. Quickly, he took a bath, using only cold water, put on clean clothes and went to find Mary. She was in her bedroom with a book in hand.

"What are you reading?"

"A library book," Mary replied, looking up and setting the book face down on the bed.

"Which one?"

"A Home Medical Advisor, if you must know, though it's none of your business."

"Oh," J.T. ignored her frosty attitude and picked up the book. It was opened to a chapter titled, Oncology for the Layman.

"What's oncology?" he asked, though he thought he already knew.

"I thought you knew everything."

"Geez, Mary, I'm just asking."

"It's the study of cancer."

"You learn anything new?"

"No," Mary snapped, then as J.T. frowned and sighed deeply, she seemed to lose her attitude. "Yes," she added.

"What?"

Biting her lip, she glanced at J.T., like she was debating whether to tell him or not. Finally, she exhaled loudly and cleared her throat. "Well, in general, cancer is very bad and usually is not curable, not unless you catch it early. And some kinds are better than others."

"Do you think Mother's is early?"

"I don't know for sure, but it seems like it's been going on for a long time."

"Is hers the good kind?"

"I don't know what kind she has," Mary admitted. "It's all been so hush-hush."

"I think it's something to do with the female organs," J.T. said, trying hard not to blush, but he need not have worried, Mary didn't look up.

"That still doesn't tell me very much," Mary picked up the book again. "There's more than one female organ, you know."

Actually, he did not know. "She's going to get a priesthood blessing tomorrow," J.T. volunteered, "and then she's going to Salt Lake City to see a specialist."

"I know, but there may not be much they can do."

"Maybe not with medicine, but a lot of people are cured by the power of the priesthood," J.T. insisted. "You've just got to have enough faith."

"Yeah, I guess," Mary mumbled, but sounded less than convinced.

"Faith can move mountains."

"Sure, it can," Mary said sarcastically. "I don't know which idiot said that, but I've never seen faith even move an anthill."

"I think Jesus said it."

"Oh," Mary shrugged, then sounding a little more hopeful, added, "and there's Smokey's Sing, as well."

"Yeah, whatever that's worth."

"You never know," Mary countered, "it might help."

They fell silent for a few moments, each immersed in their own thoughts.

"Is—is," J.T. blurted, wiping moisture from his eyes, "is she going to die?"

17

"I don't know," Mary also dabbed a tear from her eye. "I don't have a crystal ball."

"If she does die, what's going to happen to us?" J.T. asked, finally putting voice to his fears.

"I don't know," Mary shook her head, "I can't think about that right now."

Again, they both fell silent, pondering what they couldn't verbalize.

"You ready to go?" J.T. finally asked, his voice husky.

"Yeah," Mary seemed happy for the change of subject, "let me grab my purse."

"We've have to pick up Mickey on the way."

"Okay," Mary readily agreed, as she started pulling out drawers, searching for her handbag. "He's kind of cute, anyway."

"Geez, Mary, he's my age."

"I know. And that's too bad."

After fifteen minutes of frantic searching, Mary finally located her purse. Last night after the movie, she'd left it in the Plymouth.

They were already late, 3:05 p.m., when J.T. and Mary climbed into the old car for the five-mile trip to St. George. Inside, it was a Finnish sauna, minus the steam. From past experience, J.T. knew not to touch anything metal. Using the tail of his T-shirt, he grabbed the handle and rolled down the window. Mary did likewise, but using a handkerchief. By choking the carburetor, while simultaneously pumping the gas feed and praying, Mary finally got the Plymouth started. Then, again using her handkerchief as protection from the hot metal, she pulled down on the column gearshift, grinding the transmission into first gear. At last, they were ready to go.

After backing the Plymouth out of the driveway, and nearly getting side-swiped by a California tourist with a blaring horn, Mary released the clutch and they bucked down Highway 91 toward Mickey's house. With the windows wide open, they caught a breeze, but all that did was exchange one-hundred-and-fifty-degree inside air for the one hundred and eight-degree outside air. But even that small benefit ceased as Mary braked to a stop in front of the Graff house.

"Hi," Mickey said cheerfully as he slid into the back seat, then added, "you're late."

"Mary," J.T. explained, "couldn't find her purse,"

"The sheriff's going to be mad."

"Too bad," Mary said, while giving Mickey an appraising glance in the rear-view mirror,
"I'm sure the sheriff wouldn't want me to drive without my license."

"What's going on over at your house?" Mickey asked.

"Oh, nothing," J.T. answered vaguely.

"It looks like a Boy Scout Jamboree."

"It's just Smokey Grayman and his clan," Mary said. As she pulled away from Mickey's house, the Plymouth lurched forward, killing the engine. Obviously, she'd forgotten to downshift to first gear. Working hard, she finally coaxed the old car back to life.

"I thought," Mickey continued, "that he's a relative of your mother's."

"He is," Mary replied, as she ground the gears and got the car and the hot air moving again.

"So, what's he doin' over there?"

"Some kind of healing thing for our mother," J.T. mumbled, while wishing Mary had kept her mouth shut.

"Cool. Can I watch?"

"Uh," J.T. tried to change the subject, "uh, you still got your radiation badge?"

"Remember, I never took one."

"Oh, yeah, well anyway there's a town meeting on Monday. You ought to go."

"Why? I don't like those things."

"Father said he might bring up the Borch Rosenkranz problem to the group."

"Oh, yeah? Well, I would like to see that. See what the town's going to do about that commie spy."

"Spy?" Mary arched an eyebrow and glanced at Mickey through the rear-view mirror.

"Yeah," Mickey declared, "he's definitely a Russkie spy."

"We don't know that for sure," J.T. quickly added.

Mary glanced over at J.T. "Well, he certainly is a strange one."

"So," J.T. replied, "strange doesn't necessarily add up to a spy. Look at Weird Willie."

"Have they found him yet?" Mary asked.

"No!" J.T. said sharply. He didn't want to talk about that either.

After a moment of silence, Mickey returned to the original subject. "So, how does Smokey heal someone?"

Inwardly, J.T. groaned, but remained silent.

"He has an elaborate ceremony designed to court the favor of the Great Spirit," Mary explained, "then he gives Mother something to drink that drives the illness from her."

Frowning, J.T. muttered, "it's pretty much smoke and mirrors."

"Doesn't sound a whole lot different from our healing ceremony," Mickey observed, "except Smokey actually gives some medicine, rather than just rubbing oil on the top of the head and the laying-on-of-hands."

J.T. wanted to dispute this by saying, 'the big difference is one is done using the power of God's own priesthood', but he decided to say nothing.

By then, they had covered the five miles to St. George and Mary pulled in behind the J.C. Penny building. The Washington County Sheriff's Department was just around the corner.

After parking and depositing the key in her purse, Mary announced she was going window-shopping at Penny's and would see them back here in an hour. The boys watched her disappear around the corner, swinging her imitation, patent leather purse in time with her hips. Sighing deeply, probably for different reasons, J.T. and Mickey turned and headed for the sheriff's office.

The Washington County Sheriff's Office, which also doubled as the county jail, was located one block north of Highway 91, and just off Main Street. Constructed of grouted and rebar-reinforced cement block, the exterior was stuccoed a lime green. The passing years, along with the rain, wind and frost had weathered the once bright green walls to a faded, almost seedy turquoise.

The general floor plan was a standard rectangle, but was further sectioned into four smaller rooms. The front central space was set aside for reception, booking and the business office. To the right of the reception desk was a partially partitioned room for fingerprinting and photography, and to the left of the big desk was a modest office for Sheriff Evan Meecham. To the rear, and directly behind these three rooms, were three holding cells, sporting intimidating floor-to-ceiling steel bars.

Today, manning the reception desk was a remarkably pox-scarred officer, Deputy Blaine Fowler. An aggressive case of childhood chicken pox had scarred his face to a perpetual scowl, but somewhat belying his fearsome appearance, he seemed friendly enough and addressed the boys with respect. After explaining their business, the deputy instructed them to have a seat while he checked to see if the sheriff was available. A few minutes later, he returned and escorted them into Sherriff Meecham's cramped office.

With absolutely no frills, Meecham's office contained just the bare essentials. The furniture consisted of a scarred white pine desk fronted by a couple of equally beat-up chairs. Behind the desk and attached to the wall was a cluttered, cork bulletin board and above that the seemingly ubiquitous picture of Governor J. Bracken Lee. Off to the left of the desk was a four-by-four, west-facing window, the only one in the room. It was partially shaded by a chord-draw, Venetian blind, presently half-drawn. It appeared to be damaged, as it hung askew at a thirty-degree angle. Unfortunately, this defect allowed the hot afternoon sun to blaze in.

Seemingly a reflection of its owner, the sheriff's desk was remarkably untidy. Strewn with old candy bar wrappers, scattered manila folders, unopened stacks of mail and assorted flyers, the actual desktop was not visible. In the center of this landfill, sat an empty bottle of Coke and a half-eaten bologna sandwich, lying exposed and drying on a square piece of wax paper. The room smelled of mustard, mayonnaise and day-old, possibly-decomposing, lunch meat.

"Come in boys," Sheriff Meecham motioned them in with a beefy hand, then growled, "you're late! When I say three o'clock, I mean three o'clock." He pointed to the two high-back chairs in front of his desk, now partially spotlighted by the afternoon sunrays that had managed to slip past the malfunctioning Venetian blind. "Have a seat."

While the boys played musical chairs, the sheriff snatched up the bologna sandwich, taking a bite, his teeth leaving an almost perfect semicircle in the crusty bread. "When it gets dry enough," he said with a full mouth, "it's just like being toasted." Dropping the sandwich back on the wax paper, his attitude seemed to soften a bit. "What a night, huh? Haven't even had time for lunch." A distracting smudge of yellow mustard appeared on the corner of his lips. "Anyways, you boys get any sleep?"

Mickey nodded, yes, while J.T. shook his head, no.

"Me neither," the sheriff admitted.

"Have you found Willie yet?" Mickey blurted.

Once again J.T. was amazed by Mickey's brashness. Nobody, it seems, intimidated him. J.T. would never have dared question the sheriff like that. Anyway, it was curious that Mickey was so interested in whether or not they'd found Willie.

Oh, come on, J.T. silently chided himself, I'm interested in that too, so don't go jumping to conclusions. For now, he decided, he would continue to give Mickey the benefit of the doubt.

The sheriff looked up sharply at Mickey before answering. "No, but we're still looking. It's just a matter of time."

"What about Lenny?" Mickey asked, raising an arm to shield his eyes from the sunlight streaming through the mangled blind.

"What about Lenny?" Sheriff Meecham asked. "Why don't you tell me?"

"I mean, didn't he—uh—did the examination of his body give you any clues?"

"Such as?" The sheriff picked up the Coke bottle, put it to his lips before realizing it was empty, then set it down again. "Damn, it's hot in here," he muttered to no one in particular.

"Such as how he died," Mickey continued, "and anything he might've had on him."

"Like what?"

"You know, like any evidence."

"Awh, hah! So, you did search the body last night," the sheriff said, his eyes narrowing. "I suppose you're talkin' about the bullet?"

"Yeah," Mickey mumbled, "I guess so."

"Well, it's obvious, ain't it? A bullet like that can't be traced, 'cept maybe for partial fingerprints. The only purpose for them bullets is some kind of illegal activity. You take anything from the body?"

"No, sir."

"You sure?"

Mickey nodded his head. "Yes."

"Yes, you did, or yes you didn't?"

"Yes, I didn't."

"Okay. Well, speaking of fingerprints," Meecham continued, "we'll need to git a set from you two today.

"Why's that?" Mickey asked.

"So, we can see if anyone other than you two handled the bullet."

Quickly, J.T. tried to change the subject from fingerprints. "Do you think the poaching on Utah Hill had anything to do with Lenny's death?"

"I didn't say nothin' about no poaching."

"D—did Lenny drown?" Mickey blurted, now leaning far to his left side to avoid the constantly shifting sun.

Sheriff Meecham eyed both boys for a moment. "That's classified information, but I can tell you this much," he paused and eyed the boys for another long moment, then continued, "as you know, Doc Hilton is our county coroner."

Actually, J.T. didn't know that and wasn't even sure what a coroner was, but he kept his mouth shut.

"Well, anyways, he's already done a preliminary examination of the body with a full autopsy to follow, but it appears Lenny was strangled, probably with a rope. There wus rope burns around his neck and there appeared to be very little water in his lungs."

"So," Mickey added, "that means he was killed nearby and the body dumped into the pond."

"Or," J.T. countered, continuing that train of thought, "he could have been killed anywhere upstream, the body dumped in the canal, then floated down to Boy's Pond."

"Yeah, anyways, that's enough of the speculatin'. What I need from you two is to write down in your own words what happened last night, then I'm goin' have you sign it. That way, it becomes an official court document." He paused and frowned. "But first, I want to ask you a few questions, just so I'm clear myself on what happened." He paused to mop accumulated perspiration from his forehead with an already soiled handkerchief. "First of all, why was you two alone? What happened to Hafe?"

"He went home." Mickey shrugged, now slouching low so the pesky beam of light struck his forehead, not his eyes. "Said he had pressin' business."

"What pressin' business?"

"He didn't say."

"That so," Meecham scratched his stubbled chin and locked eyes, first with J.T., then with Mickey. "So, until you found him dead last night, you two had not had any recent or direct contact with Mister Lenny Weeks, is that correct?"

"No," Mickey shook his head, "that's not correct. We saw Lenny the night of town bell. He was arguing with Willie. We already told you that."

"Oh, yeah, and nothin' else?"

J.T. thought the sheriff's eyes would bore right through him. "Uh—uh— there was one other time." He glanced over at Mickey, but his face was solid marble. "We kinda had a run in with Lenny and Willie a few days ago."

"Oh, yeah, what kind of a run in?"

"Uh—I guess kinda like a fist fight," J.T. mumbled. Under the chair, Mickey kicked his shin. He kicked back but missed.

"You did, huh?" The sheriff nodded. "Well, now, that's very interestin'. Where wus these fisticuffs?"

"Huh?" J.T. said blankly.

"Fisticuffs, the fist fight. Where did it happen?"

"Oh, in Santa Clara," J.T. replied, as Mickey kicked him again, "right by the highway."

"So, who won the fight?"

"Huh?"

"The fight," the sheriff said. "In fights there's generally winners and losers."

"Uh—uh, I guess they did."

"They?" Meecham asked. "Who's they?"

"Lenny and Willie."

"Oh, yeah. So, I guess you could say," the sheriff concluded, "there wus bad blood between you two and Willie and Lenny."

Abruptly rejoining the conversation, Mickey snarled, "Willie was a skunk and Lenny was no better."

"Be that as it may," the sheriff said, then deliberately meted out his words. "So, wus you two plannin' some kind of revenge?"

"No, sir!" J.T. blurted.

Mickey shrugged. "I wouldn't have minded if we did, but we didn't."

Ignoring Mickey's answer, Meecham continued to press. "So, is that what this wus all about, revenge?"

"Maybe for Willie, but not for—" J.T. stopped in mid-sentence as Mickey kicked him again, harder. "Uh—no, sir, we—uh—had already forgotten about that."

The sheriff glared at them for a moment. "Are you sure now? I don't want no lies."

"Yes, sir!" J.T. gulped, looking down at the floor.

"How about you, Graff?" The sheriff glanced sharply at Mickey. "I want to heer your answer too."

"No, Sheriff," Mickey replied without blinking. "We had nothin' planned, no revenge. Lenny's death was nothin' to do with us."

Grunting, the sheriff got up and shuffled around back of his desk, then grabbed a note pinned to the bulletin board. "That so? So, then, why don't you tell me about them English stocks?"

J.T. was stunned! Quickly, he glanced over at Mickey. He looked just as surprised. How had the sheriff found out about that? There was no way. Nobody knew about the fort, much less about the stocks. J.T. could think of nothing more to say, so he said nothing. In retrospect, maybe he should've done that sooner.

"So let me see if I've got this straight." The note in hand, Meecham circled back to the front of his desk. Rather than sitting, he loomed over the boys. "So, you two lost a fist-fight with Willie and Lenny and for revenge you locked Willie up in them stocks of yours. And, as it turns out, that was the last time anyone saw Willie. Then, you two just happened to find Lenny's body in Boys Pond. Have I left anythin' out?"

"Uh—well, I guess not," J.T. muttered, shrinking further back into his chair. "You make it sound worse than it—"

"Yeah, well," the sheriff interrupted, "I just think it's quite an interestin' string of coincidences." The sheriff paused, locking eyes with the boys, then added, "don't you?"

"But—but," J.T. stammered, "that's not the way it happened."

"In my business," Sheriff Meecham continued, shaking his head, "it don't pay to believe in coincidences. Can't afford to." Again, he paused for long moment. "Let me give you boys another possible version of what happened."

The boys were silent.

"We've already established you two had a grudge agin Lenny and Willie cause they kicked the crap out of you. So, you two lured Willie into them stocks and then when Lenny came lookin' for him, you jumped him too and killed him. Maybe, you didn't even mean to; just give him a good beatin' and it got outta hand. Of course, Willie saw the whole thing, so now you had to get rid of him too, so there wouldn't be no witnesses."

"No, sir!" J.T. blurted, standing to face Meecham. "That's not what happened."

Remaining seated, Mickey calmly asked, "so, how did you find out about the stocks?"

"That's not important right now," the sheriff said, then hesitated. "Actually, it might be helpful. Maybe, you two could tell me who it wus? I might need him for a witness."

"Huh?" J.T. had no idea what the sheriff was talking about.

"Actually, I don't know who it wus myself," the sheriff continued. "It was an anonymous phone call," he held up the note from the bulletin board, "that came it at eight-fifteen this morning. It sounded like an older man with a strong foreign accent—maybe German or even Russian. I'm not very good with accents."

"That would be Bor—" J.T. never finished his sentence as Mickey kicked him again, even harder.

"What was that?" Meecham asked. "I didn't heer you."

"Uh—that's—uh—that could be almost anyone in Santa Clara." J.T. hurriedly amended his reply. "Most of the old timers have accents."

"I see," Sheriff Meecham looked skeptical, "I have a half-a-mind to lock you two up right now. And if I find you bin lyin' to me, you can bet, I'll do just that."

"A—are we suspects?" J.T. stammered.

"Whadda you think?" Sheriff Meecham replied without smiling. "I'd say right now you two are not only suspects, but you're my only suspects."

For a couple seconds, he glared at the boys, then returned to his desk, sitting back down, and rummaging through the top drawer. At last, he produced two sheets of paper, sporting the county's letterhead. Passing them to the boys along with two ballpoint pens, he added, "follow me." Grunting with exertion, he stood up again and headed for the door.

The sheriff made a beeline to the other side of the building, then immediately separated them. For Mickey, he found a space to write at the fingerprinting desk and for J.T., in the photography bay. He instructed them there would be absolutely no collusion, then further clarified that directive by adding, "you are to write your statement down with absolutely no talking to each other. Deputy Fowler," he gestured in his direction, "will keep an eye on you two just to make sure."

After the boys settled in at their assigned stations, he continued, "anyways, when you're finished, sign the papers, and give 'em to Deputy Fowler, then before you leave the deputy will fingerprint you two."

Meecham shook his head one last time, possibly in disgust, then waddled off. Abruptly, he turned back around and added, "oh, and I've finally got them fingerprints back from that catsup bottle; you know, the ones from that dummy fiasco."

"So?" Mickey challenged.

"So, now we can compare."

Gulping, J.T. said nothing, looking down at his shoes. Ever defiant, Mickey stared back at Sherriff Meecham.

"You two just keep gettin' in deeper and deeper." Meecham shook his head one more time, then turned away and was gone.

For a few seconds, the boys sat in stunned silence, then bowed their heads and began writing.

As with their school assignments, J.T. finished first, handing his paper to Deputy Fowler. While Mickey labored to finish, Fowler fingerprinted J.T.

First, he had J.T. clean each finger with rubbing alcohol. Next, he inked each finger by pressing them on an India ink pad. Lastly, he carefully rolled each finger on a white cardboard blotter. By the time he was done with J.T., Mickey had finished with his statement. As J.T. used a towel to clean the ink from his fingers, Fowler prepared to work on Mickey.

"D—do you think the Sheriff's really going to throw us in jail?" J.T. asked Fowler as he searched for another blotting card.

"Nah," Fowler shook his head, "he was blowin' smoke up your as—uh—uh, up your skirt. You two are still juveniles. If you are arrested, you won't even come here. You'll go straight to juvenile detention."

That revelation didn't make J.T. feel any better. "What about the results from the fingerprints? W—will you know about them today?"

"Nah," Fowler again shook his head, "we don't process 'em here. All fingerprints are sent to the database in Salt Lake City for matching and cataloging. All that takes a while."

"How long's a while?"

"I don't know—probably at least a week, maybe two."

"A—are," J.T.'s voice quivered, "are we really suspects?"

Mickey laughed derisively. "The sheriff was blowin' smoke on that one too, and it wasn't up our skirts."

"Well, I don't know about that," Deputy Fowler countered, as he rolled Mickey's inked thumb on the white card. "The best I can tell you two really are suspects. And unfortunately, like the sheriff said, right now you are our only suspects."

"So then, why don't he arrest us right now?" Mickey demanded, while Fowler worked on his index finger.

"Well," Fowler progressed from Mickey's index to middle finger, "to win any murder case in court, you have to show three things: motive, means and opportunity. You boys have two out of the three, motive and opportunity."

"So?" Mickey asked.

"So, if the sheriff could solve the third one, the means, you two would probably be in detention right now."

"Means?" J.T. asked. "What does that mean?"

"Means," Fowler replied, "means, uh—you know, how you did it. Not only that you did it, but you had the means to do it."

"I still don't get it," Mickey said.

"Well," Fowler continued, "if a man was murdered by gunshot, and you were a suspect, they'd have to prove you had access to a gun and even better 'thee gun'."

"Instead of us, what about them poachers?" Mickey added. "If it were me, I'd be looking into that."

"We are looking into that," Deputy Fowler replied. He'd finally finished the fingerprinting and returned the ink pad back to the drawer. "But so far that's been a dead end."

J.T. swallowed hard. Geez, how had they gotten themselves into such a mess? All they did was pull a simple prank on a most-deserving Weird Willie Wittwer. Yes, admittedly it was revenge, but it was justifiable revenge and was only meant as payback. No one was supposed to get hurt.

"Okay, we're done," Deputy Fowler handed Mickey a towel to wipe the ink from his fingers. "Now, I suppose you two can go."

Breathing a sigh of relief, J.T. and an ever-defiant Mickey walked out of the front door. J.T. was more than happy to get out of there. He couldn't help but wonder if this was how it would feel, getting out of jail after serving a long sentence; walking free after a few months, or a few years. Maybe, he'd know pretty soon.

Rounding the corner of the building, they saw Mary, waiting for them in the swath of shade provided by the north side of the J.C. Penny building. She looked annoyed as she glanced down at her fake Lady Hamilton wristwatch. However, before they rejoined Mary, Mickey grabbed J.T.'s arm and stopped him.

"So, it was probably old Borch Rosenkranz who turned us in."

"Yeah, I guess so," J.T. agreed, while keeping an anxious eye on his sister.

"How'd he know about the stocks?"

"I don't know," J.T. replied, then added, "somehow, he must have followed us. There's no other way."

"You mean the day we built them?"

"Come on, you two!" Mary shouted. "It's hot and I'm tired."

"Yeah, remember he chased us off his property," J.T. said, then looking troubled, added, "but to follow us all the way to the fort, well—well that's kind of spooky. It's almost like he was spying on us."

Mickey shrugged. "That's what spies do."

"But why?" J.T. asked. "I'm sure Moscow doesn't care what we're doing."

"I don't know why," Mickey replied as they continued walking toward Mary and the car, "but I do know who. It had to be Borch Rosenkranz who ratted on us."

When everyone was back in the Plymouth, Mary headed toward Santa Clara. After letting Mickey off, Mary ground the Plymouth back into gear and continued to their home. As she pulled into the driveway, J.T. noted with some chagrin Smokey's clan was still there. Of course, he knew they would be, but one could always hope. At the moment, however, there was no chanting or beating of the drums. Instead, the clan was milling about in the backyard, talking, and probably getting ready to prepare dinner.

Staying well clear of the whole affair, J.T. went directly to the service room, collected his milk pail and egg basket, then headed across the highway for the corrals. It was still a little early, but believe it or not, he'd rather do evening chores than mingle with the clan.

Though he tried to stretch it out as long as he could, he eventually did finish his chores and had to go on back. Just as he was placing the strained milk in the fridge, Mary grabbed the Mason jar.

"They need this out back."

"Okay," J.T. shrugged, "what's for dinner?"

"Mutton stew, fry bread and fire roasted corn on the cob."

Looking around the kitchen, J.T. saw no mess, no pots or pans on the stove top and smelled no aroma of boiling corn or mutton stew.

"Don't look so blank, J.T.," Mary said, heading back out the door. "I'm not fixing dinner. We're eating outside with Smokey and the clan."

Inwardly, J.T. groaned, but said nothing. You'd think Mary would be capable of fixing at least one meal.

“Anyway,” Mary continued, “Mother wants us to come and see some of the ceremony and meet our relatives.”

“Why? We’ll never see them again.”

“Of course, we will.”

“Not if Father has his way.”

“Don’t be such a grouch. Surely, you can do that much for Mother.”

Trying to will himself into a better mood, J.T. deposited the eggs in the fridge, then went to wash up. Mary was right, of course, it wouldn’t kill him to do something nice for his mother. Sighing, he dried his hands and headed out the door.

J.T. had to admit, though somewhat grudgingly, the meal wasn’t half-bad and his Navajo cousins were pleasant enough. Talking to a fourteen-year-old boy and a fifteen-year-old girl, he realized they weren’t a whole lot different from other teenagers he knew. Like all of his Caucasian friends, they too worried about school, grades, overbearing parents and of course the opposite sex.

After conversing with them for a few minutes, J.T. wandered over to the big tent. Smokey was busy putting the final touches or re-touches on the last scene of his series of sand paintings, but when he saw J.T. he motioned him in. With a flair for the dramatic, Smokey mixed some coarse red sand with some powdery white sand, then deftly poured it into the painting. Satisfied, he looked up and grinned. The obvious gaps in his picket fence smile still annoyed J.T.

“You seem troubled, little shił naa’aash,” Smokey said, sitting cross-legged in front of the mostly finished sand painting depicting the Hero Twins.

“Nah, it’s nothing,” J.T. shrugged. “I’ve just got a lot on my mind.”

“It shows. Your hozro has vanished.”

“It—it’s just that I’m worried about Mother and—and I’ve kinda gotten myself into a mess.”

“No one can say about your mother, but whatever happens she will return to hozro, walk in the way of beauty, either in this life or the next. As for your other problems, you also need to find your way back to harmony with man, with nature, and the universe.”

“It’s not nature or the universe,” J.T. sighed, “that’s the problem.”

“So, little brother,” Smokey said, looking up from the painting, “why don’t you tell me about it.”

“Well, it’s more like with my father and—uh—the law.”

“Nothing is gained from butting heads with biligaana laws. Believe you me, my people know. Man’s laws change with time, only the laws of the Great Spirit always remain the same. There is some good in man’s laws. But regardless of good or bad laws, truth and harmony are always the same, that’s the blessing way.”

For a moment, J.T. continued to sit there and watch Smokey's deft brown hands pour more multicolored sand, blending and smoothing it into a picture. It was nothing short of amazing. With no canvas, no paint and no brush, the Hero Twins magically appeared.

Would he ever be at peace, like Smokey seemed to be? Certainly, Smokey didn't pretend he was something that he wasn't. He was just as comfortable smoking a cigarette under a cedar tree as he was sitting in a Mormon pew singing hymns, or squatting in an old army tent reproducing an ancient sand painting of his ancestors. Smokey was just plain old Smokey, take it or leave it.

"Well," J.T. finally sighed, "tomorrow, I'll work on getting things back in harmony, but tonight I'm going to bed."

"Life is a hard journey, my little shił naa'aash, especially when you go it alone," Smokey stood up, stretched, then lit a cigarette. "If you need my help, I'm always here for you. I am your soaring hawk; I've been assigned to this for life." He paused, the cigarette dangling from his lips, as he searched for another pouch of colored sand. "We finish the ceremony tomorrow at sunrise, I know your mother would like you to be here."

"Okay," J.T. nodded.

"Go get some sleep, little cousin." Smokey smiled through his picket-fence. "Even the mighty hunter must at times rest."

After the short and most unsettled sleep of the previous night, J.T. slept deep and well. If he dreamed, he did not recall. It was early, about four-thirty, when his mother shook him. Her face was still covered with black soot, but this time it did not seem so alarming.

"Come, Jackie," she whispered excitedly. "You'll want to see this, the finale, the end of the blessing way."

Still rubbing sleep from his eyes, J.T. rolled out of bed, pulled on yesterday's clothes, then stumbled out of the house.

In the predawn darkness, a bonfire was blazing in roughly the center of the circle of tents. Clan and family members, including Mary, had already gathered. After depositing J.T. at the fire next to Mary, Mrs. Kunz disappeared inside the main tent with Smokey.

An old Navajo man with leathery brown skin and braided gray hair explained to J.T. and Mary what would happen next. "In the tent," he pointed, "your mother will wash the soot off her face, indicating her return to hozro. Together, with Smokey chanting a sacred prayer, they will march out of the tent. Your mother will drink from the sacred pot, a bitter emetic. Then just at sunrise, she will vomit up the last traces of her ghost-sickness, signaling her complete return to the beauty way."

To J.T., it all sounded pretty simple, but also seemed just a little weird, particularly the vomiting part.

Almost the second the old man finished his commentary, the chanting began. Dressed in traditional deer leathers, Smokey appeared at the entrance of the tent holding a small clay pot in his right hand and two prayer sticks, intricately carved and adorned with colored feathers, in his left hand.

Following closely on Smokey's heels, Anita Kunz also exited the tent, now all traces of soot washed from her face.

Holding the feathered pathos high, Smokey solemnly crossed their shafts, all the while continuing to chant and dance.

The first few lines of the prayer, the old Navajo man interpreted for J.T. and Mary.

"Now our daughter will drink this brew,

"Now our daughter, being the daughter of Black God,

"Now our daughter, being the daughter of Talking God—

After a bit, the old man fell silent, obviously caught up in the drama of the moment.

Smokey continued to chant the prayer. When finished, he offered the small earthen pot to Mrs. Kunz who eagerly drank it down. Off to the east, the horizon was getting brighter, now sporting a glowing corona of bright orange, the promise of a rising sun.

Almost immediately, Mrs. Kunz looked as though she was going to heave, but struggled to hold it. It was not yet time. A hush settled over the crowd. Collectively they held their breath. The tension grew. Mrs. Kunz looked very sick.

At that moment, the corona crowned above the purple horizon and the first vanguard photons pierced the camp. Immediately, Mrs. Kunz ran out of the compound and regurgitated all her bitter ghosts!

Exhaling with happiness, the spectators enthusiastically cheered and clapped their hands.

Even J.T. had to admit, it was a very powerful moment.

Caught up in all the drama, J.T. did not hear the truck pull up, or the door slam, and apparently none of the clan had either. Instead, they were all caught up in the glory of the emerging sunrise and focused on Anita Kunz's dramatic return to hozro. The golden light of redemption now splashed down on her upturned face.

"What in thee hell," someone loudly shouted, "is going on here?"

18

It was Sunday morning and J.T. was on his way to priesthood meeting at the Mormon chapel. For a change, he was early. Not because he particularly enjoyed the priesthood meeting, it was often pretty boring, but it was a relief to get out of the house and away from all that early morning drama.

His father had arrived home just as the blessing way ceremony reached its climax. Why he arrived three or four hours early, J.T. still did not know, but needless to say he was not happy. Perhaps furious and extremely rude would be a more accurate description. Among other things, he accused Smokey of desecrating and demeaning the Lord's holy day with his pagan rituals, then continued his tirade by hitting various other theological high points. The very first commandment given to Moses on Mount Sinai was, thou shalt have no other gods before me. In the Book of Romans, it was written, vengeance is mine, saith the Lord. The Apostle James in his epistle taught us, to pray one for another that ye may be healed. And lastly, Joseph Smith wrote, the Melchizedek Priesthood is the channel through which all knowledge is revealed from heaven.

"This is more than mere sacrilege," Mr. Kunz had roared, his eyes ablaze like a tent evangelist. "You'll all be lucky if you do not suffer the wrath of the Almighty God along with his eternal retribution."

Smokey, as usual, took it all in stride and quietly went about breaking camp, taking down the tents and packing up the gear.

As expected, Mrs. Kunz was both mortified and livid. She went straight to her bedroom and locked the door. The much sought after hozro had abruptly vanished in a swirling dust devil of family discord.

J.T. and Mary didn't know what to do. Even though they'd had nothing to do with the planning or execution of Smokey's ritual, Mr. Kunz treated them as co-conspirators, guilty by association. It was a no-win position and J.T. couldn't decide whether to help Smokey take down the big tent or not. If he did, it might get them out of the backyard faster, but on the other hand his father could possibly consider that as aiding and abetting. After standing around for a few awkward and indecisive minutes, both he and Mary compromised by also fleeing to their bedrooms.

For the next couple of hours, a tense, uncomfortable silence settled over the house, and it seemed as if they'd carefully avoided each other, or at least J.T. had. This was made easier because it was Fast and Testimony Sunday and therefore there would be no family breakfast, no reason to gather.

Traditionally, on the first Sunday of every month, Mormons fast for the morning and noon meals, donating the estimated cost of those two meals to the poor. And though it was only eight o'clock, J.T.'s stomach was already complaining. He suspected there was no way he was going to make it to the evening meal. Somehow, he would have to sneak in a slice of bread or wedge of cheddar cheese.

When the clock struck 8:30 a.m., J.T. noted with some relief it was time to get ready for priesthood meeting. Unfortunately, while he was brushing his teeth and combing his hair his father walked into the bathroom.

For a few seconds neither of them said anything. Mr. Kunz turned his attention to filling the bathtub and J.T. finished combing his hair. Finally, the prickly silence got too much for J.T. and after a few seconds he blurted, "so, are the elders still coming tonight to give a priesthood blessing?"

At first, Mr. Kunz didn't reply, but eventually growled, "she needs it more now than ever."

Quickly, J.T. finished in the bathroom, leaving his father to his bath. He donned his Sunday clothes, a short-sleeve white shirt and dark slacks, then started for the front door. With his hand on the doorknob, he stopped. There was no one around. Mary and his mother were still in their respective bedrooms, and he could hear his father in the bathroom. Abruptly, changing course, he went straight to the kitchen. After locating a bread knife, he cut a thick slice, then replaced the loaf in the bread box and headed for the fridge. Looking over his shoulder one last time, he broke off and hunk of cheese, then hurried for the front door.

Once he was well away from the house, he slowed his pace. After making a sandwich of the bread and cheese, took a small bite. Of course, he knew he was breaking his fast, but he was starving. Anyway, fasting was one of God's minor commandments, not at all in the same category as having other Gods before me, or using the Lord's name in vain, or coveting your neighbor's ass, whatever that meant. J.T. just hoped the Almighty would not be too upset, but he couldn't wait. Maybe, he could make up for it by strictly obeying his other commandments. He resolved to covet nothing. Then he filled his mouth.

"Hey, John Tobler, hold up!"

Cringing, nevertheless, J.T. slowed his pace.

Quickly, he swallowed the remaining bread and cheese, then without turning around, he growled, "what do you want, Michael T?"

Behind him, he could hear Mickey break into a run, then come sliding in behind, just missing his heels. Still, he did not turn around. He knew who it was.

KA-BOOM!

There was a mini-explosion not three inches from his right shoe. Through his thin cotton socks, he felt the concussion from the little blast, then immediately, smelled the acrid odor of burning nitrates.

Trying hard to keep a neutral face, J.T. turned around to see a grinning Mickey. Reaching into his pocket, he fished out a small round sphere, a little larger than a cherry pit and lime green in color. After showing it to J.T., he flung it down onto the sidewalk.

KA-BOOM!

The little green ball exploded with a fury, belying its small size. Reflexively, J.T. jumped backward. He couldn't help it.

"Wow! What was that?"

"Cracker balls," Mickey replied with a lopsided grin.

"What do they do?"

"You just saw what they do."

"But how?"

"Well, they're like little firecrackers," Mickey picked out a red one and handed it to J.T., "'cept there's no fuse. You just throw it down on somethin' hard, like the sidewalk. Go ahead, try it."

Cradling the little red orb in his hand, J.T. eyed it, rotating it with his fingers. Satisfied there was no fuse, he raised his arm, then threw it down on the pavement.

KA-BOOM!

"Where'd you get them?"

"Same place as the cherry bombs," Mickey replied. "They're my brother's. He got them through the mail from Wyoming."

"You got another one?"

Mickey handed J.T. a jet black one. Once again, J.T. studied it. "Do you have to throw them to make them explode?"

"Whadda you mean?"

"Well, what if you stomped on them?"

"You mean like this," Mickey dropped a purple cracker ball on the pavement, then raised his foot and slammed it down.

KA-BOOM!

"Hum-m-m, that's very interesting."

"Why interestin'?"

"Oh, nothing," J.T. replied vaguely. "I just had an idea."

"Well, let's hear it," Mickey said re-pocketing the rest of the multicolored balls.

"Let me think on it some," J.T. replied, as they crossed the highway.

The boys entered the church house through the back door, then headed straight to their priesthood meeting classroom.

In the Mormon Church there are two tiers of priesthood. The Melchizedek is the higher priesthood, the Aaronic the lower. Within the Aaronic Priesthood, there are three more layers or subdivisions: deacon, teacher, and priest. Mickey and J.T. were still deacons but were soon due to graduate to the rank of teacher.

Today, the topic for class discussion was the restoration of the Aaronic Priesthood in the latter days by Joseph Smith. According to Mormon doctrine, due to iniquity and mismanagement during the early Christian era, the priesthood had been lost. God had simply taken it back; eventually to restore it under the auspices of Joseph Smith.

About halfway through priesthood meeting, J.T. leaned over and whispered to Mickey, "I think I've got it."

"Got what?"

"I have an idea for the cracker—"

"Brother Kunz!" the instructor barked, suddenly looming over him. "Brother Kunz, maybe you could answer that last question?"

Of course, J.T. had not heard the question, but nevertheless guessed at the answer. "John the Baptist came back as an angel."

"Humpf," the teacher snorted, then added, "there will be no talking during the lesson," then proceeded on with a full description of Joseph Smith's encounter with the angel, John the Baptist.

J.T. tried to listen but he'd heard it all before. Instead, his mind wandered back to the cracker balls. Slowly a plan began to evolve and firmly gel in his mind.

After a closing prayer, the priesthood class filed out into the foyer.

"So, what about the cracker balls?" Mickey asked.

"Come on," J.T. whispered, grabbing Mickey by the elbow, "we've got to hurry. Sunday School starts in fifteen minutes."

The commencement, or opening exercises, of Sunday school, directly followed priesthood meeting and consisted of an opening prayer, a couple of hymns and two five-minute inspirational talks. After the opening exercises, which were held in the main chapel, the congregation then separated for individual classroom instruction. The classes were organized by age, from toddler to senior citizen. Each class was provided a lesson manual, a teacher and was assigned a specific topic of study for the year, i.e., the New Testament, the Old Testament, church history, church doctrine, Pearl of Great Price, Book of Mormon, etc.

This year the sixty-five-and-older group were assigned to study church history from its inception with Joseph Smith's Sacred Grove vision to the present. Considering their age, often suffering with sore muscles and arthritic joints, the seniors had naturally been assigned the classroom with the softest seats, Classroom # 1. Here, the concrete floor was not topped with Linoleum, but with a soft pile carpet, and the chairs were not the standard hardback or metal folding chairs. No, instead these seats were constructed of hardwood but with permanently attached thick cushions and padded backrests. When not in use, the seats sprang up, like theater or stadium seats, but when sat on they dropped down to horizontal, coming to rest on a sturdy metal platform.

Eschewing Sunday School's opening exercises, J.T. and Mickey hid outside the building until they could hear the organ music and singing begin, then slipped back inside, heading straight for Classroom # 1. At the moment, the halls and classrooms were quiet, devoid of foot traffic. The only sounds were coming through and around the closed door of the chapel as the organ played and congregation fervently sang the words of the opening hymn, Onward Christian Soldiers.

After checking up and down the hall one last time, the boys entered the classroom. A quick survey confirmed the room also was empty, after which the boys closed the door and immediately went to work. On each of the metal support pedestals, directly under the now levered-up seats, they placed two cracker balls. They were positioned just right, so when sat on, the seat would slam down and crush the tiny bombs.

At Mickey's suggestion, they divided the room down the middle aisle. J.T. took all the right-hand seats; Mickey took the left. Working fast, but carefully, they placed a total of forty-two cracker balls on the seat platforms. When finished, they backed off and surveyed their work with a critical eye. Unless you knew they were there, the little cracker balls were barely noticeable. Satisfied, they quietly exited the classroom.

Back in the foyer, they milled about, nervously waiting for the opening exercises to end.

"Do you think it will work?" Mickey asked as he examined a glass display case attached to the wall and warehousing the ward's many trophies. It contained assorted trophies, cups, and plaques, which had been awarded to their ward for winning church league, or district, competitions in basketball and softball or the annual roadshow contest.

"Yeah, of course," J.T. nodded, joining him at the trophy case. "No way it won't."

"Then this should qualify as an original prank and count towards beatin' Judd and Howie."

"Nobody could argue otherwise," J.T. agreed with a wry smile, but he was already having second thoughts. This insidious flareup of remorse happened every time they pulled a prank. Not only did his conscience seem to come out of hiding, but it ratcheted up a level. Seriously though, what could happen? Could anyone be hurt? Not with these little cracker balls. Their bark was a heck-of-a-lot bigger than their bite. Would anyone find them out? No, not if they were careful. Would they get into big trouble again? No, probably everyone would just get a good laugh. So, why worry? No reason to, but he couldn't help it.

Mickey asked, "so, how many will this make?"

"Huh?" J.T. had been lost in his own thoughts.

"How many pranks will that make for the summer?

"Well," J.T. verbally did the math. "There were the school cherry bombs, that's one. The mannequins, that's two. Then. this will be three."

"You forgot about Weird Willie and the stocks. This will be four, just one short of tyin' the record."

J.T. scowled. "I don't know about counting the stocks." Somehow that didn't seem right.

"Why not? It was good enough. Better'n some of Judd and Howie's."

"I don't know," J.T. shook his head, "what if something bad has happened to Willie? Then it wouldn't be much of a prank anymore."

"If somethin' happened, it wouldn't be our fault."

Still frowning, J.T. shook his head no.

As usual, Mickey persisted, "well, I think we should count it."

"Well, I don't," J.T. stood his ground, "not till we find out what happened to Willie."

Again, he eyed Mickey closely, looking for signs of self-incrimination, but saw nothing but stubbornness. In his mind, he still hadn't totally cleared Mickey of any wrongdoing with Willie. But regardless, there was simply no way they could count the English stocks—at least not yet.

"Well, then," Mickey said, finally backing off, "let's just leave it open for now. See how everythin' works out."

At that moment, the doors opened, and a flood of people streamed out of the chapel and into the foyer. For a few minutes, it was a swarming, confusing melee. They bunched and churned like penned up bucking stock at the rodeo, then slowly began to separate and disperse; each age group making its way toward their respective classrooms. Dressed in Sunday best, dark suits and ties for the men and ankle-length, long-sleeved summer dresses for the ladies, the seniors hobbled, some using canes, toward Classroom # 1.

Obviously, J.T. and Mickey did not immediately go to their assigned classroom. They hung back, then surreptitiously followed the old folks down the hall to Classroom # 1.

After the senior citizens entered their classroom, they didn't immediately head for their chairs. Instead, they continued to mill about, gossiping, and fanning themselves with anything that would move air.

Sporting a full bank of windows, the outside wall of Classroom # 1 faced east, thereby catching the early morning sun. As a consequence, the room was already hot and rapidly getting hotter.

Upon his arrival, the instructor did not close the hallway door but left it open, then immediately set about opening all the windows, trying to capture a cross breeze. With that accomplished, he paused to mop his forehead with a lapel handkerchief, then marched up to the podium, positioned at the head of the class. Loudly, he cleared his throat.

"Brothers and sisters," he said, clearing his throat again. "Brothers and sisters, it's time we get started. Could you all please take your seats?"

Peeking through the open door, Mickey and J.T. held their breath as they watched the aging classmates slowly shuffle toward their respective seats. A heavy lady, Sister Edith Hafen, with blue-tinted hair and dressed in a full-length, floral-print dress, was the first to reach her seat, but the others were not far behind. Slowly and with great dignity, she gathered the folds of her long dress around her legs, then slowly sat down. With her considerable weight, the levered seat immediately rotated downward with much more than the required force, simultaneously crushing the poor orange and purple cracker balls against the metal pedestal.

KA-BOOM!

"Oh, my God!" she screamed, jumping up. "Oh, my God! Oh, my God!" she cried out again and again, clutching her hands first to her fleshy cheeks, then her ample chest.

KA-BOOM! KA-BOOM! KA-BOOM! KA-BOOM! KA-BOOM! KA-BOOM!

Instantly, almost like a Korean battlefield, the room reverberated with near-simultaneous explosions. Seniors jumped up from their seats (as fast they could), looking both confused and shell-shocked. Fortunately, none fell or fractured any bones.

Hiking their dresses up around their knees, the ladies looked down at the floor, like there might be a snake or a rodent on the loose. Springing up from their chairs, as fast as their arthritic knees would allow, the men looked visible shaken. Stooping as low as they could (which was not that low), they cautiously checked under their chairs.

Still confused at not finding anything under their chairs, the seniors changed their focus from the floor to the chairs themself, eyeing them suspiciously as if they feared they might explode again. Instantly, the acrid smell of burning gunpower permeated the room, accompanied by the thin, gossamer smoke from combusting nitrates. A moment later, the smoke got caught in the cross current and floated directly towards the boys and the open door.

On the front row, Sister Hafen was still moaning loudly and clutching her chest. Suddenly, her eyes rolled back and like a cut tall timber about to fall, she started to sway.

Still peeking through the open doorway, J.T. and Mickey were enjoying the lively peep show. Silently snickering, they elbowed each other, amazed at how well their prank had worked. The scene in Classroom # 1 was nothing short of comedic chaos. It was bound to be a classic. It would be talked about for years!

Then abruptly, the tall timber fell! Sister Hafen's knees buckled, and she fell forward with a resounding thud. Her blue-tinted head narrowly missing the podium.

Rushing to the fallen sister's side, the class instructor rolled her over (with a great deal of effort) onto her back, then placed an ear on her abundant chest, while groping her neck for the carotid artery. Apparently not happy with what he found, he began pumping on her chest, periodically stopping to rotate both arms above her head to expand her chest, thereby drawing air into her lungs. Quickly, he lowered her arms back to her side, then resume pushing on her chest.

Brother Stucki!" he shouted between compressions. "Go get your car. We've got to get her to Saint George—to the hospital. Now!"

"I—I walked," Brother Stucki replied sheepishly.

"Well then, who's got a car?" the instructor asked, not taking his eyes off Sister Hafen, or abandoning his chest compressions.

Nobody answered.

"Brother Orson Gubler?"

"I walked too."

"Did anybody bring a car?"

Almost in self-defense, a sister answered, "it's not that far to walk."

"We need the exercise," another septuagenarian added.

Stepping forward, Sam Reber volunteered, "I brought my John Deere."

"Geez!" the instructor blurted. "Did you all walk? Then go find me a car, even if you have to flag someone down on the highway."

Quickly, J.T. and Mickey stepped aside as a couple of men hurried out of the classroom as fast as their ancient legs would carry them.

"And," the instructor shouted at their receding backs, "and, have them pull up to the front entrance, right on the lawn."

"Now," the instructor continued, remaining surprisingly calm, "I'll need some help to carry her out of here. Some of you younger, stronger ones."

Though they did not look up to the task, several frail old men gathered around Sister Hafen who weighed nearly two hundred pounds.

Frowning, the teacher then spied J.T. and Mickey still lingering in the doorway. "Come here," he motioned to them, "you two big strappin' farm boys. It's Brothers Graff and Kunz, isn't it? Come in here and give us a hand."

"Come on." J.T. nudged Mickey. "We've gotta go help."

"But—but they'll know it was us."

"Hurry up," the teacher urgently motioned them in. "Time is critical!"

"We can't worry about that now," J.T. whispered to Mickey as he started forward. "We've gotta help."

Reluctantly, Mickey followed.

"And someone call Doctor Hilton," the instructor shouted, as his lifting help gathered around, "and tell him to meet us at the hospital."

"I just live across the street," Sister Ada Leavitt responded, then apparently left to make the phone call.

The instructor positioned J.T. and Mickey opposite each other, both assigned a massive thigh. With the boys and the instructor doing most of the work, the group somehow managed to lift and lug the bulky Sister Hafen out of the classroom. At the door, they had to tilt her sideways, almost dropping her, to get through the door Once in the hallway, they struggled toward the foyer and the front door. Like a high school marching band, they tried, but did not always succeed in marching-in-step.

J.T. couldn't help but think the proceedings looked a lot like a Keystone Cop routine. Several times they stumbled, nearly dropping her, and when someone wasn't tramping on his toes, he was stomping on theirs. Inadvertently, they slammed Sister Hafen's right shoulder into the jamb as they again had to tilt her to get through the front door. The impact made J.T. nearly lose his grip, but by quickly repositioning his hand, he managed not to drop her left leg. He worried, however, about a possible shoulder injury.

As soon as they got her outside, J.T. noted a dark, four-door sedan was parked right on the lawn just four feet from the front door. Obviously, some of the elders had succeeded in flagging down a passing motorist. In the heat of the battle, however, J.T. didn't pay much attention to the car. Instead, he focused on trying to maintain his grip and hopefully save Sister Hafen's life.

One of the brethren jerked open the back door and like an ungainly centipede, they shuffled forward and somehow slid or jammed her into the back seat. Following her into the sedan, the instructor again palpated her carotids, then as best he could, considering the tight quarters, resumed pushing on her chest.

"You two!" the instructor shouted in between compressions.

Reflexively, J.T. and Mickey turned around, wondering who he might be talking to.

"No!" the instructor yelled, "not you Brother Reber, but young Messrs Graff and Kunz, you two hop into the front seat, then when we get to the hospital you can help carry her in."

Reluctantly, the boys did as instructed. Mickey opened the front door on the passenger side and nodded for J.T. to slide in. As J.T. attempted to scoot across the bench seat, his progress was impeded by several random items: a Kodak Folding Hawkeye Camera, a half-dozen manila folders and a familiar looking Geiger counter.

With a start, J.T. recognized two of these articles. Quickly, he glanced up, locking eyes with the tall driver. Meanwhile from behind, Mickey kept nudging him forward, trying to make room for himself.

"Hurry up," the instructor barked from the back seat. "I'm losing her!"

Momentarily, however, J.T. was rendered both immobile and speechless. For the driver was none other than old Borch Rosenkranz or Boris Romanoff, or whomever he was. Today, as usual, he was wearing his trademark short leather pants, a ruffled long-sleeve shirt, dark suspenders, and a green fedora with a pigeon feather wedged in the hatband.

Geez, what were the odds? With all the cars traveling up and down Highway 91, and they managed to flag down Borch Rosenkranz!

Actually, the odds were probably not all that astronomical, considering the number of times he went up and down the highway every day.

Without question, Rosenkranz also recognized him. Frowning deeply, he grunted something unintelligible and with a boney hand gathered and slid the items across the seat, bunching them next to his bare thigh.

Gulping, J.T. got in the sedan with Mickey following close behind.

"Let's get going!" the instructor shouted from the back seat. "Dixie Pioneer Hospital in St. George. Hurry, please!"

To make enough space for everyone on the bench seat, J.T. was forced to relocate the bunched items, the camera, manila files, and Geiger counter, onto his lap, then once Mickey was aboard, he was forced even further up against Rosenkranz's tanned thigh. He was so close he could smell old Borch. It was not the spicy odor of a men's cologne, but rather an odious mixture of pipe smoke and—and what? Maybe fermented grapes.

Again, mumbling something incomprehensible, at least to J.T., Rosenkranz ground the gears, then gunned the sedan down the highway toward St. George. Within seconds, he was going twenty miles over the speed limit, flying around cars even when no passing was allowed.

At first there was almost total silence, just the steady whine of the Ford's V-8 engine and the occasional grunt coming from the instructor in the back seat as he continued to perform CPR on Sister Hafen.

For his part, Mickey hugged the door and stared out the window. J.T. couldn't tell if he realized who their driver was or not.

Finally, Rosenkanz spoke. "Wie ist die paketa?"

"Huh?" Anxiously J.T. glanced up at Rosenkranz.

"Die paketa—uh—" Borch hesitated, apparently taking a moment to think. "Die Rakete."

"Huh?"

"Rakete—uh—roket." To illustrate, Borch removed his hands from the steering wheel and mimicked a rocket blasting off.

Simultaneously, a horn blasted, and Borch re-grabbed the steering wheel, jerking the Ford back into its lane.

"Oh, the rocket!" J.T. breathed a sigh of relief. Not only because Borch again had both hands on the steering wheel, but also because he wasn't bringing up the matter of them repeatedly sneaking into his compound. Maybe, hopefully, he didn't realize it was them.

"Uh—I'm still working on it."

More silence, then to fill the void, J.T. blurted, "nice camera." And it was. J.T. had seen them advertised in the magazines. They were expensive, but reportedly could take pictures of anything—maybe even atomic blasts.

"Jawohl," Borch nodded, "es ist."

More awkward silence. A minute passed, then two. Now they were in St. George proper, turning down 3rd South heading toward the new Dixie Pioneer Memorial Hospital. In another minute, they would be at the hospital and Borch hadn't said a word about them prowling around his place. Taking a deep breath, J.T. relaxed. All this worrying was for nothing.

Rosenkranz pulled up to the emergency entrance, then as the instructor and Mickey moved to get out of the sedan, he reached over and clamped a talon on J.T.'s shoulder, slowly tightening his grip.

"Ihr schreckliche Kinder," he whispered tersely, his blue eyes suddenly turning cold as polar ice caps. His grip on J.T.'s shoulder continued to tighten, as he dug his claws in so deeply they were likely to draw blood.

Terrified, J.T. struggled to leave, but Borch kept him pinned. With his free hand, he reached over, retrieving his Kodak camera, the Geiger counter and the six manila files from J.T.'s lap.

"I could use some help," the instructed shouted from outside the car, "now!"

Under Borch's long fingernails, J.T. saw a splotch of red appear on his Sunday-best, white shirt. He struggled, but still Rosenkranz did not loosen his grip.

"Left mein place alone," he hissed, then slipped totally into his native tongue. "Bleib weg von meinem Haus, wenn du weißt, was gut für dich ist."

Frantic now, J.T. tried to break free and join Mickey, who was already safely outside.

19

GLANCING AT THE CLOCK ABOVE THE WASH BASIN, J.T. NOTED THE HOUR, 7:08 p.m. He still had plenty of time. The town meeting was scheduled to begin at 8:00 p.m., but he'd needed to keep an eye on the clock. He didn't want to miss it.

By dunking his big toe, he checked the water temperature; it felt about right. Slowly, he eased into the tub, sinking to the bottom, then shivering as his back and shoulders slipped over the cold ceramic rim. Once he'd fully acclimated to the temperature, it felt good and he could almost feel the tension of the day, of the whole week, melt away.

Earlier today, he'd finished hoeing the cantaloupe patch and even though he'd hated the task, he was surprised at the sense of accomplishment it gave him. Next week, he would start weeding the tomatoes and thin the rapidly growing Alberta peaches. Also, by then the second cut of hay should be ready to haul, and of course irrigation of the fields and orchard was a weekly chore. Obviously, he was in no danger of running out of gainful employment, which he supposed was good, because as of right now he was nowhere close to having enough money to pay off all his debts.

Sinking deeper into the water, up to his chin, he tried to relax even more. It had been a chaotic and difficult week, but mostly with no one to blame but himself—

When he and Mickey had returned to Santa Clara last Sunday (the instructor's wife had driven over to St. George to pick them up), church services were still in progress. Sacrament meeting had already started with the opening hymn being sung. Not wanting to go back into the chapel and not daring to go home till the church services were over, they decided to head to the fort. Both boys were in a sober mood and neither said anything till they reached the safety of their sanctuary.

With his face drawn and ashen, J.T. finally asked, "d—do you think she will die?"

"Nah," Mickey replied quickly, though not with much conviction.

Sinking down to the dirt floor, the boys again lapsed into a pensive silence, reflecting on the earlier fiasco.

"But suppose she does die," Mickey finally said, breaking the silence, "what would that be? A crime or just an accident?"

"How should I know?" J.T. replied crossly. "I'm not a lawyer."

"Well, what do you think? You do a lot of readin'."

"Well, it certainly was no accident. We planned the whole thing."

"But," Mickey argued, "we didn't plan on hurtin' anyone. That part was an accident."

"Yeah, I know," J.T. muttered, "but that might be what's called splitting hairs."

"So, if it was a crime," Mickey persisted, "which one would it be?"

"Geez, I don't know," J.T. growled, then after a moment's thought added, "it probably wouldn't qualify as murder, cause we didn't deliberately plan to kill her, but I really don't know what it's called if you kill someone and you don't mean to."

"Do you think Sheriff Meecham will find out?"

"Geez, how would I know?" J.T. growled again, his mood souring even more. "But if he does, he'll probably lock us up and throw the keys away."

"Why?"

"Why, what?"

"Why would he throw away the keys?"

J.T. was dumfounded. "You still don't get it? We're suspects in Lenny's death, and before that there was the mannequin fiasco, and before that the cherry bombs and now this. There's no doubt in my mind if they can, they're going to put us away."

"Nah," Mickey waved it off like a pesky blue bottle fly, "nah, we're just kids."

"That excuse begins to wear a little thin after a while."

Again, they lapsed into an uneasy silence. In his mind, J.T. could almost hear the steel door slamming shut behind him and feel the immediate surge of claustrophobia. Was prison as bad as he'd heard? Were there really sexual predators in there? Would he go with Mickey? Or would they be separated? How long would they be in? Would they still be able to go to school in prison? What would happen when they finally got out? Would it completely ruin their lives?

Obviously, the answer to those questions in large part depended on what happened to Sister Hafen, but right now things didn't look so good.

J.T. glanced over at Mickey. Though pretending not to be concerned, J.T. thought he looked troubled.

Suddenly breaking the silence, Mickey asked, "do you think we should count this one?"

"What?"

"Do you think we should count this one, this as a prank?"

"You must be kidding!"

"Well—it was pretty damn good."

"No! Absolutely not."

"But what about the record."

"No more damn records," J.T. blurted, but quickly amended his answer. "No more darn records! Let Judd and Howie have it—"

Sighing out loud, J.T. turned on the hot water again. Now that his body had fully adjusted to the warmth, he could stand a little more heat. After adding a bit more water, he settled back, then his mind leap-frogged back to the fort.

In spite of J.T.'s objections, after leaving the fort, they'd headed for their usual shortcut through Borch Rosenkranz's place. Stopping briefly at the back fence, they surveyed the compound, no black Ford in the driveway, at least the part they could see.

Once again J.T. objected. The recent ride and the tongue-lashing of Borch Rosenkranz was still fresh on his mind. What had he said, 'left mein place alone,' and J.T. suspected he meant it. But Mickey insisted backtracking would take too long, as they both had to get home to do evening chores, and it was safe enough, as the dark sedan was not in the driveway. As usual, Mickey prevailed.

Rotating the loose board, they cut across the backyard, passing the shed that previously housed the shortwave radio. Not being able to resist, Mickey motioned to J.T. to stop and they alternately peeked through the loose board.

As best they could tell, the hanging deer was gone, but once again there were red, white, and green electronic lights! In less than forty-eight hours, the shortwave radio had returned to the shed. Where it had been in the interim, J.T. had no idea, maybe out for repairs. But regardless of why the absence, it appeared Borch Rosenkranz, or Boris Romanoff, was back in business! Again, now able to communicate with Moscow.

After exiting the compound, he and Mickey parted company, each heading for their respective homes. Without talking to anyone, J.T. managed to finish his evening chores, then further avoided his family by steering clear of the family room and heading straight for his bedroom. Closing the door, he pulled a Webster's Dictionary from his bookcase, then sitting cross-legged on the bed he thumbed through the book until he came to the 'M's'. Here, he turned the pages more slowly until his finger came to rest on the word he was looking for, Murder! Holding his breath and with hands shaking, he read, then reread the various definitions.

Murder-in-the-first degree - the unlawful killing of a person with deliberation, or premeditation, or occurring during the commission of another serious crime.

He breathed a sigh of relief. Certainly, that did not at all fit with what they'd done to Sister Hafen. Yes, it was a premeditated prank, but nobody planned on murder.

Murder-in-the-second degree - the unlawful killing of a person with intent, but without deliberation, or premeditation.

That didn't fit either. They had not intended to harm anyone.

Murder-in-the-third degree—similar to manslaughter.

Rapidly, J.T. flipped back a couple of pages until his finger came to rest on the word manslaughter.

Manslaughter - the unlawful killing of a human being without malice, or forethought.

If Sister Hafen did die, that could be it. They did not hate her, they hardly knew her, so there was no malice. And they had not planned to do her harm, so there was no forethought. But what the dictionary did not make clear was the potential penalty for manslaughter. Maybe, J.T. reasoned, that depended on your past record and was left up to the discretion of the judge. That thought, however, did not make him feel any better. Their past record was getting more checkered by the day.

Replacing the dictionary, J.T. flopped on Chris's bed, under the air conditioning vent, and fretted. Ten minutes later, he was called for dinner, signaling the end of the Sunday fast. Though he hadn't eaten anything since the purloined bread and cheese early this morning, now he'd pretty much lost his appetite. He shuffled off to dinner anyway; it would look too suspicious to do otherwise.

At first nobody brought up the Sister Hafen disaster. Everyone was starving from their two-meal fast and concentrated on their food. Picking at his food while surreptitiously watching the others, J.T. was more subdued than usual. And for a few minutes, he thought he might actually get away with it, then Mary, between skewering and forking a combo of roast pork and string beans into her mouth, raised the subject.

To no one in particular, she asked, "did you hear what happened to Sister Hafen today at Sunday school?"

"That was just terrible," Mrs. Kunz replied, slowly shaking her head. Like J.T., she had not eaten much either, instead she randomly rearranged her piles of food. "I heard it was a heart attack."

"Has anyone heard how she's doing?" Mary stabbed a piece of pork, then topped it with a layer of mashed potatoes.

"Some of the relief society sisters came by this afternoon to check on me," Mrs. Kunz replied, "they said it was touch and go, but she's still alive. At least she was as of a couple of hours ago."

Thank God, J.T. said silently, but did not join in the conversation.

Looking up from his bowl of bread and milk, Mr. Kunz said, "I heard the whole thing might've been caused by a damn prank." Pausing, he refocused his gaze on J.T. "Apparently, somebody set off some firecrackers in the classroom."

Still examining his plate, J.T. didn't answer. Instead, he immediately over-filled his mouth with pork, making speech impossible.

"Sound familiar?" Mr. Kunz asked, still looking at J.T. "That's seems just a little bit too much like the cherry bomb fiasco, don't you think?"

Now, J.T. couldn't answer; he was chewing.

"I'm talking to you, John Tobler."

Pointing at his full mouth, J.T. mumbled something unintelligible.

"Did you have anything to do with Sister Hafen?"

Gulping while trying to swallow, J.T. choked on his food and started coughing. "I—I—uh," he croaked, then after clearing his throat, he added, "Honest, I did not set off any firecrackers." And technically, he told himself, that was true because they were cracker balls.

"That's not what I asked," Mr. Kunz said, his eyes narrowing. "I'm only going to ask this one more time, did you have anything to do with the Sister Hafen tragedy?"

Sighing out loud, J.T. reached for the bar of soap, then lathered his hair, neck and chest. Sinking until totally submerged, he rinsed off the soap, then rested his head back on the porcelain rim. Again, his mind wandered back to the dinner.

Before J.T. could be forced to answer the question, there was a loud rap on the front
door.

J.T. exhaled a breathe of relief as Mr. Kunz got up to answer the door.

"You're early!" J.T. heard his father's voice echo from the living room.

"No, Brother Kunz," an unseen male voice answered, "we're right on time."

"Then I guess that means we're running late," Mr. Kunz grudgingly admitted. "Give me a minute and I'll go get my wife."

Returning to the kitchen, Mr. Kunz announced, with unmistakable irritation, the Elders had arrived early.

Leaving their plates and half-finished meals, J.T. and Mrs. Kunz got up and followed him back to the living room. Mary paused long enough for a couple more bites, then hurried to join them. No introductions were necessary as they all knew each other, nevertheless they proceeded with the customary ritual of shaking hands.

Dressed in a dark suit and tie, and looking like an encyclopedia salesman, Elder Hans Leavitt took charge. Elder Axel Frei, similarly dressed, stood back, and smiled amicably.

"We'll need a chair we can place right here in the center of the room," Elder Leavitt announced, walking to the spot.

"J.T.," Mr. Kunz passed on the request, "go get a chair from the kitchen."

When J.T. returned with the aluminum-tube chair, Elder Leavitt positioned it right in the middle of the room, directly under the solitary ceiling light fixture, which bore a passing resemblance to a circle of clamshells.

"Sister Kunz," Elder Leavitt continued after he'd gotten the chair just right, "would you please sit here?"

Nodding, Mrs. Kunz headed for the chair.

After Anita Kunz was seated, Elder Leavitt continued, "Elder Frei, will you and Brother Kunz join me in the prayer circle?" Pausing for a moment, he looked directly at J.T. "Do you hold the priesthood, son?"

"Yes, sir—uh—Elder Leavitt," J.T. stammered, "the Aaronic Priesthood."

"Okay, then, would you like to join us in the circle?"

Proudly, J.T. joined the circle of men standing around his mother. Elder Leavitt fished a small vial of consecrated oil from his pocket, screwed off the cap and sprinkled a few drops on the crown of Mrs. Kunz's head. Her gray hair had thinned so much most of the oil went directly on her surprisingly white scalp. Following this, the men solemnly placed both hands, often overlapping, on Anita Kunz's head.

As Elder Leavitt cleared his throat, the room became quiet, even Mary quit chewing, then he began to recite his prayer.

"Oh, God, by the power of the holy Melchizedek Priesthood, I invoke your presence here tonight as I offer a prayer for, and in behalf, of Sister Anita Kunz. As you know, God, she is battling the deadly scourge of cancer, and also as you know she has a young family and is desperately needed here on earth to care for them. Sister Kunz is a good woman, has a good heart and is true to the principals of the holy gospel as restored by thy modern-day prophet, Joseph Smith."

In his mind, he couldn't help it, J.T. started running a silent commentary on the prayer. Maybe she is true to the gospel today, but yesterday she was true to the pagan ritual of the shaman Smokey Grayman and his Navajo Sing. Hopefully, this double dipping won't anger the Almighty.

"Now, if you don't have more pressing plans for her in heaven," Elder Leavitt continued, "then we would like to humbly request that you consider—"

How could there be more pressing plans in heaven? J.T. thought, again he couldn't help it. Heaven was for eternity. Therefore, how could time be an issue? There was always plenty of time in heaven. How could anything at all be pressing in heaven?

"Surely letting her tarry here on earth for a few more years to care for her family would be find. However, as in all things, not our but thy will be done." Before the finale, Elder Leavitt paused for dramatic effect, then continued. "But of course, we are thankful for all thy blessings we have received. And we beseech these favors using the power of the holy Melchizedek priesthood as restored by Joseph Smith, and we ask them in the name of Jesus Christ, Amen."

Solemnly, and with great dignity, the men withdrew their hands from Anita Kunz's head, smiling down on her with kindness and compassion. As Mrs. Kunz stood up, each member of the prayer circle shook her small brown hand once again.

Almost instantly, J.T. felt better and couldn't help but think this would surely work. He was positive he'd felt the presence of the Holy Spirit in the room, at least he had when he'd managed to conquer his own negative thoughts. This priesthood prayer was not at all like Smokey's lengthy drum and chant liturgy. This was the real thing. They had used the power of God's own holy priesthood for this blessing. Nothing on earth was more powerful. With the Melchizedek Priesthood, they had a direct pipeline to the Almighty. Surely, He would have compassion and listen to his own elders. Surely, He could see the wisdom in letting his mother tarry here on earth. Actually, it was kind of a no-brainer. Finally, J.T. concluded, he would put the power of the Melchizedek Priesthood up against Smokey's blessing way any day.

Also, Mr. Kunz seemed satisfied with the proceedings and even remarked, "God is pleased."

After the elders departed, John Kunz's mood steadily improved. He seemed to have forgotten about Smokey's Sing, the earlier Sister Hafen conversation and even about his unfinished bowl of bread and milk. After the healing-prayer, he picked up the Sunday newspaper and settled into his favorite chair.

Also, in a better mood, J.T. wandered back to his bedroom, dropped down on his knees and silently offered his own prayer: this one for the health of Sister Hafen.

Once again J.T. stirred in the tub. The warm water had cooled. He pulled the rubber stopper, drained two or three gallons, then he added back approximately the same amount of hot water. Glancing up at the clock, he noted it was nearly 7:30 p.m. He still had a little more time. Unlike Mary, it didn't take him long to get ready. Slowly, the tension in his muscles was starting to melt away—just five more minutes. Sighing with relief, he sank back into the soapy water and closed his eyes—

After the Elders' priesthood blessing, things went remarkably well.

Almost immediately, his mother seemed to rally. She started spending more time out of bed, began doing some light household chores and even cooked a couple of the evening meals. And surprisingly, Mr. Kunz's rare mood also continued. In a very real way, J.T. thought, it was indeed a miracle!

On Monday, he and his father hauled hay together, the second cut. J.T. drove the old International while Mr. Kunz, using a pitchfork, heaved piles of loose hay onto the flatbed. This year, J.T.'s feet could easily reach the pedals: the gas feed, the clutch, and the brake. Last year, it was a struggle; he had to slide way forward on the bench seat and then half-stand on the floorboard to reach the clutch and the brake.

When the stack of hay got too high or unbalanced, J.T. would stop, put the truck in neutral, climb up on top of the stack and stomp it down. Hauling hay from the orchard, however, was a prickly, if not a painful chore. The reason: that piece was infested with grass burrs, which had an amazing affinity for any kind of fabric, including socks and pant legs. Plucking them from garments usually required donning thick leather gloves.

In late afternoon, on the last load, J.T. bounced over a deep furrow and pitched off half the load. He'd expected a verbal tongue-lashing, but his father said nothing. Almost cheerfully, he started forking the fallen hay back onto the truck. J.T. couldn't believe it. Indeed, God did answer prayers!

And even though his father continued to inspect his fieldwork every day when he was home, he just nodded his approval and had no specific criticisms. Also, to J.T.'s relief, he had not again brought up the Sister Hafen fiasco, or for that matter J.T.'s school fine, or payment for the washed-out lower half of the Loren Reber piece. In fact, the only subject he broached during this unusual sanguine period was that of Borch Rosenkranz and the upcoming town meeting with the Atomic Energy Commission and Deputy Director, Rudy Popovich. For some reason, his father seemed particularly absorbed with Borch, or Boris, whom he now referred to as Comrade Romanoff.

Feeling a bit like a snitch, after all Mr. Rosenkranz had tried to help him solve his rocket problems, J.T. told his father everything. In detail, he informed him about the shortwave radio and the deer hanging in the shack. Then, somewhat fearing reproach, J.T. took a deep breath, and told him about sneaking into the house and finding the cabinet files and the Geiger counter. Also, he related how they'd found in the bedroom closet the same foreign military uniform Borch had worn that night a few weeks ago. And, in that closet they'd seen the spread-eagle pennant, with the eagle clutching a hoop in its talons. Lastly, J.T. showed him the manila folder he'd pilfered from Borch's study. Accepting the folder, Mr. Kunz quickly thumbed through it. Without comment, he nodded and took possession of it.

Much to J.T.'s relief, he never said a thing about their illegal breaking and entering, or their petty larceny. J.T. could only assume this was one of those rare cases where the end did indeed justify the means.

On Wednesday, their brief foray into the utopian realm of Camelot, came crashing down. Just as John Kunz was preparing to leave on his weekly produce run, two marines showed up. Immaculately attired in dress uniforms, midnight black pants, navy-blue coats with gold brass buttons, they knocked on the door. Not suspecting a thing, J.T. let them in. Considering the convulsive and protracted effect this event would have on their lives, the visit was surprisingly short.

"I'm regret to inform you," the marine officer reported, with no overt show of emotion, "that PFC Christian Kunz was killed in Korea at Pork Chop Hill. And even though it was determined he was killed by friendly fire; he should still be considered an American hero." The marine paused, then stiffly added, "you should be proud of his sacrifice; he died defending our country."

J.T. sank up to his chin in the water. Now that he'd had a couple of days to think about it, he wished he'd ask the marine officer, how that made Chris an American hero? Sure, he was fighting the North Koreans and the advance of the deadly scourge of communism, but this seemed more like a colossal screwup, since we were the ones who had killed him. Did being in the wrong place at the wrong time qualify as heroism?

After receiving the news, John Kunz clenched both jaw and fists for a long moment but said nothing. Briefly, his eyes misted over, then abruptly they turned hard as blue topaz.

Crying out, Anita Kunz buried her face in her husband's chest, then continued to sob. However, resembling marble statues, J.T. and Mary sat rooted to the gold-leaf couch, staring down at the carpeted floor and saying nothing.

With his mind a blur, J.T. tried to comprehend what had just happened and he supposed Mary was doing the same.

Twenty minutes later, Mr. Kunz announced he still had work to do. With jaw still firmly set and blue eyes not only reflecting pain but also determination, he stood up and headed for his already-loaded flatbed. After he was gone, Mrs. Kunz fled to her bedroom, and in the coming days seldom left it.

Evidently, the morbid news finally registered with Mary as she started weeping inconsolably. Being just two years younger than Chris, they had always been close. At times, J.T. had envied their tight bond. He was four years younger than Mary and had never experienced that kind of closeness with either of his sibs.

In a very real and confusing way, J.T. was puzzled, even embarrassed, by his own reaction, or lack thereof. Yes, he was sad, but certainly not devastated.

Probably because of their huge age difference, six years, he and Chris were never that close. In fact, he had at times resented his older brother, especially when his father held up his perfect image, then in frustration asked, 'why can't you be more like Christian?' Also, he and Chris never played or palled around together, like Mickey and his older brother. With the death of Chris, he didn't think his life would change much more than it did when he left for the marines. Now he had his choice of beds and dibs on the air conditioning vent. Sure, he would miss Chris, and sure it was a terrible thing, but he was not as distraught as Mary, and that was both confusing and troubling.

Quickly, J.T. checked the clock one more time. Now it was 7:40 p.m. Time for one last dunk, then he really did need to get out. Holding his breath, he sank beneath the water, rinsed the soap from his hair, then resurfaced, but as he settled back, almost immediately his mind began to wander.

To complete the traumatic week, yesterday evening, just after J.T. had returned from the fields, Sheriff Meecham had showed up at their doorstep. When he answered the door, the sheriff asked to come in, then requested J.T. go fetch his mother.

After they'd all found seats, no lemonade this time, at first Sheriff Meecham was silent, staring down at the billed-officer hat resting on his prodigious thigh. After a few seconds, he sighed out loud and spoke. "I just wanted to tell you how sorry I am about Chris. He was a fine young man. Never gave me no trouble."

J.T. breathed a sigh of relief. It looked like the sheriff was here on a sympathy/condolence mission.

Instantly, Anita Kunz's eyes welled up. She started to say something, but it came out as a half-sob. After which, she simply clasped her hands tightly in her lap and nodded.

Meecham fiddled with his hat for another moment, then continued, "well, anyways, I truly am sorry, but that's not the only reason I am here."

J.T.'s heart sank.

"Well," Mrs. Kunz blurted, "what did they show?"

"Huh?" Meecham frowned.

"Oh, for heaven's sake, Evan," Anita Kunz said, "the fingerprints. What did they show?"

"Which ones?"

"The ones from the catsup bottle."

"Oh," the sheriff replied, "they're not back yet."

"Well, then, Sheriff, why are you here?"

"Uh, I hate to bring this up at a time like this, but I need to talk to J.T. about Sister Hafen and I know you," he nodded at Mrs. Kunz, "don't like me doing that without you being present."

Sighing, Mrs. Kunz dried her eyes and managed to say, "how is she doing?"

"Who?"

"For heaven's sake, Evan, Sister Hafen."

"Oh," the sheriff replied, "she was getting better, but I heard just today she's took another turn for the worse."

"I do hope she makes it," Mrs. Kunz added, "she's such a nice lady."

"Yes, ma'am," Meecham nodded, "she's my great aunt by marriage."

Again, they lapsed into silence.

After an uncomfortable moment, Anita Kunz asked, "so, what does any of this have to do with Jackie?"

"Well, anyways," Sheriff Meecham replied, finally re-locating his police hat to the arm of the chair, "it seems Sister Hafen's heart attack was brought on by a sudden fright. Someone set off firecrackers in her classroom on Sunday. Doc Hilton says her heart just couldn't take it."

"I'm praying for her," Mrs. Kunz said, "but once again, what does this have to do with Jackie?"

"Well, in my investigatin'," the Sherriff replied, "when I ask people who they think done it, the same two names keep coming up, J.T. Kunz and Mickey Graff."

"Really, Sheriff, what does that prove?"

"Nothing," Meecham admitted, "but they are getting quite a reputation."

"Oh," Anita Kunz said, drying her eyes again, "what kind of a reputation?"

"The two worst kids Santa Clara ever produced!"

"That's ridiculous," Mrs. Kunz snapped, nevertheless all eyes focused on J.T.

Squirming in his chair, he looked down at his already scuffed, new, birthday work shoes.

Thankfully, a moment later Meecham spoke. "Actually, we found a couple of 'em under an empty chair, one that nobody sat on. Technically, they're called cracker balls. They explode on impact, when crushed or thrown." He refocused his prosecutor-eyes on J.T. "Do you know anythin' about these little cracker balls?" Fishing a couple of the tiny spheres out of his shirt pocket, Meecham handed one to J.T. and the other to Mrs. Kunz.

J.T. swallowed hard. It seems he was getting in deeper and deeper. "Nah," he shook his head, "those aren't mine." Which was technically true. He discovered he was better at lying when the lies were part-truths or half-truths. Of course, they were Mickey's.

The sheriff glanced at Mrs. Kunz for confirmation.

"I don't know," she rotated the little green ball in her fingers, "I've never seen them around here Is possessing cracker balls a crime."

"It's not the cracker balls per se; it's Sister Hafen," the sheriff replied. "What we've got here, at best, is criminal mischief, and that is if she recovers. But if she dies, what we've got is manslaughter."

J.T. took little consolation in the fact he'd already figured that out.

"Criminal mischief is a Class A misdemeanor, punishable by up to six months in jail and a one hundred dollar fine. Manslaughter, on the other hand, is a felony and the punishment can be from one to five years in prison." Pausing, the sheriff again locked eyes with J.T.

This time J.T. was able to meet his gaze.

"Are you gettin' this, J.T.?" Meecham asked sharply. "Is any of this sinkin' in?"

Abruptly, Mrs. Kunz stood up. "Sheriff, I can't take any more of this. Not right now." She burst into tears. "Not at this time."

In silence, J.T. and Sheriff Meecham watched as she dropped the green cracker ball on the carpet and fled from the room. When they were alone, the sheriff's impeaching eyes slowly swung back to J.T.

"It's kinda like that corral you keep puttin' off cleanin', ain't it?"

"Huh?"

"The shit just keeps gettin' deeper and deeper." The sheriff picked up the dropped cracker ball. "Evidence," he added, re-pocketing it.

J.T. didn't respond. What could he say?

"I'm sorry to say this, John Junior," Meecham continued, though he didn't sound particularly sorry, "but you and your buddy Mickey Graff are both sinkin' in a mess of quicksand. Not only are you two my prime suspects in the mannequin incident and the death of Lenny Weeks," pausing, he held up the other cracker ball as a prop, "but now for this."

"We're just kids," J.T. blurted. "You can't honestly believe that we would kill someone!"

"Right now, I don't know what to believe," Meecham replied, stone-faced, "but I do know them California jails are full of teenage murderers. And I'm guessin' Utah's not far behind."

"I swear," J.T. looked the sheriff in the eye, "we had nothing to do with the murder of Lenny Weeks."

"That so?"

"Yes, sir."

"Then prove it."

"I—I thought that was your job."

"It is, but if you don't like being suspects, prove to me you didn't do it."

As kind of a Mexican standoff, they glared at each other, but said nothing.

"Son," the sheriff finally continued, but more softly now, "I know you're scared, and I know you feel like you're in way over your head, and you are, but

I promise if you'll come clean, tell me everything, things will go a lot easier and clear up a heck-uv-a-lot faster."

Biting his lip, J.T. again looked down at his high-tops, and said nothing.

Meecham abruptly changed the subject. "Are you and Mickey Graff still tryin' to break that silly record for the most pranks?"

"No!" J.T. blurted, more forcefully than he'd intended.

"Well, I can tell you right now you two are in danger of breakin' another one of Judd and Howie's records."

"Huh?"

"Yeah, the one for the most time."

"The most time?" J.T. frowned. "The most time for what?"

"Yeah, they both did two years at the Utah Juvenile Correction Facility," the sheriff replied, then added, "you two could easily beat that."

20

"They really did two years?"

Sheriff Meecham nodded. "Both of 'em at the youth facility in northern Utah."

J.T. was stunned! No, he didn't know. No one ever mentioned that.

"Well, anyways," the sheriff said, hauling his big frame off the couch, "you think about it. If you want to talk, you know where I am." Picking up his hat, he lumbered toward the door.

Even after the sheriff was gone, J.T.'s head continued to spin. At first, he couldn't think clearly, but eventually his thoughts began to crystalize. Did the sheriff actually think they were involved in murder? And in manslaughter? And in criminal mischief? They were just teenagers (and just barely) playing a few pranks for laughs. None of it was intended to be malicious. It was all meant in good—well if not good—then at least in harmless fun. Didn't Santa Clara have a long tradition of practical jokes? Weren't they just upholding that tradition?

But wait a sec, hold on. Don't be in such a hurry to give up; get locked away in the slammer. What had the sheriff said? If you don't want to be a suspect, then prove it; prove that you're not. With the mannequin incident and with Sister Hafen, that, of course, would be impossible, because they indeed were the perpetrators. However, they were also the leading suspects in the death of Lenny Weeks, which they had nothing to do with, at least not directly. So, how could they prove they had nothing to do with Lenny's murder? The only way J.T. could think of was to find the real killers. Sure, technically, that was the sheriff's job, but if they could identify the killer or killers, that would certainly let them off the hook. He decided he would run it by Mickey tonight at the town meeting and see what he thought.

It bothered him, however, that Judd and Howie had both done time. Nobody talked about that when they told their stories and laughed at their antics. And something else Sheriff Meecham said still stung, like his father pouring alcohol on the raw sores of athlete's foot, were they really worse than

Judd and Howie? Were they seriously the two worst kids the town of Santa Clara had ever produced? Like their heroes, Judd, and Howie, were they too on that slippery slope of malfeasance that slid straight through the front doors of juvenile prison—

With a start, J.T. checked the wall clock again. It now flashed an alarming 7:50 p.m.! Jumping out of the tub, J.T. chided himself for daydreaming. He pulled the drain-plug, toweled off, then raced for his bedroom. Though he might be a little late, if he hurried, he could still make most of the Deputy Director's meeting.

J.T. threw on his Sunday best clothes, then had to frantically search for his radiation badge. After a few minutes, he found it still clipped to a soiled t-shirt stuffed near the bottom of the dirty clothes hamper. Obviously, he hadn't been wearing it lately and just as obvious, no one had done laundry in some time—another of Mary's household duties that she'd let slide. And though he was relieved that Mr. Popovich had not witnessed his careless disregard for his radiation badge, he, nevertheless, was worried his negligence might skew the final results. Sheepishly, he clipped his radiation badge to the pocket of his white shirt, then dashed out the front door, sprinting all the way to the schoolhouse.

As J.T. burst into the foyer, he was instantly greeted by a garbled buzz of crowd chatter. It was a chaotic scene, the kind he liked to avoid. Either people were milling about or congregating in tight knots and engaging in fervent conversation. J.T. stayed at the periphery, out of the fray, taking a moment to scan the room. Off to his right he spotted his father, who had cut his produce run short to be here. He was wedged in the center of a large cluster of men and seemed to be doing most of the talking, often with his hands. Off to his left, and somewhat to his chagrin, J.T. spied Smokey Grayman, on the very first row, sitting quietly by himself. Geez, why was he here, J.T. wondered.

The foyer was arranged much the same as it was on Mr. Frei's last day of school when Deputy Director Popovich showed them the Atomic Energy Commission film. Also tonight, a Bell and Howell projector with an accompanying pull-down tripod screen was set up at the north end of the foyer. Directly in front of the white screen was a wooden lectern, sporting the official seal of the ATC. Surveying the rest of the room, it looked like every chair was taken, or at least spoken for, and the townsfolk who were not able to claim a chair were leaning against the walls or sitting cross-legged on the hardwood floor.

Finally, on the very back row, J.T. spied Mickey Tobler Graff. Standing up, he motioned to J.T., indicating he'd saved a seat.

"The whole town's here," J.T. muttered, sitting down beside his friend.

"Yeah, the words out about Borch. Everyone wants to see what happens."

"How do you know that?"

"Cause that's been the scuttlebutt around town."

"How do you know what the scuttlebutt is?"

"Cause, I talked to Curley, who talked to Suzie, who talked to—"

"Okay," J.T. cut him off; he'd already heard enough. But at that moment, he noticed Easy Earl and Curley were sitting on the row directly in front of them, just two chairs to the left. Quietly, he pointed them out to Mickey.

"So," Mickey shrugged, frowning. "I didn't invite 'em; they can sit wherever they want."

Abruptly, big Easy Earl pivoted around in his folding chair and looked right at Mickey. "Just want you to know, Suzie's not your girl."

"Never said she was," Mickey snapped back.

Easy continued, "I know you were following us the other night."

"Oh, yeah, what night?"

"Right after town bell," Easy Earl replied, leaning even further back on his chair so he could lock eyes with Mickey. But now, his chair was precariously balanced on its back two legs. "And Suzie knows too."

"I was just heading home to do chores."

"Sure, you was. How come you were so far outta your way?" Easy Earl asked, teetering back even further. "I don't appreciate being spied on and neither does Suzie."

"You're getting' pretty good at speaking for Susan."

"I'm giving you fair warn—"

Suddenly, Mickey jerked back on the balanced chair, toppling Easy Earl over and slamming him into the chair directly behind. After loudly thrashing around, Easy finally managed to extricate himself, then came at Mickey with both fists doubled.

"May I have your attention!"

Looking up, J.T. saw Rudy Popovich had moved behind the podium. Dressed casually, he wore dark slacks, a white shirt with sleeves rolled up, but no coat or tie. Loudly, he cleared his throat as a signal.

"This ain't over," Easy Earl hissed, slowly lowering his fists, and righting his toppled chair.

"You better hope it is," Mickey muttered.

"May I have your attention!" Rudy repeated one more time, again clearing his throat. "Okay, folks, it's time to get started. Actually, we're a little late," he added, glancing down at his wristwatch.

Slowly the buzz in the room died down. Now, the only sound was the clamor as everyone tried to find a chair or wall space.

Only half listening to Popovich, J.T.'s mind was racing. So that's where Mickey had gone that night after town bell, the night he'd delayed their return to the fort to release Willie. All along, J.T. had suspected he was lying about having to do chores, but until now he had not known the truth. So, Mickey had been spying on Easy Earl and Susan. He must have it bad for her! But of course, that exonerated Mickey. More than likely, no, surely, he had nothing at all to do with the early release or the subsequent disappearance Weird Willie.

Feeling like a first-class heel for suspecting his friend, J.T. glanced over at Mickey. Sitting stone-faced, he appeared to be concentrating on the back of Easy Earl's head. Hopefully, he had no idea J.T. had ever considered him a suspect in Willie's worrisome and still unsolved disappearance. Silently, J.T. vowed to never again question the veracity of his cousin and best friend.

"First of all," Mr. Popovich continued, as he paused to survey the overflowing foyer, "first of all, I would like to thank you all for coming. Honestly, I didn't expect this large of a crowd and I apologize that we don't have enough seats.

"Anyway, to begin, let me quickly go over tonight's agenda. First, I'm going to show a short movie. After that, I will give you a brief update on the latest activities of the Atomic Energy Commission and the tentative schedule for future Shots. Next, I will take a few moments to collect the radiation badges from those children who patriotically volunteered for that project. Oh, by the way, if any of you forgot your badges, you should have time to run home and get them right now."

Immediately, three kids got up and scurried out the front door.

"Lastly," Rudy Popovich continued, "I will open the meeting up for a brief question-and-answer session. But, before we get started, are there any questions about tonight's agenda?" Rudy paused for a moment to survey the crowd. "No? Okay then, let's get started. Could I get someone to turn off the overhead lights, once I get the projector going?"

After sliding the podium out of the way, Rudy Popovich fiddled with the projector for a few minutes, threading the film through rollers, then snapped it on. As a white light spotlighted the screen, almost simultaneously someone flipped off the overhead lights.

Produced by Fox Movietone News, the promised feature was nothing more than a newsreel. Filmed in black and white celluloid, the commentary was provided by the matchless, baritone of Lowell Thomas. The gist of the newsreel, it seems, was to provide an update of the ongoing nuclear arms race, plus there were some spectacular shots of atomic bomb detonations.

To J.T., the opportunity to view a nuclear blast in its entirety, in all of its stages, and in slow motion, was nothing short of mesmerizing. Initially, the massive blast sucked up loose sand and gravel, incinerated all vegetation and excavated a large cavity in the desert floor. A giant stem emerged from this cloud of chaos, as all the sucked-up debris whirled about its base, giving the appearance of a ruffled skirt. Immediately after that, the stem was capped with an enormous mushroom-shaped head, and the incinerated loose debris, still rising up from the base, morphed up from a circling skirt to a shaggy beard attached to the chin of the mushroom head. Less than a minute later, the mushroom cloud started to break apart.

In another particularly troubling segment, Lowell Thomas informed the viewers the Soviet Union was on the verge of developing their own hydrogen nuclear bomb, and to J.T.'s surprise, Mr. Thomas also announced that we (the USA) already had a functional thermonuclear weapon. Next, Mr. Thomas announced that President Dwight D. Eisenhower had refused clemency for the convicted spies, Julius and Ethel Rosenberg and they had been sentenced to be executed.

Lastly, after detailing our recent advances in nuclear technology, the movie (newsreel) abruptly ended with an American flag flapping proudly in a brisk breeze. Abruptly, a white spotlight reappeared on the projector screen. For the moment, the only sound was the terminal end of the celluloid film slapping against a metal post as the collection reel continued to rotate.

Mr. Popovich snapped off the projector and asked for the overhead lights. After which, he slid the podium back in front of the movie screen.

For the next ten minutes, Rudy gave an overview of what the AEC had accomplished in the past year and in general terms, of course, the plans for the future. Nuclear tests were scheduled, roughly every month, for the next two years. Presently, they, the AEC, had just finished the Ivy Series and were ready to commence with the Upshot-Knothole Series. These Shots were much larger than either Nagasaki or Hiroshima and would undoubtedly yield vital scientific and military information.

Deputy Director Popovich then went on to say how much the AEC appreciated the citizens of southern Utah for their past cooperation and was looking forward to their continued support. Lastly, he assured the citizens the Shots were totally safe, then with a lighthearted laugh, he recommended everyone take some time to view at least one of these marvelous, history-making events.

After pausing for a couple of seconds, the Deputy Director abruptly changed topics. "It's time now for me to collect the radiation badges. While the kids are coming up, I just want to tell all of them, and you parents as well, how much I appreciate their efforts. The data from this study will be a big help to our scientists. So, let's give all who have participated in this vital project a big round of applause."

Enthusiastic clapping, as well as some cheers erupted as the kids came forward. Everyone, including J.T., turned over their radiation badges. When he had collected all the badges, Rudy placed them in a leather grip, then returned to the podium.

"Thanks again," he said, glancing again at his wristwatch, "I have just a few minutes now, so I'll open it up to questions." Leaning forward in anticipation, he rested his elbows on the lectern.

Surprisingly, Smokey Grayman was the first to speak. Wearing faded jeans, cowboy boots and a collarless white shirt, his graying hair was parted and neatly braided into two pigtails. As he stood up, he politely removed his black reservation hat, holding it in front of the rodeo belt buckle. Before speaking, Smokey eyed Popovich for a long moment.

J.T. couldn't help but stare; he'd had never seen Smokey look so—well, quite so clean. Quickly, he glanced over at his father. No surprise here, John Kunz looked thoroughly disgusted.

"I just was wondering," Smokey finally said in perfect English, no trace of reservation pidgin, "if we will ever know the results of those badges."

Popovich frowned. "What do you mean?"

"I mean, will we ever know how much radiation these kids got?"

"I don't know for sure," Popovich said, smiling condescendingly "but usually that kind of information is classified."

"Why?"

"Why, what?" Popovich asked with a trace of irritation.

"Why would that be classified?"

"Obviously," Rudy replied curtly, "for national security concerns." Quickly, he surveyed the room. "Anyone else?"

"I'm worried," Smokey continued, refusing to yield, "about the health of these kids."

"Why?" Popovich frowned. "The Shots are perfectly safe."

"Then why do these tests on the kids?"

"Uh—uh, to further science."

"When these things go off," Smokey spoke in barely a whisper, "all the chindis gather around."

"What?" Popovich barked. "Speak up, I can barely hear you."

"This is," Smokey declared, his eyes now ablaze, "the work of skinwalkers, the yee naaldlooshii, the coyotes, and the chindis."

"I didn't understand any of that," Rudy said disdainfully, turning away. "Next!"

Grunting, old Fritz Ence stood with the help of a hand-carved cane. Seemingly unfazed by Smokey's portentous words, he blithely asked, "so, when's the next Shot due and what is it called?"

Briefly, Popovich consulted his notes. "Next will be Shot Baker, scheduled for two weeks from Monday. And after that will be Shot Charlie, in roughly another thirty days. Of course, these dates are provisional, depending on the weather conditions."

"Why on the weather?" Another man shouted from the middle of the room.

"Obviously," Rudy replied, "we can't have any storms in the forecast and the winds have to be just right."

"What's just right?" the same man asked.

"No gale force winds, and they have to be blowing due east."

"Why east?"

"I don't know why," Popovich shrugged, "but that's what the protocol calls for," then he quickly added, "any other questions?"

Someone leaning against the east wall muttered, "could it have anything to do with Los Angeles being directly to the west?"

Popovich ignored that comment. "Anyone else?"

"Do we have to do anything special with the fruit or vegetables we pick after one of them Shots?" Sam Stucki asked from the second row.

"Nah," Rudy shook his head, "not really. Just wash them, like you usually do."

Sam mumbled, "don't usually wash 'em," then sat back down to a chorus of laughter.

"Anyone else?" Popovich asked after the chuckles died down.

Slowly, and with great dignity, John Kunz rose from his chair, loudly clearing his throat. "I don't have a question, but I do have a matter of some urgency that I need to bring before the group." He paused for dramatic effect, looking over the crowd.

Most leaned forward in their chairs as an expectant hush blanketed, like wet snow, over the group.

"Well, go ahead." Popovich nodded, again glancing at his wristwatch.

"First of all," Mr. Kunz continued, "I would like to commend you on this meeting and the fine job you are doing in general, Mister Popovich."

Sporadic applause arose from the crowd.

Smiling modestly, Rudy Popovich thanked the group.

"Is this hydrogen bomb race with the Russkies real?" Mr. Kunz asked after the applause faded.

"Sure, it is," Mr. Popovich agreed, looking puzzled.

"A matter of life and death?"

"Yes, it is for southern Utah, and the whole country."

"A race so critical that both sides would do anything to win?"

"Yes," Rudy acknowledged, "I think that would be a fair assessment."

"Maybe even send spies to make sure the other side is not getting ahead in this so-called arms race? And try to steal their secrets?"

"I can almost guarantee that's what's happening."

"Well then, considering all of that, I'm pretty sure we've got our own Julius Rosenberg right here in Santa Clara!"

"What?" Popovich blurted, raising an eyebrow.

"Yes, sir, we've got our very own Russkie spy right here in Santa Clara!"

A collective gasp emanated from the crowd, followed by an edgy silence. Again, everyone leaned forward in anticipation.

At first Popovich seemed taken aback, but quickly recovered. "Are you sure about that, John?"

"Pretty darn sure."

"Well, can you at least tell me who we are talking about?"

"Sure, except his name is not Rosenberg, it's Rosenkranz."

"Right here in Santa Clara?"

"Yeah, he lives in Fritz Ence's old place, on the east side of town by the Chevron gasoline storage tanks."

"Well now," showing a bit more interest, Popovich leaned forward on the podium, "why don't you give me the details."

"Sure," Mr. Kunz pressed on, "he's new to the town, claims to be Swiss and a distant relative of the Reusch's, but they've never heard of him."

Rudy frowned. "That's not particularly damming."

"And he was seen wearing in a foreign military uniform, probably Russian, and he has a shortwave radio for sending messages."

"So?" Popovich looked confused.

"And I personally saw him coming down from Utah Hill right after Shot Able."

"Hmmmm," Rudy stepped to the side of the pulpit, "that's all very interesting, John, but really not very incriminating. You got anything else?"

"Yeah, he owns a Geiger counter and a Kodak Folding Hawkeye Camera."

"Oh, really," Popovich said facetiously. "I wonder where in the world he could get those things?"

"Also, my son tells me he's a rocket expert," Mr. Kunz continued, undeterred, "and knows a lot about rockets motors, propellants and explosives."

"I see," Popovich replied thoughtfully, but still looked dubious.

"And he has a shortwave radio."

"You already said that, John," Rudy said, then turned to the group. "Anybody else had any dealings with Mister—uh—uh—"

"Rosenkranz." Mr. Kunz supplied the name, then sat down.

"Oh, yes, Rosenkranz. Have any others here had dealings with this Mister Rosenkranz?"

With the help of his cane, Fritz Ence stood up again, then almost regretfully added, "uh, well, he is living in my old place."

"Yeah, okay," Popovich replied, looking perplexed. "So?"

"So, I guess I'm sorry for that and want to apologize to my neighbors, but—but he did pay for a whole year in cash."

Popovich sighed out loud. "Anyone else?"

"I'm not done!" Fritz snapped, refusing to yield.

"Oh, sorry," Popovich replied insincerely, "please continue."

"So, anyway, I'm the postmaster for Santa Clara."

The Deputy Director simply nodded.

"Anyway, at the post office one day I got a letter addressed to Boris Romanoff, but with Borch Rosenkranz's address, you know the address of my old place on it. When Rosenkranz came to pick up his mail, he took the letter, just like it belonged to him and never said a word and never returned it as a mistake."

"I see," Rudy said, "and what am I supposed to make of that?"

"Don't you see," Fritz replied, a bit exasperated, "nobody but the Russkies name their kids Boris. And Romanoff, you can't get any more Russian than that."

"So?"

"So, Borch Rosenkranz is an alias!"

"Okay," Popovich frowned. "Anyone else?"

Madge Reber stood. "I—I own the mercantile here in town," she said, glancing nervously around the room.

Deputy Director Popovich nodded. "Go ahead."

"O—okay. My sister-in-law is Sonja Lukin—uh—Reber, and her grandparents are from Russia. She understands a few words."

Popovich nodded.

"Anyway, Sonja works for me sometimes when I need time off, like to go to the doctor, and—and she's heard Borch, or Boris, or whatever his name is, mumble a few Russian words when he thought no one was listening."

"Geez, everyone knows he's Russian," Sid Graff, Mickey's dad, shouted from his position, against the west wall.

A chorus of agreement erupted from the crowd.

"Anything else?" Popovich asked, looking over the group.

With a flair for the dramatic, John Kunz rose again and marched forward, depositing the manila folder in Popovich's hands. "This came from Comrade Romanoff's house."

Somewhat hesitant, Popovich accepted the folder, looked it over, then cautiously opened it. After taking a few minutes to thumb through the contents, he said, "I don't suppose I want to know how you got this."

"So," Mr. Kunz replied, ignoring Popovich question, "what is it?"

After scanning the document again, Rudy answered, "well, at first glance it appears to be radiation fallout data on Shot Able. The total rads are recorded three times a day for fifteen days following the Shot."

"Why in thee bloody hell," Hafe Hafen fumed, jumping up, "would he be wantin' with that stuff?"

Popovich stroked his trimmed goatee, ""Well, I don't know for sure, but I suppose it is possible, by knowing how much fallout a Shot produced, that you could back-extrapolate and determine how big it was."

Fritz Ence jumped up and shouted, "then he sends all that data back to Moscow!"

Sid Graff added, "using that friggin' shortwave radio."

"So, what we goin' to do about this?" Mr. Kunz demanded. "We can't have a Russkie spy operating right here in Santa Clara, right under our noses and right in the shadow of our National Test Center!"

"Well, to be honest, John," Popovich chose his words carefully, "I'm not absolutely sure what to make of this, but any allegations of spying I take seriously, very seriously. I promise I will look into it." He glanced down at his watch again. "I'm so sorry, but I've got another engagement, so I'll have to bring this meeting to a close."

Without another word, he collected his newsreel, the leather grip of radiation badges and the manila folder, then headed toward the door.

"But what should we do about Boris Romanoff?" someone yelled at his back.

"Uh," Popovich stopped at the door, turning back around. "Uh, for now do nothing. I'll look into it, I promise. Probably, even get the FBI involved." Then he was gone.

"Bloody hell," Hafe Hafen shouted at the closing door, "and that is it?"

"Well," Sid Graff said sarcastically, "he sure was a big help."

Some shouted from the back, "them government types never are."

The room fell silent; for the next few moments, no one said anything. The abrupt and anticlimactic ending of the meeting seemed to have confused and deflated the crowd.

"May I say something else?" Mr. Kunz finally said, standing up again and facing the group.

"Sure," Mayor Leavitt replied, instinctively taking charge in Popovich's absence, "go ahead, John."

"As—as most of you know, I lost my son Christian earlier this week," Mr. Kunz said, his voice breaking up. "He—he died in Korea fighting for our country, fighting against the spread of this godless communism." Pausing, John Kunz tried to regain control of his emotions before continuing. "And—and I'll be damned if I'm goin' a sit by and let a communist agent, a Russkie spy, operate right here under our noses. Him being here, makes—uh—uh, kind of makes a mockery of my son's sacrifice!"

"Right on, John!" Adolph Staheli shouted from the fifth row.

"And by God, I swear on my son's grave," Mr. Kunz continued, his voice now hard as basalt, "if our government won't do anything about Comrade Boris Romanoff, then I will!"

A loud chorus of support erupted from the crowd. Now on their feet, the masses were growing restless.

"So, John," Ludwig Jaussi shouted from somewhere in the pack, "what we goin' to do about it?"

"Let's go down to Fritz's old place right now," Hafe blurted, while rubbing his bloodshot eyes, "and git 'im the hell outta there!"

"Well," John Kunz added, raising his voice a few decibels, and taking command, "we should at least go down there and see what he has to say for himself. I, for one, would like to hear it right from the horse's mouth."

"Right on, John!" Sid Graff shouted, moving toward the door.

"Damn them red Commies!" Another man screamed, also pushing toward the door.

"When?" another shouted from the far side wall. "When we goin' to do this?"

"What's wrong," John Kunz roared, "with right now!"

"Not a damn thing!" another man shouted back.

Like an angry swarm of bees, the crowd streamed out of the schoolhouse. Illuminated by the overhead streetlights, their eyes glinted, like feral dogs, and their faces glowed with the righteousness of Christian crusaders. Though their step was asynchronous and erratic, it was nonetheless resolute and with direction; their boots echoing off the asphalt like a small army on the move.

With a mixture of confusion and horror fixed upon their faces, the women seemed reluctant to join the mob. Most did not, however, a few did.

"No—more—Commies, no—more—Russkies, no—more—Reds," the men chanted as they spilled out onto the sidewalk, then onto the highway.

Their advance down Main Street was both fitful and fluid, almost amoeba-like. A phalanx, or vanguard pod would flow forward, then the body would surge to catch up. Periodically, a man would peel off, dash to his house, then quickly return with a flashlight or a pitchfork or baseball bat, and often with a pint. Most of the women remaining, voiced their disapproval, then taking their children with them, left, and headed for home.

Not wanting to miss a thing, however, J.T. and Mickey tagged along.

As the angry amoeba flowed down the highway, not only did the mob grow, swell in size, but it became more raucous, more unruly, and more inebriated. Fortunately, the night traffic was sparse, but what little there was, had to brake down and creep along, or try to work around or push through the multitude. Beams from handheld flashlights punched holes in the night sky as pints were passed around.

"No more Commies, no more Russkies, no more Reds!" The chant continued and got louder as they worked down the highway. At Ence Lane, they paused and pooled for just a moment, then poured down the lane toward the Rosenkranz house. At the front gate, the mob again stopped, milled about, momentarily unsure of their next move.

By now J.T. knew what to look for. The dark sedan was indeed parked in the driveway, that meant Borch was most likely home. The house, however, was dark, but there was something he had never seen before, a light effluxing between the boards of the shortwave radio shack. Obviously, someone was in the shed.

The moment of indecision continued as the crowd bunched in front of the white picket fence, then almost as an act of defiance, John Kunz marched forward and threw the gate open. Following him, the mob surged forward, spilling into Rosenkranz's yard.

"He must be asleep," someone shouted, "no lights."

Shaking his head, Mr. Kunz gestured at the lighted shed. "No, he's over there. That's where the shortwave radio is. Comrade Boris is sending a message to Moscow right now!"

"Kill the damn Russkie!" someone shouted. Instantly the rest joined in. "Kill the Russkie; kill the Red; kill the Commie!"

With Mr. Kunz now firmly positioned in the lead pseudopod, the mob flowed forward, down the gravel driveway, oozing past the dark sedan, then bunching up in front of the board shack.

Again, they hesitated. And as before, John Kunz stepped forward. "Boris Romanoff!"

No answer.

"Borch Rosenkranz!" he yelled even louder. "We know you're in there."

Nothing stirred within the shack.

Then someone picked up a rock, probably Hafe Hafen, and hurled it. With a loud thud, it banged against a shack board, then clunked to the ground.

Still no response came from inside.

Then almost as if cued, and sounding like a barrage of large hail on a tin roof, a volley of rocks clattered against the pine boards, then those with bats and pitchforks began banging on the wall. It was loud and nerve-wracking.

"BORIS!" Mr. Kunz bellowed, "come out, or we're coming in."

As the mob pushed toward the door, Borch Rosenkranz, looking pale and shaken, emerged from the shack. Instantly, all flashlights trained on him. He was dressed in a green corduroy hunting jacket, a ruffled long-sleeve white shirt and tan lederhosen. Perched on his head was his trademark feathered fedora, and in his hand was a ceramic smoking pipe, fashioned like a miniature Swiss alphorn.

"Was willst du? Uh—uh—vha—vhat do you vant?" Borch's voice trembled so badly his English was barely understandable.

As usual, John Kunz took the lead. "What you doin' in there, Boris?"

"Ich—uh—Ich kenne keinen, Boris—uh—nein, no Boris," Rosenkranz stammered, while shaking his head.

"Don't get cute with me," Mr. Kunz roared, "I asked you what you were doin' in there."

"Das betrifft sie nicht." Borch now reverted exclusively to a foreign tongue.

"English," Mr. Kunz thundered, taking a step forward, "speak English, you damn Commie."

Directly behind John Kunz, Fritz Ence, who knew German, began translating. "He said, it's none of your business."

"None of my business, huh?" Mr. Kunz took a threatening step toward Rosenkranz. "Listen here, Comrade, we know what you're up to. And we know you're a Russkie spy."

"Nyet," Rosenkranz emphatically shook his head. "Nein, nyet, nein."

"And we know all about the Geiger counter and the radiation fallout files," Mr. Kunz added, his voice loud and menacing.

All Borch could do was shake his head and mutter, "Nyet, nein, nein."

"And we know all about the shortwave radio you've got in there," Sid Graff shouted, pointing at the shack.

"Nein, klien Radio," Borch mumbled, taking a step backward.

Fritz interpreted. "He says there's no radio."

"Liar!" someone shouted.

Another man bellowed, "we ought'a string him up right here and now!"

"Damn red Commie!" Hafe spat out the words as he hurled a baseball-size rock, narrowly missing Rosenkranz's head.

"No radio, huh?" Mr. Kunz challenged, taking another step forward. "My boy here, J.T., says you do."

Suddenly, and now with the spotlight on him, J.T. shrank back into the crowd. Silently, he hoped Borch didn't know he was John Kunz's son.

Rosenkranz emphatically shook his head again. "Nein, nyet, nein, kein kurzer welle-Radio."

Fritz translated. "No, no shortwave radio."

"Well, if you've got nothing to hide," Mr. Kunz said, his eyes aflame, "then you won't mind if we take a look."

There was no response from Rosenkranz. Though he was quaking with fear, he managed to stand his ground.

"Sid," John Kunz ordered, "go in there and take a look. And Boris, if you know what's good for you, you'll stay out of his way."

Picking up a baseball bat, while keeping a wary eye on Borch, Sid slipped past Rosenkranz to the shack door, then hesitated. John Kunz motioned for him to get on with it. Then with the hinges squeaking loudly, Sid opened the door and disappeared inside.

A hush fell over the mob as they waited for Sid. Rosenkranz's face was unreadable. Inserting the alphorn pipe into his mouth, he sucked a couple of times, producing a puff of white smoke, which spiraled up from the pipe's bowl.

A few seconds later, Sid returned. Still holding his bat in one hand, he glared at Rosenkranz as he passed, then slowly shook his head. "Nothing, John. There's nothing in there. Just a kerosene lantern hanging from the ceiling."

Puzzled, John Kunz turned to J.T. "How about it, son?"

Once again, all eyes focused on him.

J.T. gulped, then stammered, "uh—uh, it was there last Sunday," he mumbled, glancing down at his feet, afraid to look at Borch.

"I saw it too," Mickey chimed in, obviously not wanting J.T. to get all the credit.

"Then," Hafe Hafen brayed, "he must've bloody moved it."

"Yeah," Sid Graff agreed, "probably somebody tipped him off!"

Again, there was a moment of hesitation, as the group looked to Mr. Kunz for direction. He remained silent for a couple of seconds, then took another menacing step toward Rosenkranz.

"Look here, Comrade Romanoff," he hissed through clenched teeth, "this is our country, the United States of America—"

"Land that we love," Hafe added.

"And," Mr. Kunz continued, "we know all about you. We know who you are and what you're about. So, let this be fair warning, we don't want your kind around here. We don't want no commie spies in our town."

"Right on, John!" someone shouted.

"So," Mr. Kunz continued tersely, "if you know what's good for you, you'll go back to Mother Russia. Vamoose! Disappear! Get the hell out of our town!"

"And take your friggin' hammer and sickle with you," someone else shouted.

"You got one week," Sid Graff growled.

"And not one day more!" Mr. Kunz placed his hands on Borch's chest and shoved hard.

Staggering backwards, Rosenkranz slammed against the board shack, then slumped to the ground.

"And not one bloody day more," Hafe added, then for emphasis, he hurled his empty pint. It missed Borch's head by inches, shattering against the shed wall and showering him with glass shards.

21

THE OLD FLATBED INTERNATIONAL SPLASHED ACROSS GOLDSTRIKE CREEK, this time of the year no more than a trickle, then headed roughly north by northwest.

Looming in the distance were the twin, but otherwise quite dissimilar peaks of Flattop and Windy. They, along with Utah Hill (home the Kunz's summer range), were part of the Mormon Mountain Range, straddling the Utah/Nevada border. Flattop's name pretty much defined its physical characteristics, but Windy's name gave no hint of its topography. It was, however, a near-perfect inverted cone.

Though strikingly dissimilar in topography, the vegetation of both peaks was virtually identical: blue sage, rabbitbrush, thickets of Gambel oak and scattered stands of Utah's pygmy forest, junipers, and Colorado piñons. Niche-matched fauna included small herbivores, such as mice, squirrels, rabbits along with their paired carnivores, kit foxes, and the highly adaptable coyotes. The peaks were also prime habitat for larger herbivores, such as mule deer, along with their seemingly ever present, but seldom seen predator, the mighty mountain lion or cougar. The only standing or running water in the area was the diminutive Goldstrike Creek, which they had just splashed across.

Yesterday evening a thundershower had rumbled through the area and the cool morning air still carried the distinctive aroma of wet sage, as well as the spicy fragrance of wet rabbitbrush.

"So, why do they call it Goldstrike?" Mickey asked as the remarkably serpentine road crossed the little creek yet again.

"I guess years ago," J.T. replied, his blanched knuckles gripping the steering wheel, "they found gold somewhere up this creek."

"Really! Any left?"

"Nah, it played out years ago." J.T. gunned the flatbed as they headed up the arroyo's steep west bank. "I don't think it was ever a very big strike."

"So, where does this creek go?"

"It runs into—" J.T. spoke haltingly; he was trying to concentrate on his driving, "I—I think it runs into Slaughter Creek, then on into the Virgin."

"Oh, it makes it that far, huh," Mickey said doubtfully, then after a moment he asked, "you sure he said Windy and Flattop?" Mickey was seated on the passenger's side, his arm resting on the frame of the open window, his blonde hair rippling in the cool mountain breeze.

"Don't you remember?" J.T. replied, gripping the steering wheel even tighter, while trying to see through the green/yellow splats on the windshield. The locust swarm had been particularly bad going across the Shivwits Indian Reservation. "It was the day after the cherry bomb fiasco; we walked to school with him that morning."

"I wouldn't call it a fiasco."

"Well, that's what it was."

Mickey shrugged. "Anyway, your memory's better than mine. Tell me z'actly what he said."

"Well," J.T. replied, double clutching as he tried to downshift in preparation for the equally steep downslope. Failing with that, he rode the brakes all the way to the bottom. The smell of scorched brake pads drifted up through the rusted holes in the floorboard.

Mickey frowned. "You're goin' to burn out the brakes."

"Can't help it," J.T. replied, grinding the gears again, "I can't shift this darn thing."

"So, anyway," Mickey continued, "remind me what Weird Willie said."

"Remember, he said that he and Lenny were going to make a lot of money up Goldstrike Road, up by Flattop and Windy."

"Yeah, now I kinda remember, but he never said what they were goin' to do, did he?" Mickey asked, as J.T. struggled to get the laboring truck up the far side of the arroyo. When J.T. didn't answer, he added, "maybe you oughtta shift out of fourth."

"I'm trying!"

"So, did he say how they were goin' to make all that money?"

"No," J.T. replied as he ground the gears one more time, trying to shift to a lower gear, "but everyone thought it was something to do with poaching, either for the meat or for antlers or both. I'm not sure why the antlers."

"I heard it was somethin' to do with the Japanese."

"Oh, yeah, they were going to make some kind of medicine from the antlers."

"An apro-dee-z-iac," Mickey replied confidently. "And all that fits with the unmarked bullets we found on Lenny Weeks."

"And the one we found at the fort too."

"But maybe not the ring," Mickey added, frowning. "I'm not sure how that fits in."

"Maybe, just maybe," J.T. replied sarcastically, "poachers wear rings too."

"Not a ring like that one, smart ass!"

"How would you know?"

They were both silent for a minute as J.T. brought the International to a complete stop, forced the gearshift back into first, then lurched forward again, double clutching as he once again tried to work his way up through the progression of gears.

"You're not very good at that," Mickey observed.

"At what?"

"Shifting."

"Well, I don't drive much on the road," J.T. replied, grasping the steering wheel as he rounded an 'S' curve. "In the hay field, I basically keep it in first gear all the time."

"I still can't believe you took it."

"Took what?"

"Geez, what we bin talkin' about, the truck."

"Desperate times call for desperate measures."

"Man, that's a pretty cool sayin'. Did you just make that up?"

"Nah, I read it somewhere."

"Do your parents know?"

"Know what?"

"That you took the flatbed."

"No."

"Well, they're goin' to find out."

"Nah," J.T. missed another gear, "they're in Salt Lake City for the week. My dad took the week off."

"Salt Lake City? What's in Salt Lake?"

Frowning, J.T. hesitated for a moment. He didn't like talking about it, but Mickey knew almost everything anyway. "They're up there seeing a cancer specialist. Someone called an oncologist."

"Oh!" Mickey turned away and stared out the window. "I thought she was doin' better."

"She was for a while, but not so good lately."

"What about Mary?"

"She's gone for the week too, visiting our cousin Beth in Provo. They trade staying in each other's houses every summer. This summer it's Provo. She rode up with my parents."

"And they left you by yourself!"

"They offered to have me stay with Uncle Jack, but he lives in St. George, and somebody still has to do the chores and take care of the farm. I'd rather do that than stay with Uncle Jack."

Again, there was silence. Mickey glanced over his shoulder and out the rear window, then changed the subject. "Well, anyway, I sure hope we don't run into no cops."

“Not likely way out here. When we go back, we’ll do the same thing, stick to the back roads.”

“I hear if they catch you drivin’ before you get your license,” Mickey added, “they make you wait another full year, till you’re seventeen.”

“Well, I’m not worried about that right now,” J.T. replied, braking hard for an unexpected hairpin turn. Once again, he neglected to down shift, consequently the engine strained, bucked and stalled until he finally managed to grind it down to third. “We’ve got other problems, bigger problems. We won’t need a driver’s license in jail.”

“I thought,” Mickey replied, “that’s why we’re up here, to find Lenny’s killer.”

“It is, but all I’m saying is we’re running out of time.”

“You don’t know that for sure.”

“Yes, I do!”.

“Yeah, how do you know?”

“Deputy Fowler told his girlfriend, Sue Ann Marsh, who told Bonnie Ashton, who is best friends with Mary. Anyway, the sheriff just as much as told us that himself the other day.”

“I wouldn’t go too much on what Bonnie Ashton says,” Mickey mumbled. “She’s nothin’ but a big-mouth.”

Again, they fell silent, with J.T. concentrating on his driving. This was a lot harder than he’d thought. Steering was no problem, just like the tractor or driving the truck in the field. The big difference, however, on the road you were going much faster, had to react faster and try hard not to over steer. Early on, he’d discovered over-correcting could result in skidding and loss of control, but he still hadn’t mastered the shifting. Even with double clutching, changing gears was a big problem. He had to push the clutch pedal clear to the floorboard to disengage the transmission and unfortunately his legs were barely long enough for that. And even doing that didn’t always work. Though he wasn’t a mechanic, J.T. suspected the clutch was going bad.

“Sounds like your transmission’s goin’ out,” Mickey volunteered.

“I think it’s the clutch.”

“No way, John Tobler,” Micky said, then out of the blue asked, “so, you’re really not goin’ to count the cracker balls?”

“Geez, would you drop it. That’s not a prank, that’s a felony!”

“What’s a felony?”

“A serious crime. The kind you go to jail for.”

“Then,” Mickey sighed, “we’re never goin’ to break Judd and Howie’s record.”

“Who cares? We’ve got bigger problems,” J.T. replied, as he tried to bring the truck out of another major skid. Once again, he’d over-corrected. Too much talking! He’d nearly rolled them on that last curve.

Holding tight to the window frame to keep from sliding off the bench seat, Mickey observed, "you need to slow down for the curves."

"Really?" J.T. retorted. "Geez, I never thought of that."

You know what your problem is?"

"What?"

"You can't take criticism."

"Yeah, well, anyway, we're here." J.T. sounded relieved as he steered the flatbed off the road onto a flat area devoid of vegetation. "Right here, I think we're about halfway between Flattop and Windy."

After parking the flatbed, J.T. pocketed the key and reached for a canteen and binoculars. "Might as well get started."

Mickey frowned. "You got some kind of a plan?"

"Well, for starters let's climb Flattop and see what we run into."

"Not much of a plan."

"You got a better one?" J.T. snapped, getting out of the International.

Shrugging, Mickey closed the door and fell in step.

After a bit of searching, J.T. found a faint game trail that seemed to ascend the steep slope, while periodically dodging around lava rocks and granite boulders.

For the next thirty minutes, the two boys struggled up the near-fifty-degree incline, fighting through hip-high tangles of blue sage, scattered brambles of mountain mahogany, thickets of Gambel's oak and isolated knots of junipers and piñons. Perspiring, and with chests heaving, they finally reached the summit. The top of Flattop slanted significantly to the east, and was traversed by multiple drainage arroyos, but it was relatively flat, at least compared to its craggy neighbors. From the rim, however, it was difficult to see into the interior of the plateau. Up here, the pygmy forest was thicker and the trees were a bit larger.

Proceeding counterclockwise, the boys slowly worked around the rim, searching the periphery, as well as an occasional foray into the interior. Sporadically, through windows in the dense pygmy forest, or by standing on a jutting peninsula, they were rewarded with panoramic views of the surrounding terrain, some six hundred feet below.

There was nothing. Nothing out of the ordinary on top or below. There was no telltale evidence of recent activity, illegal or otherwise. No signs of new hunting camps or recent wood cutting, no fire pits or decaying buck carcasses scalped of their antlers, and no unmarked or spent 30/30 cartridges.

"Well," J.T. wheezed, as they stopped for a rest after completing the entire circuit around the rim, "there's nothing here. Let's cross over to Windy."

Mickey eyed the neighboring peak. "You bring any lunch?"

"Yeah, but it's back in the truck."

"Let's go eat first, then do Windy."

"But then we'd have to go all the way down and all the way back," J.T. argued, as he eyed the hogsback that bridged the two peaks. "It's a lot closer if we just go straight across."

"I don't think we'll find anythin', anyway," Mickey argued. "Maybe, we ought to just call it a day and head back."

"Head back and do what?"

"Maybe search Boris Romanoff's place again. I still think he's somehow mixed up in all this. I'll bet the shortwave radio's in the house, and remember that poached deer in the shack?"

"Well, if we don't find anything on Windy." J.T. nodded at the peak, while offering Mickey the canteen, "then that's just what we'll do."

Mickey took a long gulp. "Do you think he's split?"

"Who?"

"Geez, who we bin talkin' about, Comrade Romanoff?"

"If he knows what's good for him, he will." J.T. accepted the canteen back and took a swallow. "The whole town's pretty fed up with him."

"Well, your dad sure is."

"So is yours," J.T. retorted, then uncharacteristically tried to defend his father. "You know with Chris dying and my mother's illness, Father's had about all he can take."

"Do you really think they'd lynch him, like in the movies?"

"I don't know. Maybe, if he doesn't leave," J.T. sighed and stood up, "but I hope not."

"You're kiddin'! Why not? He's a commie spy."

"I don't know, I just don't think lynching is the American way."

"Actually, it's very American. They do it all the time in the westerns."

"I don't know," J.T. replied, wanting to change the subject, "maybe it is American, but that still doesn't make it right. Come on, let's get going."

Shouldering the canteen, J.T. zigzagged down the steep slope of Flattop, heading for the hogsback natural bridge. Grudgingly, Mickey followed.

It took another thirty minutes for them to work across the land bridge, then up the equally steep slope of Windy. However, unlike Flattop, at its summit Windy offered almost no level ground. The cap rock consisted of a solitary granite spire thrust upward, like the cap sculpture of a Roman Catholic cathedral or a Mormon temple. From this precarious perch, however, the boys were afforded an unparalleled, nearly three-hundred-and-sixty-degree view of the surrounding terrain. And true to its name, the wind whipped and howled constantly around the pyramid-shaped spire.

"You see anything?" J.T. asked, the wind whistling in his ear.

"Huh?" Mickey cupped his hand around his ear.

J.T. shouted, "do you see anything?"

"Nah," Mickey shook his head. Transferring his hand from his ear to shield his eyes from the glaring sun, he continued to search.

Battling the wind, while probing for stable hand and footholds, the boys cautiously circled the granite monolith. As they inched around, they continued to survey the ground far below.

"Over there!" J.T. shouted, pointing. "Over there, right above Goldstrike Creek."

"Where?" Mickey shouted back.

"See Goldstrike Creek," J.T. pointed again, "about a half-mile up, there's a little tributary running more to the west."

"Yeah, okay," Mickey said after a moment.

"Then follow that creek up to the top."

"Oh, yeah, I see it. What is it?"

"Don't know for sure, but it looks like it could be a camp." J.T. fished the Bushnell binoculars from their leather case and scanned the area. After a few seconds, he handed them to Mickey.

Micky refocused the lenses. "Yeah, it's a camp all right."

"Anybody there?"

"No, not than I can see, just tents, but no people or vehicles. Nothing's movin'."

"Maybe," J.T. re-cased the binoculars, "we ought to head over there and check it out."

"Okay," Mickey shouted above a particularly strong gust of wind, "and stop for lunch on the way."

Carefully, they weaved their way down the near-vertical slope. Once J.T. slipped, sliding a few yards. But other than a raspberry abrasion on his right forearm and a dent in the aluminum canteen, he came out no worse for it.

Mickey offered very little sympathy. "You should be more careful, Grace."

At the flatbed, they paused for five minutes to wolf down two Spam sandwiches and a couple of bottles of lukewarm Coke, then headed northwest up Goldstrike Creek.

In early July, the runoff from melting snow was long gone, and even here in the mountains, daytime temperatures could often soar to ninety degrees. Still, that was considerably less than the one hundred, sometimes one hundred and ten degrees of the desert valleys. However, those two factors, the summer heat combined with no remaining snowpack, had reduced Goldstrike Creek to a shallow, almost ditch-like stream the boys could easily jump across.

The stream bed itself, composed of exposed Jurassic sandstone, was relatively devoid of vegetation. However, both banks, formed from the very same eroding sandstone, sported dense groves of cottonwoods, as well as almost impenetrable thickets of skunk bush and coyote river willows. With no obvious game trails and with the banks being virtually impassible, that left only the streambed as an option to get to the camp. Actually, the slickrock made for fairly easy going. They simply hiked the upsloping, almost step-like sandstone of the creek bed, while still enjoying the shade from the nearby towering and looming cottonwoods.

As they splashed upstream in two-to-three-inch water, J.T. spotted a school of tiny woundfin minnows darting for cover under half-submerged rocks or driftwood. Up ahead, he caught a glimpse of a mule deer, drinking from a pool. Raising her head, the doe made brief eye contact, then gracefully bounded up onto the bank, immediately disappearing. Navigating the thick bank vegetation seemed to be no problem for her.

Also, J.T. spotted an occasional black or smudge mark embossed on the slickrock. Though not terribly obvious, they seemed to be traction, or skid marks burned into the sandstone. At the moment, J.T. didn't know what to make of that.

In relative silence, the two boys trudged on, the only sounds came from sloshing of water or the squeaking of their wet sneakers. When they reached the point where the two streams diverged, J.T. pointed to the left hand or the West Fork. As they splashed on, the terrain gradually got steeper and the tiny creek ran faster, and even more shallow. Fifteen minutes later, the boys topped the layered, sandstone bluff to discover a flat area, almost the size of a football field. Through portals in the thick vegetation, they spotted three canvas tents.

Stopping, then backtracking a few steps, J.T. motioned for Mickey to huddle.

"I don't think it's a good idea we head in there without giving them warning." J.T. nodded at the camp, once again invisible, blocked by a thicket of skunk bushes.

"Why?" Mickey whispered.

"They've probably got guns."

"So? Nobody goes campin' without guns."

"But if they're poachers, I'm not sure what they'd do if we surprised them."

"Then what do you suggest?"

"Let's just let them know we're coming."

"Well, if they're the poachers," Mickey countered, "they may not like that either."

"Yeah, maybe," J.T. agreed, "it looks like they've gone to a lot of trouble to hide their camp."

"Anyway, it looks like nobody's home."

J.T. thought about it for a moment. "Yeah, probably, but in just in case they are, we should let them know."

"Okay," Mickey reluctantly agreed, then added, "but get ready to run if you see a gun."

Cupping his hands, like a megaphone, J.T. shouted, "hello, the camp!"

No answer.

He shouted again; this time louder. Still no answer.

"It looks like they're gone," J.T. waited another moment, then continued, "and remember we saw no vehicles from on top of Windy."

"Then what are we waitin' for?" Mickey started forward, fighting his way through the skunk bush. "Let's go see what we can find."

"And let's be careful," J.T. added, falling in behind Mickey. "We still don't know what we're getting into."

The camp consisted of three, white canvas tents, arranged roughly in a triangle around a central firepit. In closer to the pit, three metal folding chairs were set around a crude plank table. A cursory open-flap inspection of the tents' interior revealed all were empty, containing only cots, sleeping bags, various personal items and assorted dirty clothes.

Cautiously, the boys entered the first tent for a more thorough inspection. There was nothing much of interest; nothing that would help their cause, nothing that would help solve the murder of Lenny Weeks or absolve them. A little braver now, they split up. Mickey took the tent on the left, and J.T. entered the one on the right.

Inside his tent, J.T. couldn't help but notice how hot and stuffy it was. The air felt stale and was saturated with several distinctive odors: oiled canvas, stale cigarettes, and the classic smell of locker gym clothes. On closer inspection, J.T. noted this tent was just like the first one with a couple of major differences. This one was not nearly as messy and setting on the cot was a brand-new cowboy hat. Picking up the straw Stetson, J.T. rotated it in his hands. It looked identical to the one the cowboy was wearing the night he was arguing with Borch Rosenkranz. So, did that mean the cowboy was up here? Probably. Setting the hat back down, precisely as he'd found it, J.T. turned and exited the tent.

While waiting for Mickey, he began searching the surrounding area. As expected, there was assorted camping gear: a couple of kerosene lanterns, Dutch ovens, a cast iron fry pan, metal plates and utensils, and a large washbasin. But not to be expected at a recreational campsite, there was also an assortment of hand tools: picks, shovels, rakes, pry bars and even sledgehammers. Those things typically were not included in standard camping gear.

Enlarging his circle of investigation, J.T. refocused on the periphery of the camp. Curiously, there was no road leading in or out, and obviously the camp would not be visible from the Goldstrike Road. The only way in, it appeared, was the very same way they'd just come, straight up the slickrock streambed of Goldstrike Creek. To say it was well hidden was an understatement. They were lucky to find it and if they hadn't climbed atop Windy, they would never have seen it. The only way this camp would be visible to the outside world was from atop of Windy or by airplane, and that plane would have to be flying directly overhead.

Returning to the camp center, J.T. saw Mickey was finally backing out of his tent but carrying a rifle with him. Once outside, he paused, drawing down the lever-action and ejecting a bullet. Picking it off the ground, he held it high, rotating it in the afternoon sun. The brass casing glinted like fools' gold.

"Well, looky here!" he exclaimed, as he continued to rotate the cylinder.

J.T. hurried to join him. "What you got?"

"Take a look." Mickey handed over the shell.

It was a wholly intact, unfired bullet, still retaining its lead projectile. But on closer examination, it also appeared to be a 30/30, a central fire primer, with a long-range ballistic head and absolutely no manufacturer's markings.

"This," J.T. exclaimed, "is exactly the same as those other bullets!"

"Nothin'," Mickey said sarcastically, "gets by you, Sherlock, does it?"

Ignoring, Mickey's barb, J.T. asked, mostly to himself, "I wonder what this all means?"

"It means we've found our poachers!"

J.T. nodded, still examining the casing.

"And," Mickey added, "the bullets we found on Lenny and down by the fort probably came from these guys."

"Yeah," J.T. agreed, then continued in the same train of thought, "and it means these guys must somehow be involved with Weird Willie's disappearance."

"And with Lenny Weeks."

His face now ashen, J.T. nodded. "And the m—murder of Lenny Weeks!"

"Yeah, there's no doubt about it."

"Then, we—we probably ought to get out of here."

"Nah," Mickey countered, "as long as we're here, let's see what else we can find."

"But—but, we may be in way over our heads!"

"Over our heads or not," Mickey countered, "we still need to prove our innocence. Let's see what else we can find."

Snatching the bullet back, Mickey pocketed it, then set the rifle on the crude table. After that, he immediately started exploring. Reluctantly, J.T. followed.

Employing ever-widening circles, the boys searched the remainder of the compound. In the little creek, just above the camp, they found a crudely constructed diversion dam. Using boulders, sticks and mud, the dam effectively blocked the little stream, creating a shallow, but sizeable pool. Over a spillway, the creek continued on down the slope.

On the west bank, just below the surface, J.T. spied a four-inch galvanized pipe. As it exited the diversion pond, it ran through a large screw valve, then continued on down the slope. J.T. tried to rotate the wheel/valve clockwise. It didn't move, indicating it was presently closed. By turning it counterclockwise, however, he opened it a crack and could hear water rushing through the pipe. Satisfied he understood how the system worked, he closed it again, then motioned to Mickey.

Together they began tracking the pipe. After leaving the pool, the pipe immediately sloped downward, eventually leaving the creek bed altogether and veering off to the west. In due course, it crossed over a low ridge and disappeared into the next ravine.

Along its surprisingly lengthy course, the pipe had to cross a couple of minor uphill sections, but the overall grade was consistently downhill. Therefore, J.T. concluded, the initial, or head pressure would force the water over the high points. Eventually, the pipe crossed the low hillock of the first ravine, then still slanting downward, vanished into a second arroyo. Puzzled, the boys continued to follow the pipe. On the crest, above the second ravine, they paused.

"What the heck!" J.T. blurted with a mixture of awe and confusion.

"Well, I'll be damned!" Mickey exclaimed, then asked, "what is it?"

"I'm not sure," J.T. started down the slope, "but let's go find out."

At the bottom of the ravine, the pipe dumped into a long, rectangular wooden box. Also slanting downward, the box was approximately four feet wide by twenty feet long with three-inch riffles nailed transversely across it at roughly two-foot intervals. At the far end, a short span of pipe provided an outlet, a way for the box to empty back into the arroyo. Randomly scattered around the arroyo were more picks, shovels, sledgehammers, and a wheelbarrow. Also, there were a couple of two-by-four foot rocker boxes and three or four circular metal pans.

"What the hell," Mickey blurted, sighting down the long wooden box, "is this stuff?"

"I'm not sure." J.T. scooped up a little residual sand trapped behind a cross-riffle. "This is just sand—well—well, would you look at this!" He picked out a yellow speck about the size of a grain of wheat.

Snatching it, Mickey held it high. Like the bullet casing, it glinted in the bright afternoon sun, like—well, almost like fool's gold—or—or, maybe like real gold!

"Now," J.T. gestured in a circular motion around the compound, "I know what all this stuff is. It's tools for mining. This," he pointed at the rectangular wooden box, "is what's called a sluice box and the pipe bringing the water in is called a flume. Over there," he pointed again, "are a couple of rocker boxes and those metal pans are for panning."

"So," Mickey said, wide-eyed, "this is a gold minin' operation!"

"Appears so."

"So, why are they tryin' to keep it a secret?"

"I don't know," J.T. paused to think, "unless they don't have a valid claim, or this is private land, or they're claim-jumping on someone else's claim."

"So, what's this got to do with deer antlers and poachin'?"

"I'm not sure," J.T. frowned, "I really don't know, except miners have to eat too."

"Well, while we're here, let's look around a little more," Mickey said. After pocketing the tiny nugget, he climbed right in the sluice box and started sifting through the sand trapped behind the riffles.

J.T. watched him for a few seconds, then walked away and began studying the rest of the operation.

The mine was located right at a horseshoe bend in the dry wash. In the middle of the 'U', the men had tunneled through very large sandbar and into the adjacent rock wall. As they excavated, it looked like they shoveled gravel, fine rock debris and sand directly into the sluice box, then turned on the water. The on-rushing water would wash away the lighter elements, such as the sand, small rock, and organic debris, leaving behind the much denser gold flecks and nuggets. For confirmation of his theory, J.T. checked the sand in arroyo above the sluice box; it was bone dry. But below, it was still damp. That meant more than likely the sluice box had been used recently, maybe even this morning.

Apparently, the rocker boxes operated on much the same principal. The rocking motion winnowed away the lighter material, leaving the heavier gold behind. The main difference, however, the rocker boxes did not need flowing water to operate.

On closer inspection, J.T. thought the rock wall looked like it had been blasted, leaving behind a jumbled pile of rock and loose rubble. Sure, the larger chunks would have to be sledgehammered and pulverized, before shoveling into the sluice box, but that also meant there were probably explosives somewhere nearby.

Once again, J.T. circled the operation, searching for dynamite, probing all potential hiding places. And there it was! He'd missed it the first time around, but on the opposite side of the arroyo, tucked away in a shaded cutback, was a square 2 by 2 foot pine box.

Kneeling, he cautiously slid back the lid. Inside, stacked in neat horizontal rows, was a half of a case of dynamite. Some of the top sticks were beaded with oily drops, as though they'd been sweating. Taking care not to jar anything, J.T. slowly slid the lid back through the grooves, closing the box. From helping his father dynamite old tree stumps (to clear a dying orchard, in order to plant alfalfa), J.T. knew a little about explosives and he knew sweating dynamite was a dangerous thing.

At that moment, off in the distance, came the faint drone of a combustion engine. Instantly, Mickey's head popped up. The noise appeared to be coming from the southeast and was probably less than a half-mile away. And as improbable as it seemed, it sounded as though a vehicle was coming right up Goldstrike Creek!

"Sounds like they're comin' back," Mickey said, dropping a handful of sand back into the sluice box.

"Time to go," J.T. added urgently. As he turned from the dynamite, he noted with some concern the sun was already well along on its downward arc. Sunset was less than two hours away.

Staying well to the north (the vehicle was coming up from the south), they made a wide arc around the camp, hoping to eventually work south toward Goldstrike Creek, entering the creek bed well below the oncoming vehicle. The north boundary of the plateau was densely wooded with piñons and junipers, making for slow going, but at the same time providing good cover.

The boys continued their general circle around the camp without problems, but on the east side of the plateau their progress was abruptly halted. A sheer sandstone cliff blocked their way. There was no way forward and no way down!

Backing up and re-routing, they tried to work a little further south, but still ran into the same problem, the same impassible cliff. If they headed straight south, they would end up back in the camp. If they backtracked on the same arc from which they'd just come, they'd never make it back before the vehicle arrived. They were trapped!

Frantically, they searched for an alternate route. The sandstone cliff blocked any thought of going east and heading north took them further away from the flatbed, not a good idea with sundown looming. Unfortunately, it appeared the only way out was back through the camp, then down Goldstrike Creek; the very same route they'd earlier used and the same path the vehicle was now laboring up. With no other choice, they headed due south, hoping to get through the camp before the vehicle topped the incline.

A couple of minutes later, the engine noise ceased, not necessarily a good sign. Unfortunately, J.T. assumed that meant the miners were already back in camp. Still, with no other option, the boys picked their way forward, trying to stay as far away from the miners as possible. Maybe, with any luck, they could pass just to the west, circling the periphery of the camp, and still staying mostly out of view of the miners.

Taking great care where they placed their feet, the boys shuffled on. Through windows in the dense skunk bushes and thick junipers, they occasionally got a glimpse of the camp. Now they were close, very close. The camp was not more than twenty-five yards away. Briefly, J.T. caught sight of a man, but then he was gone. Carefully, they inched on.

Suddenly, inadvertently, Mickey stepped on a dry juniper twig.

"Hey, Sweeney!" a man from the camp shouted. "Go check that out. Sounds like someone's," he pointed in their direction, "out there."

"Why?" Sweeney asked, evidently not too enthused.

"Cause the Cowboy says so."

Through a small portal in the skunk bushes, J.T. caught sight of a thickset man wearing a Yankee ball cap. Reaching down, he appropriated the 30/30 from the table where Mickey had left it, then headed in their direction.

"Probably just a deer," he muttered, but nevertheless kept coming.

"Hold up, Sweeney!" A bareheaded man with a full beard now came into view. Pausing, he grabbed a handgun from a tent, then added, "Cowboy says I should come with you."

Breaking into a cold sweat, J.T. crouched even lower, while keeping an eye on the advancing miners. There was nowhere to run. He glanced over at Mickey. Looking pale and frightened, Mickey said nothing. For once, apparently, he had no suggestions.

Quickly, J.T. went over their alternatives. They couldn't go forward. They couldn't go east. They couldn't go west. With the miners advancing from the north, if they tried to go south, they would undoubtedly be spotted and gunned down.

Out of viable options, J.T. hunkered down and waited.

22

THROUGH A SMALL WINDOW IN THE SKUNK BUSHES, J.T. WATCHED THE men advance. Guns held high to keep them free of snags, they fought through the dense undergrowth. Just before they reached J.T. and Mickey's thicket, the two men split up. Sweeney, the rifleman, went left; the bearded guy with the pistol angled to the right.

Burrowing like a pocket gopher, J.T. tunneled deeper into the bush, then tried to calm himself by concentrating on his breathing. He could only imagine what the miners would do when they found them, but it was a safe bet they would not be happy. Obviously, the men did not want to be found, that's why they'd gone to such great lengths to hide their camp, and that also meant that more than likely what they were doing here was illegal. And—and, they weren't carrying those guns for show or recreation. If he and Mickey jumped up and tried to run, there was a good chance they'd shoot them in the back.

In desperation, J.T. glanced around. In the thick foliage, he'd lost track of the bearded, handgun miner, but Sweeney, the rifleman, was now so close he could almost reach out and touch his boot. There simply was no way out. Standing up and surrendering would be better than getting shot in the back; although it was possible all that would accomplish would to be shot a few seconds later in the front, the chest or the abdomen.

Or, possibly, the miners would take them prisoner and let the Cowboy decide their fate. That thought was not particularly comforting either. But regardless of the consequences, he decided the lesser of the two evils was to surrender, and he might as well get on with it before Mickey did something rash.

Just as J.T. was kneeling, preparing to stand, he heard another twig snap directly behind him. This crack was immediately followed by a brushing sound, as though someone, or something was pushing through the thick vegetation. Momentarily, J.T. froze, remaining on his knees. Had a third man joined the search party? Or maybe, the revolver miner had succeeded in circling behind them, and if he stood up, he'd might get shot in the back anyway!

Expecting the worst, J.T. slowly managed to squirm and turn around, then suppressed a cry of surprise. For there, astride his brown and white paint, was none other than his Native American cousin, his Navajo godfather, Smokey Grayman.

Cradling his 30/30 carbine on his lap, behind the saddle pommel, he emerged from the brush directly behind, coming up from the south. And in spite of the late afternoon heat, he was wearing a fringed buckskin jacket and leather-riding chaps. Of course, on his head he sported his trademark, flat-brimmed black Stetson, with silver-band conchos sparkling in the bright afternoon sun.

Instantly, Smokey put a finger to his brown lips, then patted down the air, motioning for them to stay down. Nudging the paint forward, he continued to pick his way through the heavy undergrowth, heading directly for the miner's camp.

"Halt!" Sweeney shouted, his voice loud and threatening. "Not another step or I'll shoot."

"Yaa' eh t'eeh," J.T. heard Smokey reply, as the brush portal behind him and the paint closed again. Now he couldn't see either Sweeney or Smokey, though they were not more than ten or fifteen feet away. However, he could hear them clearly.

"What the hell you doin' heer, Injun?"

"What does it look like, Biligaana?"

"Don't git cute with me, Injun! Speak American."

"Hunting deer," Smokey replied more softly, then added, "my white brother."

"I ain't your brother," Sweeney snapped, then sarcastically added, "wrong time of the year for huntin', brown brother."

"Not for me."

"That so?"

"Government land," Smokey explained, gesturing in a circle. "I can hunt when and where I want."

"Well, not heer, you can't. This happens to be a private camp."

"Not a problem." Smokey replied, his rifle still cradled across his lap. "I can hunt somewhere else. You've probably scared off the deer anyway."

"Go on, then, Injun," Sweeney growled, "git the hell outta heer!"

From his hiding place, J.T. could hear the paint slowly moving off, angling more to the southeast, his metal shoes scraping on the sandstone as his big body pushed through the sunk bushes. For a moment, everything was quiet except for the sounds of Smokey's horse. Gradually, however, those sounds became fainter, finally disappearing altogether.

"You just going to let him ride off, Sweeney?" the revolver man demanded after the two of them had rendezvoused right in front of J.T.

"He didn't see nothin'."

"How'd you know? Them Injuns see a lot more'n you think."

"No," Sweeney insisted, "he came up from the south. He didn't see nothin'."

"Well, the cowboy ain't goin' to like it; you just lettin' him go."

"So, he ain't ever goin' a know," Sweeney swung the barrel of his 30/30 so it pointed directly at the other man's chest, "now is he?"

"Okay, okay! Geez, Sweeney, just aim that damn Winchester somewhere else," the revolver man growled, then stomped off back toward camp.

Mumbling to himself, a moment later Sweeney followed.

Although the miners were gone, J.T. and Mickey stayed rooted where they were for another ten minutes. When it looked for certain all was clear, they slipped out of the thicket and started down the slickrock stream bed.

"Darn, that was close!" J.T. whispered when they were out of earshot.

"Yeah, it sure as hell was," Mickey agreed, then added, "thank God for Smokey!"

"Yeah," J.T. said half-heartedly. At the moment, he had conflicting emotions over what had just happened, and of course about Smokey in general. Though he hated to admit it, he was still embarrassed by his Navajo cousin, and very much resented that Smokey considered it his sacred duty to look after him. Furthermore, it more than annoyed him Smokey was always hanging around. It seemed, he could/would turn up almost anywhere and at any time. On the other hand, J.T. had to admit, although somewhat grudgingly, his Indian godfather had more than likely saved their lives today.

Stopping only long enough to kneel for a drink of water, they continued downstream until they came to Goldstrike Road. From there, it was only a short, quarter mile hike south to the International.

On arrival, J.T. immediately inspected the flatbed. He felt a huge sense of relief when nothing seemed amiss, no obvious sign of breakage or sabotage. Apparently, the miners had not found, or at least had not paid much attention to the truck. Jumping into the over-heated cab, J.T. rolled down the windows and cranked the engine, then waited for Mickey to climb in and close his door. With the slam of Mickey's door, he ground the old International into first gear and stepped on the gas feed.

As though it was protesting being disturbed, the old flatbed bucked and lurched as J.T. released the clutch, but eventually it leveled out. With things now seemingly under control, J.T. headed south, back down Goldstrike Road.

Off to the west, the sun had slipped behind the pewter gray Mormon Mountains, leaving the valley in a dull flat light. Directly overhead, however, the heavens were afire. A low carpet of cirrus clouds suddenly combusted, then slowly progressed through a kaleidoscope of color. First, the clouds blazed a brilliant sunflower gold, then slowly rifled to a rich ruby red, gradually evolving to a more subdued lilac purple or lavender. During the spectacular light show, a kind of awe or reverence settled over the cab.

For the next fifteen minutes, the boys said nothing, mesmerized by the constantly changing sky. Somehow, the progressing sunset seemed to reflect, or mirror J.T.'s mood. At first, he was buoyed, everything seemed brighter, more hopeful, then as the light continued to dim, his mood became progressively darker and more pessimistic.

Finally, Mickey broke the spell. "So, you know, Smokey really saved our bacon today."

"Yeah, I guess so."

"You don't seem very grateful."

J.T. snapped, "well, I am!"

"What you got against Smokey?"

"Nothing," J.T. replied curtly, "could we just drop it?"

"Why?

"Why, what?"

"Why drop it."

"Cause," J.T. said tersely, "I don't want to talk about it. Okay?"

"You don't need to get so touchy."

"I'm not touchy!"

"Whatever you say."

Silence returned, but just briefly.

Mickey started in again. "You think I don't know you're part Injun?"

Scowling and looking straight ahead, J.T. didn't reply.

Again, they rode in bumpy silence.

"Well, it don't matter to me."

More silence. Instead of answering, J.T. pushed down even harder on the accelerator.

With worry lines deepening on his forehead, Mickey finally asked, "don't you think you ought'a slow down?"

"Nah," J.T. replied, finally glancing over at Mickey, "there's never any traffic on this road," He was surprised to see Mickey was nervous. Mickey thrived on danger. Maybe, he really was going too fast.

"What's the hurry, anyway?" Mickey asked, as J.T. skidded around another U-turn, tires sliding sideways and spitting gravel. "Your father's out of town."

"Well, if you must know, he called to check on me last night," J.T. replied. After negotiating that turn, just barely, he punched down on the accelerator again.

"So?"

"So, he told me he was going to try to call every night while they were in

Salt Lake City, just make sure everything was okay; see if I needed anything."

"Probably, just worried about you," Mickey exhaled loudly after the flatbed was safely back on a straightaway, "you know, about leavin' you alone."

"Probably, but I think he's not just checking on me, as much as he's checking up on me."

"Geez, I wonder why," Mickey mumbled sarcastically, while clinging to the window frame as J.T. accelerated out of another turn, "seems he'd have no reason to do that."

"What are you trying to say?"

"Nothin'. What time did he call last night?"

"Nine o'clock."

"So, you think he's going to call again at nine?"

"Probably."

"Then you'd better hurry," Mickey replied, after checking his wristwatch, "it's already eight-thirty."

"What do you think I'm doing?"

With the sunset now stonewashed to a faded, gunpowder gray, J.T. focused strictly on the road. There was just enough light, barely, to see the outline of the road, but probably not enough to go this fast. He really should slow down, but he did not.

Instead of going slower, J.T. discovered if he braked hard going into the turns, then stomped on the accelerator coming out, he wouldn't lose much momentum. Unfortunately, this maneuver, often resulted in the backend fishtailing, as the rear tires fought for purchase in the loose roadside gravel. On the infrequent straightaways, J.T. floorboarded it, and in spite of the jaw-rattling washboard, at times reaching speeds of fifty miles-per-hour or more.

Just as J.T. entered a rare, quarter-mile flat, he thought he could make out a telltale dust plume, ballooning up in the distance. It appeared to be headed their way and coming fast. In most places, J.T. knew the Goldstrike Road was too narrow for cars to pass side-by-side. At least one of them had to pull off onto the shoulder.

Taking his foot off the accelerator, J.T. slowed and started to veer off onto the right shoulder, but the approaching car did not reciprocate. Barreling down the middle of the road, it looked like it was going to slam into them. Braking hard, J.T. swung even further off the road, his tires crushing a blue sage and a beaver tail cactus. As he bounced over a football-size rock, his head hit the ceiling hard enough to momentarily fog his vision. Without braking or slowing, the other car roared on by.

"Ye-ow!" J.T. moaned, massaging his head as he glanced at the car through his rearview mirror. Unfortunately, now all he could see was the receding cloud of dust.

"Wasn't that old man Rosenkranz?" Mickey asked, also rubbing his head.

"I don't know." J.T. ground the gears back into first, then not waiting for the dust to completely settle, he bucked the flatbed back onto the road.

"I think it was a black sedan," Mickey continued, "probably Comrade Boris out doing his daily radiation checks for the Kremlin."

"Whatever," J.T. shrugged as he pushed down on the accelerator, coaxing the old flatbed back up to speed. Right now, he was more concerned with getting back to Santa Clara in time.

"Wonder why he was in such a hurry? Was there a Shot today?"

"No, I don't think so," J.T. replied.

"Was someone chasin' him?"

"Like who?"

"Like the Santa Clara mob chasing him outta town."

"Did you see anyone else?" J.T. snapped, then added, "he always drives like that."

Within a few more seconds, they were once again up to speed. After turning left off Goldstrike Road, they continued to barrel down Pahcoon Road. Unfortunately, there was almost no light and they still had fifteen miles to go. If J.T. didn't get home to take his father's phone call, then he'd have to come up with yet another excuse. Coming up with credible lies was getting harder and harder and J.T. had to admit he was getting pretty tired of trying. Determined to get home before his father called, he punched the gas feed to the floor, barely slowing for the upcoming curve.

"Don't you think you should turn your headlights on?" Mickey said.

"Yeah, probably."

Leaning forward, J.T. grappled for the light switch, then as he glanced up, suddenly there was another car in front of them. The oncoming headlights blinded him!

Instinctively, J.T. whipped the steering wheel hard to the left. His rear tires skidded on the loose gravel, then abruptly after reestablishing traction, propelled the flatbed forward again. A millisecond after that, a six-foot cut bank appeared directly in front of the windshield. With no time to react, J.T. belatedly stomped on the brakes. It was, however, too late; the flatbed smashed into the cutbank. On impact, J.T.'s chest slammed hard against the steering wheel, and his head shot forward, striking the windshield.

Responding just in time, the other car swerved hard in the opposite direction, careening off the shoulder and crashing through the roadside sagebrush, creosote, and cacti. Finally, the white sedan staggered to a stop in the sandy bed of an arroyo.

At first, everything blurred, then fogged, then faded to charcoal black. J.T. struggled to remain conscious, to keep some brain lights/activity on. Reaching out, he fumbled for the door handle, grabbing, and hanging onto it as though it was some kind of anchor that would stop the spinning. After a few more seconds, his eyes began to focus. At first, he was confused at what he saw through the windshield, nothing but the looming cutback, then like a breeched irrigation dam, it all came rushing back.

Mickey? What about Mickey!

Quickly, J.T. glanced over to his right. Mickey wasn't on the bench seat! Panicky now, he looked down and there he was, wadded-up like a first draft English paper, lying on the floorboard. He wasn't moving! Had he just killed his best friend?

Fighting back a wave of guilt, J.T. slid across the bench seat. Reaching down, he touched Mickey's shoulder. No response. Gently, he shook him.

Still nothing. Oh, God, please!

He shook him again, a little harder.

"Ug-g-g-h," Mickey suddenly groaned. "Geez, where'd you learn to drive?"

Looking upward, J.T. offered a silent prayer of thanks, then turned back to Mickey. "Can—can you get up?"

"Yeah," Mickey stirred a little, "I think so if you give me a hand."

Re-positioning his legs for better leverage, J.T. grabbed Mickey under the arms and lifted.

Grunting and twisting, Mickey slowly worked out of the foxhole between the dashboard and the bench seat.

"W—what the hell happened?" he asked, holding his head.

"We hit that." J.T. pointed through the windshield at the towering cutbank.

"Oh," Mickey said sarcastically, "and I thought you'd just stopped for a stop sign."

"No, I to swerved to miss a—"

Abruptly, the driver-side door jerked open and a man sporting a goatee and wearing a white lab coat thrust his head in.

"You guys okay?"

Though still a bit shaken, nevertheless both boys nodded yes.

"Well then," the man's voice suddenly changed from concern to consternation, "what in the hell was that all about?"

"M—mister Popovich?" J.T. blurted. In the dark, he was still unsure who he was talking to.

"Yeah?"

"Mister Popovich, it's us, J.T. Kunz, and Mickey Graff. You know from the Santa Clara Elementary School. I wore one of your radiation badges."

For a long moment, Rudy Popovich eyed the boys suspiciously. "Huh—yeah, okay, I remember. Are you guys, okay?" he asked again, his voice once again a bit more gentle.

"I think so." J.T. replied, while exploring an expanding goose egg on his forehead.

"How about you, Graff?" Popovich asked

"Yeah, I'm okay," Mickey replied, gingerly stepping out onto the running board, then off onto the ground.

Backing up, Popovich also allowed J.T. to exit.

For the next few seconds, J.T. and Mickey took inventory of their injuries. Of course, there were the expected bumps and bruises, but thankfully there were no Rorschach puddles of red, so apparently neither of them was leaking blood. And all their limbs moved freely, so that seemed negate the possibility of boney fractures.

At least, J.T. thought, as he watched Popovich walk back to his AEC sedan, it wasn't Borch Rosenkranz he'd run off the road. Running a Russian spy off the road could have been dangerous to one's health, particularly if he was on the run and desperate. No telling what he would do.

As the boys gathered around, Deputy Director Rudy Popovich started his car, put it in reverse and tried to back onto the road. Unfortunately, all he accomplished was to spin his rear tires in the deep silica sand.

"Well, I'm stuck," he announced, rejoining the boys. "Engine's okay, but I can't get her out of the sand. No traction."

"Uh," J.T. nodded at the flatbed, "I'm pretty sure I've got a chain behind the seat. Father always carries one for emergencies."

Doubtfully, Popovich eyed the flatbed. "Will your truck even run?"

"I don't know—I think so." Pivoting around, J.T. led the group back to inspect the truck.

Fortunately, the cutbank was composed of compact, but soft sand, and the truck was built like a Sherman tank. So, other than a few paint scrapes and a couple of fairly shallow dents in the hood and bumper, the old International appeared to be fine. Thankfully, as with the boys, there was no telltale bleeding of essential fluids, like water or oil. And even the locust-splattered windshield remained intact.

"Well, give it a try," Rudy said, opening the door for J.T.

Climbing back into the cab, J.T. cranked the engine. As usual, it groaned and protested for a few seconds, then when he'd sufficiently choked it, the flatbed roared back to life. Carefully, and with Popovich giving verbal and hand directions, J.T. ground the gearshift into reverse and backed the truck to the other side of the road, getting as close to the sandy arroyo and the white sedan as possible. Next, he fished the chain from behind the seat, handing it to Popovich. Lying prone, Rudy looped one end around a frame crossmember. The other end, J.T. hooked to the tow ring at the back of the International.

After Popovich climbed back in the sedan, he simultaneously waved and yelled, "okay!"

Grinding the transmission into first gear, J.T. lurched forward, snapping the chain taut, then gunned it. Like it was a matchbox car, the International easily pulled/ jerked the AEC car out of the arroyo back to safety of the more solid Pachoon Road.

"Thanks, boys," Popovich said as they gathered around their vehicles.

"Sorry about all that," J.T. mumbled, loosening, and re-coiling the chain, "it was my fault."

Popovich eyed him for a moment. "You got a driver's license, son?"

"Well—uh—well—I—"

Frowning, Popovich shook his head. "I have half-a-mind to turn you in. What are you guys doing up here, anyway?"

"Uh—uh," J.T. stammered, quickly turning away to re-stow the chain.

Never one to be intimidated by authority, Mickey boldly stepped forward. "I guess we could ask you the same thing."

"I'll ask the questions here, Graff." Popovich got in Mickey's face, then backed off. "Well, okay, I guess that's a valid question. We've got a radiation monitoring station up here and the technician assigned to collect the data got the flu, so I'm filling in. Now it's your turn, what are you two doing up here, at this hour and with no driver's license?"

"Uh—uh," J.T. mumbled, still searching for an answer.

"And," Popovich added, "is that truck stolen?"

"The truck? Oh, no," J.T. blurted, "it's my father's."

"And he knows you have it?"

"Well," J.T. hesitated, thought about lying, then quickly settled on the truth. "Well, not exactly."

"Meaning what?"

"Uh—uh, meaning he's out of town."

"But you will let him know?"

J.T. nodded.

"Okay, boys, I guess I'll let it go this time; you know, no harm no foul. But if I ever see you driving without a license again, I will turn you into the Washington County Sheriff myself."

Again J.T. nodded.

"So, then," Popovich said sternly, "I'll ask one more time, what are you doing up here, and it better be good."

Without missing a beat, Mickey answered, "we're up here checking on some leads."

"Leads?" Rudy echoed. "What kind of leads?"

"You know, leads on the death of Lenny Weeks and whole the Boris, uh—uh, Borch Rosenkranz thing. We think they might be related."

"Well, I don't know anything about the death of a Mister Lenny Weeks," Popovich said, eyeing the boys closely, "but I do know about Mister Rosenkranz. We just cleared him, boys."

Quickly, J.T. added, "cleared him of what?"

"Suffice it to say, like I said the other night at the town meeting, I had the FBI check him out. He's okay."

"What!" J.T. exclaimed. He couldn't believe it. All their carefully crafted theories suddenly, like his rocket, gone up in smoke. "What does okay, mean?"

"I really don't have time for this," Popovich said, turning away.

"Come on, Mister Popovich," J.T. pleaded. "This is important to us and is part of the reason we're up here."

Popovich eyed J.T. for a moment, then shrugged. "Okay, like I said, the FBI checked him out. The first time he shows up on their radar is in Augsburg, Germany, nineteen hundred and thirty-six. His father worked at the Messerschmitt factory and—"

"Messerschmitt?" Mickey interrupted. "What's a Messerschmitt?

"Messerschmitt was the factory that made German warplanes," Popovich explained, then continued, "and after that, the FBI could find no record of him until nineteen hundred and forty-one. It seems that's the year he graduated from Berlin Technical University with a degree in physics. Good grades. The next time he shows up on their screen is nineteen hundred and forty-three. At that time, he began working for the German V-2 rocket program in Blizna, Poland—"

"In Poland?" This time, J.T. cut in. "Why Poland?"

"Well," Popovich shrugged, "it seems at some time during the war, the Gerrys moved their main flight-testing facility to Poland, to get it out of the range of allied bombers."

"Okay," J.T. nodded.

"Anyway, at the end of the war, after the Russians captured Poland, they nabbed Rosenkranz and whisked him off to Baikonur to work on their missile program. But, by then, he was getting older and really wasn't of much help. After they released him, he made his way to East Germany, then somehow managed to sneak across the Iron Curtain to West Berlin. From there, he immigrated to Canada and from Montreal he came here."

"And that's it?" Mickey demanded.

"That's the whole story," Deputy Director Popovich turned back toward his car, then added, "I've gotta to go, boys."

"Well," J.T. continued to argue, falling in step, "Madge Reber says he speaks Russian."

"Yes," Rudy stopped again, "and so do a lot of other people. The FBI report indicates he picked up a few words while working in Baikonur, but really never became fluent. And furthermore, he never joined the communist party and as best we can tell was never much of a Stalin supporter either. In fact, one foreign source indicated he was actually kind of a pain in the butt—uh—in the neck and was never of much help to the Russians. That, plus his age, was the reason they let him go."

"Don't you see," Mickey persisted, "it's all a disguise. That's all part of his cover story. The KGB is real good at that."

Popovich simply shook his head.

"But—but what about the Geiger counter and the fallout files?" J.T. persisted, as Popovich again turned to go.

"Well," Rudy explained, "after all, he is a scientist. I guess for something to do and because he has a naturally curious mind, he was monitoring radiation fallout both in Santa Clara and somewhere here on Utah Hill. He told the FBI agents he might even try to publish a paper from the data he's collected. However, the feds may or may not let him; the data he's gathered is more than likely still classified. But regardless of that, there's nothing illegal about what he's been doing. Shoot, you guys could buy a Geiger counter and do the same."

Yeah, J.T. thought, we could if we could afford one.

"What about the letter addressed to Boris Romanoff that he picked up at the post office," Mickey demanded, "and never returned it as a wrong address?"

"My understanding," Popovich slowed his stride, "that was kind of a inside joke. His Russian coworkers nicknamed him Boris Romanoff. They thought if he was going to work in Russia, he needed a Russian name. One of them, a lady friend I think, wrote the letter after she also had defected, to Sweden I think."

"Well, what about the shortwave radio?" J.T. asked, as they gathered by Popovich's car. "Don't you think that's a little suspicious?"

"No, not really. He's also an amateur ham radio operator," Rudy opened his car door, then leaned against the fame, "and has been for many years. Lots of people are. Apparently, he now has a U.S. license and call letters. It's just another hobby, like golfing or fishing."

"But what about the Kodak Camera?" J.T. asked, before Rudy could climb into the car.

Pausing, Popovich looked incredulous. "Now that's really fishing, boys. Would you go to Germany without taking a camera?"

"Huh?"

"He'd never been to America before and there's some damn—uh—darn pretty country around here to photograph, like Zion, Bryce and the Grand Canyon for starters."

Mickey muttered, "I've never bin to Zion, Bryce or the Grand Canyon neither."

"Okay," J.T. said, then asked, "so, then, why is he here?"

"As best I can tell," Popovich replied, climbing into the sedan, "he was doing just what he said he was, a German immigrant coming to America to enjoy his golden years."

Suddenly, J.T. felt like a first-class heel, but Mickey was not ready do drop it. "But he told us he's from Switzerland."

"I don't know about that," Rudy cranked the engine. "Maybe he lied about that, or maybe he was born in Switzerland, then his family moved to Germany when his father got a job at the Messerschmitt factory. But I do know people around here like Switzers a whole lot better than they do Krauts."

Of course, J.T. knew that was true. Even though they spoke the same language, nobody here equated the Swiss with Nazi Germany.

Mickey, however, still was not satisfied. "But isn't that illegal?"

Popovich shook his head. "If I tell you I grew up in Albuquerque, New Mexico, and I actually grew up in Salt Lake City, there's still no law against it unless I write it on an official government form."

Mickey raised an eyebrow. "On a government form?"

"You know, falsify my immigration papers, then it's a crime."

"So," Mickey persisted, "his immigration papers said he was from Germany?"

"No," Rudy replied, "I actually think they said Canada."

"I still don't like it," Mickey grumbled, "that he lied to us. Said he was from Switzerland."

"Maybe he was from Switzerland," Rudy replied, putting his car in gear, "I don't know. Look boys, it's late and I still have to collect data from Bull Valley, then change things over for the next Shot."

"Wait," J.T. blurted, as his mind quickly jumped from Rosenkranz to radiation and then the next Shot, "I've got one more question."

"Okay," Popovich said, impatiently.

"Have you heard anything about the badges?"

"Badges? What badges?"

"The radiation badges," J.T. replied. "Have you got any results?"

“Oh—not yet—and maybe I never will. That stuff’s all classified.”

“So,” Mickey frowned. “Borch was measuring radiation, wasn’t he?”

The Deputy Director nodded.

“Why isn’t that classified?”

Looking more than a little exasperated, Popovich replied, “do I really have to answer that?”

“Yeah,” Mickey nodded, not backing off, “to me, it seems the same.”

“Well, one was measured by the government and one by a private individual.”

Frowning, J.T. said, barely above a whisper, “that makes no sense.”

“Look boys, I’ve really got to go.”

“So,” Mickey blurted, his voice getting louder, “it’s not like the government never makes a mistak—”

“So,” J.T. cut him off; Mickey was getting in one of his moods, “so, Mister Popovich,” J.T. said, still trying to wrap his head around all this news, “so, what does this all mean?”

“What it means,” Rudy Popovich said impatiently, “is Mister Borch Rosenkranz is no more a Russian spy than you, or me, or President Dwight D. Eisenhower!”

23

Stunned, the boys watched the white sedan disappear around an "S" curve heading north.

"Maybe he is a legal German or Canadian immigrant," Mickey muttered, "but I still think he's up to somethin'."

"I don't know." J.T. sighed, scanning the west horizon. The earlier golden sunset had completely vanished, now replaced by the evening star, Venus, shining like a lighthouse beacon in a black celestial sea. "Maybe we really did jump to conclusions."

"Nah, there's somethin' wrong with him," Mickey declared. "What about the cowboy and the poached deer? We forgot to tell Mister Popovich about that. There's somethin' goin' on here; I can feel it in my bones."

"Well, come on," J.T. said, nudging Mickey forward. "We've got to go."

The boys drove the rest of the way mostly in silence. After the near collision with Popovich, J.T. slowed the flatbed down considerably. There was no way he was going to make it home by nine o'clock anyway. As an unanticipated benefit, however, the slower speed gave him more freedom to mull over what had just happened.

So, was it really true that Borch Rosenkranz was not a Russian spy? And Boris Romanoff was just a nickname? Apparently, it was. Was he, in fact, just an innocent old man looking for a place to retire, to spend his last few remaining years in peace, after spending a lifetime in the midst of political and civil turmoil? Was the reason he hadn't mixed so well with our community because we hadn't let him? So, if what Popovich had said was true, then the angry mob scene from the other night was not only unnecessary but was downright embarrassing and completely un-American. The whole town, at least the male half, had falsely accused Borch Rosenkranz of being a Russian spy and ordered him to leave town.

Suddenly, J.T. felt sick to his stomach. If all that was true, they, he and Mickey, had played a major part in arousing suspicions and fanning the flames of intolerance. Now, it appeared the only thing Borch had personally done to him was give him some advice about his rocket problems. And if he ever found the time, he would like to try implementing some of Borch's suggestions. It was all terribly confusing and very upsetting. He felt like a first-class heel.

But on the other hand, if Borch was who he claimed, then as Mickey said, how did you explain his apparent shady association with the cowboy? Obviously, the very same cowboy who was presently involved in the highly suspect and probably illegal gold mine. Was Borch involved in the mine too? There had to be some association. He and Mickey had seen the cowboy at Rosenkranz's place twice and he'd probably been there more than that. And he and Rosenkranz had been arguing about something, maybe money. So, regardless of Popovich clearing him, like Mickey said, there was something about this whole affair that still didn't pass the sniff test.

Also, it still bothered J.T., if in fact Borch was a German immigrant, then why did he tell the town he was Swiss? Why did he claim to be a relative of the Reusch's? Why didn't he just say he was German?

Well, maybe, like Popovich said, it was because of the war. Since the end of the war, there was a lot of lingering resentment for Japanese and Germans, or Japs and Krauts as they were disparagingly called. Maybe that's why he claimed to be Swiss.

"So do you think your dad will notice those new dents in the front end?" Mickey asked, suddenly breaking the silence.

"I don't know," J.T. forced his mind back to the present, "but I doubt it. There's so many other scratches and dents on this old truck, I don't think so."

"For your sake, I sure hope not."

"It's just a hay truck and it'll still work fine for hauling hay."

"What you goin' to tell him about being late tonight?"

"I don't know," J.T. replied glumly. "I still haven't come up with anything yet."

"Tell him you were out playin' Town Bell."

"I'm not sure that would help."

Again, the boys lapsed into silence and once again J.T.'s mind began to wander, this time leapfrogging three hundred miles north to Salt Lake City.

Obviously, he was worried about his mother. She hadn't looked well for quite some time. And this trip to Salt Lake City to see an oncologist, what was he to conclude from that? Was it some kind of last-ditch effort? Or was there a real chance it might help? J.T. desperately hoped it was the latter.

And even though he tried not to think about life without his mother, he couldn't help it. What would happen to them, to their family if she died? Mary would surely leave in another year or two, either to college or get married, then it would just be him and Father—cats trying to live with dogs, capitalists trying to live with communists. If indeed that happened, what effect would it have on his father? Would the ordeal mellow him some, or make him even more bitter? Shuddering at the thought of losing his mother, with all the attendant possibilities, J.T. forced his mind in a different direction.

It was totally frustrating, but they, he and Mickey, still hadn't a clue who killed Lenny Weeks and furthermore, Weird Willie hadn't turned up either. And to compound the problem, they were likely running out of time. If what Mary told him was true, the sheriff was close to arresting them for the murder of Lenny, and the clock was ticking; then figuratively speaking, it was way past midnight.

In the miners' camp, they'd found the same unmarked bullets that were on Lenny's body and in the bushes by the fort. Somehow it all had to be connected, but how? Unfortunately, the gold mine appeared to be another random and frustrating clue, which led nowhere. However, they'd better start connecting the dots soon, the blood hounds were nipping at their heels.

Finally, J.T. thought about his seemingly fast fading goal of making a functioning rocket by the end of summer. Like everything else, he was failing miserably at that too. In his mind, thanks to Borch Rosenkranz, he thought he knew how to make a two-chamber rocket, so combustion would not occur in the fuel storage chamber, and he'd figured out how to make a better motor. He just needed the time to work on it.

And if all that was not enough, the end of the summer was just around the corner with its first-date tradition looming. For a while, he'd thought Annie Leavitt was a real possibility, but now she seemed more interested in Curley Reber. Oh, well, it's not like he wanted to go anyway.

But there was one thing of which he was certain, so far this summer had been a total bust. Probably, worse than a bust if you added in their disastrous attempts to break Judd and Howie's prank record.

In the gloom of the cab, J.T. shook his head as he mentally replayed the cherry bomb-school fiasco, the ill-fated mannequin caper, and the near-fatal cracker ball prank. Yes, this summer had been a more than a bust, it had been a total and unmitigated disaster.

The only silver lining, if you could call it that, was now he had earned fifteen of the twenty dollars, exactly three-fourths of the money he would need to pay off his share of the school damages. And thankfully, his father had not yet presented him a bill for flooding and nearly destroying the Loren Reber piece. Maybe, hopefully, he never would.

In silence, they passed through the small town of Gunlock, then on down the road to the turnoff to the Shivwits Indian Reservation. The last five miles from the Reservation to Santa Clara was the only time J.T. was required to drive on the highway, U.S. Highway 91. After entering Santa Clara, he breathed a sigh of relief. No cops, no tickets, not tonight. Maybe his luck was changing after all. He dropped Mickey off, then took the backstreet, Corral Street, home and parked the flatbed in back of the house.

As J.T. opened the service door and walked into the house, the phone was ringing. Taking a deep breath, he picked up the phone, then held his breath.

"Where you been?" his father demanded, not bothering with pleasantries.

"Uh—uh—"

"This is the third time I've called," he snapped. "The first time was over an hour ago."

"Uh—uh, we ran into Mister Popovich and got to talking," J.T. stammered, which was mostly true.

"Who's we?"

"Me and Mickey Graff."

"I should have known," Mr. Kunz growled, "that kid would be involved."

"Anyway, they've checked out Borch Rosenkranz," J.T. blurted, desperately trying to change the subject.

"Who's they?" Mr. Kunz asked, taking the bait.

"Popovich and the FBI."

"And?"

"And they say he's not a spy!"

There was a long moment of silence, then Mr. Kunz spoke, slowly meting out his words. "So—just how—did they—determine that?"

Over the next couple of minutes, J.T. recounted the details of the day with two major exceptions: instead of divulging he took the International, he said Mickey's older brother Darrell drove them up to Goldstrike Creek, and of course he didn't breathe a word about seeing Smokey Grayman.

"Sounds like," Mr. Kunz said sarcastically, "the FBI did their usual thorough job."

"Why?" J.T. was confused.

"Well, obviously, they didn't get the whole story. Regardless of what they say, something's not quite kosher here."

"Kosher?"

"You know, legit."

"Oh, so why would they try to hide their gold mine?"

"Well," Mr. Kunz replied after another moment, "I can think of two possible reasons. One, they don't have a valid claim or two, they don't want to sell their gold to the government."

"What?" J.T. was not following any of this. "Why not the government?"

"Well, son, the price of gold is regulated by the government, thirty-five dollars per ounce. That's all you can get, unless you sell it on the black market, then you can get a whole lot more.""

"The black market?"

"You know, illegal trade, under the table. The law says you have to sell all gold to the government and at their price, then they can keep it or resell it to private companies, like those that make jewelry or to dentists."

"Why would the government want to keep it?"

"Son, the paper dollar is backed by gold, that's called the gold standard. Every paper dollar in circulation is backed up by that same value in gold and that gold is stored at Fort Knox."

"I still don't get it," J.T. said. This was all new to him.

"If you control the value of gold, then you also control the worth of the dollar. It stabilizes our money system. Understand?"

"Yeah, I guess, but what's that got to do with Mister Rosenkranz?"

"I don't know for sure," John Kunz admitted, "but Borch and those other miners are definitely up to something. Keep an eye on them, son, but don't do nothing stupid."

"Okay."

"But," Mr. Kunz continued, "it is a pity the FBI are such damn incompetents that they can't even…" His father's voice trailed off and he never finished his thought.

When the conversation lagged, J.T. asked, "so, how's mother doing?"

"Oh, she had her second visit with the cancer specialist today. I think they're going to start cobalt treatments tomorrow. Looks like we'll be up here a little longer than we thought. Are you okay with that?"

"Yeah, I'm fine."

"Are the animals okay? Are you doing your chores?"

"Yes, Father."

"You're going to need to pick the Bartlett pears. They should be ready and maybe even the early cling peaches."

"Okay."

"Sid Graff's fruit stand said they would take all we can pick."

"Okay."

"And the hay should be about ready. Do you think you can cut and rake it and I'll ask Uncle Jack to help you haul it?"

"Yes, Father."

"And don't forget about the watering turns."

"I won't."

"And keep an eye on Romanoff or Rosenkranz, or whatever his name is, but be careful. He might very well be dangerous."

"I will, Father." J.T. was planning on keeping an eye on him anyway. There just had to be a connection between Borch and the cowboy and Lenny's killer.

"I'll call you tomorrow at nine."

"Okay."

"Don't be late."

"Okay."

After hanging up the phone, J.T. went to look for something to eat. There was nothing in the fridge and he didn't want to cook, not this late. He settled for his father's ulcer meal, a bowl of soggy bread and milk, then he headed out to do his chores. No flashlight was needed, as the night was aglow, peppered with countless rhinestones and the bright aurora of the Milky Way. After chores, he tumbled into bed.

The next morning J.T. picked eight lugs of Bartlett pears,then delivered them to Graff's fruit stand, but the early cling peaches weren't quite ready. He declined the offered money and told Sid he could pay his father when he got back. That afternoon, he cut the hay, minus the Loren Reber piece he'd previously trashed, then dashed home to do his evening chores.

After finishing his chores and completing the obligatory nine o'clock phone call with his father, no new news on his mother, he met Mickey on Highway 91, right where it intersected with Ence Lane.

"So," Mickey asked, "what's your plan?"

"Find something to tell us what's going on," J.T. replied, then added his father's words, "something's not quite kosher here."

"Kosher?"

"You know, not legal."

"Where do you get them big words?"

"I read a lot."

"Yeah, well, that's not much of a plan."

"You got a better one?"

"So, do you think he's still in there?" Mickey asked, nodding toward the house. The only light appeared to be coming from the back porch.

"I don't know," J.T. shrugged. Though he agreed with his father, something wasn't kosher, he still felt bad about the whole affair. "Maybe he's gone," he finally replied. "The mob only gave him a week."

"But that was before Popovich cleared him," Mickey argued, "so, that may not still apply."

"Yeah, I guess, but maybe Borch doesn't know he's been cleared."

"But remember, we saw him yesterday on Goldstrike Road," Mickey argued, "so he's still around."

"Yeah, probably that was him, but he could have been out collecting his monitoring equipment before leaving town."

"Well, there's one way to find out," Mickey said, starting down Ence Lane. "We've gotta know for sure."

To J.T., the Rosenkranz house always looked creepy, particularly at night. Tonight was no exception. There was no moon and no lights on in the house or the shed, just the single porch light. Also missing was the black sedan and the driveway appeared empty. As they started down Ence Lane, the boys turned off their flashlights, then stopped at the front gate.

Mickey suggested they check the shack first, make sure the shortwave radio was still gone.

J.T. nodded, the shed still gave him the willies, then reluctantly he followed Mickey. As quietly as they could, the boys slipped down the vacant driveway. It was eerily quiet; the only sounds came from the crunch of gravel under their rubber-soled sneakers.

Though J.T. thought it a waste of time, the door was always padlocked, Mickey stopped to check it. Strangely tonight, however, it was not locked. Creaking loudly on rusted hinges, Mickey swung the heavy plank door open. Glancing over his shoulder at J.T., he shrugged, then ducked his head and entered.

"C'mon in, J.T.," he whispered, "it's okay. No bodies in here tonight."

Cautiously, J.T. stepped in and looked around. He took a deep, claustrophobic breath; before him was nothing but sea of black! Then Mickey flipped on his flashlight. Quickly, J.T. followed suit. That was much better.

Yes, the shortwave radio was still missing, but now the table it had been resting on was also gone. And, thankfully, there was no deer carcass either. The only things left behind were the frayed loop of rope still dangling from an overhead rafter and that curious low mound of dirt in the center of the shack's floor. After taking one more look around, the boys backed out. There was absolutely nothing of interest in there. Maybe Rosenkranz had split after all and taken his shortwave radio with him.

Silently, Mickey nodded toward the house. Sighing, J.T. signaled his agreement. They had to know. Turning off their flashlights, the boys headed for the bungalow. Hopefully, that same bathroom window was still unlocked.

Standing on his tiptoes, Mickey reached up and shoved the window upward. It didn't budge. He tried it again. Still nothing. Motioning for J.T. to kneel on all fours, he climbed up on his back. The added height gave him better leverage and he tried again. This time the window groaned, then raised a couple of inches. Mickey continued to work until it was high enough to crawl through. Once inside, he leaned back over the sill and helped J.T. scramble up.

Once inside, they again flipped on their flashlights and headed down the hall toward the kitchen. It looked much like it did before, with pots and pans in the cupboards, and canned food and bottles of wine in the pantry. Everything was neat and in place; it didn't look like Borch was planning to leave anytime soon.

Back in the hall, they headed for the bedroom/study. Again, there were no moving boxes, or suitcases. Nothing to herald an impending move, and as with the kitchen, everything here was also neat and clean. The Geiger counter was still in the desk drawer and the manila folders with the radiation data were still neatly filed away in the adjoining cabinet.

Satisfied nothing had changed here, the boys proceeded to the master bedroom. No surprise here either. The bed was made, the dirty clothes hamper was half-full, and Borch's clothes were still hanging in the closet, including that odd military uniform.

On the shelf right above the uniform was the matching hat. J.T. focused his flashlight on it. Looking a bit like a commercial airline pilot's hat, it was sewn from heavy gray cloth, sporting a curvilinear black bill or visor with a high-pitched forehead that sloped backward from the crown. Braided white cord, or decorative piping, was sewn around the periphery of the bill and a silver block eagle, clutching a hoop in its talons, was embroidered right in the center of the high-pitched brow.

J.T. snatched the hat from the top shelf, then on impulse slid apart the hanging clothes. Yes, the pennant was still there, pinned to the back wall. Holding the hat next to the pennant, he compared the two eagles. They were identical. Both were block eagles and both clutched the same curious silver hoop or circle in their talons.

"You still got that ring?" J.T. whispered to Mickey.

"What ring?"

"The one we found down by the fort."

"Uh—I think so, I always keep it with me." Mickey fished through his pockets. "Why?"

"I just thought of something."

After a couple more seconds of searching, Mickey produced the ring, then with Mickey manning the flashlight, J.T. compared the eagle tooled on the ring with the hat and pennant. All three block eagles were identical.

Removing the pins that secured the pennant, J.T. rolled it up and wedged it inside the military hat.

"Let me keep the ring for a day or two," he whispered to Mickey, as they turned to go.

"Why? What are you —"

Suddenly, there was a pounding on the kitchen door.

The boys froze, then snapped off their flashlights.

The pounding started again, this time even louder, then someone grabbed the door handle, jerking on the door. Apparently, it was locked.

"Come on," Mickey tiptoed toward the hall. "Maybe, we better get the hell outta of here."

Still holding onto the hat, pennant and ring, this time J.T. didn't argue.

At the bathroom door, Mickey seemed to have a change of heart. "On second thought," he whispered, "let's sneak back into the kitchen and see who it is."

Vigorously, J.T. shook his head, but as usual Mickey ignored him. Dropping down on hands and knees, he crawled toward the kitchen. Reluctantly, J.T. placed the hat, pennant and ring on the bathroom commode and followed.

Stopping under a west-facing window, Mickey rose on bended knee, lifting the corner of the Venetian blind just enough to peek outside. After a couple of seconds, he dropped down again, motioning for J.T. to look. With his heart racing, J.T. inched over to the window, raising the blind just a slit.

What he saw both surprised and puzzled him. For there, standing on the kitchen landing, spotlighted by the porch light, was none other than the cowboy, wearing his trademark white Stetson. And he was not alone. Accompanying him was that same short, heavy man they'd seen earlier at the mining camp, and once again he was wearing a Yankees ball cap. It took a moment, for J.T. to remember his name—oh, yeah, it was Sweeney. Impatiently, the two men shuffled about the landing, often glancing over their shoulders. Grabbing the door handle, the cowboy rattled it one more time.

"Let's get closer," Mickey whispered, "so we can hear what they're sayin'."

Before J.T. could protest, Mickey was on the move again. This time he crawled over to the outside door, the one leading to the porch. With growing trepidation, J.T. followed. By placing an ear right on the door panel, they could hear most of the conversation coming from outside.

"Where the hell do you think he is?" the cowboy asked.

"Beats me," the ballcap man, Sweeney, replied. "He's never around when we need him."

"Yeah, I know, but now's a good time to go check on it," the cowboy said. "See if it's still there."

"Huh?"

"Yeah, with him gone, now's a good time to go check."

"Huh?" Sweeney repeated a second time.

J.T. got the feeling Sweeney wasn't too bright.

"Damn it!" the cowboy exploded. "Are you really that friggin' dumb? I'm talkin' about that shed." He paused and apparently pointed at the shed. "Go look."

"Oh! Oh, yeah," Sweeney said, seemingly without resentment. "Yeah, I'll just go and do that right now."

"Then git on with it," the cowboy growled, "and don't take all friggin' day."

Again, rising to their knees, J.T. and Mickey raised up a corner of the half-window, Venetian blind.

Stepping off the landing, Sweeney flipped on his flashlight, then walked straight to the shack. Swinging the unlocked door open, he disappeared inside.

Almost immediately, within a couple of seconds, he reappeared, then rejoined the cowboy on the landing.

"Yeah," he nodded, "it's still there."

"You sure?"

"Just like we left it."

"Good." The cowboy turned and rattled the door one more time.

"What we goin' a do?" Sweeney asked, loudly yawning.

"Wait right here till he gets back," the cowboy replied, sitting down on the top step, "no matter how long it takes."

"But I'm tired," Sweeney complained. "Didn't get no sleep last night. Damn coyotes."

"Too bad," the cowboy barked, "you can sleep now."

"No way, I can't sleep standin' up."

"Then stretch out."

Nudging J.T., Mickey pointed toward the bathroom. Quietly, they crawled across the kitchen to the hallway, then tiptoed into the bathroom. After retrieving the hat, pennant, and ring, they exited through the open window, no belly flops this time, and this time they remembered to close the window.

Once outside, and keeping the house between them and the two men on the landing, the boys sneaked out of the compound and were soon back on the Highway 91 (Main Street). When they were well-away from Borch's place, they stopped under a streetlight.

"What the hell was that all about?" Mickey asked when they were well out of earshot.

J.T. shook his head. "I have no idea."

"Did you heer that ball cap guy say, it was still there?"

"Yeah, right after came out of the shed."

"We were just in there," Mickey continued, "and there's nothin' in there."

"I know," J.T. replied, "there's no table, no shortwave radio, no nothing; just a piece of rope hanging from the rafters."

"Weird," Mickey said.

Frowning J.T. added, "we must be missing something."

"There wus nothin' to miss."

Shrugging, J.T. started walking down Main Steet. Mickey hurried to catch up.

"So, what you goin' to do with them?" Mickey nodded at the hat, pennant and ring still cradled under J.T.'s arm.

"I don't know for sure, probably talk to my father. Maybe there's some kind of a clue in this stuff."

"I sure hope so," Mickey sighed, "cause we're gettin' nowhere fast."

"I expect the sheriff any day."

"Yeah, maybe, but I've gotta get home," Mickey said, yawning. "My parents are gettin' tired of me stayin' out late. They say you're a bad influence."

"Me? That's what my dad says about you."

"Oh, yeah," Mickey smiled, "I've been nothin' but a saint 'round you." Playfully, he pushed J.T. away. "Get away from me, you bad influence. I gotta git home."

"I've got to go too," J.T. replied, but he wasn't sure why; there was nobody home and his chores were done. For a moment, he watched Mickey dissolve into the black night, then sighing, reversed directions, and headed toward his equally dark and empty home.

As he shuffled home, the overhead streetlights toyed with his shadow. When he approached a light pole, his shadow progressively shrank to that of a midget, then right under the light, it disappeared. Then as he walked away, his shadow started ballooning once again, to become a Goliath. Normally, he was fascinated with the play of light and shadow, but tonight his mind was elsewhere. He was debating whether to call his father tonight or wait till morning.

While in Salt Lake City, his parents were staying at Uncle Howard's, on the East Bench and fairly close to the University Hospital. His father had, of course, given him the phone number in case of emergency, but this hardly constituted an emergency, plus it was late, and he didn't want to wake everyone at Uncle Howard's. Although J.T. really wanted to talk with his father tonight, he reluctantly decided to wait until morning.

For J.T., however, it was another hot and sleepless night. Even stripped down to his underwear, with no overlying covers, not even a sheet, he still perspired like midday in the fields. It was impossible to get comfortable. Tossing and turning, he tried to clear his mind, but that was impossible too. Even moving over to Chris' bed, directly under the swamp cooler vent, didn't help. It was not just the oppressive heat and the high humidity (thanks to the arrival of the summer monsoons) that kept him awake, but also the constant rehashing of the day's events.

In between frequent body rotations, he relived the evening over and over, but he kept coming back to one sticking point. Why had the cowboy asked the ball cap miner, Sweeney, to go over and check the shed? And why had Sweeney returned and said it was still there? What was still there? Less than thirty minutes earlier, he and Mickey were in the very same shed, flashlights on, and there was nothing. It was driving him crazy. Somehow, they were missing something, maybe even something important, but what?

Even though J.T. was convinced in some way all of them, the cowboy, Sweeney and Rosenkranz, were tied in this together, whatever this might be, try as he might, he couldn't connect the dots. Without ever falling asleep, he felt the warmth of the sun's first intrepid rays stream through his window and splash down on his face. Groaning, he got up, struggled back into yesterday's clothes, and headed outside for morning chores.

By the time he finished straining the milk and storing it, along with a half-dozen newly gathered eggs, in the fridge, it was 7:58 a.m. Now it was safe, he figured, to call his father. Picking up the phone, he gave the number to the long-distance operator, then waited.

"Hello," a gruff, and maybe even sleepy, voice answered. It was Uncle Howard. Suddenly, J.T. remembered Howard worked the nightshift at Kennecott Copper.

Hoping he hadn't gotten him out of bed, J.T. identified himself, then after exchanging the required pleasantries, he asked if he could speak to his father. He waited nearly five minutes.

"What's wrong?" his father demanded, not bothering with a 'hello'.

"Nothing, I just needed to talk with you."

"Oh," his father said, then more softly added, "so, what's up, son?"

For the next five minutes, J.T. explained the events of last night, including looking in the shed, sneaking into the house and the appearance of the two men on the landing, the same two men that were at the gold camp. He finished by confessing he had stolen the hat, ring, and pennant from Rosenkranz's closet.

His father was silent for a long moment. "You know, what you did is illegal."

"But—but we had to do something."

"Be very careful who you tell this to."

"I will."

"So, what do they look like?" his father asked, "the hat, ring and pennant?"

J.T. took a minute to describe them.

"I don't know," his father said slowly. J.T. could almost see him shake his graying head. "But I'll tell you what, old Fritz Ence, down at the post office, was in World War Two. Why don't you take those things over there? Let him take a look at 'em. See what he thinks."

"Okay," J.T. responded, already feeling a little less alone, a little less burdened. At least, now he had a plan.

"Then," his father added, "we'll talk again tonight."

"Okay."

"Don't hang up yet," his father said quickly. "I was about to call you anyway. I have something I need to tell you." He paused.

"What?" J.T. asked, fearing the worst.

"Well, your mother started to bleed last night, either from the radiation treatments or the cancer, and—and, well anyway, she's in the hospital now."

"Bleeding? Bleeding from where?"

"You know, from down there."

"Oh," J.T. replied, then with his voice trembling, he asked, "is—is she going to be okay?"

"I don't know," his father said, then quickly amended his answer, "yes, I think so. I've gotta get ready to go to the hospital now. I'll call you tonight." Then he hung up.

For a couple of seconds, J.T. sat quietly, flooded with emotions. Wiping a tear from his eye, he thought about his mother. This sounded serious, very serious. She was bleeding enough to be hospitalized! Certainly, that couldn't be good. Was she going to die? She had always been his advocate, stood up for him, had been kind of a buffer between him and Father. But if she died—

He couldn't think about that now. Reaching for a kitchen towel, he dried his eyes and started for the door. At least now, he had a project, something to do to keep his mind occupied. Holding back a sob, he stepped outside.

When the post office opened at 9:00 a.m. sharp, J.T. was there waiting. The second old Fritz opened the customer window, J.T. greeted him. Fritz seemed to be in a good mood, as J.T. offered him the hat, ring and pennant. Still smiling good-naturedly, Fritz accepted them, then his smile instantly vanished. His face suddenly contorted with rage, and he shoved/threw them back at J.T.

"Where in the bloody hell," he yelled, "did you get that stuff?"

"I—I'd rather not say," J.T. stammered, taking a step backwards.

"Tell me!" Fritz shrieked.

"Uh—uh."

Instantly, Fritz jumped to his own conclusions. "They belong to that verdammt Borch Rosenkranz, don't they?"

"Uh—uh, I guess so." Suddenly, J.T. wished he'd never shown them to Fritz.

"All that stuff is pure evil, straight outta hell," he screamed, wild-eyed. "These are symbols of Lucifer, the archangel of Dachau!"

"W—what?" J.T. sputtered, retreating even further from the customer window.

"Those things," Fritz jabbed a crooked, arthritic finger, "are Nazi SS, the German Wehrmacht. They've been soaked in innocent blood. Get 'em the hell outta my post office!"

Shivering, in spite of the unusually warm morning, J.T. hurried back home. It was still early, only 9:30. If he was lucky, maybe he could still catch his father before he left for the hospital.

Out of breath from running, he wheezed the number to the operator.

"What is it, J.T.?" his father asked, also slightly out of breath. Apparently, he'd just been backing his car out of the driveway when Uncle Howard stopped him.

"I just talked to old Fritz!"

"And?"

"He says they're all Nazi SS things," J.T. blurted, "and he got real mad."

There was a long moment of silence. The only sound was the crackle of static along the three-hundred-mile phone line.

"Father?" J.T. finally said, wondering if he was still there.

"Yeah."

"So, what does it all mean?"

"Well," Mr. Kunz said after another long moment of silence. "It probably means that during World War Two, Borch Rosenkranz was a Nazi officer, likely serving in one of them SS death squads."

"So?" J.T. asked, though he was not sure if he wanted to hear more.

"So, by definition, that makes him a war criminal!"

"Then what's he doing here?"

"I can only assume he's on the lam."

24

"On the lam?" Now J.T. was even more confused. "Father, I don't know what that means?"

"What it means, son, is he's on the run."

"If he's on the run, then what's he doing in Santa Clara?"

"I assume he's hiding from the law!"

"Why does he have to hide?" J.T. asked. "The war's been over for years."

"After the war," Mr. Kunz explained, "the Allies established the Nuremberg Court to punish the Nazi war criminals. And even though those trials are over now, the Jews, particularly the Jewish Mossad, are still actively searching for Nazi's who escaped detection and are bringing them to justice."

"What's a Mossad?"

"They're Israel's version of the CIA."

"Are they looking for Mister Rosenkranz right now?"

"Yeah," Mr. Kunz said, "probably."

J.T. paused for a second, trying to digest all this new information, then steered the conversation in a slightly different direction. "So, why did old Fritz get so upset?"

"Could be for a couple of reasons," Mr. Kunz replied. "Not only was Fritz in World War Two, but so was his brother Heinrich, uh Henry. Henry was killed in the Battle of the Bulge and Fritz was captured and tortured in an SS prisoner of war camp. I don't remember which one, but it could have been Dachau."

"How did Fritz get away?"

"He didn't. The Allies freed him at the end of the war," Mr. Kunz replied, then added, "so, Fritz, for good reason, has no time for Germans, especially the Nazis."

"Okay," J.T. said, shifting the phone to the other hand, "but he got pretty mad."

"You can hardly blame him. Most people in America hate the Germans and the Japanese. It's still too close to the war."

"But grandpa spoke German and so do a lot of the other old people in town."

"Speaking German and being German are two different things."

"What do you mean?"

"Well, they speak German," his father said, "because they're from the German part of Switzerland, but that's where the comparison stops. The Swiss refused to join Hitler in World War Two and remained neutral. They had nothing at all to do with the SS, or the death camps, or any of the other atrocities against the Jews."

In a war like that, J.T. couldn't help but think, remaining neutral was probably nothing to be proud of, but he kept that thought to himself. "So, what does the cowboy and the gold camp have to do with all of this?"

"I don't know for sure," Mr. Kunz replied, pausing for a couple of seconds, "but on the spur of the moment, I can come up with a couple of possible scenarios. One, the cowboy found out about Borch's true identity, a Nazi war criminal, and is blackmailing him."

"You said two scenarios," J.T. reminded him.

"Oh, yeah. Well, rumor has it there is a big colony of escaped Nazis living undercover in South America. They are attempting to rebuild the Third Reich, or this time around I guess it would probably be called the Fourth Reich. Anyway, the price of gold in the United States is cheap, much cheaper than black-market gold, that's because the government regulates the price." He paused, then added, "are you following me?"

"Yeah, so far."

"Well, it's possible, Rosenkranz is buying illegal cheap gold from the cowboy and smuggling it into South America, where it is much more valuable to help finance the Nazi cause."

J.T. took a few seconds to take all that in. Even though he could understand his father's logic, he was still having trouble thinking of Borch as a Nazi war criminal, rather than a communist spy. He couldn't decide which was worse. "So, what should I do now?" he finally asked, suddenly wishing his father were home. He was definitely in way over his head.

"Well, son," his father replied, "if you go to the sheriff, you will have to explain how you got those Nazi things. Unfortunately, what you did is a crime, breaking and entering, and theft. You could get into big trouble for that." He paused a moment, then added. "It sounds like you get along okay with Rudy Popovich, don't you?"

"Yeah, pretty much."

"Why don't you get hold of him and have him look into it. Apparently, he has connections with the FBI."

J.T. considered this for a moment. "What if he won't talk to me? Or they won't even let me make an appointment to see him?"

"Tell them it's a matter of national security. That always gets their attention."

"D—do you know when you're coming back?" J.T. asked, silently hoping, maybe for the first time ever, he'd see his father soon.

"Hard to say for sure. It depends how things go with your mother. Anyway, I should get going and check on her now."

"But—" J.T. hesitated, then blurted, "but, I sure wish you were home now."

"So, do I, but you can handle it, son. Just do like I said."

"Okay, Father."

"I'll talk to you tonight."

"Okay, Father."

After hanging up the phone, J.T. didn't immediately move away from the kitchen counter. Obviously, he knew he was in way over his head, in more ways than one, and had been for some time. But even though he was in over his head he somehow managed to keep digging deeper and deeper. That took real talent.

However, if one good thing was to come of all this, he did seem to be getting along a little better with his father. Sure it was by long distance, but they had actually been communicating, working as a team, trying to figure all this out. That was a first! But, on the negative side was the very reason they had to communicate by long distance, his mother's deteriorating health. He could, and probably would, spend all day worrying about that. Thankfully, he had things to do. He had to contact Mr. Popovich and there was still hay to cut.

But—but, Borch Rosenkranz, a Nazi war criminal. And on the lam! He never expected that. He'd so firmly pigeonholed him as a spy, it was hard to think of him as anything else. If he had a choice, now that he had time to think about it, he would rather him be a spy, than a SS Nazi war criminal. No telling how many innocent people he'd killed and would probably do so again if cornered. Were they actually going to rebuild the Third Reich? A shiver raced down his spine. Undoubtedly, Borch already knew they'd been snooping around his place. He and Mickey had better be careful.

Sighing out loud at the enormity of it all, J.T. pulled out the phone book and looked up the number for the St. George field office of the Atomic Energy Commission. With continued, even growing misgivings, he had the operator connect him.

"Mister Popovich is not in," a secretary told him, using her most professional voice, "but, whom should I say called? You may leave him a message if you like."

"Uh—uh, this is J.T. Kunz," J.T. said, using his deepest voice, "I need to talk to him about a matter of—uh—a matter of national security."

"I see," the secretary replied evenly, but definitely seemed more interested, "and what would that be?"

"Huh?"

"What is the matter of national security?"

"I—I," J.T. stammered, "I can only talk to Mister Popovich about that."

"I see. I'll give him your message. And your phone number?"

"Huh? Oh, Orchard, two-two-five-five."

"That's Santa Clara, isn't it?"

"Yes, Ma'am."

"Actually, I think Mister Popovich is scheduled to be in your area later today," the receptionist continued, "it's possible he might want to stop by and see you. Where do you live?"

"On Main Street, about halfway between the post office and Graff's fruit stand. He can ask anyone; they can show him."

"And the street number?"

"Uh—uh, there is no street numbers in Santa Clara." She must not be from around here, J.T. concluded as he hung up the phone, or she would have known that.

Now, he had a decision to make, whether to wait for Mr. Popovich or go cut and rake the hay. After waiting a half-hour, he decided he had to work while it was still relatively cool. He tacked a note on the front door explaining where he had gone, then put the hat, ring, and pennant in a flour sack, climbed on the old Massey-Ferguson and headed down the Vineyard Road.

The hay mower was an old horse-drawn machine, which had been retrofitted with rubber tires and converted to tow behind a tractor. The cutting mechanism consisted of a retractable arm, or lever, sporting two rows of serrated teeth, riveted so they opposed each other. Through a series of transfer gears, the rotating wheels powered the teeth, as the machine moved forward. When in motion, the two rows of opposing and overlapping teeth would rapidly oscillate, but slightly out of phase. The end result was a very efficient cutting machine that could slice through almost anything in its path. With the lever arm extended, the mower would cut a six-foot swath through the alfalfa, parallel, but to the immediate left of the tractor's path.

Cutting hay was a hot job and it always stirred up a cloud of pollen and swarms of flying, biting insects. Over the years, J.T. had also seen a variety of other animals scatter in front of the gnashing blades, including pheasants, skunks, snakes, raccoons and one time two small deer who had hunkered down in the waist-high alfalfa. Occasionally, one of them, often the pheasants and hopefully never a skunk, would get confused and not move away fast enough or in the wrong direction. The mower showed no mercy. He hated that.

J.T. was about halfway finished with the south field, directly below the orchard and adjacent to the Loren Reber piece, when he had his first visitor. Deputy Director Rudy Popovich pulled up in his white sedan, sporting AEC logos. Dressed in beige slacks, Rudy also wore a short-sleeve white shirt, no tie and a Panama straw hat. Removing his hat and using it as a fan, he carefully stepped over the furrows and cut alfalfa toward the tractor. Killing the engine and grabbing the flour sack, J.T. hopped off the tractor and walked over to meet him.

"So, this is what you do when you're not running people off the road," Popovich joked.

"Yeah, I guess so."

"I love the smell of fresh cut hay," Rudy said, inhaling loudly through his nose.

J.T. shrugged but didn't comment. There was not much about farm work he liked, including the smell of cut alfalfa.

"Hot work, though," Popovich said, as he continued to fan himself with his hat.

"Yeah," J.T. shrugged, "you get used to it."

"But probably less stressful, "he added, almost wistfully, "than what I do."

"If you say so," J.T. replied, but without conviction. Right now, he had plenty of stress.

"So, my secretary informed me this is a matter of national security. I called, couldn't get you, so I came right over and saw your note on the door."

"Yeah, I guess," J.T. stammered, "uh—uh, that's what my father told me to say."

"What?" Popovich snapped, no longer smiling. "I cut a staff meeting short."

Gulping, J.T. proceeded to tell the Deputy Director everything. He related how he'd sneaked into Borch's house and found the hat and pennant. Not looking Popovich in the eye, but examining his shoes, he then admitted he and Mickey had pilfered those things, the hat and pennant. And how they'd found the ring by the fort. Next, he went on to explain how, on his father's suggestion, he had showed them to old Fritz Ence, the postmaster, then described Fritz's reaction when he saw those things. Lastly, he told him of the gold mine and his father's theories about the mine.

"Well," Popovich paused for a few seconds, apparently trying to process it all, "it seems to me as of late you've developed a healthy disregard of the law."

"Huh?"

"It seems every time I see you, you're breaking the law," Popovich said sternly. "Let me see, we have you driving without a license, reckless driving, and now breaking and entering and stealing. Son, do you not know the law, or do you just not care?"

"Uh—uh," J.T. stuttered. "Uh—usually—uh, I'm not like this."

"Really? You couldn't prove it by me."

Looking down, J.T. checked out the alfalfa stubble; it was cut short and clean with no pheasant legs, at least none in the immediate area. Silently, he dragged his shoe over the short stalks, then finally mumbled, "so—so other than that, what do you think?"

"Well," Rudy replied, his voice a little softer, "what you father said is entirely possible. It's true there are some Nazis who escaped to South America after the war, and also there's no question that gold mined here and shipped down there would immediately gain a substantial amount in value."

"What about the blackmail theory? You know, the cowboy blackmailing Borch?"

"Well, that's possible too." Popovich shrugged his shoulders. "So, did you bring that stuff?"

Without comment, J.T. handed him the flour sack containing the hat, ring, and pennant.

Taking each item out of the bag, Rudy examined them, then carefully replaced them. "Do you mind if I keep these for a while?"

J.T. mumbled, "no, yes, uh—go ahead." Actually, he was happy to be rid of them. "So, what do you think?"

"Well, first of all, I think you shouldn't be sneaking into other peoples' houses. It's a damn—uh—darn good thing I'm not the law."

Swallowing hard, J.T. nodded.

"But the question, is Borch Rosenkranz a Nazi war criminal? I just don't know. This stuff," he held up the flour sack, "is definitely Nazi paraphernalia, however, nothing about a Nazi affiliation came up in the FBI's investigation. Then again, they weren't really looking for that. In fact, they couldn't find much of anything about him prior to his graduation from the Berlin Technical University in nineteen hundred and forty-one. On the other hand, there's no question, he did work for the Nazi's on their rocket program, so I guess I would have to say, it is possible."

"So, what do we do now?"

"Well," Popovich replied, once again his voice stern, "you are not going to do anything. I'm going to take these things back to the office and contact the FBI. See if I can get them to take another look at Mister Borch Rosenkranz."

"Okay."

"I'll get back to you," Popovich said. Slinging the flour sack over his shoulder, he began trudging back across the already wilting hay stalks.

Abruptly, he stopped and looked over his shoulder. "And I mean it, J.T. Kunz, stay out of trouble!"

For a moment, J.T. watched him until he reached his white sedan, then sighing out loud, he started up the Massey-Ferguson.

He was about three-quarters done with the field when his second visitor showed up. It was none other than his best friend and cousin, Mickey T. Graff. As usual, he was shirtless, in fact his only clothing consisted of a pair of cutoff Levi's and sockless white sneakers. Now, in early August, his skin was so tanned, he might be even darker than Smokey Grayman.

This time, however, J.T. did not stop the tractor, but continued cutting. Timing his jump, Mickey hopped up on the running board, then worked his way up to the left rear fender. Bracing with his feet, he sat down on the fender, grabbing hold of the rolled metal edge for support.

"Looks like you're almost done," Mickey shouted above the drone of the engine and the constant clack-clack of the mower blades.

"Yeah," JT. shouted back, "another half hour or so."

"Your parents back?"

"No, not yet. Probably not for a few more days," J.T. replied, as he bounced over the furrows. Turning the tractor around, he started down the field in the opposite direction. "I told Mister Popovich about Borch and gave him the ring and the other stuff."

"Whadda he say?"

"That he would look into it."

"That means nothin' goin' to happen," Mickey said sarcastically, then added, "you want to go cool off at Boy's Pond when you're done?"

"Sure, why not?"

"Then I'll meet you there in about a half hour," Mickey said as he nimbly hopped off the moving tractor. Dodging the slicing blades, he made his way across the alfalfa field.

Forty-five minutes later, J.T. crawled through the familiar skunk bush thicket to the banks of Boy's Pond. It was midafternoon and the temperature had soared to one hundred and seven degrees. Sure, he knew the cool water would feel good on a hot day like this, but he was a little hesitant. He hadn't been back to Boy's Pond since they'd found Lenny Week's body. It was kind of like, well kinda like sleeping in a motel room after someone had committed suicide or had been murdered. He wasn't sure how the water would feel. Logically, he knew it wasn't exactly the same pond, the same water had been replaced many times over since then, but it was the same location and just thinking about it made him a little squeamish.

When he arrived at the pond, Mickey was already in the water. Didn't seem to bother him. Somewhat reluctantly J.T. shed his clothes, then cautiously dipped a toe. He thought the water might feel slimy, or oily, or weird, or somehow different, but it didn't. Slowly, he slid in all the way, then layered out. For a few minutes, they floated in silence.

"It's kind of strange," J.T. finally said, "being back here."

Mickey bobbed past but said nothing.

"A lot has happened this summer," J.T. continued, as he dog-paddled over to Mickey.

"Summer'll be over in another month," Mickey finally said.

"Have you saved enough money to pay the fine?" J.T. asked, rotating to his back again, then almost immediately got caught up in the whirlpool.

"Almost, you?"

"Still four dollars and fifty-five cents short."

Once again, they floated in silence; both got caught up in the whirlpool.

"Have you thought about who you're goin' to take for date night?" Mickey finally asked.

With all that had happened, J.T. had nearly forgotten about date night. Right now, that seemed so trivial, so insignificant. Definitely, not a high priority. "No, I've got no one. How about you?"

"Nah," Mickey replied, "I guess we're just a couple of losers."

"How about Suzie Hafen?"

"How about Annie Leavitt?"

"I don't want to talk about it."

"Me neither," Mickey admitted. "So, what do you wanna talk about?"

"How we can get out of this mess."

Mickey nodded his head, setting off a series of circular ripples. They both completed one more orbit before Mickey spoke again. "I'll tell you what, that conversation last night between the cowboy and his buddy, Sweeney, still bugs the hell outta me."

"I know," J.T. replied. For some reason, Mickey's cursing no longer bothered him. "It still bugs me too."

"He definitely said it was still there, but what was still there?"

"I don't know." As J.T. shook his head, he could feel both ear canals fill with water. "There was nothing there."

"Whatever it was couldn't have disappeared that fast," Mickey continued, rotating from floating to treading water. "We were in that shed thirty minutes earlier."

"So, it had to still be in there and we overlooked it."

"Do you think maybe we ought to go take another look?"

"I really don't want to. That place gives me the creeps."

"Well, I think we'd better," Mickey said firmly. "Somehow, it all has to be related to Lenny Weeks and Weird Willie."

"I don't know."

"You're the one who said we were running out of time."

"Yeah," J.T. sighed, "okay. When?"

"The sooner the better," Mickey replied, then resumed floating. "How about tonight?"

"Okay," J.T. replied, "but not until we've finished with our evening chores, and I'm done with my phone call with Father."

"How about nine-thirty?"

"Okay, I'll meet you at Ence Lane."

"Well," Mickey said. "if we're gonna do that, then we'd better get goin'."

J.T. had just finished with the evening chores and was looking for something to eat when the phone rang. No surprise, it was his father.

"Is everything okay, son?"

This was his father's usual greeting, but somehow tonight he seemed preoccupied, almost distant, but over the phone it was hard to say for sure. "Yeah, I got the south field cut today."

"Good," Mr. Kunz's replied, but his voice was flat and lackluster. "You get a chance to talk to Mister Popovich?"

"Yeah, he agrees it's Nazi stuff, but he's not yet ready to call Mister Rosenkranz a war criminal yet. Says he's going to have the FBI look into it."

"I hope they do a better job this time," John Kunz said, then repeated, "is everything else okay?"

"Yeah," J.T. said. He wasn't ready to tell his father about all of his other troubles.

"Well, okay," his father paused for a long second, "well then, you have a good night and I'll call you tomorrow."

There was another long moment of silence, but nobody hung up. "Are—are you okay, Father?" J.T. finally asked.

"Me? Yeah, I'm fine."

"How's mother?"

More silence.

"Actually, not so good," his father finally admitted. "She took another little turn for the worse today."

"What happened?"

"She bled again. Even more this time."

"From the cancer?"

"Yes—no—I don't know. I guess maybe it's partly from the radiation."

J.T.'s eyes misted over. He felt a lump the size of an apricot grow in his throat. "Is—is she going to be okay?"

"Yeah, sure," Mr. Kunz replied without conviction, "but this might take a little longer than we expected."

"That's okay; I'm all right."

"You sure?"

"Yes."

"Then I'll talk to you tomorrow, son."

"Okay."

After hanging up, J.T. was instantly flooded with an overwhelming sense of dread, of impending disaster. Leaving the light on, he drifted from the kitchen. For a few minutes, he wandered aimlessly about the empty house, finally settling on the overstuffed chair in the living room. Sitting down, he stared blankly out the big picture window, watching, but not really seeing, the gray light of dusk slowly morph into the ebony of night

His father had been unusually quiet on the phone. Why? Was he worried? Worried about his wife, J.T.'s mother? Worried that she would die? If she did, J.T. wondered if he would he be able to handle it. She'd been his comforter, protector, and confidante. Losing her would be like removing an arm or a leg. Would his life ever be normal again? How could life be normal with only one arm or one leg? Would he ever be a carefree teenager again? Somehow, he doubted it.

Outside, the headlights of a car briefly flashed through the window as it executed a U-turn, then pulled up to the curb, parking right in front of the house. At first J.T. paid it little attention until he saw the big frame of Sheriff Meecham struggle out the cruiser, his sagging facial features highlighted by the overhead streetlight. After hiking up his pants over his bulging belly, he re-tightened his belt, then eyed the house for a moment. Shrugging, he started forward, lumbering up the front porch steps.

Now fully alert, J.T. watched him closely. Why was he here? And at this hour? Had he heard about the breaking and entering of Borch's house? Maybe. But maybe he was just here for another round of intimidation? He knew he shouldn't interrogate a minor without their parents being present. So, why was he here?

J.T. heard Sheriff Meecham shuffle onto the concrete landing, then rap on the front door. Getting up, he moved to answer it, then abruptly stopped. Maybe, Sister Hafen had died after all, and now he was guilty of manslaughter. Or, maybe, the sheriff was here to arrest him for the murder of Lenny Weeks, or maybe he now had matching fingerprints from the catsup bottle used in the mannequin fiasco and was here for that. No, the odds were he wasn't here to interrogate, but here to arrest him for something.

In midstride, J.T. pivoted around, then walked through the kitchen and directly into the service room. Picking up a flashlight on the way, he then quietly exited the house. As he dissolved into the night, he could still hear Sheriff Meecham pounding on the front door.

In the pre-moon darkness, J.T. headed south, cutting through Frei's peach orchard till he reached the safety of the riverbed. From there, he worked upstream until he was directly below the Rosenkranz compound, then he angled north through Emil Gubler's still uncut alfalfa field. Now he had no choice, he now had to go through Borch's compound to meet Mickey on the highway. He took a deep breath and wriggled through the fence.

"You're late," Mickey growled as J.T. slipped in beside him at the top of Ence Lane.

"My mother's not doing so good," J.T. blurted. He had to unload to someone.

"Oh, geez, I'm sorry. Is she goin' a be okay?"

"I don't know. She's bleeding again, but I don't know for sure how bad."

"Well, I'm sure she'll be okay," Mickey added, then awkwardly tried to embrace J.T. Not knowing what to do with his hands, J.T. wedged them in his front pant pockets.

"I also had to dodge the sheriff."

"The sheriff?"

"Yeah, he showed up about the time I was getting ready to leave."

"What did he want?"

"I don't know," J.T. replied. "I left through the back door, then cut down through Frei's orchard down to the river."

"Then you must have come up through Borch's place?"

"Yeah."

"Anybody home?"

"Nah, I don't think so. No lights on and no car in the driveway."

"Good," Mickey said, starting down Ence Lane. "So, what do you think he wanted?"

"Who?"

"Geez, who we bin talkin' about? The sheriff.

"Oh, him, I don't know," J.T. replied, falling in step, "but probably he was going to arrest me. That's why I left; I wasn't taking any chances."

"That means we've got to figure this out fast," Mickey said, then for emphasis added, "damn fast!"

At the front picket gate, they paused for only a second. Everything still looked dark and quiet. Mickey opened the gate and they slipped into the compound. Ignoring the walkway to the clapboard house, they headed straight down the gravel driveway, past the darkened bedroom and onto the shack. Fortunately, the plank door was still unlocked. Opening it, they squeezed in, then closed it again.

With no secondary light from the house and no moon, the darkness inside was absolute, like in a bat cave. Involuntarily, J.T. shuddered, then tried hard to quash his usual claustrophobia. Extending his hand in front of him, he couldn't see his fingers. This whole thing was more than a little unnerving. He was almost ready to bolt when Mickey flipped on his flashlight. Remembering he had one too, J.T. did the same and instantly felt better.

As the twin flashlight beams punched holes into the black fabric of the night, Mickey and J.T. methodically searched the little room. They covered every square inch. It was totally empty, no plank table or chair, no shortwave radio or platform microphone. Also, there was no deer carcass, just a cut and frayed piece of hemp rope still dangling from the rafter. Other than that, there was absolutely nothing, nothing but bare board walls and an equally bare dirt floor.

Backing up to get a better look at the ceiling and the rope fragment, J.T. once again tripped over the mound of dirt in the middle of the floor.

"Darn it," J.T. exclaimed, "that's the third, no the fourth time I've done that."

Mickey redirected his flashlight to the mound. Using his shoe length to measure, he stepped it off. "It's about five to six feet long and about two feet wide," then he added, "why do you think it's here?"

"I don't know," J.T. replied, kicking at the dirt. It was fairly loose compared to the rest of the hard-pack floor. "But it looks like it's been recently turned, like a ploughed field."

"Maybe," Mickey said, "Borch redid the floor before he brought in the table and microwave."

"Why would he do that? It's still a dirt floor."

Both boys trained their lights on the odd mound, staring at it for a few moments.

Mickey finally asked, "are you thinking what I'm thinking?"

"Yeah, probably."

"Guess we need a shovel."

"Guess so," J.T. agreed. "Your place is closer."

Apprehensively, the boys took one last look, then hurried from the shack.

Now on the eastern horizon, there was just a hint of silver, suggesting a new quarter moon would soon follow. At the moment, however, it was still very dark. Running most of the way, the boys reached Mickey's house in less than five minutes. Without bothering to talk to anyone, Mickey located a shovel in a tool shed, then they raced back to Ence Lane.

At the Rosenkranz compound, everything still seemed quiet. With chests heaving, the boys entered the front gate, everything was still dark in the house, so they hurried straight for the shack. Once inside, they closed the door and again flipped on their flashlights. For a couple of uneasy seconds, they stared at the mound, then at each other.

"You dig," Mickey finally said, shoving the shovel into J.T.'s hands. "I'll hold the flashlights."

"Me? Why me?" J.T. didn't budge. He was tired of Mickey always deciding who did what and when.

“Okay, then, we’ll trade off, but you go first.”

“No,” J.T. stood his ground. “You go first.” He shoved the shovel back at Mickey.

Frowning, Mickey took the shovel and circled the mound twice. Taking a big breath, he then sunk the spade into the soft soil. It went in easily, up to the hub. Lifting the dirt, he discarded it against the far wall, then sunk the shovel in again. For the next five minutes, he dug steadily, removing most of the mound and even creating a shallow pit, then he took a breather.

“It’s your turn,” he said, pushing the shovel toward J.T.

“You need to go deeper.”

“No, it’s your turn!”

Grudgingly, J.T. relinquished the flashlights and accepted the shovel. Placing the blade in the shallow cavity, he put his foot on the steel hub and drove the spade deep into the soft earth. Lifting it up, he deposited it onto the growing discard pile next to the wall, then he sunk the blade in again.

“Hey! Hey, you in there!”

J.T. froze, nearly dropping the shovel!

“We know you’re in there!”

Suddenly, the night air was alive with cursing and yelling. The uproar was not directly outside the shed but seemed to becoming from a bit further away, maybe in front of Borch’s house. Instantly, the boys extinguished their lights. Crouching low, they dropped down to their knees. Now in total darkness, they crawled toward the north wall, peeking through the gaps in the pine boards. From this angle they couldn’t see the people, but they certainly could hear them.

Apparently, at the front gate, a large crowd had gathered. They were loud and unruly, with frequent verbal outbursts, often spiced with cursing.

Someone shouted, “damn, it’s locked!”

“Then let’s try the backdoor,” another man yelled. His suggestion was greeted with a loud howl of approval.

After that, the mob lurched from the front of the house, down the gravel driveway to the back porch. Like laser beams, their flashlights stabbed angry holes into the black night. Obviously, some, if not all, had been drinking. For a few minutes, they milled aimlessly around the porch, then one man stepped forward. In the poor light, J.T. didn’t at first recognize him, that is until he started to speak.

“We know you’re in there, Herr Rosenkranz!” Fritz Ence bellowed at the darkened house. Thank God, J.T. thought, his own father was far away in Salt Lake City.

With no lights on and no car in the driveway, to J.T. it was obvious Borch was not home, but apparently it was not to the inebriated mob.

“Come on out,” Fritz shrieked, “you damn, Nazi!”

Another man bellowed, "we don't want no swastikas 'round here!"

"Git your'se friggin' SS arse out here," Hafe Hafen cursed.

Old man Spitzer joined in. "Jew killer!"

"Child killer," another man added.

"And" Fritz roared, "you killed my brother, Henry!" He then stepped on the porch landing, pounded on the door with his cane, then screamed, "and you locked me in Dachau for eight friggin' months!"

"We already gave you fair warning!" Mr. Leavitt shouted.

"It's payback time!" someone else screamed, maybe Mickey's dad, Syd.

"And it's judgment day!" Hafe bellowed, hurling an empty pint bottle. It shattered against the neatly painted clapboards.

Suddenly, the air was alive with flying missiles: stones, sticks and bottles. Sounding like inch-size hail on a corrugated roof, they thudded off the house. Then glass began to shatter—a lot of glass.

After a few chaotic seconds, there was a brief lull as the men reloaded and caught their breath.

"If he won't come out," Fritz screamed, almost hysterically, "then we'll smoke him out!"

Another loud chorus of approval greeted this proposal. Then, seemingly out of nowhere, someone produced a can of gasoline, handing it to Fritz. Stepping up onto the porch, he liberally sprinkled petrol on the railing, across the landing and splashed some on the back door. Reversing his course, he then trailed a little rivulet of gasoline back off the porch steps onto level ground, some ten feet away.

With almost paralytic fascination, the boys watched the scene unfold. Instinctively, they knew they should do something, but what? It all happened so fast! It was like watching a disaster movie on the big screen. They were simply spectators with no ability to change the script or edit the film. It had to play itself out.

From the front pocket of his bib overalls, Fritz produced a stick match, struck it against the coarse fabric. Instantly, it flamed. He hesitated for only a second, then pitched the match toward the little rivulet of gasoline.

The gas flared and flashed onto the porch, then rapidly jumped to the back door. From there, it quickly metastasized, snaking across the white clapboard walls. With seeming delight, the flames leaped through the already broken windows and a few short seconds after that, the whole house was ablaze.

Even from as far away as they were, J.T. was surprised at how loud it was. The huge fire was almost deafening, sounding a lot like a cattle stampede or the roar coming from Shot Able.

Like a bonfire of the Gods, huge orange tongues of fire leaped thirty feet into the night, as one by one the remaining unbroken windows exploded with the fury of dynamite.

As the house burned, the jubilant arsonists danced in the light of the fire; their inebriated faces flushed and their eyes glowed a rabid red.

Though a full fifty feet away, the boys not only heard, but also felt the blast as the oil furnace, along with its reservoir exploded, hurling firebombs, and flaming shards in all directions, including the shed.

Leaning up against the pine boards, J.T. could feel the heat. It was already hot and rapidly getting hotter.

"The shed'll go too!" he shouted above the din.

25

On the Kunz's farm, as with most small southern Utah farms, the harvesting of hay was a grueling, labor-intensive, five-step process. As far back as a year ago, J.T. had heard about a new laborsaving machine called a baler and he had even seen a picture in Popular Mechanics, but they didn't own one. They're too expensive, his father repeatedly insisted, but somehow J.T. suspected the real reason they didn't have one is because they already had a cheap, laborsaving machine—namely J.T. Kunz.

Step one: cutting the alfalfa, which J.T. had already done.

Step two: after cutting, the hay had to partially dry before raking into windrows. Too green and it would mold when compressed into rows or stacked in the barn; too dry and the delicate alfalfa leaves, the most nutritious part, would fall off, leaving only the woody stalks. So, when the desiccation was just right, the alfalfa would be raked into long windrows.

Step three: once in rows, the hay was further dried, then the rows were manually dissected, with a pitchfork into individual, smaller piles.

Step four: in the early morning hours while the dew was still on the hay, another hedge against losing the leaves, the individual piles were forked onto the flatbed International.

Step five: the hay was then hauled to the barn where it was again pitchforked off the flatbed and inside the barn for storage, and for protection from future rain and mold.

Of course, the wildcard in all of this was any rain during the five above steps. Adding significant moisture at any stage increased the threat of molding. Therefore, if the hay got rained on while in the field, then additional days were needed for drying. It was not at all unusual when harvesting hay, to be caught up in the proverbial race with the weather, specifically the mid and late summer monsoons.

And, if possible, all five steps needed to be completed within a week, or before the next irrigation turn. The newly cut alfalfa plant needed to be watered in order to grow enough (and not perish), so the entire five-step process could be repeated in another month, or so.

In late July and early August, however, temperatures often approached one hundred and ten degrees, thereby decreasing the drying time considerably. And even though J.T. had finished cutting the south field only yesterday, it was already dried enough to rake. The cut alfalfa had progressed beyond the wilting stage and was now well on its way to firming up. Any drier and the leaves would surely start to drop off.

J.T. was about halfway through raking the south piece when he glanced up and noted with some chagrin the sheriff's black and white cruiser was parked at the top of the field. Due to the loud engine noise of the Massey-Ferguson and concentrating on the raking, he hadn't heard his car pull up, otherwise he might have taken off. But now he was trapped! Obviously, the sheriff had seen him, so if he ran now, it could possibly be construed as flight from justice, another felony. And that's just what he needed, another felony! Anyway, he would have to face Sheriff Meecham eventually; he might just as well get it over.

Eyeing the sheriff's slow progress, he decided to finish this row, make the U-turn, start back, then wait. That would put him closer to the sheriff anyway.

As he worked up the row, J.T. kept one eye on the cruiser. As he expected, the sheriff struggled out of the vehicle, but what happened next did surprise him. A moment later, his best friend and second cousin, Mickey T. Graff, also exited the cruiser. J.T. did a quick double-take to see if Mickey was in handcuffs. He was not. At least that was encouraging. After tripping the rake one last time and dropping down a perfectly aligned roll of alfalfa, he brought the tractor to a stop and turned off the key.

Occasionally stumbling over the deep furrows, Sheriff Meecham started toward him. Once he even dropped to his knees. Cursing loudly, he slapped any dirt from his beige slacks, then checked for any green chlorophyll stains. Covertly, Mickey rolled his eyes, but nevertheless continued to follow the sheriff at a respectful distance.

Finally, the two of them congregated around the Massey-Ferguson. The late morning heat from the still rising sun, coupled with the heat radiating from the hot combustion engine, made the ambient temperature nearly unbearable. Hyperventilating loudly, like an asthmatic in a storm of ragweed pollen, Meecham's face was beefy red and dotted with beads of perspiration. Standing directly behind, Mickey lampooned him by grabbing his chest and faking a heart attack.

In spite of the gravity of the situation, J.T. couldn't help but grin.

"Some—thin'—funny—John?" Meecham managed to wheeze out the words between gasps for air.

"Uh—no, sir," J.T. replied, quickly erasing his half-grin.

"I wouldn't be a smilin' if I wus you." The sheriff used an equally sweaty arm to smear the perspiration across his forehead. "None of this is funny business. Maybe some prison time will wipe that silly grin from your face." Grabbing it by the bill, Meecham removed his sheriff's hat, using it as a fan.

"Sorry, sheriff. It wasn't you," J.T. said contritely, then as a peace offering, he handed him his insulated Mason jar.

Gulping down the water, Meecham then splashed some on his face and offered the few remaining drops to Mickey.

"Anyways," the sheriff said, the water seemed to revive him, "I've come to heer your side of the story. I've already heard Michael's, and I want to compare versions."

Quickly, J.T. glanced past the sheriff to Mickey for guidance, some kind of silent communication or hint. Were they going to play it straight, or were they going to embellish, put themselves in the most favorable light?

Immediately, Meecham whirled around. "I don't want no collusion between you two, so don't say nothin', Graff."

Mickey shrugged.

Turning back to J.T., the sheriff added, "well?"

"Well, what?"

"Well, let's heer your side of all this," Meecham replied, returning the Mason jar.

"Side of all what?" J.T. asked, stalling for time. He needed some time to think. He needed a moment to decide on how to play this. Obviously, Mickey would be of no help.

j "Geez," Meecham blurted, "what do you think. Your side of the story of what's happened since we found Lenny Weeks' body."

"Yeah, okay, Sheriff," J.T. replied, then nodded toward the orchard, "but maybe we ought to go over there, where there's some shade."

The sheriff glanced over at the inviting orchard, then immediately agreed. Starting up the Massey-Ferguson, J.T. headed toward the trees. As Mickey tried to hop on the fender, the sheriff reached out and stopped him.

"Don't want you two to have time to git your stories straight," Meecham said. "You can walk with me, Graff."

The Kunz's orchard contained an assortment of trees: Bartlett pear, delicious and Jonathan apples, bing and Lambert cherries, Chinese apricots, Alberta and cling peaches and a variety of nut trees including almond, pecan, walnut and black walnut. Trying to make use of all available space, John Kunz had also planted alfalfa between the rows. Here, however, the alfalfa was thin, not nearly so robust, mainly due to the near continuous canopy of shade. Though the acreage was nearly the same, the yield from the orchard was less than a third of that from the south field or the pre-damaged Loren Reber piece.

Parking the tractor under the umbrella of a huge Jonathan apple tree, J.T. waited for the other two. It took a full five minutes for Mickey and the sheriff to arrive, but at least that gave J.T. a chance to decide which version of the truth to tell. Quickly, he'd reviewed what had happened, and which version would put him in the most favorable light.

No! No more slanting of the truth. At that moment, he decided he was done with the lies, even his favorite ploy, half-truths. This, a string of possible felonies, was the final result of doing that. This is where his lies and half-truths had gotten him. No, he would tell the full and unadulterated truth.

Upon his arrival, the sheriff immediately collapsed under the apple tree and rested his back against the trunk.

"You got any more of that water?" he wheezed, smacking his lips.

"No," J.T. shook his head, "that was the last of it. I wasn't expecting company."

The sheriff gave him a sharp glance. "Okay, then," Sheriff Meecham took another couple of seconds to fully catch his breath. "Well, okay, John Junior, now, let's heer your side of the story. And Michael T.," the sheriff paused to point a stodgy finger, "you go over there under that other apple tree."

"Uh-uh, that's a Bartlett pear tree," J.T. corrected, then immediately wished he'd kept his mouth shut.

"That's so? You tryin' to be some kind of a smartass or somethin'?" Meecham gave J.T. a dark look. "Graff, go over there under that pear tree and keep quiet."

Glancing sideways, J.T. again searched Mickey's face for a clue of how he intended to play it. He simply shrugged his shoulders and did as he was told.

Of course, Mickey's actions gave J.T. no clue, but he had already decided to tell the whole story and nothing but the truth, including the discovery of the gold mine and the cowboy with his ball cap partner, Sweeney, and the conversation they'd overheard that night in the house.

J.T. explained all that, then he told the sheriff how they'd sneaked into Borch's house and took the hat and pennant and how he'd showed them to Fritz Ence, who was furious. He related how earlier they'd found the unmarked bullets and block eagle ring. Then, while again reliving the shock, he explained to the sheriff how they'd watched from the shed as the angry mob burned down Borch's house. Lastly, he mentioned finding that odd mound of dirt in the shed and how they'd started to excavate it before the fire drove them away.

"Well," Meecham said, swatting at a giant horsefly. "That's pretty much the way your buddy Graff told it."

Silently, J.T. thanked God that Mickey had also decided on the truth, then out loud he added, "so, I guess that means we're innocent."

The sheriff forced a laugh. "Hah-hah-hah. No, that means you're probably tellin' the truth," the sheriff took a wild swing at the horsefly. Missed. "Tellin' the truth and bein' innocent ain't the same thing. Big damn difference."

"In this case," Mickey added smugly, rejoining them, "we're both innocent and truthful."

"You two haven't been innocent since the day you wus born," the sheriff snorted, "with all those stupid pranks." He struggled to his feet, while still fighting off the determined horsefly, then he added, "God, how I hate insects—and the great outdoors too, for that matter."

"That's why," Mickey muttered, "you have a desk job."

"What?" The sheriff turned on him.

Hurriedly, J.T. asked, "so, what happens now?"

"I guess," the sheriff replied, turning back to J.T., "we've got a hole we need to finish diggin'. We can go in my car."

On the way to the Rosenkranz compound, they made a brief detour to Mickey's house, grabbed a shovel, then drove the rest of the way in a pensive silence.

As they neared the compound, Mickey finally spoke. "Have you found ole Borch Rosenkranz yet?"

"No," the sheriff replied gruffly. "Nobody seems to know where he is."

"So," J.T. asked, "does he even know his house was burned down?"

"Not that I know of," Sheriff Meecham turned down Ence Lane, then added, "maybe he got frightened and left for good. Got scared, after your dad and his cronies threatened him that last time."

"Maybe, but I don't think so," J.T. replied. "At least if he did, he didn't take any of his stuff with him."

"How would you know that?" The sheriff glanced at J.T. in his rearview mirror.

"We were in there, you know, when we got the Nazi stuff. We already told you that."

"Oh, yeah," the sheriff nodded, "I need to remember to add another couple of felonies, breaking and entering and burglary, to my list."

J.T. couldn't tell if he was serious, but nevertheless wished he'd kept his mouth shut.

"What's going to happen to Fritz and the mob?" Mickey asked, ignoring Meecham's not so subtle threat.

"I suspect, we'll charge them with arson, but that's up to the county attorney. They're just damn lucky nobody was inside, or it would be arson and murder."

"But he's a Nazi," Mickey protested, "and a Jew killer."

"Don't matter," by then the sheriff had started down the driveway, then had to swing wide to get past the pile of blackened debris that used to be the

Rosenkranz's house, "you can't take the law into your own hands."

Needless to say, J.T. was shocked when he saw Rosenkranz's house in the light of day, or at least what was left of it. The only thing still relatively intact was the brick chimney, standing and seemingly silently guarding the devastation, like a loyal dog standing over his dead master. The house itself was nothing more than blackened rubble, a jumbled heap of charcoal, mixed with scattered items of refractory metal, like scorched pots and pans, and the aluminum kitchen table. Looking a bit like a picture he'd seen of a thermal field in Yellowstone National Park, random plumes of smoke still spiraled upward, mixing with July's scintillating heat waves, then vanishing into the hazy summer sky. Even inside from the cruiser, J.T. could feel the heat still radiating up from the smoking ruins.

The nearby shed had also burned, though not as thoroughly as the house. Nevertheless, it had been damaged enough to lose structural integrity. Collapsing inward, it now appeared to be nothing more than a jumbled pile of half, and mostly burned, blackened boards.

"Well, anyways, boys," the sheriff said, coming to a stop in front of the charred heap, "looks like we're goin' to have to move those boards first, afore we can dig." Then after they'd all climbed out of the cruiser, he added, "well, what you waitin' for? Go on. Get 'er done."

Bending over, Mickey picked up a board. "Ouch! Damn it!" he cursed, instantly dropping the plank. "These friggin' boards are still hot."

Sheriff Meecham studied the problem. "You guys go ahead and work on this for a while but be careful where you grab. I'm going to go git some leather gloves, git us somethin' to drink and maybe git some more help. You two go ahead and remove them loose boards, but no diggin' till I get back." He paused and looked them in the eye. "Comprendo?"

Mickey shrugged his shoulders indifferently; J.T. simply nodded.

"I mean it!"

"Okay," Mickey muttered, "we get the picture, Sheriff."

"Anyways, you two better still be heer when I git back." The sheriff shuffled back to his cruiser. Turning the car around, he exited the compound.

"That's just like him," Mickey grumbled when the sheriff was safely out of earshot, "leave all the hard work for us."

"What did you expect?" J.T. asked, gingerly plucking a board from the heap, and tossing it off to the side. As he reached for another board, he put voice to his pet peeve, "we're nothing but slave labor anyway."

"Why didn't he want us to dig?" Mickey asked, latching onto another still smoldering board, but staying well away from the hot end.

"I don't know," J.T. sighed, "unless he doesn't want us to contaminate the evidence."

"Contaminate, how?"

"You know, by adding our fingerprints where they shouldn't be, or maybe destroying some evidence by handling it or breaking it."

"What kind of evidence."

Suppressing a shiver, J.T. pointed downward, before answering. "whatever's down there," then he grabbed another board from the pile.

For the next thirty minutes, the boys carefully selected their boards, taking care to stay away from the blackened or hot end, then tossing them into a pile well away from the destroyed shack. Some partially burned boards were still nailed to a stud, or piece of the baseboard, or ceiling joist. Those boards had to be pried apart, or if that was impossible, then the two of them would combine efforts and lift the heavy section off the heap.

By the time the sheriff's cruiser reentered the compound, they had pretty much cleared a circle around the partially excavated mound. The top mantle of dirt was scorched and covered with soot, but there was no mistake, they were in the right spot. They could see the shallow pit, no more than a foot deep, they'd dug last night.

Squeezing out of his patrol car, the sheriff waddled over to them, carrying a pair of leather gloves and two bottles of ice-cold Coke. Even from several feet away, J.T. could see the dew droplets condensing on the chilled bottle, then sliding down the curvilinear glass. Maybe, the sheriff had a heart after all.

"You two go ahead," the sheriff said handing the bottles to the boys, "I've already had mine."

As J.T. accepted the bottle, out of the corner of his eye he saw Deputy Fowler climbed out of the cruiser from the passenger's side.

In three long, sustained gulps, J.T. drained his bottle, handing it back to the Sheriff. The cold made his esophagus go into spasm, and the carbonation made his eyes water. Mickey also quickly finished, seemingly without suffering the same consequences. Without comment, Meecham accepted the empty bottles, then handed them to Fowler, who returned them to the patrol car.

"Now you two back out of the way," he instructed the boys, "and give Deputy Fowler the gloves and some room to work."

Scowling, but remaining silent, the pock-faced Fowler accepted the gloves and shovel. As he pulled on the gloves, however, he turned back to the sheriff. "Evan, maybe it would be best if you sent the boys on home."

"And why is that, Blaine?"

"Well," Fowler carefully measured his words, "there might be—uh—things down there that would not be appropriate for them to see—you know, at their age."

"Don't let them fool you none," Meecham snorted. "They've done more and seen more than you think."

"But still, they're just thirteen."

"Fourteen," Mickey corrected.

"So?" Meecham replied. "Fourteen or not, like I said, they've done and seen more'n most forty-year-olds."

Shrugging, Fowler stepped into the shallow pit and sunk the shovel's blade into the blackened, but soft dirt. "Whatever you say, Evan, you're the boss. But I was just thinking how it might look, say to the Washington County News."

"Don't see no reporters 'round here."

"Well, they're sure to hear about it and want to do interviews. This is big news for Washington County."

While still eyeing his deputy, Meecham appeared to reconsider. After a couple more seconds, he sighed out loud. "Maybe, you two better go on home now, but I want you to stay there in case I need you."

Mickey mumbled something unintelligible.

"What?" the sheriff asked sharply, glaring at Mickey.

"Oh, nothing," Mickey muttered, turning away.

"Go on then," the sheriff waved a meaty paw in the direction of Ence Lane. "Git on outta here. I'll be in touch later. You'll need to write up your version, a deposition, of what happened."

As the boys backed up to leave, the sheriff immediately returned his attention to the scorched pit. Doing as told, the boys started to leave, but halted their retreat about thirty feet away. They couldn't leave now. This was the culmination of their investigation, and not the sheriff's.

They hovered there for a moment, then without exchanging a word, they decided to stay. Employing kind of a of Utah two-step shuffle, the boys stayed out of sight by continually dancing behind the backs of the sheriff and the deputy, while still managing to stay close enough to get a glimpse of the excavation.

After digging less than ten minutes in the punishing July heat, Fowler was dripping wet. Perspiration saturated both the front and the back of his beige sheriff shirt and his chocolate pants clung to his skinny thighs like leotards. Handing the shovel back to the sheriff, Fowler looked for water and shade. As he turned to exit the pit, the boys quickly disappeared behind the pile of blackened and discarded boards. Looking around Fowler frowned and for the moment appeared to be indecisive. The only available shade was the ribbon of a shadow cast by the sheriff's cruiser. He headed for that.

Grudgingly, Meecham accepted the spade. With absolutely no breeze, but with a few monsoon clouds gathering overhead, it was both humid and hot, like an Indian sweat lodge or a Swedish sauna.

Shading his eyes, the sheriff peeked through puffy fingers at the sun, as it played peek-a-boo with the drifting stratocumulus clouds. Sighing out loud, with sweat dripping from his bulldog jowls and large sweat halos ringing both armpits, he stabbed the shovel in the soft soil. Lifting a fully-loaded shovel, he tossed it aside, then plunged the spade in one more time. Less than ten minutes later he was exhausted and motioned to Fowler. Reluctantly, Fowler abandoned the shade of the cruiser, and an exhausted Meecham returned the spade to him.

It was obvious to J.T. neither lawman had spent the summer in the hot sun hoeing weeds; both of them appeared to be wilting in the late July sun. Undoubtedly, he and Mickey would last much longer in this kind of heat.

Scowling, but biting his lip, Fowler accepted the shovel and went back to work. Fifteen minutes later, he looked exhausted and was just about to relay the spade back to Meecham when he struck something.

"What's that?" Meecham asked, suddenly perking up.

"I don't know," Fowler replied, "but it feels solid."

"Like a rock?"

"No, more like a tree root," Fowler replied, as he dug his spade in again and struck it a second time. Setting the shovel aside, he kneeled in the pit, then went down on all fours. More carefully now, he scraped and teased the dirt away from the still invisible object.

As the sheriff leaned in closer, Mickey and J.T. silently inched forward, still taking care to stay directly behind Meecham.

Meanwhile, Fowler explored the pit with his hands. Gently, he brushed away the overlying soil, then using his fingers, he raked through the loose dirt. Suddenly, he found something, maybe that root, and latched onto it. Grunting with exertion, he pulled. Whatever it was it didn't budge. He jerked harder.

Almost in unison, J.T. and Mickey gasped, and even Sheriff Meecham drew in a quick breath. But Deputy Fowler looked stunned to the point of paralysis. For what he held in his hand was not a tree root, or even an old buried and forgotten water pipe. No, it was a human arm!

The fabric of its short sleeve-shirt had already started to decompose, fray and shred into ribbons. Likewise, the skin underlying the fabric was soiled and had started to slough, leaving bare patches of exposed muscle bundles.

Within seconds, the odor of rotting and decomposing flesh escaped from the uncovered arm, then immediately wafted outward, like pond ripples from a tossed stone. Reflexively, J.T. held his breath and pinched his nose.

Startled by the sudden and expected bright light, anaerobic insects, and burrowing worms, slithered across a white strap-tendon, then wormed in-and-out the decaying muscle bundles. Apparently, they were desperately trying to find a path out of the bright sunlight and away from the lethal oxygen.

Almost like he'd just reached into a burlap bag and pulled out a diamondback rattler, Fowler dropped the necrotic arm. Recoiling in horror, he stumbled backwards, fell on his buttocks, then scrambled out of the now three-foot deep hole.

"What is," he stammered, pointing, "uh—who—who is that?"

"What's wrong, Blaine?" Meecham scoffed. "Ain't you never seen a dead body before?"

"Y—yeah, but not like this."

Caught up in the drama, the boys had inched even closer, eventually joining the circle around the corpse.

"Keep on diggin'," Meecham ordered, then noticed the boys. "Thought I told you two to go on home. Go on now—git, and I mean it." He shooed them away, like they were annoying children, interrupting an adult conversation.

Again, J.T. and Mickey backed up until the sheriff turned his attention back to the body, then once again they stopped. Like Fowler had done previously, the boys plopped down in the thin band of shade provided by the cruiser but kept an eye on the pit.

"Go on," the sheriff nodded to Fowler. "Let's git it over with."

Reluctantly, and with his pocked face glistening with sweat, Fowler took up the shovel and again began digging, this time around the periphery of the body. In a wide circle, he carefully excavated the loose dirt. First, he fully exposed the uprooted arm, then the other one. Then he worked downward, removing the topsoil from the abdomen, the hips and lastly both legs. Fifteen minutes later, he had the entire anterior surface of the body exposed, that is with the exception of the head.

Even though now the ambient temperature had climbed to at least one hundred and seven or eight degrees, J.T. and Mickey could no longer remain in the shade. There was something morbidly magnetic about the whole scene. Like watching the body of Lenny Weeks rotate in the whirlpool or passing a bad accident on the highway, they couldn't take their eyes off the pit. Subconsciously, they continued to edge forward, trying to get a better view, eventually rejoining the sheriff at the excavation site. This time apparently Meecham was so engrossed, he didn't seem to notice them.

Slowly and meticulously, Fowler cleared down the flanks, lateral to the abdomen, then he freed both hips. Following that, he moved on to the legs. Wiping the sweat from his brow, he then offered the shovel to Meecham.

Vigorously shaking his head, the sheriff refused, pushing the spade back to Fowler. "Finish it up, Blaine," he ordered. "Yer almost done."

Once again, Fowler mopped his brow, then bending over, worked in the opposite direction toward the head. Within minutes, a soiled and decomposing chest appeared, then a skinny, badly sloughing neck and after that, what was left of the face. Mottled and caseating, it looked a bit like a tree stump after the termites had finished with it.

In silence, the foursome stared down at the now fully exposed and mostly decomposed body. And though all along this is what they'd expected, it nevertheless came as a shock.

At first, J.T. refrained from looking at the eyes, afraid of what he might see. But finally unable to resist, he peeked.

Involuntarily, and in spite of the heat, a shiver raced down his spine. They, the green cat eyes, were gone—both of them. But an accordion-shaped, white grub, probably looking for shade, inched out of one empty eye socket, then like a toy slinky, inched across the decaying flesh of the nose and into a nostril. And the neck! It was so twisted and bent, the head drooped down to the chest, like a sunflower tracking the setting sun. Quickly, J.T. looked away.

With what appeared to be an equal mix of horror and fascination, Meecham and Fowler remained rooted on edge of the pit, staring down and the decaying body. At first neither of them, not even the sheriff, said a thing.

Still holding his nose, J.T. closed his eyes tight, but unfortunately, they wouldn't stay shut. Against his wishes, they opened again.

Mickey, seemingly unfazed by the whole morbid affair, joined the sheriff and deputy on the edge of the pit, and now doubling as a grave.

However, because of the advanced state of decomposition, there was, at least in J.T.'s mind, still some question who was lying in that grave. Was it Weird Willie Wittwer? Maybe. Probably. But he couldn't say for sure.

mostly decomposed body. And though all along this is what they'd expected, it nevertheless came as a shock.

At first J.T. refrained from looking at the eyes, afraid of what he might see. [illegible], he peeked.

Involuntarily, and in spite of the heat, a shiver raced down his spine. They [illegible] eyes were [illegible]. Both of them. But [illegible] [illegible], probably looking for [illegible], had [illegible] one eye [illegible] like a [illegible] slimy [illegible] across the decomposing flesh of the nose and into a nostril. And the neck—it was so twisted and bent, the head drooped down to the chest like a sunflower against the setting sun. [illegible], J.T. looked away.

With what appeared to be an equal mix of horror and fascination, Meacham and [illegible] crouched on edge of the pit, staring down at the decaying body. At first neither [illegible] the sheriff said nothing.

Still holding his nose, J.T. [illegible] his eyes [illegible], but [illegible] they couldn't [illegible]. Again [illegible] the [illegible] again.

Mickey [illegible] the whole [illegible] the sheriff and deputy on the edge of the pit, and now [illegible] as a grave.

However [illegible] the advanced state of decomposition, there was [illegible] still some question who was lying in that grave. Was it Ward Wallie Wagner? Maybe. Probably. But he couldn't say for sure.

26

THOUGH J.T. TRIED TO KEEP HIS EYES CLOSED, HE DIDN'T SUCCEED. Opening his eyes again, seemingly against his will, he took a step closer. He couldn't help it. He took another step, then another.

As he advanced, J.T.'s eyes involuntarily focused on the hands and fingers. They had not been spared. Identification by fingerprints would also be impossible.

Next, he focused on the face, or what was left of it. Most of the distinguishing facial features were gone, vanished due to the ongoing putrefaction (nature's way of breaking down living protein). Indeed, the sloughing of the major facial features, made the usual way of positive identification most difficult.

Sure, there were exposed cheek and chin bones, but J.T. could not make a positive identification with just those bones. Though not a forensic expert, he supposed most cheek and chin bones looked much the same.

But—but, there was no mistaking the teeth, the yellow and protuberant buckteeth! No decomposition here. Though the surrounding fleshy gums were gone, the teeth remained perfectly intact. Conspicuous, like the Devil's Tower rising above the Great Plains, they also served as a distinctive landmark in a sea of decomposing jelly. So, in spite of the advanced state of decomposition, J.T. couldn't help but conclude, lying there in that shallow grave was indeed the long-missing Weird Willie Wittwer.

For a few seconds, the four of them, J.T., Mickey, Deputy Fowler, and Sheriff Meecham, remained rooted at graveside, staring at the corpse, then almost as if choreographed, they all backed off. Pinching their noses, as they walked away, they tried to block out the stench.

J.T. had smelled rotting flesh before (a wounded deer that escaped hunters before dying), but this was different; this was a human body. This was Weird Willie Wittwer! Someone he'd known since kindergarten. Turning away from the others, he walked toward the sheriff's cruiser in search of fresh and untainted air, and for a moment alone.

Though they were never that close, J.T. couldn't help but feel a twinge - no, more like a huge wave of guilt. There was no question he could have treated Weird Willie better. Sure, Willie was different, but that was no excuse for his behavior. They, all of the sixth grade, could've tried to better include him in their group.

"What you thinkin'?" Mickey asked, joining J.T. at the cruiser.

"That we could've been nicer to Willie."

J.T. thought Mickey would argue, but he didn't. "Yeah," he nodded, then quietly added, "we all could've done better."

For a long minute, neither of them said anything more, that is until the sheriff shuffled over.

"You two still here?" he asked rhetorically, his voice hollow and now no longer loud and blustery.

Nodding, J.T. focused on the sheriff, so as not to look at the corpse again. Stone-faced, Mickey stared straight ahead and said nothing.

"So, anyways," Meecham continued, gesturing back at the corpse, "now we know what happened to Mister William A. Wittwer."

"But we still don't know who or why," Fowler added, joining the group. His pocked face had lost all its color.

Grunting his acknowledgment of Fowler's point, the sheriff looked at the boys. "So, tell me again how you two put this all together?"

J.T. glanced sideways at Mickey.

Shrugging his shoulders, Mickey mumbled, "go ahead, you tell him."

"Well," J.T. began slowly, trying to organize his thoughts. "Well, we've spent a lot of time thinking about it and—and this is how we think it all fits together."

"Go on." Meecham nodded.

"Uh—uh," J.T. stammered, finally deciding no matter how bizarre it sounded to just blurt it out. "Well, we think Borch Rosenkranz is a Nazi war criminal hiding out here and buying black market gold from the cowboy and his friends. He then ships the gold to South America where it's much more valuable, using it to finance what's left of the Nazi Party hiding out down there." J.T. paused for a moment, eyeing the sheriff for his reaction. "You know, to help rebuild the Third Reich."

"Go on," Meecham repeated, giving no hint as to whether he was buying any of this or not.

"And—and, we think Lenny and Willie must have stumbled onto the goldmine, probably by accident, maybe while looking for deer shed, you know, antlers to sell to the Japanese."

"The Japanese," Mickey interjected, "make an apro-desi-ack out of 'em."

"Go on," Meecham said for a third time.

“And even though Lenny and Willie escaped from the gold camp, the cowboy saw them, found out who they were and tracked them down. When we locked Willie in the stocks the night of town bell, and though we didn’t know it, both Lenny Weeks and Borch Rosenkranz were following us.”

“You mean,” Meecham said, frowning, “they were in cahoots?”

“No,” J.T. shook his head. “Each was acting on their own and not aware of the other’s presence. So, after we put Willie in the stocks, Borch went back to get the cowboy, but Lenny remained at the fort hiding and watching us till we left, then he freed Willie.”

Still the sheriff’s face was a mask. He offered no further comment.

J.T. pushed on. “About the same time Lenny released Willie, Borch returned with the cowboy. Trying to ditch them, Lenny and Willie split up. Lenny headed up the creek and Willie doubled back towards Rosenkranz’s place, probably heading for the safety of town.”

“So?” Meecham asked.

“So, the cowboy eventually caught up with Lenny, killed him and dumped his body in the canal, or maybe did it right at Boy’s Pond. Meanwhile, Borch caught up with Willie and killed him somewhere around here, maybe right on his own compound, then buried him out of sight in the radio shack.”

Once again, J.T. paused, glancing at the Sheriff, then at Deputy Fowler for their reaction.

“That’s a bit convoluted,” Fowler finally said, then nodded his head, “but I guess it could’ve happened that way.”

His face no longer a mask, Sheriff Meecham still looked unconvinced. “Sounds to me like you two are tryin’ to pound a round peg into a square hole, or maybe it’s the other way around. Either way, it don’t fit. So, then you just pound a little harder until it does.”

“You got a better explanation?” Mickey demanded.

“Only one, and it’s a hell-uv-a-lot simpler,” Sheriff Meecham replied, closely eyeing the boys. “We’ve already established you two had a vendetta from that fight when Willie and Lenny kicked the crap outta you two. So, for revenge you killed both of ‘em.”

“How could we do that?” Mickey challenged. “You just said they beat crap outta us.”

“Well, using Willie as bait, you waited for Lenny, then ambushed him down by the stocks. Just as he released Willie, you jumped Lenny, killed him, then you chased Willie up here and did the same to him. All the rest of this is nothin’ but tryin’ to put a shine on shi—uh—on horsepucky. Borch being an escaped Nazi may or may not be true, but either way it has nothin’ to do with nothin’.”

J.T. blurted, “You can’t actually believe that we’re killers!”

“Why not? You had both opportunity and motive.”

"But what about the means?" J.T. asked, remembering the word Fowler had taught them many days earlier at the jail. "Lenny's a whole lot bigger than either of us. No way we could have overpowered him."

Shaking his head, the sheriff looked each boy in the eye separately. "Sure, you could've if you surprised him. Got the jump on him. You don't have to be very big to hit someone on the head from behind."

J.T. began to wither under Meecham's unnerving glance, but somehow managed to not look away. Mickey, as usual, stood his ground, unflinching and defiant.

"That—that," J.T. stammered, "still doesn't explain the means."

"I just told you," Meecham countered, "with a club."

"So—so, do you have the murder weapon," J.T. challenged. He knew unless the sheriff had that, the actual instrument of death, he had not yet established means.

Sheriff Meecham remained silent.

"And if all that's true," Mickey finally joined in again, "why would we lead you to the body?"

"Well, anyways," the sheriff grunted, "we're goin' to find out who did it. It's just a matter of time." Turning away from the boys to his deputy, he added, "Blaine, go ahead and get poor Willie outta that hole and I'll go find the coroner." He started to walk away, then turned back. "You boys can come with me, cause after I talk to Doc Hilton, you two are goin' to show me that so-called goldmine that you've bin talkin' about."

It was mid-afternoon before Sheriff Meecham got everything organized. First, he had to find the coroner, Doctor Hilton, insist that he cancel the rest of his afternoon patients, and attend to his forensic duties, namely the deceased and fast-decomposing Willie Wittwer.

Immediately after that, the two-car caravan headed west toward the slumping sun, and toward the distant Mormon Mountains and specifically Utah Hill. Sheriff Meecham, with J.T. and Mickey in the back seat, led the way, while Deputy Fowler, in his cruiser, followed close behind.

Racing against the setting sun, they traveled with a sense of urgency and as a consequence made pretty good time. J.T. couldn't help but feel sorry for Deputy Fowler; riding drag he had to eat dust most of the way. However, by the time they arrived at the very same pullout where J.T. had parked the flatbed a couple of days earlier, the sun sunk down to the horizon, hovering just above the Mormon Mountains.

After the sheriff and the deputy parked their cruisers, and with J.T. and Mickey leading, the foursome sloshed up Goldstrike Creek. Occasionally, they had to stop and wait for the sheriff to catch his breath and catch up. Just before reaching the camp, they left the creek bed and circled to the west, climbing the low ridge that separated the camp from the adjacent goldmine. From the crest, they could get a glimpse of the mine to the west, but also had a pretty good view of the camp to the east.

Stopping on the ridge, both Sheriff Meechan and Deputy Fowler pulled out Bushnell binoculars and scanned the camp. A few seconds later, Fowler offered his Bushnells to J.T., then he took a few seconds to scan the compound.

It appeared, even from this distance, the miners had just finished their day's work and were getting ready to start supper. Gray smoke, embedded with lively sparks, spiraled up from a central campfire. On the nearby plank table, there was an assortment of canned goods as well as what appeared to be the hindquarter of a deer, undoubtedly recently poached. From the looks of it, the miners were going to have venison tonight.

After a quick inspection of the camp, J.T. focused on the miners. He counted two—no three men. Sweeney, the thickset one wearing the Yankee ball cap, was at the fire pit, bending over the Dutch ovens. Another man, wearing a floppy straw hat and dressed in bib overalls, appeared to be stowing the mining tools and cleaning up around the camp. The third man, wearing a white Stetson, was sitting at the far end of the plank table with what appeared to be a set of balance scales. Lastly, J.T. noted with some consternation, a 30/30 rifle was in plain sight, propped against the trunk of a juniper tree and within easy reach of the cowboy.

Impatiently, Mickey nudged J.T. in the flank. Nodding, he handed him the field glasses, then a minute after that Fowler reclaimed them.

After another quick survey of the compound, Fowler broke the silence. "So, what's your plan, Evan?"

"Let's just to go in there and talk to 'em. See what they're up to."

"But," Fowler argued, "if what the boys said is true, they may not be friendly."

"That so? You got a better plan?"

"Yeah," Fowler nodded, "I would say let's start out by assuming they're dangerous."

"And that's your plan?" Meecham replied sarcastically.

"No," Fowler said patiently, "also, I think we should sneak up on them, maybe one from each side and surprise them. Go in with guns drawn, ready for anything. But of course, you're the boss."

"Not much of a plan, "the sheriff muttered, but implemented it anyway. "Okay, Blaine, you circle to the other side, then we can cover each other when we go into camp."

"What about the boys?" Fowler asked.

"What about 'em?"

“What if there’s gunplay.”

“Who said anythin’ about gunplay?”

“Well, it’s entirely possible,” Fowler replied, “and if there is, I don’t think it would look good if we involved the boys.”

“Look good to who?” the sheriff asked. “Judas, Blaine, there’s nobody heer.”

“Maybe not now, but later on when a reporter from the Washington County News starts asking around, trying to get a story.”

“Oh, them again, the Washington County blab,” the sheriff said contemptuously, but nevertheless seemed to consider Fowler’s point. “Okay, you boys better stay heer in case there’s any trouble.”

“But,” Mickey argued, “we know the lay of the land and how the camp is—”

“No!” the sheriff cut him off, “and I mean it this time. Stay here. We don’t need you kids gettin’ all shot up for the Washington County News.”

Using a circular motion, Sheriff Meecham gestured for Fowler to go ahead and loop around to the far side of the camp. When in place, he was to give a hand signal, then together they would advance on the campers.

Occasionally, over the next few minutes, through small portals in the skunk bush thickets and junipers, J.T. caught brief glimpses of the deputy’s progress. He maneuvered around the camp at what seemed to be a snail’s pace, but nevertheless managed to do so without alerting the miners.

It took a full fifteen minutes for Fowler to work his way to the opposite ridge. When he was at last in place, he took off his beige sheriff hat and waved. After Meecham returned his signal, the two lawmen started forward. Being careful not to make noise, they inched toward the clearing.

As the sheriff and deputy descended from higher to lower ground, they dropped into a denser ribbon of the pygmy forest.

At that moment, J.T. lost sight of them. Without thinking, he crept forward a few paces, trying to keep them in his line of sight. Briefly, he saw them, but then lost them again. Instinctively, he worked forward a few more yards.

Not one to miss out on the action, Mickey stayed with J.T., if not a step ahead.

Suddenly, the lawmen came back into view! The sheriff paused at the periphery of the camp, hiding behind a piñon that only partially concealed his huge frame. On the opposite side of the camp, Fowler ducked behind a large granite boulder.

Nudging J.T., Mickey nodded toward the camp, then started moving forward again. J.T. tried to grab and stop him, but Mickey pushed on. Though he didn’t think it was a good idea, J.T. followed. In the fast-fading light, the boys flitted from juniper to piñon, from piñon to juniper, only stopping when they once again had a clear view of the camp and the lawmen.

Drawing his .357 Magnum, Sheriff Meecham paused for a moment, apparently checking to make sure the safety was off, then took a deep breath. After that, he boldly stepped away from the skinny piñon into the clearing.

"This is Sheriff Meecham," he boomed, "and I have a few questions—"

Before he could finish, the cowboy dove out of his chair, rolling on the ground toward the 30/30.

KA-BOOM!

The sheriff's .357 Magnum barked and bucked, and the bullet thudded into the juniper tree just inches above the cowboy's head.

"The next one, Tex," Meecham shouted tersely, "is in your chest."

J.T. was astonished! The sheriff may not be very nimble on his feet and way out of shape, but he sure could handle a firearm!

Meanwhile, the bib overall man, who was gathering tools, latched onto a shovel and heaved it at the sheriff. The wooden handle banged against his leg, but fortunately the metal blade narrowly missed his head, then careened loudly off the trunk of a nearby piñon.

Doubling over in pain, Meecham grabbed his leg.

Seeing he'd missed, but now had the advantage, the miner grabbed a pickaxe.

At that moment, Deputy Fowler stepped away from the boulder, took a couple of quick steps forward and shoved his revolver between the man's shoulder blades. "Let's play nice, now," he said firmly. "No more throwing things."

Quickly looking over his shoulder, the bibbed man got a glimpse of Fowler's .357 Magnum, then immediately dropped the pickaxe, and held his hands high.

Still sprawled out on the ground, the cowboy hadn't yet managed to reach the 30/30, but it was only a foot away. Suddenly, he lunged for the rifle again. Just as fast, the sheriff's heavy boot came down hard on his wrist, pinning it to the ground.

"Yeow!" the cowboy screamed.

"No," Meecham wagged his finger in the cowboy's face, "I wouldn't do that, Tex."

Sweeney, the ball cap man, now holding the Dutch oven cast iron lid like a track and field discus, prepared to sling it at Meecham.

Fowler barked, "I wouldn't do that, Cookie. I seldom miss at this close range."

Thinking better of it, Sweeney lowered his arm and dropped the lid into the fire.

"Come on," Mickey whispered to J.T., "we're missing all the action."

"But the sheriff said to—"

"I don't give a damn what the sheriff said," Mickey snapped. "I ain't goin' to miss this for nothin'." Pivoting on his heel, he pushed through the thick skunk brush and right into the center of the camp.

J.T. hesitated for only a second, then followed.

"I thought I told you two to stay put," the sheriff growled as they entered the clearing.

At that moment, he had his .357 magnum was trained on the cowboy and Fowler was alternating his weapon between the ballcap Sweeney and the bibbed overall guy.

Looking down at their feet, the boys didn't immediately reply.

"Well, as long as you're here," Meecham growled, "you might as well make yourselves useful. Cuff 'em. All three of 'em."

Fortunately, Fowler had brought an extra set of handcuffs. Mickey grabbed his two and J.T. got the third one from the sheriff's belt.

Though his hands were badly shaking, J.T. did as told. Drawing the cowboy's arms behind his back, he snapped the cuffs around his wrists. Mickey did the same with Sweeney and the bibbed-overall guy.

Once all the miners had been cuffed and were no longer a threat, Meecham and Fowler re-holstered their handguns, then herded everyone to the center of the camp.

"You three sit down over by that big juniper, and no talkin'," Meecham ordered.

Bending over, Fowler picked up the 30/30 moving it well away from the juniper and setting it on the far end of the plank table.

"Well, come on," Meecham said impatiently, "let's look around a bit, but don't contaminate nothin'."

"Contaminate?" Mickey frowned and looked puzzled. "Contaminate what?"

"Yeah, don't touch nothin' without checkin' with me first."

"Why?" Mickey asked, brazen as ever.

"Cause I said so. That should be reason enough."

Turning to the boys, Fowler explained, "touching might smudge any fingerprints or make for more prints the lab has to sort through."

Pivoting, the sheriff headed straight for the plank table where the cowboy had been sitting. Picking up a pea-sized nugget from the scales, he eyed it, rotating it in his fingers. It glinted like a rhinestone in severely angled rays of the dying sun. Snatching a flour sack from the table, Meecham dumped out its contents, mainly assorted canned goods. After dropping the small nugget in the sack, he did the same with the small pile of gold grains and a nearby leather pouch half-filled with gold dust. Lastly, he also placed the balance scales into the sack.

Meanwhile, Mickey and J.T. turned their attention to the 30/30, now lying on the table. Drawing down the lever action, Mickey ejected a shell. Stooping to pick it up, J.T. examined it closely. No big surprise here. It had a central primer and ballistic tip with absolutely no manufacturer's markings.

Snatching the bullet from J.T., Mickey let out a whistle. "Well, would you looky here. It's a match. It's just like all the others."

"So," J.T. said, "that must mean—"

"Damn it," Meecham cussed, grabbing the bullet, and also dropping it into the flour sack, "I thought I told you two not to touch nothin'."

While all this was going on, Deputy Fowler went to check out the tents. Quickly, he searched the first two, apparently found nothing of interest, then disappeared into the third tent. A moment later he reappeared. "Hey!" he shouted, frantically waving them over. "Hey, Evan, I think you best come and take a look at this."

Dropping the flour sack on the plank table, the sheriff picked up the rifle and with the boys in tow, headed for the third tent.

Impatiently, Fowler waited for them, holding the tent flap open.

Grunting, the sheriff bent slightly at the waist and looked in. Directly behind him, J.T. and Mickey did the same.

In the poor and fast-fading light of late evening, it was difficult to see anything.

Simultaneously, they, the sheriff, J.T. and Mickey, all took another step forward, then leaned in even more.

At first nobody said anything.

27

"WHAT THE HELL'S HE DOIN' HERE?" SHERIFF MEECHAM ASKED, AS HE backed out of the tent, then turned to face his deputy.

"I'm sure I don't know, Evan," Fowler replied, then nodded at the tent. "Maybe you should go in there and ask him?"

"But it makes no damn sense," Meecham added, ignoring Fowler's suggestion.

To no one in particular, J.T. commented, "I thought he was long gone."

"Yeah," Mickey said, "'specially after the mob burned down his house."

"He went missin'," the sheriff said, "even before that."

To make sure he wasn't seeing things, J.T. pulled back the flap and looked in again. No, his eyes were not playing tricks. There was no doubt about it. Sitting there on his cot, bound, and gagged, was none other than the recently exonerated Russian spy, Boris Romanoff, and presently a suspect of Nazi war crimes, Mister Borch Rosenkranz!

Meecham glanced over at J.T. for answers. "Okay, John Junior, how does your theory explain this?"

J.T. shrugged his shoulders as if to say, 'I didn't see this coming either.'

Turning from J.T., the sheriff looked at Mickey. "Well?"

"We already told you our theory," Mickey replied.

"Yeah, well, run it by me one more time," the sheriff said. Suddenly, he seemed more interested in what the boys had to say.

Once again Mickey deferred to J.T. "You tell him. You understand that gold thing a lot better than me."

"Well," J.T. said after taking a moment to collect his thoughts, "we think Borch Rosenkranz is a Nazi war criminal hiding out here in southern Utah."

"Go on," Meecham said, "I remember that part. So, why's he heer and not in New York City or California?"

"Well, we think he's been buying black market gold from those guys over there at low U.S. prices and shipping it to South America where they cash it in at the much higher world market prices. Then they use the profits to fund the rebuilding of the Nazi Party."

"So, then," Meecham asked, "if'n all that is true, then why's he tied up in that there tent?"

"Uh—uh," J.T. shook his head, "that the part, we haven't figured out yet."

"That's the round peg and in a square hole part, huh?" Meecham said sarcastically, then added, "go on and tell me what you think."

"Well," J.T. hesitated, then continued, "obviously, Mister Rosenkranz has had some kind of disagreement with the miners, probably over money. Remember, we'd heard him and the cowboy arguing about money."

"No, I don't remember that," the sheriff replied, "remind me."

"It was the same night we found the deer hanging in the radio shack and later we found Lenny Week's body in Boy's Pond. Oh, and before the mob burned down Borch's place."

"So, you think Rosenkranz was in cahoots with the miners," Sheriff Meecham said, frowning, "and it was them that murdered Willie and Lenny?"

"Yes," J.T. nodded.

"Again, tell me why."

"We think Lenny and Willie were gathering antlers up here to sell to the Japanese and just happened to stumble onto their mining operation. And even though they got away the miners saw them and eventually identified them. To protect their illegal mining operation, they, along with Borch Rosenkranz, tracked Lenny and Willie down and murdered them. Lenny ended up in Boy's Pond and Willie was buried in Borch's radio shack."

The sheriff appeared to ponder this for a moment, then grunted. "So, if'n all that's true, why's he tied up in this tent?"

"I just told you," J.T. said patiently. "He had a disagreement with the miners, probably over money."

Meecham paused a moment, apparently to reconsider the boy's theory. "Well, maybe you might have somethin' there after all."

"You bet your as—uh—you damn right we do," Mickey crowed. "You should have listened to us from the start."

"Don't go and get all cocky with me, Graff," Meecham snapped. "You seem to forget that you and me still have other unfinished business."

Not backing down, Mickey glared at the sheriff, but thankfully kept his mouth shut.

"Blaine," Meecham turned back to his deputy, "go in there and untie Mister Rosenkranz, but cuff him, and bring him out here."

Fowler shook his head. "We got no more cuffs."

"And why's that?"

"I wasn't expecting this many. I only brought two and we've also used yours."

"Humpf," the sheriff snorted, "well, then go untie him from the cot, bring him out here, and tie him back up again."

Biting his tongue, Fowler ducked inside the tent, then returned a couple minutes later with a disheveled and badly trembling Borch Rosenkranz.

J.T. eyed him closely. Fear now seemed to be permanently embossed on his once proud and aristocratic face. Instead of haughty and aloof, he now looked like a broken, sniveling old man, his confidence totally shattered.

Also, from the looks of him, he'd been roughed up by the miners. The tail of his long-sleeve shirt dangled over the back of his short leather pants, but the front of the white shirt was soiled, blood stained and ripped in a couple of places. His trademark feathered Fedora was missing and his gray hair was mussed and matted with clot. Like a losing prize fighter, both of his eyes were blackened, his cheekbones were red and swollen and he sported several eggplant purple bruises about the face and neck.

After untying his hands, Fowler led Rosenkranz out of the tent, depositing him in one of the chairs next to the plank table. Immediately, Sheriff Meecham and the boys congregated in a semi-circle around Borch.

By then, it was mostly dark. Overhead, a thin layer of cirrus clouds were still aglow, spotlighted by the upward slanting rays of the recently vanished sun. However, the camp at ground level was immersed in a colorless, gray light. Unhooking a flashlight from his belt, Sheriff Meecham turned it on, shining it directly on Rosenkranz's battered face.

Normally a tall man, Rosenkranz looked small and broken as he slumped forward in the chair. Reflexively, he raised his forearm to protect his eyes from the bright beam of Meecham's flashlight.

"Go ahead, Blaine," Meecham said, briefly swinging the light to shine on his deputy, "tie him up again."

"I don't think," Fowler said, "that he's going anywhere."

"I said, tie him up!"

Though it probably wasn't necessary, certainly Rosenkranz didn't look like he was even capable of getting out of the chair, Fowler did as told.

After a couple more seconds of tense silence, the sheriff refocused the light on Borch, then said sternly, "so, now let's hear your side of the story, Mister Rosenkranz?"

With his arm still protecting his eyes, Borch seemed dazed and unable to comprehend, or at least not able to speak.

"Go on, Rosenkranz," the sheriff prompted, "tell us what happened."

"It might help," Fowler suggested, "if we removed the gag."

"Oh, yeah," the sheriff said sheepishly, "go ahead and do that, Blaine."

After Fowler removed the gag, Meecham refocused the light on Rosenkranz.

"Okay, now, Rosenkranz," the sheriff said gruffly, "tell us what you're doin' heer."

More silence, as Borch continued to duck his head and cover his eyes with his forearm.

"It might help," Fowler said, "if you didn't shine that bright light right in his eyes."

"Obviously, you don't know nothin' about interrogatin'," the sheriff growled, but nevertheless redirected the light from his eyes to spotlight Borch's left ear.

Again, there was silence, however, Borch did lower his forearm.

The sheriff nudged Rosenkranz with his boot. "Go on, tell us about this here gold mine and what a Kraut immigrant like you is doin' here."

At first nothing, then suddenly, Rosenkranz started talking. His speech was rapid, babbling and in a foreign language, most likely German. "Diese Männer haben mich angestellt, um mit ihren Explosivstoffen zu helfen.

"English!" Sheriff Meecham snapped, "Speak English."

"Ich fand das heraus, was sie taten, war unerlaubt und sagte ihnen, dass ich zur Polzei gehe. Sie schlugen mich und banden mich an disesen Stuhl fest."

"No," the sheriff barked, obviously irritated, "English! Speak English. I don't know no kraut."

With eyes wild and darting, Borch blurted, "Ich bin unschuldig. Die Männer wollten mich umbringen. Lass mich bitte gehen"

"English, Rosenkranz," the sheriff shouted, his face turning red, "speak English!"

Once again Borch started rambling incoherently in German. Apparently, he was so distraught he couldn't remember the few words of English he'd mastered.

Throwing his hands up as a sign of surrender, the sheriff turned to J.T. "You know him, don't you? See if you can talk to him?"

J.T. hesitated. "I don't know him that well."

"Go on," Meecham ordered, "try it, anyway."

Turning from Meecham to Borch, J.T., using a much softer tone and enunciating more slowly, said, "Hey, Mister Rosenkranz, it's me, the rocket kid."

Bleary-eyed, Borch looked up. "Nein, Ich will nicht über Raketen reden, diese Männer haben versucht, mich zu töten."

Shrugging, J.T. forged on. "Can you tell me what happened?"

"Ja, wie gesagt, diese Männer haben versucht, mich zu töten."

"Why did they beat you and tie you up?"

"Warum fragst du sie nicht?"

Shaking his head, J.T. turned back to the sheriff. "I can't get him to speak English either."

Sighing, Meecham turned Fowler. "Okay, for now, Blaine, but make sure your ropes are secure, and let's keep him away from the others. When we get back to Saint George, we'll have to find an interpreter."

J.T. quickly volunteered, "Fritz Ence, the postmaster, he knows German."

"The postmaster, huh?" the sheriff repeated, then added, "do you know where he lives?"

"Right by the Santa Clara Post Office."

After Deputy Fowler retied Borch Rosenkranz, keeping well away from the miners, the two lawmen, along with the boys, continued their search of the camp. By then, it was so dark any further investigation had to be done by flashlight.

Reluctantly, Sheriff Meecham called it off, saying he would have to come back tomorrow to finish up with the camp and the adjacent goldmine. Right now, however, it was too dark to do anything but mess up the potential crime scene. Furthermore, they still had prisoners to transport back to St. George.

"Maybe, tomorrow," Fowler suggested, "we should get the state police involved and possibly even the FBI."

"And why is that, Blaine?" the sheriff asked, disdainfully.

"Oh, I don't know," Fowler shrugged. "It just seems like there's a lot going on here."

"Like what?"

"Well, we possibly have an illegal goldmine, and the selling gold on the black market, and possibly across state lines. All of those are federal offenses. Then if what the boys say is correct, and they're shipping gold to south America, possibly to fund the rebirth of Nazi party, I think that's likely something the FBI would be interested in."

"So?"

"So," Fowler replied, "it just seems a lot for our little department to handle."

Meecham snorted, then added, "go get the prisoners and let's get going down the hill."

After borrowing deputy Fowler's flashlight, J.T. and Mickey led the way. Directly behind the boys, came the three cuffed gold miners, followed by a badly limping Borch Rosenkranz. Bringing up the rear were Sheriff Meecham, using his flashlight, and lastly, Deputy Fowler. In the dark, they tripped and stumbled over the slick river rocks. One time, Borch even slipped and fell backwards into the water, completely submerging. With Borch sputtering and gasping for air, Fowler helped him to his feet again.

Once they arrived back at the cruisers, the sheriff took a few minutes to figure out how to transport everyone. Finally, in the secure back seat of his cruiser, he shoved the cowboy and Sweeney, while J.T. was assigned to ride up front in the passenger's seat. Deputy Fowler locked the bibbed overall miner along with Rosenkranz in his backseat, while Mickey climbed up front with him.

In the sheriff's cruiser, the long and dusty trip back to Santa Clara was made mostly in silence. J.T. was trying to weave some logic, along with a bit of perspective, into the day's surprising and unexpected turn of events. He hadn't foreseen what happened to Borch, the beating and being held a prisoner, and was trying to make some sense of it. Sheriff Meecham's ongoing silence indicated he was probably doing the same.

However, aside from Borch Rosenkranz and his confusing fallout with the miners, there was another startling fact that was not so puzzling, two people were dead! Though they may not have been close friends, these were two young people who he knew and who should be alive today. Alive for at least another sixty years! It was hard for him to reconcile the fact they were gone - forever. Death was such a hard concept to understand.

It was a couple of hours past sunset when the sheriff pulled up in front of the Kunz's house. Suddenly, J.T. had a premonition of impending disaster; something bad was going to happen. It was like being trapped in a slot canyon when sky darkens as the rain clouds blow in. He supposed the reason he felt this way, he was finally realizing the enormity of everything that had happened. But hopefully this was the end, all of it was behind him now.

So, could things get any worse? Somehow, he doubted it. He'd already hit rock bottom, and by definition you couldn't go any lower. Or could you?

J.T.'s unsettling premonition quickly gave way to a rapid descent into depression. He supposed what brought on that rapid change was there were no warm and beckoning lights, shining through the windows, welcoming him home.

From the highway, the Kunz's house appeared dark and lifeless, seemingly underscoring the fact he was very much alone. He couldn't help but wonder if it would ever feel like a real home again? Like even before Korea, when the family unit was wholly intact. The five of them, his father and mother, as well as Chris, Mary, and him, all gathered around the dinner table. So, much had happened in just one year, really just one summer. Sighing out loud, he reached for the cruiser's door handle.

"Sometime soon," Meecham reached over and stopped him, "I'll need you and your buddy Michael T. to come into my office again and write up a report. You know, your version of what happened today."

"Okay." J.T. nodded. "When?"

"Tomorrow afternoon would be fine."

"Okay," J.T. said again. Briefly wondering how he'd get to St. George with both his parents and Mary being gone, but he'd worry about that tomorrow. Maybe, Mickey's mother could take them.

Getting out of the cruiser he closed the door, then paused briefly, again eyeing the dark, uninviting house.

"And," the sheriff said, leaning out of the open car window, "we still need to figure out a way to settle our other problems."

"What other problems?" J.T. responded absently. Obviously, his mind was elsewhere.

"Well, for starters we still have that mannequin incident and that firecracker fiasco with Sister Hafen."

"Oh," J.T. mumbled. With everything else that had happened, he'd almost forgotten about those things. With the two recent deaths, more specifically the two murders, those pranks seemed to have faded into insignificance, or at least taken a backrow seat. But now, with just those few words, like a nagging summer cold, they all came back. Unfortunately, forgetting about them, did not make them disappear. Obviously, the sheriff hadn't forgotten.

And of course, he still had all his other, non-legal problems pending too, namely, paying for his share of the classroom damage from the cherry bombs disaster and possibly also having to compensate his father for the water damage and erosion to the Loren Reber piece.

What an absolutely terrible summer this had turned out to be! And in addition to all of the above, his ongoing failure to achieve his primary goal for the summer, to make a workable rocket, really hurt. Breaking Judd and Howie's record for the most pranks in a summer was never really a goal of his, but more a goal of Mickey's.

And lastly, his complete lack of prospects for the upcoming end of the summer first date. Life just kept getting better and better.

"Yeah, okay," he muttered, finally answering the sheriff, "we'll come in tomorrow."

"One more thing," Meecham said, "how do I get hold of Mister Ence?"

"Huh?"

"You know, to translate."

"Oh, you mean Fritz," J.T. replied. "I'm sure he'll be at the post office tomorrow."

Without further comment, Meecham rolled up his window and drove off.

Still fighting a tidal wave of depression, J.T. watched the sheriff's twin taillights rapidly morph, as he gained speed, into double streaks of red, then suddenly disappear as he rounded the bend of Highway 91.

Sighing out loud, J.T. trudged up the steps of the darkened house and opened the front door. As he walked through the door, the telephone rang. Slamming the door behind him, he ran through the living room into the kitchen and grabbed the phone. He knew it was his father, and this time he was happy to hear from him. He badly needed someone to talk to.

"H—hello, Father," he said, slightly out of breath.

"Hi, son," his father replied, then went strangely silent. He didn't even ask why J.T. was late for the call or if everything was okay.

"Boy," J.T. blurted, "do I have a lot to tell you!"

His father did not respond. More silence.

"Father?"

"Uh, me too, Son," Mr. Kunz finally said, carefully measuring his words. "I also have a lot to tell."

Not waiting for his father, J.T. immediately started in. "We finally found Willie Wittwer and you'll never believe, but Borch—"

"Maybe," his father interrupted, "I should go first."

"Oh, okay," J.T. replied, deciding his news could wait.

Again, the line went dead for a few seconds and briefly J.T. wondered if they had lost connection.

"Father," he finally said, more subdued, "are you still there?"

"Yes, Son," his father replied softly, but still hesitated.

"Are you okay, Father?" J.T. asked, suddenly worried.

"Yes—uh, no—not—really," his father replied, his voice breaking up.

"What—what's the matter?"

"Son, I don't know how to tell you this..."

With his mind racing wildly, J.T. waited for his father to continue.

"Son," his father finally said, "your mother died today."

28

Like an elite 4 by 400 relay team, one season seamlessly passed to the next. Summer surrendered the cosmic baton to autumn and now autumn was reaching full stride, racing toward a waiting winter, who was looking back with outstretched arm.

Going by the calendar, however, it was late September, and the brutal summer heat had started to wane. Daytime temperatures now rarely exceeded a hundred degrees, often much less, and nighttime temperatures were downright pleasant. The blades of electric fans and swamp coolers rotated less frequently and less urgently and would soon stop altogether. Blue-bellied lizards once again perched on jutting rocks, trying to soak up the last of the season's warmth, while diamondback rattlesnakes slithered through combined wheat fields, searching for deer mice, sensing the long season of hibernation was drawing nye. Homo sapiens were also in a state of flux. Recreational activities gradually shifted from indoors, aquatic, or nocturnal to outdoors, diurnal, baseball diamonds or football fields.

Moreover, the arrival of fall also meant the farm season was winding down. There was still one cut of hay to harvest, the fifth, then the cows would be hauled down from Utah hill and let into the fields to graze on the stubble. But even after the last cut of hay was hauled and stored, there would still be one more watering turn for both the orchard and the alfalfa fields. Also, the last of the fruit, the tart Jonathan apples, were ready to pick, however the peaches, pears, apricots, and cherries had already been harvested, and—and that was about it. Of course, the cantaloupes, tomatoes, string beans, and corn had all played out some time ago.

Winter chores would arrive soon enough. There would be fruit trees to prune and the cuttings to haul away. Barnyard manure would have to be shoveled, hauled, and spread over the fallow fields. After that, poorly producing alfalfa and barley fields would need to be plowed under and readied for spring planting. Also, before the arrival of spring, irrigation ditches would need to be cleaned of weeds and any breaches repaired, but right now there was a welcome lull.

Today, as it turned out, was very close to a perfect autumn day. The temperature had topped off at an ideal seventy-seven degrees and not a breath of wind stirred through the crinkled leaves and spindly branches of the creosote bushes. Overhead, occasional, puffy, but harmless, clouds drifted by, but rather than spoil the faultless day, they only seemed to add a bit of texture, kind of a downy bas-relief, to the otherwise homogeneous blue sky.

And even though it was a weekday, a hump day, J.T. was out of school early. Unexpectedly, his last two afternoon classes had been cancelled. Mr. Avery, who taught seventh-grade English, was called away for a death in the family, and Mr. Blake, who coached J.V. football and taught P.E., had contracted a late summer cold. J.T. didn't mind the break because that left the entire afternoon for him to do as he wished. And what he wished was to test his rocket.

With a flour sack slung over his shoulder, he ascended the blue-clay slope, heading toward the crest of the Red Sand Hill. For some time now, he'd been working toward this moment, and believe it or not, he was pretty sure he was finally ready. Today was to be his big day and apparently Mother Nature, also sensing its importance, had obliged.

Also, Mickey was out of school early, as they'd registered for the same classes, and he was supposed to meet him at the launch site, but he hadn't arrived yet. But that was not too alarming, or even surprising, as J.T. was a full half hour early.

Over the last three months, J.T. had made sweeping changes to his rocket, mostly following the recommendations of Mr. Borch Rosenkranz. First, he'd finally figured out how to construct a two-chamber fuel delivery system. He separated the chambers by inserting and soldering a thin aluminum partition. Through that divider, he had bored a small hole in precisely the geometric center, thereby connecting the upper and lower chambers. Subsequently, when the fuel burned in the lower or smaller chamber, it would create space and sort of a draw-vacuum, pulling fuel down from the upper and larger storage chamber. Then add to this the effect of gravity and hopefully he would have a continuous feed system; that is, of course, until all the fuel was consumed. With any luck, by preventing all the fuel from burning simultaneously, that would solve the explosion problem, which of course is what destroyed his last rocket.

Also, J.T. had modified the fuel composition, again at the suggestion of Mr. Rosenkranz. His chemistry set did not contain powdered aluminum, so using a knife he tried to scrape shavings from a small section of aluminum pipe, but this proved to be a slow and exasperating process. After some experimentation, however, he determined the aluminum catalyst did not burn any better than sugar, so he went with beet sugar. It was easier to handle and far easier to find. Then with the dogged determination of a research scientist, he experimented with the relative proportions of sugar and gunpowder until he got it just right. And as it turned out, Borch was spot-on about that too. It made a great fuel.

Next, he'd made significant changes to the motor. Instead of simply crimping down the outlet, he found two aluminum brushings of slightly different sizes, so he could telescope them together, and also fit them into the terminal end of the fuselage. Painstakingly, he soldered these cylinders in place, which effectively narrowed the exhaust from the size of a fifty-cent piece to less than a dime, all the while maintaining the precise symmetry of a circle. This upgrade, J.T. hoped, would cure his rocket's propensity to veer from vertical flight.

Lastly, he had redesigned the cone and fins, making them more aerodynamic. He lengthened the cone tip and trimmed back the overlapping metal edges, thus making it flush with the body or fuselage. Instead of using wood, he fashioned the rear fins out of sheet aluminum, then soldered them to the fuselage. Now, he was fairly confident the aluminum fins would not burn or drop off when the fuselage was super-heated by the combusting fuel. Also, he made the fins a little smaller and increased the number from three to four, thereby, hopefully, increasing the stability.

Now, he had to admit, the rocket was a sleek, silver beauty and he was cautiously optimistic it would fly.

After completing the design and construction, J.T. had one task remaining, to name it. All ships of any size and worth, whether of sea or air, were granted names, usually female, but not always. Sometimes, they were christened for cities or states, and at other times for presidents or military heroes. And occasionally, they were named for intangible ideals like liberty, justice, or freedom. After giving it considerable thought, J.T. decided he would christen his rocket ship for this momentous, life-changing, and in many ways, regrettable summer.

At first, he'd considered naming it Willie or Lenny in honor of the fallen, but in the end that was too painful, and it wouldn't be right to choose one and leave the other out. Then he considered Borch, in honor of the wronged and the man who had helped so much with its construction, but that didn't seem to fit either. That name conjured up way too much regret. After that, he briefly considered Annie (his sixth-grade crush), but that was much too presumptuous. And of course, he considered his mother, Anita, but again that was still too raw, and he didn't like the symbolism of blasting her off into space.

So, in the end, he'd settled on Town Bell, a somewhat abstract symbol of the tragic evening that had started it all in motion.

With a pencil, he traced the letters onto the fuselage, but couldn't make it fit unless he made the letters so small you would need a magnifying glass to read them. With some reluctance, he shortened it to T. Bell, then got out his metal engraving set and meticulously etched each letter onto the aluminum fuselage. Now at last, it was ready!

After J.T. topped the sand hill, he trudged the short distance to the launch site, the same flat, sandy area he'd used previously. Fishing the wooden platform from the flour sack, he positioned it just right in the center of the clearing. Next he retrieved the rocket, carefully setting it on the platform, then balanced it against the vertical rocker arm. After that he threaded the dynamite fuse down through a small hole in the platform's floor, angling it off to the right. Lastly, he turned his attention to the nearby viewing bunker.

A few tumbleweeds had blown in since he'd last used it, and there was a small sand drift that had to be hand-scooped away from the window. Finally, after removing a wicked, inch-long scorpion, the bunker was ready for launch.

Once he'd finished with his pre-launch chores, J.T. backed off and surveyed the area. He was satisfied. At long last everything was ready, that is everything except for his best friend and second cousin, Mickey T. Graff. He still hadn't made his expected appearance. Obviously, J.T. didn't want to launch without Mickey. Half of the fun was having an audience, someone to share it with, and furthermore if the rocket actually did fly, he needed an eyewitness to verify.

Trying to be patient, but finding it difficult, J.T. wandered about aimlessly for a couple of minutes, then flopped down in the checkered shade of a thorn bush. Sighing out loud, he rested his back against its corrugated trunk, but eventually found that too uncomfortable and stretched out, spread-eagle on the red sand. Clasping his hands behind of his head, he checked out a small troupe of clouds as they slowly migrated overhead, west to east. Today they seemed particularly striking, puffs of cotton-white in a sea of azure blue. Languidly, the clouds moved about, like clumps of shaving cream in sink water. Slowly, they changed depth and contour, creating fanciful, even whimsical patterns. Mesmerized by their random movements and ever-changing shapes, J.T.'s mind began to wander.

To say that it had been a painful, an eventful, even a life-changing summer was a major understatement. It was all of that and more.

His mother's funeral had been an excruciating affair, and J.T. knew he wasn't completely over it yet. Maybe, he never would be. In retrospect, he was not at all surprised Smokey's sing had not worked, had not saved his mother's life, but he was a little surprised the Elders' priesthood blessing, along with his own frequent prayers, had been equally ineffectual. Was it all wasted breath? It appeared so. This Father in Heaven, this merciful God, was hard to understand. He'd personally witnessed very little mercy coming from on high during this whole ordeal.

The funeral service had been held in the Santa Clara Ward Chapel, followed by interment in the hot, and mostly barren, Santa Clara Cemetery. His mother's grave was located on this very same hill on which he now reclined, but about a half of a mile, or so, to the west, and her coffin was covered with this very same red sand.

Bishop Heinke had delivered a long and rather generic eulogy. According to the bishop, God had an urgent mission for his mother in heaven and that's why she had been abruptly and prematurely called back. At the time, J.T. couldn't help but think, what could possibly be urgent in heaven? Wasn't it a place with an unlimited supply of time? As in infinity? But he still wanted to believe, so he managed to quell those blasphemous thoughts.

By living good and faithful lives and adhering to the principles of the gospel, Bishop Heinke went on to assure the Kunz family, they could and would someday be reunited with their wife and mother in heaven, even the celestial kingdom. With tears streaming down his face, J.T. resolved to do just that, to live a good life. He surely wanted to see his mother again.

Lastly, Bishop Heinke looked right at J.T. and told him he knew his mother wanted him to fulfill a Mormon mission. Sometime later, J.T. learned that right before leaving for Salt Lake City, his mother had indeed confided that information to the bishop. And like a celestial branding iron, this statement instantly sealed his post-adolescent future, but nevertheless did little to quiet his troubled soul.

Of course, Smokey Grayman, the part-time Mormon, part-time shaman, also attended the service of his favorite cousin, Anita. But to J.T.'s relief, because he didn't want a scene with his father, Smokey did not sit with the family, but sat quietly by himself on a back row pew. It amazed J.T., as he watched Smokey take the sacrament, how perfectly comfortable he was mixing his Navajo religion with Mormonism. For him, the two were not mutually exclusive and there was no obvious or even an apparent incongruity, but to J.T., they were as different as January and July. Furthermore, he still was not entirely sure Smokey's sing was okay with the God of the Holy Bible, known to be a jealous God. But now he wasn't absolutely sure it wasn't either. He hadn't completely reconciled that point. Sometimes, life was so very confusing.

Nevertheless, J.T. had never seen Smokey look quite so—uh—so clean, except maybe at the early summer town meeting. At the funeral, he wore a long-sleeved, white shirt with an open collar and his black/gray hair was recently washed and neatly braided. After the service, and with an insightful smile, he told J.T. not to be sad, but to be happy that his mother had finally found hozro.

"They are not dead who live in the hearts they leave behind," Smokey had counseled, then added, "and like the soaring hawk, she will always be here for you," he paused, placing his hand over his heart, then continued, "you just need to know how to look for her."

Doc Hilton thought his mother's cancer and death might be related to the nuclear tests at Yucca Flats and the subsequent radiation fallout. J.T. was not sure, but he thought it could be a possibility. The Atomic Energy Commission, however, continued to maintain the tests were entirely safe and the Shots continued about one per month. This fall the AEC would wrap up the Upshot/Knothole Series and J.T. had heard through the grapevine the next series would be called Operation Ivy. He was, however, pretty sure he would not watch any of those Shots.

The burial itself was an exercise in agony. It took all of J.T.'s fortitude to remain grounded, rooted there at the graveside. He wanted to run; to get out of there! The maddening thud, thud, thud of the red silica sand striking the hollow-sounding casket was almost more than he could bear. It was loud; it was penetrating; it was permanent. The thud, thud, thud had the echo of eternity and carried the finality of death. It was a sound he would never forget.

For about a week after the funeral, the family wandered about aimlessly, in a protracted funk, then John Kunz abruptly announced that everyone was going back to work. After that, at the beginning of each week, and before he left on his Nevada produce run, he once again taped two work lists on the kitchen cupboard: one, fieldwork for J.T., and the other, housework for Mary. And to J.T.'s astonishment, Mary now routinely cooked dinner, did laundry and cleaned the house, and did so without complaining. Also equally surprising, it seemed now he and Mary seldom quarreled.

Also, his father eventually discovered he had taken the flatbed that day he and Mickey had gone up to Goldstrike Creek and found the miner's camp. Just like J.T. had predicted, he never noticed the new dents and scratches—no, that's not what fingered him. What did him in - one evening when his father was driving the flatbed at dusk, he flipped on the headlights. Unfortunately, from hitting the cut bank, the lights were now way out of alignment. One lamp beam swung wildly to the left, the other angled almost directly upward, and neither illuminated the road. When confronted, J.T. fessed up. His father threatened the belt, but it never happened. It seems now his father had lost his appetite for corporal punishment, but also it soon became apparent he didn't seemed capable of displaying much affection either. He was pretty much an emotional cripple.

After that, things pretty much settled into a routine. Though his father had never been a jovial man, after the funeral he became even more withdrawn, more cynical, and more distant. Who could blame him? In the space of a month, or so, he had lost a son, his favorite son, and his wife, the love of his life. J.T. decided to cut him some slack.

Abruptly rousing out of his reverie, J.T. got up and walked back to the edge of the Red Sand Hill. There still was no sign of Mickey. What was taking him so long? Mickey was usually on time or five minutes early and—and he could hardly start without him. Sighing, J.T. returned to the shade of the thorn bush and again flopped down. The clouds were still there, but now the pattern was much different, more layered, like whipped cream piled high on pumpkin pie.

Showing unexpected compassion, Sheriff Meecham delayed the mandatory visit to his office until after the funeral, but unfortunately, he did not cancel it. Roughly, a week, or so, after the funeral, the sheriff called and reminded J.T. they still had unfinished business.

Again, he begged a ride from Mary, and once again they picked up Mickey on the way. Initially, the sheriff separated them and had them write down their statements regarding that fateful day, including the events that led to finding the grave and the body of Weird Willie Wittwer, as well as how they'd stumbled onto the illegal gold mine. When finished, Deputy Fowler collected their papers, then ushered them into Sheriff Meecham's cramped office.

Like trying to find the North Star on a cloudy night, at first the sheriff's face was obscure and unreadable. After sitting them down on the two wooden chairs facing his desk, he squeezed back into his padded captain's chair. Silently, he continued to eye them, while taking a few seconds to rearrange the manila files on his untidy desk, then dispose of assorted food wrappers and junk mail into a nearby wastebasket.

"So, how you doin', J.T.?" he finally asked, his voice surprisingly soft. "I was sorry to heer about your mom."

"O—okay, I guess." J.T. was a little taken aback by the sheriff's show of concern.

"Your mother, well, I always thought—uh—that she was a fine woman. She always had your best interests at heart." Meecham paused and pursed his lips. "Well, anyways, I am sorry about all that, but we have to move on. We still have unfinished business."

Mickey, as brazen as ever, blurted, "can I ask a couple of questions first?"

The sheriff eyed him sharply, then shrugged. "Yeah, okay, go ahead."

"So, was our theory right?"

"And what theory would that be?"

"You know, our theory about how everything went down. How the gold mine, the cowboy and Borch Rosenkranz were all connected and how they killed Lenny Weeks and Weird Willie."

"Yes and no. You guys was dead wrong on Borch Rosenkranz," the sheriff said, slowly shaking his head. "He was not hiding out here and he was not a Nazi war criminal. For the record, he was never in Hitler's SS either."

"You sure about that?" Mickey asked, doubtfully.

"Yeah, real sure. The FBI checked him out again, a second time. He's clean, squeaky clean, boys."

"So," J.T. asked, "then why was he mixed up with the cowboy?"

"Well, apparently," Meecham replied, "his university physics degree, and all of those years working with solid rocket fuel, made Borch somethin' of an explosive expert. The cowboy hired him to help with the blasting. Seems they was chasing a vein of gold into solid rock."

"You tryin' to say," Mickey blurted, "that he had no idea what they were doing up there was illegal?"

"Not at first," the sheriff replied, as he picked up and apparently pondered whether to take a bite of the day-old grilled-cheese sandwich, "I guess things is different in Germany, but when he did figure it out there was a big scene and Rosenkranz threatened to expose the whole operation. The cowboy and his gang tied him up and was tryin' to figure out what to do with him. That's when we showed up."

"Okay," J.T. said, frowning, "then, why did he kill Willie?"

"He didn't," Meecham replied, "but you were right about one thing. The reason Willie and Lenny were killed is they did stumble onto that gold mi—"

"I still don't get it," Mickey interrupted, shaking his head, "then why was Willie buried in Borch's shed?"

"Well, that part was almost the way you guys figured." Setting down his cheese sandwich, the sheriff located a warm Coke, took a big swallow, then continued. "The night you locked Willie in them stocks, Lenny was following you, all right. But unbeknownst to you or Lenny, the cowboy and his cronies was followin' him. Right about the time Lenny set Willie free, they showed up. The cowboy chased Lenny up the creek bed, eventually caught him, strangled him with his own bandana and tossed his body in the canal. Eventually, he floated down to Boy's Pond where you two found him. Meanwhile, the other two miners chased Willie up close to the Rosenkranz place, killed him by breakin' his neck, then buried him out of sight in the radio shack. Apparently, Borch had no idea he was there."

"Well, at least we know Borch was not totally innocent," Mickey insisted. "If nothin' else, he was a deer poacher."

"No, not even that," Meecham shook his head. "The deer was given to him by the cowboy as kind of a bonus for his services. Again, he had no understandin' of our huntin' laws."

"So then," J.T. asked, he frown deepening, "who is he? I mean the real Borch Rosenkranz?"

"Well, it looks like," the sheriff replied, once again picking up and eyeing the cheese sandwich, "that he is just who he said he was, a German immigrant tryin' to git away from all that chaos in Europe and enjoy his retirement years."

"So, then," Mickey asked, "why did he tell us he was from Switzerland?"

"Apparently, he was, originally. His family immigrated from Bern, Switzerland to Germany when he was a baby. His father had found work in the Messerschmitt factory in Augsburg and eventually became a naturalized German citizen as did the rest of the family."

Still not convinced, J.T. asked, "okay, then why did he have Nazi uniform, and a SS ring and pennant?"

"From what I heer, he had an older brother, Adolph, who was in the SS." The sheriff now turned his attention to some stale potato chips. "He was killed in the war, on the Russian Front, I believe. And understandably, Borch, as the only living relative, was given his cremated remains along with his personal effects, which included the uniform, ring, and pennant."

"I still think it's a bit strange," Mickey said, "him saving that stuff and wearing the uniform that night, and all."

"I tend to agree with you on that," Meecham replied, munching on a stale chip. "But there ain't no law against puttin' on a Nazi uniform in private, at least not as far as I know."

"So, what's he going to do now?" J.T. asked, suddenly hit with a tsunami wave of remorse.

"I don't know," the sheriff shrugged, "but I heer he might move to Idaho, or Wyoming. I'm not for sure, but I do know he won't be comin' back heer."

"What about the cowboy and the miners?" Mickey asked. "Surely, they're not going to get off scot free."

"Far from it," the Sheriff replied. "I don't think we're goin' to have any trouble puttin' them away for a very long time. Mister Rosenkranz, of course with Postmaster Ence translating, has agreed to come back and testify at the trial."

For a moment, everyone fell silent, each lost in their own thoughts, then Mickey blurted, "so are you tryin' to tell me there are no Russkie spies here in Washington County?"

"Well, I wouldn't go that far," the sheriff replied, then added, "but not right now, at least none that we know of."

Now once again, almost two months later, while lying on the Red Sand Hill, J.T. still felt the awful sting of guilt, followed by another giant wave of remorse. They, he and Mickey, had played a big part in what had happened to Borch Rosenkranz and certainly he was not proud of it. He knew he would regret that for the rest of his life.

Sighing out loud, he got up and again walked over to the edge of the sand hill. Spread out below him was the little verdant valley of Santa Clara with its patchwork of houses and farms, but still no sign of his truant cousin and best friend, Mickey Graff.

As it turned out, like the sheriff said, Borch was exactly who he claimed to be. Johann Reusch finally did get the old parish records from Rötenbach, Switzerland that he'd been waiting for months. So, now after completing his genealogy back several generations, he discovered indeed Borch's mother

(Greta Hirschi Rosenkranz) was his maternal grandfather's (Otto Rosenthal) first cousin. Otto Rosenthal's branch of the family, as well as the Reusch branch, joined the Mormon Church and subsequently immigrated to America. The Hirschi Rosenkranz branch did not join the Mormon Church and stayed in Switzerland. But regardless of their church affiliation, that still made Santa Clara's Johann Reusch and Germany's Borch Rosenkranz second cousins, just as Borch had claimed.

Flopping back down on the sand, J.T. looked up at the variegated white and blue sky. Change the blue to brown and you'd have a root beer float with lumps of floating ice cream. But after a moment that changed too, and he continued his musings.

They, the entire town, but particularly he and Mickey, had wronged Borch Rosenkranz. Yes, sure the town bore some culpability, as they never really accepted him into the Swiss clique, but he and Mickey were the ones who had consistently stoked the fires of suspicion.

There was probably no way he could ever make it up to Borch, since he was not coming back, except briefly to testify, however in his heart J.T. knew he would if he could. But aside from the fact that restitution was unlikely, he had learned some hard lessons that would serve him well for the rest of his life. Lesson One, strange men are not necessarily bad men. Lesson Two, be slow to condemn and even slower to jump to conclusions. Lesson Three, don't blindly follow the herd; first find out where the herd is going.

Skipping from thoughts of contrition, J.T.'s mind eventually returned to that day in Sheriff Meecham's office.

"So, what's going to happen to Fritz Ence and the mob?" he'd asked the sheriff.

"Well, it's kind of ironic," the sheriff smiled and shook his head, "but as it turns out Fritz was both landlord and owner, and of course Borch was just rentin'. So, Fritz burned down his own place."

Mickey asked, "Isn't that still arson?"

"Yeah, I guess, it is, technically," Meecham agreed, "but since no one was hurt and Fritz has promised to reimburse Borch for his rent and loss of personal property, and since he has agreed not to try to collect any insurance money, and since Borch refuses to file a criminal complaint, I guess we'll probably just drop the whole thing."

"Drop it," J.T. exclaimed. "Fritz and the mob ruined his life!"

"Well, he was not alone in that one," the sheriff said, first eyeing Mickey, then J.T., "now was he?"

There was a long moment of silence as the boys checked out their shoes and the floor, then Meecham continued. "Anyways, like I said, we still have unfinished business, specifically that mannequin mess and the firecracker fiasco with Sister Hafen."

"Wasn't firecrackers," Mickey blurted, defiant as usual.

"Well, it was crackers somethin' or other," Meecham snapped.

"Cracker balls," J.T. added.

"Well, anyways, how do you want to play this?" the sheriff asked. "I've got your fingerprints on the catsup bottle from the night of the mannequin disaster, and I have an eyewitness who saw you two throw them cracker balls on the sidewalk just outside the church that morning right before Sunday school."

"That still don't prove we did it," Mickey said, still defiant.

Feeling a little less confrontational than his friend, J.T. stammered, "So—so, w—what are our options?"

"Well, actually, it's purdy simple. You can plead innocent, and we can take this all the way to trial, or you can plead guilty to two counts of criminal mischief."

"So, what happens if we plead guilty?" Mickey asked, his voice now a little less cheeky.

"In that case, you would go before a judge to be sentenced. But in situations like this, the judge often goes on what I recommend."

"W—what would you recommend?" J.T. asked, though not entirely sure he wanted to hear the answer.

Meecham rattled off the list. "Probation, restitution and community service."

With voice now trembling, J.T. asked, "S—so what does that all mean?"

For once, Mickey was quiet.

"First of all, it means no jail time, but you two will have to keep your noses clean for a couple of years, or you will go to jail. That's the probation part." Meecham paused to eyed them, then added, "and since there was no loss of property, restitution in this case would simply consist of apologizing to Sister Hafen in person and writing a letter of apology to the California tourist."

J.T. nodded and fortunately Mickey did not object.

The sheriff continued. "Community service would consist of at least a hundred hours. I could see maybe fifty hours mopping hospital floors at night or after school, and maybe another fifty hours cleaning ditches for the Santa Clara Water and Canal Company. Or something like that."

"Which do you want?" Mickey asked, turning to J.T., "the hospital floors or the ditches?"

"No, no," the sheriff shook his head, "it's not like that. It would be a hundred hours for each of you."

"We'll take it!" J.T. said quickly, then turned to Mickey, hoping for his approval.

Sighing deeply, Mickey finally shrugged and nodded.

Standing up to stretch his legs, J.T. trudged over to the crest of the sand hill one more time. Still nothing. Briefly, he considered starting the launch without Mickey, but that would be no fun, and he needed an eyewitness. Plus, he also needed someone to share his triumph or disaster. Anyway, he still had plenty of time; sunset wouldn't be for another couple of hours. Trying not to get discouraged, he sat back down and decided to give Mickey another ten minutes.

The letter of apology to the California woman was nothing; it was just a letter, but nevertheless they made sure it was a sincere letter. The in-person apology to Sister Hafen, however, had been an intense, emotional affair. He'd been nervous, embarrassed, and blubbery. She, on the other hand, was nothing short of gracious and understanding, which made him feel even worse. She was, he had decided, in spite of her advanced age, her large frame and blue hair, one classy lady.

The community service was still a work in progress, but he was getting damn (Mickey's language was starting to rub off on him) uh, he was getting—darn good at mopping hospital floors. The hours assigned for cleaning the Santa Clara Water and Canal Company ditches would be scheduled for a little later, during the winter months.

Also, at the end of summer, they'd had their much-ballyhooed first date. It was a shy, clumsy, and awkward affair. In the end, Mickey had managed to win the hand of the beautiful Suzie Hafen and yes, Annie Leavitt had agreed to go with him. With Mickey's mother as their chaperone, they had double dated. To J.T.'s surprise, Annie had dressed up for the evening. Not looking at all like her usual tomboy self, she'd applied makeup and lipstick and wore a grown-up dress with nylons and jewelry. And also, to J.T.'s surprise, she really did look pretty. Just a hint, he suspected, of the woman that was to come.

Of course, they had shared a popcorn and a Coke, and during the movie J.T. had debated whether or not to hold her hand. In the end he just didn't have the nerve. But after the movie, when he walked her to the front door, she leaned over and kissed him full on the lips, then instantly fled inside her parent's house. He was in seventh heaven, whatever that meant. His first kiss! It wasn't all that bad and the memory of it would last a lifetime.

Also, he'd written his three-page essay on the lessons he'd learned from the cherry bomb disaster and had finally paid off his share of the damage/reconstruction money to Superintendent Hartley. After that he was given a certificate of graduation from the Santa Clara Elementary and also received permission to attend school this year, the seventh grade at Woodward Junior High in St. George.

A few days before school started, he received in the mail his class schedule. His homeroom assignment and first class would be American history at 8:00 a.m. However, no teacher's name was listed, that box simply contained the letters TBA. At first, J.T. thought those must be the initials of his new teacher, maybe someone named T.B. Anderson, or Timothy Barnes Andrus, or something similar; that is until Mary smugly informed him it meant, To Be Arranged.

But the real surprise came when he walked into his homeroom that first morning. For there, sitting behind the large teacher's desk, right in front of the blackboard, was none other than Miss Stella Miller. The very same Miss Miller they'd terrorized last year with cherry bombs. Instantly, she recognized him as he did her. Hesitating at the door, the blood drained from his face. Just as he was turning to flee, she smiled and waved him in. Fighting back the tears, he silently vowed she would have no trouble from him this year.

And it goes without saying, they did not break the still timeless and still untouchable record of Judd and Howie's, but instead of the record they'd gained something much more valuable. They had learned—

"You sleeping?" a voice demanded.

Startled, J.T. opened his eyes. Looming right over him was the freckled and familiar smiling face of his cousin and best friend, Mickey T. Graff.

"No, just thinking."

"About what?"

"About everything. This last summer," J.T. got up and slapped the red sand from his pants, "and everything that's happened."

"It was quite a summer, all right."

"Yeah," J.T. nodded, "both good and bad."

"Guess we won't never get the record."

"Nah, Judd and Howie are pretty safe."

"Unless you want to try next summer."

"No way!" J.T. almost shouted, then more softly added, "you're late."

"The cows got out of our vineyard piece," Mickey explained, trying hard to suppress a grin, "been chasing them for over an hour."

Mickey seemed pretty calm, J.T. thought, for having been chasing runaway cows. He wasn't even cussing or fuming, but instead was kind of grinning. Oh well, no sense in making an issue of it; they still had plenty of daylight left.

"Well, come on," J.T. said, trudging through the red sand toward the launch site. "Let's see if she'll fly."

When they reached the site, Mickey bent over and picked up the little silver rocket from the platform. "Damn, she sure is a beauty," he whistled softly, while slowly rotating it in his hands. "Hey, what's this? You named her. What? Oh—T. Bell."

"Yeah," J.T. nodded. "I thought she needed a name other than just Rocket."

"Hubba—hubba—hubba," Mickey exclaimed, while grinning. "Teresa Bell? Good choice!"

"No—no!" J.T. stammered, turning red. Believe it or not, when choosing the name, he hadn't even thought of Teresa Bell, a well-developed ninth grader and Woodward Junior High's answer to Marilyn Monroe.

Just then there was a sound of a twig breaking and following that a blur of activity. Suddenly, all the bushes seemed to come to life. Kids pushed into the clearing from every direction. Annie Leavitt was there and so was Susan Hafen. A couple of seconds later, Alan, Greg, Curley, and Easy Earl materialized, standing at the periphery. In fact, after that, nearly the entire sixth grade class of last year showed up.

Then up the sand hill trudged Mr. Frei, leading his new crop of fifth and sixth graders into the clearing. He certainly looked a lot better than the last time J.T. had seen him. His face had more color and he had put on a little weight.

"All the kids wanted to see this," Mr. Frei explained. "We'll call it a science class field trip."

Confused, J.T. turned to Mickey.

"You can't have a momentous occasion like this," Mickey said, still grinning, "and not have an audience. That would be—uh—like playing the World Series with no fans."

So, that's where Mickey had been, J.T. realized, out gathering spectators.

Spontaneously, a cheer erupted from the group, then out of the corner of his eye, J.T. saw another person walking toward the launch site. Coming in from the west and leading a paint horse, was none other than his Navajo godfather, Smokey Grayman! How Smokey had found out about the launch, J.T. had no idea. Maybe, from Soaring Hawk, but somehow his Godfather had a knack of always showing up at the right time. But J.T. was happy he came.

Then right behind Smokey came his sister Mary. After topping the hill, she went over to stand beside Smokey. J.T. knew his father would not be coming, he was on his Nevada produce run, but he was happy to see Mary. She must be skipping school to be here.

Suddenly, J.T. felt something catch in his throat, also there was something in the corner of his eye, probably blowing sand, except there was no wind. Well, whatever it was, it made his eyes water.

"Okay, then, let's do it," his said, his voice husky.

Taking the silver rocket back from Mickey, he held it high, displaying it to the crowd. More cheers. Then with hands shaking, he repositioned it back on the launch platform, so the dynamite fuse dangled through the hole and angled slightly to the right. Lastly, he repositioned the stabilizing rocker arm.

After motioning to Mickey to take cover in the bunker, J.T. instructed the rest of the crowd to back up a safe distance, then he paused to take it all in.

Almost like a hot and humid summer day, the air was thick and palpable. Today, however, it was not hot and there was no threat rain. No, the air was heavy with anticipation.

Surrounding the little launch site, the spectators suddenly became graveyard quiet, as everyone held their breath. Throwing a little bit of sand in the air, like a professional golfer, J.T. checked the direction of the wind. Still there was none. Silently and with eyes wide open, he glanced upward and uttered a brief prayer to both the Mormon God and Smokey's Great Spirit, hoping one of them might be listening.

After taking in one last deep breath, he set his jaw, then fished a book of matches from his pocket, the ones with the flamingo-feathered woman on the cover. Kneeling down near the platform, he struck the match on the abrasive pad. Quickly inverting it, he gave it a couple of seconds to burn strong, then touched it to the fuse and dove for the safety of the bunker.

The fuse hissed, then hesitated, and looked like it might flame out. Then suddenly it flared!

From the bunker, J.T. could easily follow the telltale powder sparks and the tiny plume of black smoke as the flame flashed underneath the platform, then up into the rocket's fuselage.

At that moment, T. Bell shuttered and J.T. held his breath.

Would she hold together? Or would she blow?

Copious black smoke belched from her new motor, billowing off the launch platform and almost totally engulfing the silver bird. The aluminum ship hesitated for another second, then like the mighty phoenix, began to inch upward off the platform and away from the desert floor. Slowly, it gained altitude, majestically rising above the plumes of swirling smoke and to the loud cheers from the crowd. It was a magnificent sight!

Then the ship started going faster and faster, exponentially gaining velocity. Straight as an arrow, T. Bell pierced a lacy cloud, then gently arched to the left.

Within seconds, the rocket was no more than a silver speck, then it completely disappeared into the perfect September sky.

READERS GUIDE

1. What purpose does the PROLOGUE - CIRCA 1932 serve?

2. What are J.T. and Mickey's somewhat less than lofty goals for the summer?

3. Why does John Tobler Kunz prefer the moniker J.T.?

4. Why does J.T. and Mickey's sixth grade class end up with a substitute teacher, Miss Miller?

5. Of which government agency is Rudy Popovich the assistant director?

6. What is the purpose of the radiation badges Mr. Popovich clips on the students?

7. Why do the sixth-grade boys dislike Weird Willie?

8. Reportedly Borch Rosenkranz is Swiss, the same heritage as the townsfolk, so why is he not accepted by the citizens of Santa Clara?

9. After the cherry bomb fiasco, the boys see Rosenkranz wearing a foreign military uniform. Which country do they think it represents? Ultimately, which country does it signify?

10. Why does Mr. Kunz think Borch Rosenkranz is a Russian spy?

11. How does Superintendent Hartley find out the identity of the six cherry bomb bombers?

12. What penalty is imposed on them for that prank?

13. What is J.T.'s hobby/passion? What is his summer goal for that hobby ?

14. J.T.'s given name is John Tobler; Sheriff Meecham calls him John Junior; what is his mother's pet name for him?

15. Why does the first test flight of the rocket fail? What is Borch Rosenkranz's suggestions to correct the problem?

16. Why does Mr. Kunz despise Smokey Grayman?

17. How are Smokey and Mrs. Kunz related?

18. On a trip to Utah Hill, they observe the detonation of an atomic blast (Shot). What is Smokey's reaction to the blast? Mr. Kunz? Mrs. Kunz? J.T.?

19. The Kunz's leave Utah Hill earlier than planned. Why?

20. On the way home they are nearly run off the road by a black sedan. Who is the driver?

21. After a fistfight with Willie and Lenny, J.T. and Mickey cut through Borch's property on the way to their hideout. What do they find in Rosenkranz's backyard shack?

22. While at their hideout, the boys build English stocks. Why?

23. What is the mannequin prank? Though no one was hurt, why does the sheriff get involved?

24. The next prank is cracker balls under the seats in Sunday School. What goes wrong?

25. What happens to J.T.'s brother, Chris?

26. What is town bell? Where did it originate?

27. After J.T. and Mickey lock Willie in the English stocks, he disappears. Why does J.T. initially suspect Mickey might be involved?

28. When Willie does not show up, the sheriff organizes a search party. The boys do not find Willie. Who do they find?

29. At a town meeting Mr. Kunz accuses Borch Rosenkranz of being a Russian spy. What evidence does he present? And what does Mr. Popovich propose to do about it?

30. Not waiting for Popovich, the town mob descends on Rosenkranz's property. What ultimatum do they give him?

31. In looking for Willie, the boys find a body hanging in Borch's shed. Who or what is it?

32. Continuing to look for Willie, they stumble onto a goldmine up Slaughter Creek? How are the goldmine and Rosenkranz connected?

33. The FBI vindicates Borch. he's definitely not a Russian spy. What now do Mr. Kunz and the boys suspect he is? And the gold from the goldmine is being used for what purpose?

34. The town mob burns down Rosenkranz's house, and eventually Willie is found. Where?

35. So, how do J.T. and Mickey put it all together – the murders of Lenny and Willie, the goldmine and the involvement of Rosenkranz?

36. From what does Mrs. Kunz die?

37. What does J.T. christen his rocket? Why?

38. So, who is the real Borch Rosenkranz?

39. During this unforgettable summer, two of J.T.'s friends are murdered; he is largely responsible for running an innocent man out of town; both his mother and brother die; and he's placed on probation for all his ill-advised pranks. Nevertheless, the story ends on an upbeat or positive note. What is that upbeat? Would you consider this a happy ending? Or merely a satisfying ending? Or an anticlimactic ending?

9 781632 935502

29. At a town meeting Mr. Kunz accuses Borch Rosenkranz of being a Russian spy. What evidence does he present? And what does Mr. Popovich propose to do about it?

30. Not waiting for Popovich, the town mob descends on Rosenkranz's property. What ultimatum do they give him?

31. In looking for Willie, the boys find a body hanging in Borch's shed. Who or what is it?

32. Continuing to look for Willie, they stumble onto a goldmine up Slaughter Creek? How are the goldmine and Rosenkranz connected?

33. The FBI vindicates Borch, he's definitely not a Russian spy. What now do Mr. Kunz and the boys suspect he is? And the gold from the goldmine is being used for what purpose?

34. The town mob burns down Rosenkranz's house, and eventually Willie is found. Where?

35. So, how do J.T. and Mickey put it all together – the murders of Lenny and Willie, the goldmine and the involvement of Rosenkranz?

36. From what does Mrs. Kunz die?

37. What does J.T. christen his rocket? Why?

38. So, who is the real Borch Rosenkranz?

39. During this unforgettable summer, two of J.T.'s friends are murdered; he is largely responsible for running an innocent man out of town; both his mother and brother die; and he's placed on probation for all his ill-advised pranks. Nevertheless, the story ends on an upbeat or positive note. What is that upbeat? Would you consider this a happy ending? Or merely a satisfying ending? Or an anticlimactic ending?

9 781632 935502

www.ingramcontent.com/pod-product-compliance
Lightning Source LLC
Chambersburg PA
CBHW010747310726
48980CB00004B/395

* 9 7 8 1 6 3 2 9 3 6 4 0 0 *